THE GORKHA URN

by

Matthew S. Friedman

FIRST EDITION

Copyright 1997, by Matthew S. Friedman
Library of Congress Catalog Card No: 96-90808
ISBN: 1-56002-712-6

UNIVERSITY EDITIONS, Inc.
59 Oak Lane, Spring Valley
Huntington, West Virginia 25704

Cover by Whitney Eskew

Dedication

To my mother and father who have always been an inspiration to me. And to my loving wife Radha, who has had to put up with my endless hours of typing away on my computer—I love you.

PART ONE

1

"Matt, you asshole, you got us lost again, didn't you?" asked Thad with that usual sour look plastered across his face. "Where the hell are we?" Thad was funny that way. He didn't like surprises and being lost in the forest in the late afternoon was very much of a surprise for him.

"I don't know where we are," I replied back. "Why don't you ask Butthead over there. He's the one with the damn compass." I was pissed that Thad, once again, blamed me for one of Mark's screw-ups. Mark was the one supposedly leading the way.

"Mark, you asshole, where the hell are we?" asked Thad in his most whiny voice. He paused for a moment to tie one of his shoe laces which kept coming undone. He was the only person I knew who could double tie his shoe laces and still have them come undone.

"Hell if I know," said Mark with a big wide smile. "I guess you could say we are a wee bit lost. Such is life."

I walked up to Mark and watched what he was doing. He kept tapping the side of the compass to get the needle to move in the direction he thought it should be pointing. No wonder we were lost, I thought to myself. He didn't have the foggiest clue how to use the stupid thing.

Unlike Thad, who was obviously bothered by their predicament, Mark looked at the situation from a different perspective. Being lost in one of West Virginia's largest forests was great fun—just another adventure. For him, he would have preferred that the forest be an untamed jungle with hundreds of man-eating animals. Mark took everything in stride—nothing was a problem.

"Well, what are we going to do now, Butthead?" asked Thad. From the high pitch in his voice, it sounded as if Thad's anxiety level was on the rise once again. "It's getting late and in a few hours the sun will go down. I can't believe I let you talk me into this. I should be home studying or something. You know we have finals coming up in two weeks." Thad paced back and forth like an expectant father as he talked. This was just one of his many nervous habits.

"Shut up, Thad, and stop your damn complaining," Mark demanded. "We'll camp here for the night and find my uncle's cabin tomorrow morning. No sweat." Mark walked around the area looking for a place to settle for the night.

"What about a tent?" asked Thad with his arms pulled tightly over his chest. "Do you have a tent? I don't see any tent." He had that pouting expression on his face which always looked so condescending. Thad was a first-class complainer, one of the world's finest—a champion.

"We don't need a stupid tent," replied Mark. "It's not going to rain tonight, look at the sky. It's an absolutely clear day." We all looked up. "We'll sleep out under the stars like men. Only fags sleep in tents." Standing there in his bright red flannel shirt, old faded blue jeans and army surplus marching boots, Mark looked like a regular mountain man.

"Well, I guess I'm a fag then because I'm not sleeping out in the open here," said Thad defiantly. "No way, Butthead! Do you know how many mosquitoes there must be out here, not to mention bears, snakes and all kinds of other wild creatures. What about you Matt? Are you going to sleep out here like a caveman?"

As always, Thad was trying to get me to side with him against Mark. Since Thad and I both had at least one foot in the rational world, it usually wasn't hard to recruit my support. But this time I couldn't help but agree with Mark. I was glad to be out of town and wanted to go fishing the next day. I was tired of high school, tired of studying and tired of the same old routine. I needed a change. I had no desire to return anywhere.

"I don't think we have much of a choice this time, Thad," I confessed. "You got a better plan? And besides, it's only May. The bugs and other critters aren't that bad now. I'm sure no ones been eaten by any man-eating bear in this area for at least a week or so." I couldn't resist teasing Thad about such things. He was such a baby.

"Come on, let's just go home," Thad whined. "That's my plan. If we start walking we can probably make it back to Butthead's truck by around seven. We all have flashlights. This was a stupid idea to come all the way out here to go fishing. I knew we'd have a terrible time. I told you so."

"You know something, Thad, you're such a pussy," yelled Mark as he came storming over to give him a piece of his mind. It didn't take much to set Mark off when Thad was around. "What makes you think that we're not having a good time. I'm having a great time. The best time I've ever had in my whole entire life. So why don't you just shut up. If you want to go home then go. I'll point you in the right direction. I'll even give you the keys to my truck. Here take them." Mark threw the keys and the compass on the ground right in front of Thad.

From the way he was standing, it was clear that Mark was really pissed at Thad. In the five years that I had known both Mark and Thad, I couldn't think of a single time when we'd been together when they didn't argue at least once. As always, it

8

was up to me to come between my two best friends to restore the peace until the next incident. I was always the peacemaker. I knew my role well and was always there on cue.

"Would you guys just grow up and shut up," I said as I reached for the keys and the compass off the ground. I wiped them off and handed them over to Mark again. "I'm so sick and tired of hearing you fight like little girls. You should both be wearing bright pink dresses with nice white bows. Now listen, we are stuck here and we're going to have to make the best of it. There is nothing we can do about it now. Butthead screwed up again. What do you expect for someone with shit for brains." Of course, I said this with a smile. Mark was pretty good about accepting my many insults. He liked the attention. Thad, on the other hand, got up and walked away with his feelings hurt.

After my little scolding, the three of us began to settle in for the night. We found a small pine grove which was relatively free of back breaking rocks. The area was covered with small pine needles which made a nice natural mattress. There were also a number of large Hemlock trees nearby which acted as a shield from the cool spring wind.

It felt good to be outdoors again. I hadn't camped outside for several years since quitting the boy scouts. There was something about being in a forest which allowed one to really relax. A person could do, say or think anything they wanted and not worry about the consequences.

After spreading out our sleeping bags, Thad and I walked around looking for small branches and twigs to start a fire, while Mark collected rocks to prepare a fireplace. Mark was always willing to do any job which required physical strength. In an earlier life, he must have been a work horse or something.

"Matt, I don't know why it is that I let you guys talk me into these stupid trips," said Thad as he shook his head. "I could be home studying or reading a good book. Something like this happens every trip we go on. We run out of gas, the truck breaks down, we run out of money—what is it with us?"

"Can't answer that, Thad," I replied. "Maybe we're just cursed. Hell if I know."

"We are cursed," said Thad as he pointed over at Mark. "How the hell did we get Butthead for a friend. The guy is truly a Neanderthal from another age. Just look at him. He's really embarrassing."

As we both stopped and stared at Mark, I couldn't help but agree that in some ways Thad was right. As Mark carried over a giant rock from the forest, one much too big for him to comfortably lift, he did look like something out of the stone age. His body was not just "well" developed, it was overdeveloped. Every muscle was well defined and prominent. At the age of sixteen, he was already six feet tall, weighed nearly 180 pounds and his enormous barrel shaped chest protruded out of all of his clothes like a comic book super hero. He was also hands-down considered one of the best looking guys in the junior class. While his face was nothing special, most of the girls were spellbound by his massive dimensions.

Because of his incredible size and strength, Mark became one of Elkins, West Virginia's finest wrestlers ever, with an undefeated record of wins since starting high school three years before. Even as a freshman, he was whipping seniors equal to his size and weight.

Mark got the nickname "Butthead" because he used to have this nasty habit of butting heads when he first learned to wrestle as a kid. Although he stopped this tendency years ago, the name stuck with him. Mark never took offense when anyone called him that. For some reason, it never occurred to him that his nickname might have more than one meaning.

While Mark's body was perfect in every detail, his mind represented another matter. Like many "big" boys, Mark didn't have as much in the brains department. Despite this fact, he was always accepted by all. His sheer size was enough to ensure his inclusion into any group he wanted. He also never took life all that seriously. He always had a joke for every occasion and was never without a smile. His way of never letting anything bother him also made everyone feel at ease. The only person who got under his skin was Thad. But he was not alone in this regard. Thad had this way of bringing out the worst in nearly all who knew him, including myself.

Compared to Mark, Thad was from another planet all together. He was a small, scrawny guy who looked like he spent many of his formative years in a concentration camp. But what Thad lacked physically, he made up for intellectually. He was Elkins High School's top junior when it came to grades. No one could touch his smarts. Because his body was weak and non-responsive, he whined about anything that required any physical activity. Choosing things to do which satisfied both Thad and Mark were often nearly impossible.

Standing there in his dark blue flood pants, checkered polyester shirt, complete with a ballpoint pen, wearing black socks and bright, brand new white K-Mark sneakers, I couldn't help but feel that Thad could win, hands down, the award for being the most authentic nerd alive. He was truly the real thing. If he could only see himself through my eyes.

As for me, I guess you could say that I fell somewhere in-between the two of them. I had always been fairly competitive on the playing field and could also hold my own in the classroom. But I could never decide whether I wanted to be known as a jock or a nerd. Being friends with the two of them always allowed me to have contact with both worlds without committing myself to one or the other. If it wasn't for me, Mark and Thad never would have become friends. I'm the only thing they had in common. That and the fact that they were both from Elkins, West Virginia.

*   *   *

"Matt, are we really going to waste an entire weekend out here?" Thad protested. It was clear that he hadn't given up hope that he could somehow change my mind. I sometimes gave into him just to stop his damn whining. "Let's forget about this fishing trip and head home tomorrow morning. We never catch anything anyway. And besides, what is it about some stupid fish biting a hook and being hauled to shore which gives you guys such a vicarious thrill. Does it make you feel like big men to torture defenseless creatures. I mean really. When you think about it, it's truly barbaric. What if you were sitting here and a chocolate Eskimo Pie fell in front of you and you bit into it and a massive hook punctured your jaw. The next thing you know you're being hauled in the direction of a pond. After holding out as long as you could, you are pulled into the water where this big fat fish tosses you into a pile with a bunch of other human saps. At that point you slowly suffocate from lack of air. But moments before you croak, your miserable life flashes before you. I mean really, isn't that what you do to those pathetic, helpless fish?"

"I guess I never thought about it that way," I laughed out loud. "I'll have to remember to stay away from those Eskimo Pies the next time I see one dangling in front of me."

Before Thad could hit me with another one of his many justifications for why we should return, I decided to cut him off at the pass. It was time to put him out of his misery.

"Listen, Thad, both Mark and I like being fish-killing barbarians for a day. It's early in the season so we might even catch something this time. Just remember, we told you not to come out with us. Every time we take one of these wilderness trips, you say you want to tag along and then you complain the whole time. So you're getting no apologies from me. Just forget about it. You're here, so make the best of it."

Thad just stood there and stared at the ground. I could tell he was about to go into one of his pouting moods. To prevent this from happening, I decided to razz him a bit. Without knowing what hit him, I grabbed his neck from behind and started playfully messing up his hair. I thought this might snap him out of his sour mood. As always he became furious with this act of affection and tried to push me off.

"You homo," he yelled as he finally managed to free himself. His hair was in a state of disarray and his glasses were hanging off one ear. "I hate it when you do that to me you big jerk. I expect childish behavior like that from Butthead, but not from you. You should stop hanging around with him, Matt, he's beginning to affect your mind."

Before either of us knew it, Mark came running up from behind and grabbed both of us into his massive arms and lifted us like we were nothing.

"Did someone say homo?" asked Mark as he laughed and twirled us around in the air. "I saw you two standing here looking so damn cute in those tight pants you're wearing and I just had to get me some."

"You're disgusting," yelled Thad as he tried to free himself.

"You're all talk, Mark," I replied as I puckered my lips. "I'm ready for you right now big boy. Just let me down so that I can drop to my knees."

"I always thought there was something funny about you, Matt, so the truth finally comes out," said Mark. He let us both down. "You should stop wearing your sister's dresses."

"Only when you give them back to me," I responded back on cue.

We had gone through this same routine a thousand times with little variation. But each time, Mark still got a kick out of it. Both Mark and I enjoyed exchanging insults—the cruder the better. Thad, who never really understood the fundamentals of humor, seldom joined in. It wasn't that he didn't want to. It's just that the few times he tried, his timing was all off and his teasing nearly always sounded so serious.

*　　*　　*

The sun was setting fast as we all returned to the camp site. After starting a massive bonfire and heating up some canned beans and corn we had brought along, we all sat back, mesmerized by the dancing flames. It was a spectacular night. The sky was filled with a trillion flashing stars, there was a gentle breeze blowing through the trees and there wasn't a single insect to be found. As always, we eventually ended up discussing those familiar topics which were so much a part of our thoughts at that point in our lives.

"I still think that Cindy is the best looking babe in school," said Mark full of excitement. "I mean, have you ever seen such massive boobs before? God, they are monsters." Mark used his hands to mimic the size.

"What is it about Cindy's chest?" asked Thad. "I mean really. If you ever stopped and looked twelve inches higher at her face you'd notice that she could win first prize in any bow-wow show. She's really not that pretty if you ask me."

"I don't know about that, Thad," I said as I came to Mark's

defense. "I have to agree with Mark on this one. Cindy is pretty fine. Have you ever seen her in a bathing suit. Man, she's a real knock out. I think you probably need to get those glasses of yours checked." As I talked, I sat there pulling pine cones apart and tossing the remains into the fire.

"That's my point. If she didn't wear a size triple D bra you guys would never even give her a second look," said Thad. "So she has a little extra fat on her mammary glands. What's the big deal?"

"Thad, if we really have to explain it to you, then I truly am sorry," said Mark as he put his arm on Thad's shoulder. As always, Thad quickly pulled away.

"So, finals are coming up in two weeks. You know I think . . ." Thad started to say in an effort to change the subject.

"Shut up, Thad," I said as I threw a handful of pine cones at him.

"What'd you do that for?"

"I don't want to talk about school. We can worry about that on Monday. We came out here to forget about school for a while, remember?"

There was a long pause in the conversation. Off in the distance an owl could be heard hooting. As I stared at the sky, I saw two consecutive falling stars. I was about to tell Thad and Mark about it, but decided to keep it to myself.

"So Mark, did you manage to get a donation from your father's liquor cabinet?" I asked with a bit of anticipation. "It just wouldn't be right us going out into the woods like this without something to keep us warm. Since Cindy decided not to come, I'll settle for something else."

"Well, now that you mention it, I do think there is something here which will make you feel all warm inside," Mark admitted. He walked over to his knapsack and pulled out a quart of cheap blackberry brandy. "I was waiting for just the right moment. I guess this is as good a time as any."

Before taking his first swig, Mark turned to Thad and asked, "Do you want some before I put my scummy lips all over it. You wouldn't want that white crud from my lips to touch the bottle before you have your turn, do you?" Mark knew exactly what Thad was going to say in response.

"You know I don't drink that piss," replied Thad with a grimace on his face. He shoved the bottle away in disgust. "It always makes me sick. Yuck! That stuff makes toxic waste look like Kool-ade."

"Well, it's time to waste away," said Mark as he took a big swallow. As always, Mark gulped the fluid too fast and some of it spilled all over the front of him. I'm sure every shirt he owned had some kind of stain across the front. He wiped his mouth with his shirt sleeve and offered me the bottle.

13

I grabbed it out of Mark's hands and took a big gulp myself. It was Friday night and I was determined to get good and toasted.

"Matt, you are as bad as the Butthead with that stuff," said Thad in a self-righteous manner. "You know something, you both are going to turn out to be drunks when you get older. Your livers will become diseased, your stomachs will be filled with blood-oozing ulcers, and your families, if you ever get that far, will leave you. You'll both die alone in some gutter somewhere. You just wait and see. That's what happens when you drink like that."

Mark turned to me and paused as if to think about what Thad had just said. For a moment he almost had a serious expression before turning to Thad and saying, "Sounds pretty good to me. What about you, Matt—should we begin our descent into a life of misery tonight?"

Not wanting to miss an opportunity to razz Thad a bit, I replied, "Maybe Thad's right. Maybe our futures are so dismal that we ought to end our pitiful lives right here and now, this very moment—you know, to spare our families and friends from all of the pain and suffering we will cause them." I took another swig from the bottle and handed it back to Mark who did the same.

Thad picked up on the sarcasm right off and turned his back to me. He was obviously hurt that we didn't respond to his sincere concern for our well-being.

"You're right, Matt. We should end our pathetic lives right now. No sense being a burden. I recommend we both jump into that fire and burn ourselves alive," Mark said with a smile. He was trying his best to hold back his laughter.

"No, we want to leave something behind for our families to feel guilty about," I said. I looked around for a better plan. "I think we should both climb one of those trees and dive head first onto a big rock. Of course, Thad would have to deal with the mess. Oh, and I forgot, he doesn't know how to get back. You know something, Mark, I guess we'll have to postpone our deaths until after we get him back to civilization. No sense in allowing someone who's got such a brilliant future ahead of him as a lawyer or rocket scientist to get eaten by wild bears. It will be our last unselfish act before ending it all. God, aren't we thoughtful."

"You're right, Matt," said Mark as he finally gave into his laughter. "We can kill ourselves next weekend. Have another drink."

"You two are truly pathetic," said Thad angrily. He was clearly irritated—it was written all over his face. "I hate you both. Every time I try to give you advice you make fun of it. Well, go ahead and kill yourselves. See if I give a flying fuck.

When I'm off somewhere living like a normal human being, you'll be wasting your lives away and then one day you'll be old and grey and look back and wish you took my advice."

"Come on, Thad, we were just kidding," I said as I reached out to shake his hand. "You have to learn to take a joke."

Mark and I both knew that Thad was probably not going to say another word for the rest of the night. He was not very forgiving and when he had that pouty expression cast all over his face, it was nearly impossible to change his mood.

"Well, I'm going to take a piss," said Mark as he yawned and stretched. His yawn sounded like a grizzly bear in heat. He got up, staggered to his feet, and walked over to a small patch of trees not far from the campsite to relieve himself.

"Come on, Thad," I pleaded. "Forget about it. Can't you take a little joking around?" Once again I accepted the diplomatic role in an effort to snap him out of his mood.

"Screw you, Matt," he snapped back. "You're as bad at Butthead. You say that I can't take a joke? Well, when it's me who is always the joke, how do you think I'm supposed to feel?"

What could I say. Thad just didn't get it. I figured the best thing to do was just drop it until the morning.

*   *   *

Moments later, without a warning, Mark shouted at the top of his lungs, "Shit, what the hell is this! You guys better come over here now . . . and bring a light." Both Thad and I nearly jumped out of our skins. It was not like Mark to get so excited about anything.

"Sure, Mark, like I'm really going to go over there so that you can try to scare me with one of your goofy, juvenile tricks," Thad shouted back, not believing that Mark had really seen anything at all. Thad had been duped too many times to take Mark seriously about anything.

At first, I also thought it was one of Mark's childish pranks, but the tone of his voice was all wrong. He truly sounded spooked. I grabbed one of the flashlights and ran over to where he was standing. As my light found the spot, a mild shiver slowly crept up from the base of my spine to the hairs on my neck which, without hesitation, stood at attention.

There, three feet in front of me, was a full-grown middle-aged man lying on his stomach. His face was turned towards us. His eyes were fixed open as if in a perpetual stare. From the way he was dressed, with a light blue dress shirt, dress pants and black wingtips, he looked like a businessman. His back was completely covered with blood. There seemed to be a hole in his shirt—it looked as if he had been stabbed or shot from behind.

Thad, realizing that he was left alone by the fire, finally

15

stood up and reluctantly came over to us despite his feeling that Mark was up to something. When he caught sight of the man, he paused just long enough to throw-up beans and corn all over his shoes. None of us had said anything for what seemed like an eternity. I finally broke the silence, "Do you think he's really dead?"

"Don't be stupid," said Mark as he poked at the body with a stick. "Only dead people let ants wander in and out of their mouth, and besides look at him, he's as hard as a rock." Mark kicked the body with a thud. The sound brought up more of Thad's recently eaten food—this time on my shoes.

"How could you pick a campsite next to a god damn corpse? Didn't you see him lying there, Butthead?" I yelled at Mark as I used some pine needles to clean off my shoes.

"Well, excuse me for living, I forgot the first rule of being a good boy scout. Check the campsite for dead bodies," he replied back sarcastically. "Do you think if I really saw this guy lying here that I'd save it until now?"

"Well, what are we going to do now?" I asked somewhat bewildered.

"We'll have to go back and tell the police in the morning," said Mark in a matter of fact tone. He walked over to the campsite and returned with a small hand towel which he draped over the dead man's face.

"What? The morning—did you say the morning?" asked Thad, not believing what he just heard. He tried to hold back another hurl. "I'm not sleeping in the woods next to some dead guy. You've got to be out of your mind if you think I'm staying here." Thad began pacing back and forth again. His nervousness was building exponentially.

"Well, we just can't stroll out of here tonight," I answered back. "We'll never find our way back in the dark."

Thad grabbed my arm and turned me in the direction of the body as he pointed his light on the man's back. "Matt, take another look at that guy," he insisted. "Does all of that blood on his back suggest to you that he died of natural causes? It looks to me like this guy was shot in the back. Unless he managed to find a way to shoot himself that way, which I'm sure you'll agree is highly unlikely, I would venture to guess that someone was kind enough to do it for him. And judging from the fact that he hasn't been eaten by any animals yet, he doesn't smell, and the blood is still not completely dry, it probably happened fairly recently—like sometime today."

"Thad's right," said Mark after inspecting the blood. "This guy hasn't been here too long. And look at this, there is a trail of blood leading here." Mark pointed the flashlight along a track of blood which led off into the forest. "He wasn't shot here. He must have ran away from whoever did it. You know something, they may still be looking for him out there somewhere."

We all turned and stared into the darkness which seemed to surround us. At the mention of a potential killer lurking out there somewhere, every noise took on a new meaning.

"I say we get the hell out of here now," urged Thad. "Mark can find the way back. All cavemen know how to find their cave in the dark."

"Do you think you can get us out of here?" I asked as I turned to Mark. At that point I, too, was spooked and felt that it was time to move on.

"Well, if we walk east for awhile, we should hit a stream that leads to the main road," replied Mark. "It's a bit out of the way, but at least we'll know we're going in the right direction." Mark gently bit his lip as he looked around for some bearings. He did this every time his mind was forced to think about something—which wasn't very often.

"Then let's do it," Thad pleaded. "Come on, let's just get out of here now!"

"Wait a minute," I said. "Shouldn't we try to find out who this guy is? We need to tell the police something about him." I reached down and fumbled to retrieve his wallet from his hip pocket. I used the tips of my fingers as if he had some kind of horrible disease. After finally wrestling it out, we all gathered around as I opened it up.

"Holy shit, look at all of that money he has," yelled Mark. "There must be a thousand dollars there. What does a dead guy need with that much money?"

"Forget about it, Mark, your truck's carburetor is going to have to wait another year," I said in a serious voice. I knew what Mark was thinking. "Look, his name is Robert Carter, he's from New York. What is he doing all the way down here?" His driver's license gave an address in New York City. We quickly looked through the rest of the wallet, but didn't find anything else of interest.

"Could we just get out of here," cried Thad as he tugged on my shirt sleeve. "Take the god damn wallet and we'll bring it to the police. Whoever did this could still be on his way here right now. So let's just go."

Mark, after realizing how freaked out Thad had become, walked away, came up from behind him and grabbed his side. Thad was nearly airborne. While Mark thought it was one of the funniest things he had ever done, I thought under the circumstances it was in pretty poor taste.

"Cut it out, Mark," I scolded him. "Let's make a move."

"Wait, wait, wait. How will the police ever find this place?" asked Mark. "If we leave now in the dark, it will be hard for us to explain where it is. Shouldn't we try to mark it with something?"

We all looked for some kind of landmark nearby. But everything around us looked so ordinary. They'd never find the location without some help, I thought to myself.

"I have an idea," I finally said after thinking it over. "Thad, go grab my red T-shirt out of my pack and bring it over to me. Mark, get some of your fishing line and your knife." After bringing the shirt and the line over, I wrapped the line around a number of trees which surrounded the body. The circle I created was more than twenty feet in diameter. I then ripped the shirt into small strips and tied the strips onto the fishing line.

"This should be easy enough to find," I said, pleased with myself.

We also decided to leave a trail of "Doritos" to the site. Mark had brought a bag with him and volunteered to drop chips along the way as we headed for the main road.

It's funny how finding a dead body in the woods only a few yards from your campsite has a way of immediately sobering a person up. One minute I had a good buzz going and the next minute I felt absolutely nothing. Before leaving, Mark picked up the brandy bottle and tossed it into the forest. It landed off in the distance with a loud crash. We had only killed about a third of the bottle—what a waste.

It didn't take long for us to pack up our things. We frantically went around the campsite and picked up as much of our stuff as we could find. Fortunately our packs were small since most of the gear we needed was at Mark's uncle's cabin.

Before finally departing, we argued about whether or not to keep the fire burning. Thad thought that we ought to put it out because whoever carried out the hideous crime might find the body if he saw the fire. Mark, on the other hand, felt that if the fire was out that there wouldn't be much body left for the police to find—some hungry animal out looking for a meal might find it and drag it off somewhere. But it was his other point which convinced me. He said that no self-respecting murderer would expect to find the person they had just shot sitting next to a fire toasting marshmallows. I tended to agree—the fire was left burning. While Thad ordinarily would have continued to argue his case, his strong desire to flee the site was too compelling to worry about something so trivial.

"Okay, let's get the hell out of here," I said. We all had our packs on, the area had been well policed and it was time to depart.

"Finally," Thad sighed with an expression of relief.

*   *   *

Twenty-five minutes out, Mark located the stream he was looking for. Under pressure, his mind was incredible when it came to knowing which direction to go. It was almost like he had this ability to draw from a primitive part of his brain which was controlled by instincts rather than reason. He also appeared to be taking the situation in stride. He was like a warrior going off to battle—he was ready for whatever came his way. In fact, I think at some level, he wanted to meet up with the murderer. To him, it would have been just another adventure.

On the other hand, Thad and I were both utterly hopeless. Between the two of us, we couldn't muster up an ounce of courage. All I could think about was that at any moment some crazed madman from the darkness of the forest would drag me off to some horrible place where I'd be brutally murdered. It wouldn't be something as simple as a shot to the back—no, with my luck, he'd use a chain saw to cut me into tiny ity-bity pieces or stab me to death with a table fork. Maybe there was some truth to all of those horror movies I had seen throughout my life.

Thad was so frightened that he had to pee every ten minutes. He was known for having what he described as a "nervous bladder." It seemed like we were always stopping to allow him to relieve himself. Most times when he tried, nothing came out. On the few attempts when he was able to manage a drop or two, it usually dripped onto his leg because he couldn't keep his hands from shaking.

At different points along the way, the forest became thick with underbrush. As much as we tried, it was nearly impossible to pass through branches, leaves and vines without making a serious racket. With every step, the cracking sound beneath our six moving feet seemed to call forth to the forest—"we are coming."

To conserve our batteries, we decided to use only one flashlight at a time. After only a half hour, the first set of batteries lost all of their juice. I walked close behind Mark to take advantage of what little light was available. Since Thad was unable to see very well in the dark, he maintained a firm grip on my belt to help lead him along. This arrangement was less than satisfactory. Every fifty yards or so, he somehow managed to give me a massive "wedgy." As much as I tried to stop him from doing this, every time he yanked at my belt, my underwear found a way of squeezing my private parts.

*   *   *

It was Mark who first noticed a flickering light off in the distance. He stopped so abruptly, that I nearly fell on top of him. Needless to say this resulted in another tug on my undershorts by Thad, the "wedgy master."

"Hey, look, there is someone up ahead," said Thad in a loud voice. His head was bobbing back and forth as he tried to get a better view. "We're saved."

Before Thad could say or do something stupid, Mark grabbed his arm, put a hand over his mouth, and whispered into his ear, "Did it ever cross your mind, smartboy, that maybe they are the ones who iced that guy back there. Are you ready to make friends with them right away? If you are, then be my guest." He removed his hand from Thad's mouth and turned back in the direction of the campfire.

"Oh, shit," said Thad as this potential was revealed. "What are we going to do now? I have to pee again."

While Mark and Thad were talking, I scanned the area with what little light was available from what appeared to be a campfire up ahead. I then tapped Mark on the shoulder and moved close to him so that I could quietly whisper something into his ear.

"I think we should make a big circle around them," I said as I pointed off to the left of their campsite. "Since the stream is on our right side, and that would be too difficult to cross in the dark, I say we go left. Let's not take any chances. It looks as if there are at least three of them."

"Okay, then follow me," Mark whispered. "I'm going to have to turn the flashlight off. Whatever you do, don't make a sound, you hear me? We are going to do this nice and slow—a regular snail's pace."

"But I can't see without the flashlight," Thad complained. "It's dark out there."

"Well, you're not going to be able to see if they put a bullet between your eyes," Mark responded back. Thad got the point.

After tossing the bag of "Doritos" Mark had been using to leave a trail back to Carter's body, he crouched down on all fours and began feeling his way along the ground to avoid making any sound. Both Thad and I tried to follow his every move. As I made my way, Thad had such a tight grip on my ankle that I thought if I pulled suddenly my foot would come right off.

Mark led us along a wide, circular course that took us well over a hundred yards outside the campsite. We went over rocks, through bushes and around trees like a giant caterpillar. I kept wondering if I was going to put my hand on a rattlesnake. Ordinarily, I would have mentioned something like this to Thad, but he was already so freaked out I kept this little thought to myself.

We could hear what sounded like a group of men talking and laughing off in the distance. But their voices seemed insignificant compared to the sound of a twig cracking or a leaf being crushed beneath us. Our packs also seemed to make all kinds of loud squeaking noises. It was as if every sound we made was amplified a hundred times over in our minds. The anxiety this created was immense.

After nearly thirty minutes of snailing along, everything was going fine—we were nearly out of their range. When all at once Thad yelled "shit!" at the top of his lungs.

Before he knew what hit him, Mark jumped on top of Thad and once again threw a hand over his mouth. The force of this immediate response was so great that it threw Thad's glasses clear off his face a few yards away.

"What the hell are you doing," whispered Mark. "Are you trying to get us killed? Now I'm going to take my hand off your mouth and I want you to "quietly" tell me what the hell is wrong with you."

"Look at my hand," said Thad as he placed it in front of Mark's face. "It's covered with shit. I'm going to puke—it stinks." Thad was the only person on the entire planet who could manage to put his hand in the only bear shit for ten miles. If we weren't in such a strange predicament, Mark and I would have died laughing.

While Mark and Thad were clearing up the mystery of why the word "shit" came out of his mouth at such an inopportune time, the men sitting around the fire had stood up and were pointing flashlights in our direction.

"Who is out there?" shouted one of them. "Go check it out now. Hurry up! It could be him."

As the three men made their way towards us, it was clear from a pistol in one of the guy's hands that they were not your average recreational campers. I felt Mark hesitate as if he was preparing to make a run for it. But we all knew it was hopeless. Mark and I could have possibly run away without too much trouble, but Thad would have been left to the wolves. With nothing else left to do, Mark motioned for us to try to quietly move under some shrubs which were situated five or six feet directly behind us. We did the best we could to conceal ourselves, but it still felt like we were right out in the open.

As I laid there on the ground waiting to see what might happen, for the first time in my life I really knew what it was like to taste a bit of reality. This was not a bad dream that would go away when I woke up. It was real and the course of my life, or death for that matter, could be changed in those few minutes that followed. I was terrified.

As they came closer, I could see the outline of their bodies clearly from where I was lying. One of the guys was over six feet tall with broad, massive shoulders. The one next to him was much smaller. It was difficult to make him out because the big one was always standing in the way. The leader of their pack was a squirrelly man who stood a few feet behind the others, without a gun. He seemed to be one of those real nervous types who always moved around a lot.

Their flashlight beams passed by us once and then again. They didn't see us. I kept asking myself, how could they have not seen us? The beam was pointed right at us. I could hear Thad crying softly. Mark was poised as if to jump up and take them on if he had to. I was simply praying to God. To spare my life, I promised to give up some of my vises, including my entire Playboy collection and the box of tissues I kept under my bed.

"I know someone is out there," said the squirrelly man. "I can feel it. I know it's him. You find his ass and bring him to me now. We need him to tell us which one it is—or else we're screwed." From the tone of his voice, it sounded like he was very frustrated about something.

I focused on every word in an attempt to make sense of it all. Who were they talking about? Was "him" the dead man in the forest? Why did they want him?

"Where do we look, boss?" asked the tall one.

"I don't give a shit where you look, just find him. The guy has a bullet in his back for Christ sake. He's got to be around here somewhere!" The squirrelly guy slapped the big one on the back to get him moving.

Both men walked right past us as they ventured off into the darkness. The squirrelly guy stayed behind and watched them as they disappeared. He then turned, but as he was beginning to walk back to the fire, he stepped on something which cracked beneath his shoe. It was Thad's glasses. He stared at them for a long time before he slowly leaned over to pick them up. Before he was able to grab them off the ground, Mark was airborne and on the guy with one of his best wrestling moves. The man never knew what hit him. Within a quarter of a second, the guys' face was pressed against the ground so that he couldn't yell out.

"Quick, take the flashlight and get the hell out of here now," Mark commanded softly. "Follow the stream. It leads right to the main road. I'll meet up with you at the truck in a few minutes. Now get the hell out of here. And hurry!"

Without hesitating, Thad and I were off. It's funny what a person on the cutting edge of fear is capable of. Both of us were breaking land speed records as we ran through the thicket. Our packs flew back and forth on our backs with every step. Whenever we fell, we'd get right up again—the pain of bruised muscles and scratched skin would have to wait. Thad didn't even have his glasses. For the first time, the athlete inside of him found a reason to come alive—our gym teacher, Mr. Ryan, would have been proud of Thad.

As it turned out, the main road was closer than we had expected. When we reached it, we turned left and ran in the direction of Mark's pick-up truck. It was parked about a quarter mile along the edge of the Cheat River. We arrived there in no time flat. As we sat on the bumper, gasping for air, it took us a while before we could utter a single word.

"Where the hell is Mark?" I blurted out in-between gasps. "How could we have left him there? He's going to get himself killed."

"Let's go get help," Thad insisted. From the terrified look painted across his face, it looked like Thad was going to have some kind of breakdown any second. "Where are the keys?"

"I don't have them," I said frantically. "I thought you had them. Oh great. After they kill Mark they'll come here and finish us off for sure."

"We've got to get out of here," Thad pleaded as he pulled on my arm. "We can't stay here. They're going to come for us. They'll be here any minute." Thad was bordering on hysteria. I'd only seen him like this once before when he thought he got a "C" on a term paper back in the seventh grade. Of course, it was a big mistake. Thad never got less than an "A" on anything.

"And leave Mark behind?" I asked surprised. "No way. He saved both of our asses. And besides, he said to wait for him by the truck. I'm staying right here until he comes."

"Great, another Rambo," cried Thad. "Well, I've had enough of all of this bull shit. A dead man ten feet from our campfire, guys with pistols wandering around the woods, Mark playing Mr. Macho, I can't take this. Let's just start running." Thad couldn't manage to stand still. He was moving around like a spinning top out of control.

"And go where? By foot it would take us over an hour to reach anywhere," I said. "We're in the middle of nowhere, remember?"

"Well then, what are we supposed to do?" asked Thad. He kept walking around in a circle. I was getting dizzy just watching him. He also kept smelling his hand.

"Wait a minute, I got an idea. Let's climb up on that rock over there and wait for Mark. If he doesn't come in the next fifteen minutes we'll head out. We just can't leave him here."

I may have appeared to be in control on the outside, but inside my mind I was hopeless. My common sense, do-what-you-have-to-do-to-save-your-own-hide part of myself kept telling me to get the hell out of there. But at some level I knew I couldn't run. Mark was my best friend. If it hadn't been for him, I probably be dead by now. I couldn't abandon him. Maybe there was a little courage inside of me after all, I thought to myself.

We tossed our packs into the bed of Mark's pickup and then both climbed up onto this massive rock which overlooked the vehicle and the surrounding area. From where we were situated, we had a good view of everything around us. The river was on the other side of the road. The gentle sound of the water trickling along was in stark contrast to the fear which was roaring inside both of our minds.

We crouched down to make sure that we couldn't be seen from the street. We also gathered a small pile of fairly hefty stones, just in case we needed to defend ourselves. I'm not sure why Thad collected them. He could hardly see two feet in front of himself without his glasses. But having them nearby seemed to comfort him.

Neither one of us said a word. I was so scared I could hear my own heart pounding. With every beat, a moment passed and then another. Every minute felt like a lifetime.

After a while, I began to wonder whether we should be so close to the truck. If they did manage to find this place, they'd know we were nearby because of our packs. As I looked around for a better location, I noticed a silhouette coming out of the woods in our direction. I whispered to Thad that someone was coming and for him to be quiet. After the incident in the woods, an entire battalion of half-crazed soldiers couldn't get him to utter a word. The guilt of having caused this mess by screaming out was weighing heavily on his mind.

At first, I thought it was Mark, but in the darkness it was hard to tell for sure. It wasn't until I heard him whisper our names that I realized that he was okay.

"Up here," I whispered back. "We'll be right down."

After climbing down, Thad and I both ran up to Mark and spontaneously hugged him—some kind of male bonding thing, I guess. I had never been so happy to see someone in my entire life.

"What the hell happened?" I finally asked. "How did you get away?"

"I'll tell you later," said Mark as he looked behind him. "They're still out there. We're going to have to haul ass."

We all jumped into the truck. But when Mark tried to turn the engine over, that old carburetor on his 1973 Dodge pick-up refused to kick in.

"Matt, turn it over when I tell you," Mark said as he leaped out and frantically opened the hood.

After pulling off the air filter and sticking a twig down the mouth of the carburetor to hold open the butterfly valve, I gave it another whirl. For a moment it almost started, but then the battery began to grow weak.

"Try it again," he shouted frantically. Once again it almost started as if to tease us. We could all smell the gas, a sure sign that the motor was becoming flooded. We had gone through this routine a thousand times with Mark's old truck. We knew we had about a fifty-fifty chance she'd fire up.

As I sat in the driver's seat, waiting for Mark to give me the okay to try again, out of the rear view mirror, our worst nightmare was coming to life. Two of the men from the campfire were running down the road in our direction. Both were wielding pistols in their hands.

"Mark, they're coming, they're coming, oh shit!" I yelled. Thad let out a loud scream.

"Again," Mark shouted. "Try it again, now."

I don't know what he did to it that time, whether he just "willed" it to start, but it did. Mark slammed the hood and jumped in the back area of the pickup just as I was flooring it. With tires screeching and dust from the road flying in every direction, the two men stopped running and began shooting at the moving vehicle. One of the bullets struck the rear brake light. Another hit the back window shattering it completely. By this time, Thad was on the floor of the front seat screaming at the top of his lungs.

After getting out of range, I could still hear Mark yelling, "Faster, faster—go faster."

At one point I flew around a corner and nearly ran over a fisherman who was walking along the side of the road. The guy had to jump three feet to avoid being hit. But this didn't phase me one bit. I drove that truck like there was no tomorrow. Even after we got into town, I kept going until we reached the safety of Mark's shed. After pulling inside, Mark jumped out and quickly shut the two wooden doors behind us. For the first time that night, we all felt safe.

2

As the three of us stood there in Mark's shed, he described what happened after Thad and I ran off. In some ways, Mark's story was almost too much like a cheap detective novel to be believed.

After Thad and I headed for the truck, he managed to somehow gag the man he had jumped with one of his socks which he pulled from his pack. Believe me, there could be no worse punishment than having one of Mark's socks shoved in your mouth. He also managed to use his belt to tie the man's hands behind his back. As his captive kicked and tried to free himself, Mark dragged him even further into the woods to avoid being seen or heard by his two companions.

Mark tried this best to make out who the man was. But since he had given his flashlight to us, he was unable to get a good look at his face. One thing was for sure, he wasn't from around here. The guy wore some kind of sweet smelling aftershave. Most men in Elkins either smelled like firewood, sweat or chewing tobacco. He also said the guy had on a suit, dress shirt and necktie, complete with a bright, shiny gold tie clip. No self-respecting "good ole boy" would be caught dead in the forest with anything less than a good flannel shirt and an old pair of blue jeans—the uniform of the great outdoors.

Just as he was preparing to run off himself, Mark noticed that the two other men were returning to the campsite. With dancing flashlight beams and the distinct sound of feet trudging through the thick underbrush, they were pretty obvious. As they came closer, Mark held his victim tightly using one of his best wrestling holds to avoid allowing him to move at all. Only after there was a safe distance between him and them did he release his captive as he quickly drifted off into the darkness of the forest.

It only took a few seconds before he started hearing some shouting behind him as he raced through the woods toward the main road. The man had somehow gotten loose and alerted his two buddies. But by that time, Mark was well on his way.

"You know, the only really bizarre thing was that I could hear that guy yelling at me as I ran through the woods," Mark explained. "He kept saying stuff like 'I'll find you, you son-of-a-bitch. And when I do, I'm going to rip your heart out.' He sounded like a real lunatic."

After finishing his story, Thad and I just stared at him not knowing what to say. It was Thad who finally broke the silence.

"As much as I hate to admit it, you were really great out there," he conceded. "I just couldn't believe it when you picked that guy up and threw him down on the ground. That really took some balls. You probably saved both of our lives. I'm . . . I'm grateful." This was one of the few times I had ever heard Thad say something nice about Mark. I could tell it wasn't easy for him, but I was glad he made the effort. Mark was all smiles.

"Thad's right, we both owe you big time," I finally jumped in. "You were like superman out there." I grabbed his hand and shook it several times. I couldn't think of anything else to do to express my sincere appreciation.

"You guys would have done the same for me," said Mark confidently. Both Thad and I looked at each other as if to convey the message—No Way.

"So what's the plan?" asked Thad in an attempt to change the subject. "Shouldn't we go call the police right away? Those guys are going to get away if we don't hurry." I could tell he was still a bit shaken up from all of the excitement. He just wanted the whole bad experience to be over with as soon as possible.

"Don't worry about that, I'm sure those guys are long gone by now. Actually, I've been thinking about this whole thing," said Mark reluctantly, as if he knew he'd be facing some resistance. "To tell you the truth, I'm not sure we should go to the police after all."

"What?" asked Thad, not believing what he was hearing.

"Just wait a second and hear me out. Like I said, I don't think these guys are from around here. They must be city boys. Who knows, they might even belong to some mob. Well, I don't think we should get involved. Besides, if we go to the police, these guys might find out who we are and come after us. They've already killed one person we know about."

"But what about the dead guy?" I asked. "How are the police going to know that he's out there if someone doesn't tell them?" I wasn't sure I wanted to hear Mark's answer to this question.

"Forget about him," said Mark as if he didn't care if anyone ever found the body. "Just think about this thing for a moment. They didn't even know who we were and they started shooting at us. This bunch is really bad news. I don't think we should do anything to piss them off. Besides, I didn't get a good look at them. Did you? We don't have any names. We don't have nothing. What the hell are we going to tell the police anyway?"

To a certain extent, I couldn't help but agree with Mark. A few years back, an uncle of mine witnessed a car accident involving a drunk driver. He had to testify in court to describe what he saw. The whole legal thing dragged on for weeks. My uncle used to tell this story and then he'd say to me 'Boy, I don't care what it is, never admit to seeing anything to those damn cops. It's not worth the god damn time and trouble—believe me.'

"I don't believe what I'm hearing here," Thad exclaimed totally dumbfounded. "Mark, you are totally nuts. There is a dead man lying in the woods right now and you want to just pretend it didn't happen? I say we get the police over here right this second. We know most of the cops in town. They'll protect us. That's their job for Christ sake. No one is going to come after us. Mark, you are just paranoid."

"Forget it, Thad," Mark replied back sharply. "I wouldn't trust those cops to guard my grandfather's blind dog and he's already dead." Mark and the police were like vinegar and water—they didn't mix very well. From the time he was a kid, Mark always had this problem getting along with authority figures. He just couldn't stand having an adult tell him what to do. He even had trouble dealing with his wrestling coach. If he hadn't been such a terrific wrestler, his coach would have kicked him off the team months ago.

At that point, the inevitable happened. Both Mark and Thad took that all so familiar stance with their hands tightly across their chest as they stood facing each other—a clear sign that neither was willing to budge on this one. Once again, lines had been drawn in the sand on both sides and it was up to me to somehow break the deadlock. After thinking it over, it occurred to me that maybe there was a way to let the police know about the body without revealing our names.

"So what about an anonymous phone call?" I asked, as I sought some kind of compromise. "We can make the call, disguise our voice and tell them what we saw without giving our names. That will work, right?"

I could tell from the way Mark relaxed his posture that he wasn't going to have a problem with it. It was Thad I was more concerned about. He was never much for compromise.

"Well, Thad. What do you think?" I asked, hoping for a positive response.

"I don't know. I still think the cops should know all of the details."

"Then we'll tell them over the phone. The only difference is that we won't give them our names. Believe me, it will work out fine."

"I guess that will work," Thad conceded.

So without any further discussion, we all agreed that we'd make a phone call to the police and tell them about the murder without revealing our identities. At the time, it seemed like the right thing to do. To prevent Thad from thinking any further about our decision, I immediately changed the subject.

"So, Butthead, what are you going to tell your father about

the truck's broken window?" I asked as I walked over to inspect the damage. The truck seat was covered with glass from the impact of the bullet. "You know, with a truck this old, you're going to have a hell of time finding a replacement for that."

Without answering me, Mark walked over to his truck and just stood there staring at the broken window for nearly a minute as he rubbed his chin. He then opened the driver's door, reached inside and grabbed the cheap K-Mart AM/FM Cassette player, shook it a few times, pulled it right out of the dashboard, and then threw it behind the tool bench. "Needed a new one anyway. Well, I guess it looks as if someone broke into my truck and stole my radio," said Mark with a big smile. "Shit, did they have to break my rear window to get it out?" Mark may not have been all that bright when it came to passing exams or writing term papers, but he did have an advanced degree in knowing how to cover for himself.

"Hey, wait a second, I just thought of something. What about the license plate?" I asked as I walked to the back of the truck. "Maybe those men saw your plate before we took off."

"No chance in hell," said Mark confidently. "My license plate lights don't work and when you hit the gas, there was so much dust flying, I nearly choked to death."

"Okay, then what about the wallet?" Thad chimed in. "They'll never know who the guy was unless we give it to them. How are we supposed to do that with our little anonymous phone call?" It looked as if Thad had not yet completely conceded after all.

I took the wallet out of my pocket to look at it. Before I knew it, Mark grabbed the wallet from my hand and pulled out all of the cash. "We'll tell them the guy's name and address over the phone. And as for this money, it's going to pay for a new window and the pain and suffering we all had to endure. We deserve it."

"That's disgusting, stealing a dead man's money," said Thad as he tried to grab the wallet and the money back again.

"That's the point, Thad, the man is DEAD, gone, finished," said Mark. He held the money out of Thad's reach. "What does he need with this money now?"

"What if he has a wife and kids?" asked Thad. "Did you ever stop and think about that? Maybe that's all the money they have in the world."

"If he's such a good family man, then the prick shouldn't have gone out and gotten himself killed. He should have stayed up there in New York."

"Mark, give me the money and the wallet until we figure this out," I insisted. When he realized that I was serious, he reluctantly yielded to my demand. Mark seemed to respect my judgment. I put the money back inside the wallet and started looking at what else it contained.

"Before we do anything else, let's see if there is anything else in this wallet," I suggested. "Maybe it will give us some clues as to why someone would want to plug this guy."

The black, eelskin wallet looked like new and was full of all kinds of business cards and papers. We pulled everything out and lined it up on the hood of Mark's truck. In addition to $872, there were eleven business cards representing a range of different companies and organizations, a driver's license, some credit cards, two or three Mastercard receipts, a drug store photo receipt and a few pieces of paper that had phone numbers written all over them. At the time, none of it seemed all that useful.

"This pile of junk isn't going to tell us anything," said Mark. "I say we keep the money. We nearly got ourselves killed tonight, remember? And how am I going to pay for a new window and brake light without it. Someone owes us."

"Listen, Mark, Thad is right about the money, it doesn't belong to us," I explained. That was the eagle scout in me talking. "I say we hold onto it and the wallet until we see how this whole mess plays out. We'll decide what to do with it once things settle down." I went over to one of the tool-bench drawers at the back of Mark's shed and placed the wallet and its contents inside. "We'll leave it here for now." Then I locked it up and put the key in my pocket. Although Mark looked a bit frustrated by my decision, at some level, even he knew it was the right thing to do.

"See, Butthead, I told you it was a stupid idea to take the money," said Thad in an attempt to once again prove that he was infinitely smarter than Mark. As always, Thad's better-than-thou attitude resulted in a good smack on the head.

"Sorry about that, Thad, just a nervous twitch," said Mark with a bit of satisfaction.

"Okay, so let's go call the police and put this night behind us," I said anxiously. "Mark, we can probably use the phone in the kitchen. Your parents will already be upstairs, won't they?"

"Are you crazy?" asked Thad. "We can't use the phone here. The police probably have some kind of tracing device. Don't you ever watch TV?"

"Elkins police trace a call?" Mark laughed out loud. "I'd be surprised if they even knew how to use a phone, the dumb fools."

"If we are going to do this thing, let's not take any chances," said Thad. "I say we drive over to the shopping center on the other side of town, make the call at one of the those pay phones there and then head home." Thad looked at me in an attempt to gain my support. His plan sounded reasonable.

"Sounds good to me," I replied. "Let's go do it."

*   *   *

Minutes later, we were back in Mark's truck again, driving over to the shopping center. None of us said anything as we made our way through the empty streets. Since it was already past 10:00 pm, the town was comatose, with only a few late night dwellers wandering around.

"Who's going to make the call?" asked Thad. I could tell by the way he posed the question that he was certain it wasn't going to be him.

"I'll do it," I volunteered. I figured that Thad was too uptight to say the right things and Mark was too unpredictable when it came to dealing with the police.

We pulled into the shopping center parking lot adjacent to the Taco Bell restaurant. Instead of stopping near the phones, Mark drove right up to the dumpster in back.

"Why are you stopping here?" I asked. "The phones are over there."

"I've got to get rid of all this glass. Don't be a baby. Go ahead and walk over there you wimp."

As I slowly headed for the phone, Mark and Thad were busy pulling the broken glass from the truck seat and throwing it into the dumpster. Because the entire window was shattered, they had to remove all of the glass.

"Hey, wait for us," shouted Mark as he and Thad came running over. "We can finish that later. Can't have you doing this thing all by yourself now. Besides, I want to hear what those turkeys say to you."

"What's the number for the police?" I asked after inserting my quarter.

"Don't be stupid, Matt," said Mark. "Everyone knows it's 911."

"I mean the regular office number asswipe," I said. "911 is for god damn emergencies."

"Well, what the hell do you call a man laying dead in the woods with his killers still running around shooting at people?" asked Mark. "I think they won't mind you using that number to tell them about it." I always hated it when Mark was right.

While I stood there with the receiver in my hand, my palms began to sweat as my heart went into full throttle. After dialing the number, the phone rang three times before someone finally picked up at the station.

"Hello, Elkins police station emergency, how may I help you?" answered a young woman. I somehow expected that the person on the other end of a 911 line would be a bit more interested. Whoever it was sounded bored with her job—or maybe with her life in general.

31

"I'd like to report . . . a . . . murder," I somehow managed to say. I tried to lower my voice to sound older.

"Who is this?" asked the woman. "Please state your full name and address."

"Never mind that. There is a dead body in the Monongahela Forest around three miles south of Badger Creek in the . . ."

"Please sir, I need your name," she insisted.

"I said I'm not giving you my god damn name," I insisted. "Now do you want the information or not?"

A moment later someone else at the station got on the phone. "Okay, sonny, this better not be some kind of joke. Now what do you want?" asked one of the other cops.

"I'm trying to report a murder. There is a guy in the . . ."

"Who is this?" asked the cop.

At that point Mark, who was listening to what I said, lost his temper and grabbed the phone out of my hand. "Now listen asshole and listen good 'cus I'm only going to say this once. There is a dead man in the Monongahela National Forest near Badger Creek about three miles in the forest to the right. He was shot in the back with a pistol. There are markers there to show you where the body is. He was killed by three men who probably came from another state. The dead guy's name is Carter and he came from New York City. If you want to find him, you'd better get your butts out there before some animal comes along and eats him up. This is no joke."

Before the cop could say another word, Mark hung up the phone. "Let's get the hell out of here," he hissed. For some reason the phone call got him real fired up. "I told you those cops were idiots. They couldn't solve a god damn crime if they committed it themself—the dumb fucks."

Minutes later we drove right past the police station on our way home. I guess in my mind, I expected to see flashing lights or groups of men getting organized to send out search parties to locate the corpse. But it looked as quiet as ever.

"Do you think they understood what you were trying to say," asked Thad as if to imply that maybe Mark hadn't spoken clearly enough.

"Shut up, Thad," Mark responded angrily. "You heard what I said. Were you able to follow it?"

"Let's forget about it," I said trying to restore the peace. "It's late and I'm exhausted. Take me home."

"Matt, why don't you stay at my house tonight," Mark offered. "My parents are probably asleep and your folks will wonder why you didn't go to my uncle's cabin. You know how your father is. He'll drill you to death if you come home unexpected like this."

"Well, what about me?" asked Thad.

"What about you?" replied Mark. "I'll drop you off on the

way." Mark had had enough of Thad for one night. Thad lived only a mile or so away from Mark's house so it was easy to swing by. Thad was disappointed that he was not invited over. Even though he wanted to go home, he would have liked to have been invited to Mark's house anyway.

3

It was Mark's mom who came in and woke us up the following morning. With her bright orange hair which resulted from not following the directions on the hair color box, her puffy rabbit slippers, and her light blue robe which did a nice job of covering up her oversize body, Mrs. Clark resembled the stereotypical bon-bon eating, soap opera watching housewife depicted so often on TV.

"Mark, Mark, wake up," she whispered as she gently shook his shoulder. It was nearly impossible to get him out of bed at that particular time of the day. It was like waking the dead. "Mark, I want you to listen to me. Thad's on the phone. He says it's real important and he needs to talk to you." When there appeared to be no sign of life coming from Mark's bed, she turned to me and asked, "Matt can you see what you can do with him?"

"Sure thing, Mrs. Clark. I'll do what I can."

"By the way, I thought you boys were going up to uncle's cabin to fish last evening. What happened? You all seemed so excited about the trip." She tried to straighten Mark's room up a bit while she talked.

"Well, um, we decided to fish Cheat River instead," I responded. "Old man Wilson said they stocked the run near the bridge off Route 11. We thought we might get lucky there instead."

"Did you catch any?" she asked timidly. By this time she was used to the fact that we spent a great deal of time fishing without ever really catching anything. A couple of high school age boys from West Virginia who couldn't fish—that was a real embarrassment for the entire family.

"The usual," I muttered under my breath.

"You'll have better luck next time," she said as she patted me on the head like one would a small child. "Now, Mark, go talk to Thad. He's been waiting on the phone for quite a while now."

She left the room before Mark stirred in his bed. From years of experience, he had learned that the best way to deal with his mother in the morning was to just play dead.

"What time is it?" asked Mark as he reached for his alarm clock. "Shit, look at this, it's only seven o'clock in the morning on a Saturday. Shoot." After tossing the clock into a pile of clothes on the floor, he turned over and covered his head with the sheets. "Matt, you go talk to Thad. I can't deal with him this early in the morning."

"What if it's something about last night?" I asked nervously.

For a moment Mark raised his head and thought about something. He then mumbled, "Yesterday was ancient history, forget about it. We'll worry about it later."

It looked as if there was virtually no chance that Mark was going to make any effort to pull himself out of bed. So I climbed out from under the covers, threw on a pair of pants and decided to talk to Thad myself. As always, Mark's room was a complete disaster area. Along with heaps of clothes distributed all over the place, his school books and papers were scattered in multiple piles on top of piles. Mark's infinite number of sports trophies were everywhere. He had long since run out of room for all of them. Like most people who have an overabundance of something, they no longer held any meaning for him. To get myself out of there, I had to watch my every step to avoid falling over something. Mark's mother had given up trying to introduce order into the room years before—it was truly a hopeless case.

As I went to pick up the phone near the refrigerator, I noticed that Mark's dad and brother were at the kitchen table feasting on scrambled eggs, smoked sausage, home fried potatoes and sweet butter rolls. The incredible smell given off by these fat-filled foods seemed to overwhelm the entire house. In Elkins, unlike the rest of the world, those foods were still considered good for you. The word "cholesterol" to most folks sounded like something you spread on an open cut before putting on a Band-aid. While other Americans bought all that talk about giving up fatty foods, the people of Elkins just went on enjoying this pleasure in life. Course this meant that many of us were blimps. But I guess life is full of trade offs.

"Hey, Matt, how's it going," asked Mark's dad as I reached for the receiver. Mark and his father were the splitting image of each other. They both had the same easy-going mannerisms and the same infectious smile. Looking at Mark's dad, I could almost guess what Mark would be like in twenty-five years.

"Fine, Mr. Clark, just fine," I replied back in an attempt to act as if nothing had happened. I tried to look relaxed, but I'm not sure I was all that convincing. Mark's brother kept staring at me kind of funny. "Hello . . . hello."

"Mark, is that you?" asked Thad with a half-crazed voice. It sounded like he was teetering on the edge of hysteria. "It took you long enough."

"No, it's me, Matt," I said. The sound of Thad's voice alarmed me. I couldn't help feeling that the proverbial shit had hit someone's General Electric fan. I knew that what he was about to say had to be pretty bad. "So, what's up?"

"Jesus, did you see the newspaper this morning? They found the wrong guy. They say they found some fisherman who was beaten to death, not shot. They're going to think we did it . . . shit we're in big trouble. We should have just gone to the police like . . ."

"Yes, Thad, I'm over here at Mark's house in the kitchen with his family." I then whispered to him, "I can't talk now, meet us at Scotty's Restaurant in twenty minutes and for god sake calm down." I hung up the phone and calmly walked over to the kitchen table.

Mark's brother was still looking at me suspiciously. He never really liked me all that much. Maybe that's because I spent the last ten years harassing him. These days, he always seemed to have that look in his eyes which communicated "someday I'll get back at you." At twelve, he was already a big kid. I knew that one day he'd probably pay me back big time.

"Is everything alright?" asked Mrs. Clark. She had a worried expression on her face. "Thad sounded a bit upset this morning."

"Oh, he's fine. You know how he gets right before finals."

"I suppose so," she said. "Matt, do you want some breakfast?" As good as it looked and smelled, I couldn't concentrate on food just then. Thad's phone call really had me spooked.

"No thanks, Mrs. Clark," I responded back in a nonchalant manner. "We're meeting Thad over at Scotty's for a quick bite. Um, Mr. Clark are you finished with the paper? I want to see the basketball scores." The paper was lying on the chair next to him.

"Sure thing. Oh by the way, Michigan won and it looks as if the Bulls are going to win the series again," he confessed with a certain degree of disappointment. "Can't say I'm happy about it. Those Bulls are too damn conceited if you ask me." He handed me the sports section which was lying on top of the pile.

"Actually, could I have the whole paper if you don't mind?" I asked. "I um, I also want to see what's happening in the news."

Mr. Clark hesitated for a moment, took off his glasses and then handed all the loose sections to me. "Taking an interest in the world, uh Matt?" he asked as he chuckled under his breath. "Thad must be rubbing off on you guys. By the way, did you hear about that Bantum man killed over in the park last evening. It happened right in Elkins own back yard. World's getting pretty ugly these days."

"Yes, sir, it sure is," I replied back before leaving. At some level, I was kind of hoping that Thad had somehow got it all wrong. But hearing it come from Mark's dad confirmed that Thad didn't have some wild nightmare after all.

The moment I got back to Mark's room I frantically searched for the front page. They had somehow managed to twist the paper all inside out. Mark had fallen back to sleep again.

I couldn't believe my eyes when I finally saw the headlines "Bantum Man Murdered Near Cheat River." The story read as follows:

"Elkins police reported that early Saturday morning they located the body of a Bantum man near Badger Creek within the Monongahela National Park. The man was found beaten to death with multiple bruises to his head and abdomen. His identity is being withheld until his immediate family can be notified.

Police say that the man's body was discovered late last night after an anonymous phone call directed them to the scene of the crime. Police suspect that some type of radical religious cult may have been responsible for the murder. The body was surrounded by a circle of fishing line which had small pieces of red cloth tied every two or three feet. Authorities speculated that this might be some kind of makeshift alter for the murder. Several feet from the body was a fire which was still burning upon the arrival of the police. In addition, local authorities also found several items of clothing presumably belonging to the killers. In an unusual twist in the case, the police noticed that a collection of rocks were used to spell out the number 666. This number is often associated with the worship of satan.

Police suspect that the man was probably fishing along the Cheat River when he was abducted and taken into the woods. He was wearing a full fishing outfit, complete with a bag which contained several rainbow trout. Authorities also reported that they found the tail of a trout protruding from the victim's mouth. Apparently, a small brown trout had been forcibly lodged down the man's throat following his death. Authorities believe that this might have been part of the ritual.

Because of the unique circumstances of the case, police have called in representatives from the Federal Bureau of Investigation's special cult task force unit to assist in the investigation. The fact that a phone call was made to the police to report the crime leads authorities to believe that the group wanted to publicize their misconduct.

Citizens of Elkins and surrounding areas should keep a look out for anything which appears out of the ordinary. Anyone with any information which might help the authorities solve this case are urged to contact their local police station."

After reading the article, I ran over to Mark and frantically tried to wake him up. "Mark, Mark . . . get your ass up, we've got major problems."

"What is it . . . get away from me and let me sleep," he said as he tried to push me aside and roll back onto his stomach.

"Mark, I said we're in deep, deep shit man," I repeated in a very serious tone.

A moment later, Mark sat up and paused before saying, "What are you talking about?" His eyes were still half shut. He looked like he had just woken up from a six month hibernation. "This had better be good, Matt. It's Saturday morning remember?"

"Take a look at this," I said as I tossed the newspaper onto his lap.

"So what, our taxes are going up again, big deal."

"Not that story, you jerk, look at the other headline," I said as I pointed toward the article.

It took him a while to read the entire article, but every few lines he became more and more alert. "What the hell is going on?" he nearly shouted. "This is bull shit. They say there the guy had on a fishing suit. I didn't see any god damn fishing clothes on Carter. He was wearing dress pants. They also said his head was beaten and that there was a fish shoved down his throat. We didn't see any of that . . . they must have gone to the wrong spot."

"Come on, Butthead, think about it. It says that they found the guy surrounded by fishing line which had small pieces of red cloth on it. It had to be our spot."

"Shit, what's going on here then?" Mark was totally baffled. "None of this makes any sense."

"Don't you see, those guys we bumped into last night are trying to frame us. I think the dead guy they found in the woods was that man who was walking along the road last night. Remember, the one I nearly hit with the truck—that fisherman. He probably heard the shots, ran up to see what was going on and they bumped him off to keep him quiet."

"But how did they find Carter's body in the first place? It was out there in the middle of the woods."

"They probably just followed the Dorito trail you left behind. Remember? Since they thought we'd go and tell the police about them, they changed bodies to discredit us."

"What do you mean discredit us?" asked Mark not understanding what I was talking about.

"Listen, if we called the police and said that some guy from New York was laying there and then it turns out that someone else was there instead, it makes us look like liars," I tried to explain.

"Shit, shit, shit . . . I can't believe this is happening," said Mark as he covered his face with his pillow. I never saw Mark so affected by anything before.

"It was Thad who called and told me about the article," I said as I started pulling Mark's clothes together. "He's half out of his mind. I told him to meet us at Scotty's in twenty minutes so get your ass up. We need to figure out what to do next."

"Wait a minute, so where's the other body, that Carter guy's body?" asked Mark. "They didn't mention it in the newspaper."

"I don't know. I haven't figured that out yet."

*   *   *

Mark and I decided to walk to Scotty's because of the broken window on his pick-up truck. He wasn't ready for his father or anyone else to see the damaged goods. As we made our way through a small patch of forest behind his house in the direction of the town center, I couldn't help but feel somewhat responsible for that poor man's death. If we hadn't drawn those guys out of the woods when we did, he'd probably still be alive today, I kept thinking to myself. As much as I tried to put the thought out of my mind, the guilt my parents had taught me to feel about such things kept creeping back.

"You know, Mark, we are partly to blame for that Bantum man's death," I confessed with a bit of remorse in my voice.

"What the hell are you talking about?" asked Mark, not understanding what I was trying to say. He stopped walking and turned towards me before saying, "That's an incredibly stupid thing to say."

"Well, just think about it. It was because of us that they came running down that road. If they hadn't seen us last night, the poor guy would still be alive."

"I'm not taking any responsibility for that man being dead," Mark insisted. "If you are looking for someone to blame, talk to your good buddy Thad. He's the asshole who started this whole mess. You know, I should have made him eat some of that bear shit when I had the chance."

"I know what you're saying, but I still feel bad."

"Forget about it. There is nothing we can do about it now."

Mark and I started walking again, this time in silence as we passed through old man Taylor's back yard on our way to Cedar Street. As always, Taylor opened his kitchen window and yelled out obscenities at us for trespassing on his property. Mark and I just went about our business as if nothing was happening. After ten years of the same routine nearly every day, Taylor's ranting and raving had long since been reduced to nothing more than background noise for us.

"Do you think that those men last night would recognize us

if they saw us walking around town?" I asked as I kept an eye out for strangers as we made our way along the road.

"Probably not," Mark replied back. "It was too dark for them to see anything. The only one I really got close to was the squirrelly man. I'd probably be able to ID him if I ran into him again, being so close and all. But I doubt he'd ever recognize me."

When we finally arrived at Scotty's Restaurant, Thad was nervously pacing back and forth out in front. He had on his old pair of glasses to replace the ones that had been broken the night before. With tired looking, bloodshot eyes, it appeared as if he hadn't slept much since we last saw him.

Since Scotty's was overcrowded, with a line of people waiting to get inside for some of the best food in town, we decided to head down the road to the Burger Barn Restaurant instead. The place always had plenty of empty booths available on Saturday mornings, which would offer some semblance of privacy.

"So what the hell took you two so long?" Thad complained as we made our way together along the main street in the direction of the restaurant. "Matt, you told me twenty minutes. It's already over forty-five minutes. Look at my watch."

"Shut up, Thad," Mark snapped back. "We're here now, alright?"

"Did you see the paper this morning?" asked Thad.

"I say we talk about it after we get inside," I suggested. "I want to sit down before we get into this whole mess."

After arriving and ordering three cups of black coffee, we found a small, secluded booth away from all of the families who were sitting around, stuffing their faces with greasy hashbrowns and sausage muffin "thingies." Although I hated taking my coffee black, everyone else in town I knew seemed to drink it that way. I figured I might as well get used to it straight up. What else could I do?

From the moment we sat down, it was evident that Thad was on the verge of losing it. Whenever he got nervous or excited about something, the left side of his nose twitched up and down. Mark and I made a fortune off him playing poker since it always happened whenever he tried to bluff. This time, the way his nose was bobbing all over the place, it looked like at any moment it would fly right off his face.

"So, did you see the newspaper?" asked Thad again.

"Yeah, we read it," I admitted.

"So what the hell is going on?"

"You read the article, you tell us what's going on," responded Mark. Both Mark and Thad looked at me for an answer to the question—as if I knew more than they did.

"I told Mark I think they were trying to set us up," I

explained. "Those men last night must have found Carter's body and knew that we would tell the police about it. I think they didn't want anyone to know about him so they put another body there in his place. When the police came, they found this guy from Bantum and now they won't be looking for anyone else."

"But how could they have possibly found Carter's body?" asked Thad. "He wasn't anywhere near their campsite."

"Think about it, Thad," I explained. "If we weren't trying to hide something, wouldn't we have just walked right past their campsite as if nothing were going on. They must have figured out that we were scared of them by the fact that we hid in the woods. Mark jumping that man only added to this impression."

"That still doesn't answer my question," Thad repeated himself. "How could they find Carter's body way out there?"

"Don't you remember the Doritos?" I asked. "We left a trail that led right to his body."

"Oh, I forgot about them. Shit."

"They must have found the trail and just followed it there. So anyway, if we had gone to the cops, they wouldn't have found Carter there and we'd have been really screwed. They would have thought we were the ones who did him for sure."

I could tell Thad understood my little theory, but even after explaining it twice to Butthead, I wasn't sure he fully followed my logic. He had a confused look all over his face.

"So what are we going to do now?" asked Thad as his nose twitched in full gear. "The police are going to figure out we were there. It's just a matter of time."

"And how are they going to do that?" asked Mark. "They've got no proof we were there."

"By our fingerprints, stupid," said Thad. "Don't you ever watch TV or read books."

"First of all, what is there that has our fingerprints on it?" asked Mark. "And second, did anyone ever take your fingerprints before, Thad?" He shook his head no. "They can only determine if it was your prints if they have prints to match them with. There is no way they can possibly connect what happened out there in those woods with us." It was bizarre to actually hear Mark say something that made logical sense. This was a rare occasion indeed.

"I don't know, Mark," I said feeling a little skeptical. "What if they find Thad's glasses out there in the woods? Have you ever seen anyone else in town wearing thick glasses like Thad's. All they have to do is take them down to the local eye shop to find out they belong to him."

"So what does that prove?" asked Mark defiantly. "Thad could just say he lost them out there. You guys are too paranoid. Now let's just forget this thing ever happened and get on with our lives."

"I don't get my glasses here in town," said Thad in a quiet voice. "We go to an eye specialist in Washington, D.C."

"See," said Mark as if redeemed. "Even if they found them out there, they can't track them to us. They'll never know we were anywhere near that place."

"I don't care if they'll never be able to track us down," said Thad. "I'm going straight to the police right now. All we have to do is tell them our story and they'll believe us. I know they will. That way we won't have to worry about them someday coming after us. It's the only way."

"Oh, yeah," said Mark sarcastically. "Then how are you going to explain why we didn't tell them about this thing until now? And what about the fact that the body we saw there hasn't been found? What are you going to say—the dead guy we saw with bugs coming out of his mouth must have just gotten right up and walked away?"

"We tried to tell them last night on the phone," Thad explained. He was trying to piece together something, anything which would provide a solution to this mess. "They probably put it on tape or something. That will convince them. Right?"

"Fat chance," replied Mark. "If we go in there now, our asses will be fried. Believe you me. All they're looking for is someone to pin this thing on. You want to be that person?"

"You know, I just can't believe this shit," said Thad as he put his head between his hands. "I know it, we're all going to get caught and they're going to take me off to some jail and I'm going to become someone's boy-toy for the next ten years. You know what happens in those prisons. I don't care what you guys say, we should have gone in and told the police the truth from the beginning. We should go report this thing right now and take our chances. It's the right thing to do."

"I told you," Mark explained. "It's too damn late. If we go there now we're going to end up in jail for sure. Now forget about saying anything to anyone. Believe me, those stooges at the cop station will never be able to figure this out. They are all mindless bums. I say we lay low and ride this thing out."

"I don't know, Mark, they think some kind of a cult was involved," I finally jumped into the conversation. I kept finding myself siding with Mark and then with Thad and then with Mark again. I couldn't make up my mind who was right. "The cops aren't going to let this one go unsolved. Too many people are going to be terrified until someone is caught. Besides, the paper said they have already called in the FBI. Even if the Elkins police are complete fools, the Feds have ways of finding these things out."

"So big deal, a few boys from the "Federal Bureau of Idiots" are here," said Mark as he laughed out loud. "Listen Matt, you've seen those 60-Minute type shows on TV where a few teenagers are picked up for some bizarre cult crime. They are always people that no one would ever suspect—an honor student or some kind of do-gooder. Before we had a chance to tell our story, which I might add is hard to believe now that Carter's body is gone, I think everyone would automatically believe that we were guilty as sin. I think our only chance is to just lay low. Now if we knew where Carter's body was, that would be another story, but we don't."

"I still think they'll find out," declared Thad. "I don't care what you say, I'm going to the police. We'll tell them what happened and take our chances. It's the only way."

As Thad started to stand up, Mark grabbed him by the collar and forced him to sit down again. Thad made no attempt to resist.

"Now, Thad, despite the fact that you irritate the hell out of me most of the time, for some strange reason I still consider you my friend," Mark whispered to him softly. "Now, let me say one more thing before you decide to blab to the world that we were wrapped up in this mess. Those men last night, whoever they were, shot at us and then killed some innocent bystander at the drop of a hat. What makes you think that they're going to allow us to say bad things about them? They could be living right here in town for all we know. What if we tell the police everything and these guys decide that they don't like us? Um? You know that our pictures will be in all of the papers, on TV. What's to stop them from doing the same to us? And remember what that guy said to me in the woods? Do you remember? He kept saying over and over again 'I'll find you and you'll be dead meat.' Those were his exact words I swear. Now if we go to the police, we will either end up in jail or dead. Do you want that to happen? I know I don't. I still think we have a good chance of getting off if we just stick together and keep our traps shut." I had never seen Mark more articulate and clear about something in his entire life. It was scary to see him making so much sense.

"Mark's right, Thad," I said reluctantly, finally choosing sides after all of my waffling back and forth. "I don't see any other way out of this one. At least not for now."

Feeling overwhelmed and defeated, at that point Thad covered his face with his napkin and started to cry. Up to this point in his life, Thad's biggest fear was getting anything less than an A on an exam. He was totally unprepared for the "real" world to show its ugly face in small-town Elkins. It was in stark contrast to his "perfect" life. This was not part of the plan.

"Thad, come on now," said Mark with one of his big smiles. "Everything is going to be okay. I promise you, I won't let anything happen to you. Don't worry about those guys, we'll just stay away from them. And as for those prisoners, I wouldn't let them have that cute bod of yours, it's all mine." Mark reached over and tried to tickle Thad to snap him out of his mood.

"Get the hell off of me, Butthead," said Thad as he pushed Mark away. "You joke about everything. Well not this time. This is for real, Butthead. We are in some real big trouble and I'm scared shitless."

"Cool it, Thad," I said as I looked around the restaurant. "You're talking too loud. People are starting to look over here. I'm also scared. We're all scared."

There was a long pause while we all sipped our black coffees in silence. The more I thought about it, the more my mind began circulating different scenarios about how we'd be hunted down and killed by those men from the woods. I kept imagining a car driving up with them wielding shot guns. They'd force us inside the vehicle and take us someplace to execute us. With every replay of this event in my mind's eye, I began to feel myself becoming more and more terrified.

"So if we're not going to the police, then what do we do now?" asked Thad after regaining control of his emotions. "I'm not going to just sit here and wait for the police or those mad-dog killers to come for me. I'll go completely insane."

"Thad's right about that, Mark," I agreed, rejoining his side once again. "Both the cops and those men might be out there searching for us right now. I don't want to just sit around and wait to see who comes for us first."

"So what the hell do you think we should do?" asked Mark defensively. I could tell he was beginning to get frustrated by all this nonsense. "Have you got some kind of plan in mind?"

"Wait a minute, I think I got an idea." All at once something Mark had said seemed to make sense to me. "And before you say anything, just hear me out. Maybe we can go to the police at some point, but before we go, we can try to find out what happened to Carter's body. Once we know where he is, then we can go to the police and explain everything that happened. You said so yourself, Mark, if we knew where Carter's body was, it would be another story. Without Carter, either the media will try and convict us if we turn ourselves in or we'll be hunted down by those chumps . . . or both."

"So how the hell are we going to find him?" asked Thad not quite believing what he was hearing. "We don't even know who it was who took the body. It could be anywhere by now."

"Well, let's just look around a bit and see if anything turns up," I explained. "I say we go back to Mark's house and check out what's in Carter's wallet again. Maybe there's something we overlooked. If we don't find anything then we'll just drop it. What the hell do we have to lose? At least we'll be doing something."

Both Mark and Thad looked at each other before getting up and walking toward the door. My suggestion was the perfect compromise to break the stand off between the two of them. At the time, I was only half serious and never thought that anything would come from it.

*   *   *

From the Burger Barn, we returned to Mark's garage again and spread the contents of Carter's wallet all over the hood of the trunk. After inspecting each of the business cards, there didn't appear to be any kind of pattern. Some belonged to antique store owners in New York and New Jersey. Others came from service contractors such as Sears Carpet Cleaners and the like.

There was a small sheet of paper which had all kinds of numbers written all over it. But this also yielded no clues about Carter. The numbers were in random order with no real pattern.

"Wait a minute," I said full of excitement. "I think I have something here. Look at this Mastercard receipt."

"What about it?" asked Thad as he tried to look over my shoulder. I had to push him away because he kept pulling my shirt like a little kid.

"It's for the Gateway Motel on Main Street here in town," I said as I inspected the receipt. "He must have been staying there. The slip says that he took out a room for three days starting yesterday afternoon. And look at this one, there is also a charge slip for a Hertz Rent-A-Car . . . it says they gave him a red Toyota Camry, license number MF4423. He rented the car for a week, beginning Thursday, May 12th. That was two days ago. He must have rented the car in New York and came here on some kind of business."

"So what?" asked Mark not quite understanding the importance of such a find. "He's dead. How is that stuff going to help us now."

"At least we know where he was before he was murdered," I said optimistically. "We might be able to find something out from the people who own the motel."

"Isn't that motel run by those Indians?" asked Mark. "Remember how freaked out everyone was when some foreigners came in and bought that place from old Mr. Cleaton? People kept talking about how within a few years the entire town would be bought out by outsiders. Don't you remember that?"

"I remember that family," I laughed out loud. "The old guy wears some kind of diaper wrapped around his head and his wife always has a red dot between her eyes and that funny dress wrapped all around her."

"It's called a saree," Thad casually remarked. Mark had no idea what Thad was talking about.

"What's sorry?" asked Mark.

"I said saree, not sorry," Thad explained. "That's what women in India wear."

"Whatever," said Mark totally uninterested in this bit of cultural trivia. "So what do we do now?"

"I say we go over to the motel and see if we can find anything there." I knew it was a long shot. But there was nothing to lose.

"What are we looking for?" asked Mark.

"I don't know, I'll tell you when we find it."

With that, we were off once again, this time to the Gateway Motel in search of clues to Carter's whereabouts.

*   *   *

None of us could believe our eyes after arriving in front of the Gateway Motel. There, parked right in front of room number "Two," was a brand new red Toyota Camry with a Hertz Rent-a-Car sticker plastered right smack in the middle of the bumper. The license plate also matched the Mastercard slip. Carter had been staying there alright.

The three of us stood on the sidewalk across the road as the heavy traffic on Main Street raced by. We watched as a cleaning woman left the first room and walked over towards room "Two." She was a large black woman who had a hard time moving about because of her excessive size. She must have weighed in at over 300 pounds. Her light-blue uniform, which was obviously one or two sizes too small, looked as if it was going to burst off her body at any moment. From the sour grimace which seemed to be pasted onto her face, she wasn't overly thrilled to be working there—or perhaps anywhere else.

"That must be where Carter was staying," I said as I pointed to the second room. "You don't think they would have put the body back into his room, do you?" Mark pushed my hand down. I was looking a bit too conspicuous standing there pointing across the street.

"If he is in there, we'll know in about a second," said Mark with a bit of a laugh. We all watched as the cleaning woman knocked on the door. "That poor lady will probably have a complete heart failure herself if she finds Carter sprawled out dead on the bed with bullet holes through his back."

"Shhhit," said Thad nervously. "Look, she's taking out her keys. Oh, man, she's going inside. She's going inside!" We all watched and waited as she finally used her key to unlock the door and enter. For some reason, Thad seemed to be totally convinced that Carter was in the room. I could see him lose all the color in his face while waiting for the outcome. I must admit, I was also kind of expecting to see the poor woman come screaming out of that room any minute. The anticipation of the

46

moment was awesome.

Seconds later, she came waddling out carrying a handful of towels which she dropped into a small bucket before locking the door behind her. So much for that theory, I thought.

"Actually, if you think about it, if they were trying to erase Carter from this planet, don't you think they'd have gotten rid of his car if they knew it was here?" I asked in an attempt to rationalize the situation.

"They must not know about the car or that Carter was staying at this place," replied Thad in support of my assumption.

"Or, what if they are keeping the car here to see if we will come looking for it?" asked Mark. I could tell he was looking around to see if anyone was watching us. "They could be staking out this place right now. Just waiting for us to fall into their little trap."

Thad and I had this habit of making eye contact whenever Mark said something incredibly stupid—this was one of those times. That fairly rational person I observed over at the Burger Barn Restaurant seemed to have vanished. Mark had somehow miraculously returned to his old dumb jock self.

"Think about it, Butthead," Thad explained slowly so Mark could clearly understand. "You don't really think that they would believe that we'd be stupid enough to try to track down Mr. Carter or any of his killers, do you?"

It took Mark a while before he figured out that Thad was making fun of him. He must have realized that his statement sounded kind of ridiculous because he didn't reply back.

"So what now?" asked Thad impatiently. "We know that Carter stayed here. We know he's not in the room. Big deal. We still don't know where they stashed his body and we never will. This has all been rather pointless, wouldn't you say?"

"Wait a minute, don't you see?" I responded back full of enthusiasm. "He probably left some of his stuff inside that room. We have to find a way to get inside. Maybe there is something in there which will lead us to him."

"Yeah, like the motel owner is going to just let us waltz right into his room and look around through his things," said Thad with that annoying tone of his, which bordered on being obnoxious. "Or are we going to add breaking and entering onto our list of crimes they will charge us with when they finally get around to picking us up?"

With Thad's arms crossed tightly across his chest and his nose twitching in full gear, I could tell I was in for a good deal of resistance.

"We don't have to break in," I answered back defensively. "We'll just ask for permission to wait inside the room."

Both Mark and Thad stared at me as if I had three heads. I'm sure they were convinced that I had completely lost my mind.

"What the hell are you talking about?" asked Mark before Thad could say anything. "And how are we going to do that?"

"Well, one of us will just go up to the owner and say that he is Carter's nephew," I explained. "We'll tell the guy that Carter left his wallet at our house after visiting and he called and asked us to drop it off. We know enough about the man to be fairly convincing, don't you think?"

"And then what?" asked Thad, still totally unconvinced. "How are you going to get them to let you inside the room? Who'd be that stupid?"

"I don't know, I'm sure we can think of something which will convince them," I replied. "All it takes is a little imagination. That's all."

"So where is his wallet?" asked Mark. "Didn't you lock it up in my tool bench again?"

"No," I pulled the wallet out of my back pocket. "I brought it along just in case we needed it." Actually, I didn't really trust leaving it in Mark's garage. All that money was too much of a temptation for someone with his questionable scruples.

"So who is going to do this wonderful thing," asked Thad, knowing very well that it wasn't going to be him.

I was afraid they were going to ask that question. I could tell from the way they were both looking at me that they expected me to do the dirty deed. Yes, it was my idea but why should I be the one to carry it out, I thought to myself. At some level I knew I didn't have a choice. There was no way that Thad could pull it off. And even though Mark was the master liar among the three of us, he was never all that convincing when asked to play someone other than himself.

"I think Thad should do it," I said in a semi-serious tone. Even though I knew it was a crazy idea, I wanted to see his reaction, which was always very predictable.

"No way, no way, no way," said Thad as he waved his hands back and forth, and backed away from me. "It's your lame-brain plan. You do it. You can keep me out of this one. You're the one who feels it necessary to track Carter down, not me. And even if I wanted to, they'd never believe a word I said. I always break out in a sweat whenever I try to lie. Forget it, Matt."

I turned to Mark. My expression must have betrayed what I was about to suggest.

"Don't even say it, Matt," said Mark before I could even get a word out. "You know I'm not afraid of anything, but they'd believe you before they'd believe me. You have that trusting face." He reached out and pinched my cheek as he said it. "Actually, I say we drop all of this nonsense and just head on home. I'm perfectly content to completely forget about Carter's dead body and go on with my life."

"Okay, then I'll do it," I said reluctantly. "But if it looks as if this scheme isn't working, I'm just going to run like hell. I don't think you guys should hang around here. If they see you, they might think something's up. Go wait somewhere else."

*　　*　　*

Mark and Thad decided to wait over at the Burger Barn Restaurant while I made an effort at pulling off my little hair-brain scheme. It just didn't feel right having them so close by—knowing they were near would have made me even more nervous than I already was.

All kinds of thoughts traveled through my head as I made my way across the busy road and walked in the direction of the motel's registration office. "What makes you think you can get away with this?" that little voice in my head which had always kept me out of trouble, repeated over and over again. "Don't be stupid. Give this thing up." But despite my better judgment, something deep inside me, something new, wild and unexplored, rejected this call for reason and allowed me to forge ahead. I had to do this thing.

It took every bit of courage I could muster to open the screen door. I could feel my hand trembling as I reached for the door knob which separated me from the office inside. The handle felt stuck at first when I went to turn it. But with a little more effort, it gave in to my force and permitted me to pass.

The small registration office was dimly lit and had a strong, almost spicy smell which was foreign to me. This unusual aroma, which only added to my anxiety, seemed to be coming from an adjoining room. The walls were covered with an assortment of tacky posters depicting mountain scenes from Asia and Europe. Next to the reception desk was a small couch and a coffee table which accommodated a collection of magazines which were more than a few years old. In the upper corner, to the right of the desk, there was what appeared to be a small shrine of some type with colorful pictures of elaborate gods dressed in bright colored clothes. One of the gods was red and had an elephant's head on what appeared to be a human body. Ashes were scattered in front of the shrine from incense which must have been placed there for some unknown purpose.

Moments after entering the office, an attractive, middle-aged Indian woman entered from a side door, and stood by the counter. She was wearing a bright yellow "saree" which exposed her mid-section. That bizarre red dot was placed squarely on her forehead. I couldn't help thinking that it looked as if someone had shot her between the eyes with a small caliber rifle. I guess the events of the night before caused me to think of such things.

"Can I help you?" she asked with a strong Indian accent. She seemed incredibly serious to me. I didn't get the sense that she was all that trusting.

"My uncle, uh, Mr. Carter left his wallet at my house last night and my dad told me to bring it to him," I replied nervously. "Has he come back yet? I knocked on his door but there was no answer."

She looked over to the key rack and said, "No, he is still out."

"My dad said that if he wasn't back that I should wait in his room until he returns." I tried to smile as I struggled to prevent my lips from quivering. They felt like they were flopping up and down all over the place. I wondered whether she noticed them as much as I did. She maintained a continuous glaring stare which felt like a laser beam that was capable of cutting a hole right through my head.

"Please give me the wallet and I'll see that he gets it when he returns," she said, reaching out her hand. I couldn't help but notice the dozen or so gold bangles which encircled her arm. The clinking sound they made when they came together created almost a musical melody.

"I'm afraid I can't do that, ma'am," I replied back politely "You see he has a lot of money in it and my father told me to make sure to hand it directly over to Uncle Rob." I pulled the wallet out of my pocket and showed her all the money.

"Your uncle did not stay here last night," she noted. She looked at me the way my mom did when I was about to be accused of something.

"I know he didn't, but he is paid up until tomorrow, isn't he?" I said confirming what I knew to be true from the Mastercard receipt. "He has many friends here in town who insist that he stay with them. He is supposed to return in the next hour or so. I'm not supposed to leave until he comes. He is going to drive me home with his car." I pointed to the red Camry parked outside—another fact verified.

"You can sit there and wait for him until he comes back," she said, motioning her head in the direction of the couch directly behind me.

"Actually . . . if you don't mind, I'd rather wait in his room," I said respectfully. "My school is supposed to compete in one of those school scholastic competitions on TV and I really don't want to miss it. I'm sure Uncle Rob will be back real soon." I thought that if she believed I was the scholarly type, I might win a few points with her.

"I can't let you in his room," she said firmly. "I have never seen you with your uncle before. Do you have any identification?"

"I'm not sixteen yet ma'am," I lied. "I don't carry a license or anything like that." I took Mr. Carter's license out of his wallet and held it next to my face in one last ditch effort to convince her. "Look at his picture. Can't you see the resemblance." I forced another smile on my face and tried to appear as sincere as a church choirboy.

She studied the picture and then me for a long time before she finally walked over and handed me the key. We were right, he was staying in room number Two.

As I left the office, I couldn't believe she actually bought my story. It must be real easy to be a criminal in this town, I thought. I also couldn't believe I was about to break into this poor guy's room. Yesterday the biggest crime I had ever committed was stealing gumballs from the Dollar Store when I was just a kid. Sixteen hours after finding Carter, I was lying to get into the room of a guy who I knew was dead to rummage through his belongings. I couldn't help but wonder how low I'd fall by the end of the week.

As I endeavored to open the door to the motel room, I dropped the keys. My heart was still beating at full throttle and my ability to coordinate was a bit off kilter. Although I couldn't tell for sure, I sensed that the Indian woman was watching me from the registration office window.

Once inside, I quickly shut the door and then immediately turned on the TV. After flipping the channels, to my surprise, I managed to find a station on cable which actually had one of those nerdy school scholastic competitions going on after all. I couldn't believe my good luck.

Based on the way Carter maintained his possessions, he appeared to be some kind of neat freak. He had three pairs of shoes perfectly lined up next to each other. They all looked as if they were standing at attention the way they were carefully placed against the wall. You could almost see your reflection in their shine. He had also taken all of his clothes and very carefully placed them either in the closet on hangers or within the available drawers. Each and every garment looked pressed and cleaned by some anal recessive dry cleaner who strived for perfection. I was also surprised to find that even his socks and underwear looked as if they were ironed—I could swear they all had creases. I laughed to myself at the thought of pleated underwear. In the bathroom, his toothpaste, dental floss, shaving cream and other hygiene accessories were lined up as if a choreographer had been brought in to create the most appropriate configuration.

The only luggage I could find was an empty garment bag and a red, eelskin briefcase which was locked. I shook it several times. I could tell that it contained a bunch of papers and what sounded like a large set of keys. From the moment I discovered it, I felt like the answers we were looking for must be in that case.

51

As I was desperately attempting to open it with a nail file I had found in the bathroom, there was a loud knock on the door. The first thing that came to my mind was that I was caught—they must have found out I wasn't who I claimed to be. I carefully peered out the front window and could see that it was the motel owner—the guy who wore the turban on his head. The man had a long black beard and a humongous belly. He wore a two piece white outfit which reminded me of a pair of pajamas I used to have when I was a kid. Of course, mine had little bunnies all over it.

I walked over to the door and slowly opened it. I wasn't sure what to expect next.

"You can't stay in here," said the man with a heavy Indian accent as he pushed the door open and entered the room. I noticed that his gums were stained red, probably from years of chewing something gross. I couldn't stop looking at them—they were so incredibly ugly. Imagine having to kiss that guy, I thought to myself.

"But my school is competing," I said, pointing to the TV. "It will be over in another five or ten minutes. Please let me stay until then."

He walked up to the television and stared at the screen. There was a commercial on. He was waiting to see if I was telling the truth. Finally, the show came back on again. Luckily he didn't notice the schools were from another part of the state altogether. Aside from Thad, there was no one nerdy enough to participate in that kind of thing at Elkins High School. We had our pride.

"I will put you in another room until he comes back," he said in a strong Indian accent. "You can't stay here. I don't know who you are."

Shit, what was I supposed to do now? Come on, think fast, Matt, I kept saying over and over in my head. What can you say to convince him to let you stay for just a little longer?

"Listen, sir, I would prefer not to stay in another room," I said. "My father told me to wait in Uncle Rob's room until he returned. If you don't believe me, call my father."

"What's the number?" he asked as he tried to read my expression. I never thought he'd take me up on my offer.

"The number?" I asked timidly

"Your father's number?" he repeated impatiently.

I knew that short of telling him a number, he was never going to let me stay. The number is 521-9678."

He walked over to the phone and dialed the number. I could tell he was watching me in the mirror. I tried to look relaxed and natural as I pretended to be interested in the TV program. "What is your name?" he asked.

"My name? . . . it's Kevin," I replied. "Kevin Carter." When he looked away, my eyes kept darting back and forth searching for a way out if I had to make a run for it. Beads of nervous sweat began to form across my brow. One freed itself and slowly made its way down the side of my face. It tasted salty as it ended up on my lips.

"It's busy," he said after trying the number several times.

"My sister must be on the phone again. She can talk for hours. Why don't you try again."

After making a kind of grunting noise, he put the phone down and took one more good look at me before leaving without saying another word.

After he left, I knew I had to get out of there quick. I could tell that he didn't trust me and would keep calling that bogus phone number I gave him. Eventually, the phone line to the Subway Sandwich shop would be free. It always took me about ten calls before I finally got through. It was a long shot that panned out.

I grabbed the briefcase and rushed over to the door. The only thing I could think of was to take the case and open it up somewhere else where I could get my hands on some proper tools. I was afraid the motel owner would come back again and I'd lose my chance to find out what was inside.

I slowly opened the door with great care and tried to peer outside. There didn't seem to be anyone around so I casually strolled out and closed the door. It locked behind me. I then turned right and began to walk in the direction of a small side street that ran along the motel. Before rounding the corner, the door to room number One opened and there standing directly behind me was that Indian dude. Because I had the case in front of me, I wasn't sure whether or not he saw it.

Without waiting to see what would happen next, I made a mad dash out of there. I was always a pretty good runner and was able to put a sizable distance between me and the motel in a matter of seconds. He could have been following right behind me for all I knew. For some reason it never crossed my mind to turn around and look back.

*　　　*　　　*

I must have made quite a spectacle with that eelskin briefcase swinging back and forth as I raced down Colt Street, past the Dollar Store and the billiard hall, and finally up a back alley which led to the rear entrance of Fred's Pawn Shop. Mark and I used to go there often to smoke cigarettes and read Playboys when we were younger because no one could see us from the main street.

While I sat down on a beat-up, wooden crate in an attempt to catch my breath, the stark reality of what I had just done hit me hard. If the police came looking for me, I could get arrested for being a thief and could actually go to jail. I could even end up losing my entire future. "How come I hadn't thought of this before going through with this crazy plan of mine?" I asked myself. As much as I wanted to just forget that the incident had occurred, it was too late. It wouldn't just go away—it was already a part of history now. To clear my conscience, my mind began to quickly rationalize that this wasn't really a misdeed with malice intent. I only did this thing to solve another crime—to find out who killed Carter and to send them to jail. What I did was a noble act. It had to be done to move the process along. But despite all of this mental haggling going on in my head, I couldn't escape the fact that I was feeling ashamed for having done something terribly wrong.

One fact was perfectly clear to me. I knew I had to get out of the area fast. I was sure the motel owner had seen me taking the briefcase. He was probably contacting the police that very moment. Before long, I imagined that the streets would be crawling with cops. My only hope was to get Mark and Thad to somehow pick me up.

After stashing the briefcase under a large pile of discarded cardboard boxes next to a big green dumpster, I cautiously left the alley and made my way around the corner to a pay phone located directly in front of the Mister Donut Shop. It was the only public phone for blocks which I knew was actually in working order. As I was dialing the Burger Barn number, which I was able to retrieve from the phone book, something really awful happened. I could see in the reflection on the stainless steel plate attached to the phone that a local police cruiser had just pulled up right behind me. One of the police officers got out of the car with his nightstick in hand and started walking in my direction. I couldn't help but feel that my life was about to end. "Should I make a run for it or just take it like a man?" I asked myself. I figured if I got caught, I'd just lie like hell. It would be my word against the motel owner's. I hoped that an accusation from some foreigner would not stand up against a local resident's word. Besides, I didn't have the suitcase with me. They'd be looking for some kid with the case in hand.

But to my surprise, the officer walked right past me as he entered the shop. In fact he gave me a big, friendly smile as he passed by. What was I thinking? I'm standing in front of a god damn donut shop. Thousands of cops a day must walk through those doors in search of jelly filled donuts and hot coffee. He was probably having some kind of withdrawal—it was time for his daily donut "fix."

When it looked like I was off the hook, at least for the time being, I turned my attention back to getting in touch with Mark and Thad.

"Hello, Burger Barn, how can I help you?" answered some hamburger flipping toad.

"I need to talk to someone who is at your restaurant now," I explained. "His name is Mark Clark. He is wearing . . ."

"I'm sorry, we don't allow the phone to be used by customers," said the man in a cocky, matter-of-fact manner. What a prick, I thought to myself.

"Are you the manager?" I asked in a scolding tone. He didn't respond. "I asked if you were the manager?" It didn't take a rocket scientist to tell from my voice that I was pissed.

"No, I mean yes, I'm the acting manager," he responded with a little less confidence. "The manager is on his break."

I tried to sound more official this time out. "I'm calling from the hospital. Mark's father has been in a terrible car accident and I need to tell his son to get over here immediately so that he can donate some blood. His father has a very rare blood type and is very close to death." The lies were really pouring out like sweet molasses that day.

"Hold on, I'll try to find him," he said as a sense of urgency seemed to grip him. All at once he was on a mission of mercy. "Oh, um, what does he look like?"

"He's sixteen years old and should be wearing a pair of blue Levis, with a red T-shirt which says 'Go Ahead and Make My Day' printed across the front. Now hurry. It's a matter of life and death."

I waited for a few minutes before I heard Mark's voice on the other end of the phone. The prick had obviously told Mark what I said because he sounded terrified.

"Is my dad okay?" he cried. "Which hospital are you at?"

"Shut up, Butthead, and listen to me. It's me, Matt. Your father's not dying. The stupid burger boy wouldn't let me talk to you so I made up that crazy story. If he's standing there you'd better look worried or something. Now listen carefully to me, I'm in a bit of trouble and need you to get me out of here fast. I ripped off a briefcase out of Carter's room and I think the owner of the motel saw me take it."

"You did what?" Mark asked, totally surprised.

"Just shut up and listen. I'll explain what happened later. He may have already called the police by now. In fact there's one parked right behind me. You got to get Thad's car somehow and pick me up in front of that alley behind Fred's Pawn Shop. You know the place where we used to smoke butts and read those girlie magazines. And make it fast, man. Pretty soon the place will probably be crawling with cops."

"Okay, we'll be right there," he said. I could hear him laughing to himself as he hung up the phone. I'm sure he couldn't believe that I'd sink so low. I could only imagine what the little burger man was thinking when he saw Mark laughing after hearing such a horrifying story about his father.

*   *   *

It took those assholes nearly forty endless minutes before they finally pulled up in Thad's mom's car. You could hardly see Thad's head over the dashboard as he drove up. I ran over to the car and jumped into the back seat keeping my head down. My hands shook as I clung to the stolen briefcase. Even before I had the door closed, Thad started his verbal assault on me.

"Are you crazy Matt?" Thad shouted as he drove off. "You just can't go around breaking into people's rooms and stealing their stuff. And Butthead said you let that guy see you. You are really in trouble now. You're going to go to jail for sure."

"Shut up and drive," I said. I wasn't in any mood for one of Thad's stupid moralistic lectures. "Did you drive past the motel on your way over here?"

"Yeah," said Mark. "There weren't any cops or anything. The place looked pretty dead."

"Drive by again," I insisted. "Maybe they're there by now."

"Are you kidding?" asked Thad, not believing what I was saying. "Let's stay as far away from that place as we can. Do you want to get yourself caught?"

"Just do it," I demanded. I was so wound up by that point, anything would have set me off. As we drove past the motel, there didn't seem to be any cops around anywhere. The place was perfectly quiet.

"So now you've taken up stealing, Matt," Thad started up again. "I expect that kind of criminal behavior from Butthead, but not you. See what happens? It starts with one small crime and before you know it you're getting deeper and deeper into trouble. A week from now, you'll be going around attacking helpless old people or robbing banks. It's like . . ."

"Would you just shut the hell up and drive," I finally yelled with some conviction. "It was worth the god damn risk. I think whatever's in this case will help us learn who this Carter guy is. After we've figured this thing out, we'll explain it all to the police. They'll understand. So just stop your god damn complaining."

"You mean who this guy was," Thad corrected me.

"What are you talking about?" I asked.

"You just said we'd find out who this Carter guy 'is,'" Thad explained. "I'm just pointing out that you should be using the past tense 'was' since the guy is already dead." I decided to leave that one alone. Leave it to Thad to give me English lessons during a time like this.

"So what do you think is in the case?" asked Mark.

"Hell if I know," I admitted as I shook it a few more times.

"I couldn't get it open at the motel. That's why I took it with me. We're going to have to break it open with something. I say we go over to your garage, Mark. Do you have anything that will rip this thing open somehow? It's pretty well built."

"Are you crazy?" asked Thad. "You can't rip that thing open. That's a very expensive briefcase. Isn't it bad enough that you took it? Now you're going to ruin it? Eelskin cases cost a small fortune."

"Well, what do you want us to do with it now that we have it?" asked Mark. "The only way we're going to find out what's in it is to get inside."

There was nothing Thad could say. As much as he didn't like the idea, Mark was right. I also thought that although he'd never admit it, Thad too was dying to see what the case contained.

*   *   *

After arriving at the car shed, I described to Mark and Thad what happened to me at the motel. As much as I tried to tell the story straight, the temptation to stretch the truth just a bit was too compelling. I just gave them what they wanted to hear, a good story—that's all. Going into that motel and taking the briefcase took a lot of balls—I deserved some credit. It wasn't often that I was the center of attention and I wanted the tale to become legendary.

I started off by describing how I was allowed into the room by the owner's wife. It was following this point in the story that the actual version of what occurred began to change somewhat. I went on to explain how the man with the turban came in later and for no reason began accusing me of stealing from his motel. I recalled in great detail how he tried to corner me as he kept waving a big wooden stick in my direction. To defend myself, I grabbed the briefcase to fend off his blows. It took a drop kick to his right thigh to lay him out. As I tried to run past him out the door, he grabbed my ankle in an attempt to pull me back inside. He was yelling something in this bizarre foreign language. I had to smack him on the head with the case to get him off of me. I then ran as fast as I could down the road to the alley.

They both listened to me with their eyes wide open. They hung onto my every word and actually believed it all. As I was telling this highly exaggerated version of what really occurred, I kept expecting them to refute it, but they didn't. If they had, I would have told them that I was only kidding. I guess people will believe just about anything.

"He didn't call the police because he's probably dead from being hit by the briefcase," said Thad in disgust. "I told you, you'd start killing people."

"Don't worry, he was fine," I said in my defense. "The guy

had that cloth diaper thing wrapped around his head for Christ sake. Besides, I saw him getting up as I was taking off."

"Hey, wait a second. I thought you told me over the phone that you weren't sure whether he saw you taking the case or not?" asked Mark in an attempt to clear the record.

"I didn't want you to worry," I admitted. I thought for sure Butthead would call me on this one, but he didn't. To the very end I was prepared to own up to the truth, but they didn't seem to think that what I was saying was all that far fetched. Maybe after Mark's adventure the day before, my story didn't sound all that unbelievable.

For a long time, none of us said anything to each other after that. As if in unison we all felt the need to just think about things for a while. Thad was the one who looked most caught up in some deep far-off thought.

"You know something, maybe that guy never made a call to them after all," Thad finally said out loud.

"Call to who?" asked Mark.

"The cops, you moron," remarked Thad back. "Think about it for a second. It was his wife's fault that Matt was able to get into the room in the first place. If they admit that fact to the police, then they become responsible for whatever was missing. It's probably easier for them to just pretend they don't know anything about it. Besides, maybe they don't have a green card or something and don't want to have anything to do with the police."

"Hey, maybe you're right about that," I said in full agreement. "They've been in West Virginia long enough to know what us folks think about outsiders. It's probably not worth the trouble to get involved."

"What the hell's a green card?" asked Mark, once again confirming that he had no clue about things outside Elkins. Both Thad and I just looked at him with an expression which clearly reflected our utter astonishment that he could be so ignorant. He didn't pursue it.

"Okay now, I said as I walked over, picked up the briefcase and began fiddling with the locks. "Let's just forget what happened at the motel for now and get down to business here. I think it's time to open this sucker up and see what's inside. I bet it's important stuff."

At first we tried to open the case with a screwdriver, but we couldn't seem to fit the end into the lip. We then tried breaking the locks with a hammer and chisel. This only resulted in our crushing them. Finally, Mark grabbed his father's Craftsman heavy-duty electric drill, put on a quarter inch bit and made a dozen holes directly into each lock. When it popped open, we all began grabbing things from inside the case.

"Here's what made all that jiggling noise," I said, while

lifting a set of keys. "There must be at least fifty keys on this thing." The keys were on a large stainless steel ring. Each one was numbered in consecutive order.

"What do you think they open?" asked Mark. He inspected them for some clue. They didn't look like ordinary house or car keys.

"I don't know," I remarked. "All I know is that they are pretty tiny. Hey wait a second, the keys to Carter's rental car are also in here." I picked them up and showed them to Mark and Thad. Neither one of them seemed all that interested in my find.

"Wow, look at this," said Mark as he opened some kind of pamphlet. "I think I got something here. It looks like our friend Carter ran an antique shop in New York City. Listen to this—'The Orient Express, one of New York's finest locations for rare treasures from the orient, features a vast collection of antiquities from India, Nepal, Tibet, China and Burma.'"

"What are you reading from?" asked Thad as he tried unsuccessfully to grab it out of Mark's hands.

"It's a brochure for his store," announced Mark as he handed one to each of us. "His shop is called the Orient Express. Look, there's a picture of the place and on the back is a photo of Carter himself. Man this guy must really have bucks. Check out the kind of junk he sells."

We all inspected the brochures without saying anything. I kept trying to make a match between the dead body I saw in the forest the day before and the man standing there in the picture. If it wasn't for his name under the photo, I never would have believed they were the same person. He looked so much different from his driver's license, which made him seem much younger.

"Who's that other dude in the picture?" I asked.

"It must be his business partner," replied Mark. "According to the caption below, his name is Dr. Shyam Sinha. He looks like some kind of foreigner."

"Well, that explains all of these antique magazines," Thad remarked with a handful of glossy publications which depicted a wide assortment of antiques from around the world. "And look what else I found." Thad handed me a pile of around twenty extra-large color photos. Each had some kind of metal statue or bowl on it. On the back of them was what appeared to be background information on the item, including a price. A lot of the statues were of topless women with over-sized breasts standing or sitting in strange positions.

"Wow, check this out," I said full of excitement. "This guy must be really rich. Some of these things are worth over $50,000."

"Let me see those," said Mark as he grabbed the collection of photos out of my hand. When he realized the erotic nature of the snapshots, he seemed to lose interest in our little quest for answers.

"Hey, there's an address book in here," declared Thad.

"Let me take a look," I said. Thad handed it to me and I quickly flipped through the pages. There were hundreds of names and addresses. I didn't see anything which looked like a clue so I tossed it back into the briefcase. I was anxious to find something a bit more compelling.

"Here's something," I said as I picked up a large file which contained a collection of folded newspapers. The file was labeled "Nepal Project—Confidential" and had a large red ribbon carefully tied around it. On the front page of the first newspaper was an article which was circled with a bright yellow highlighter.

"What's that?" asked Mark. He seemed to have finally lost interest in looking at the erotic statue photos.

"It's some kind of foreign newspaper called the Rising Nepal," I said as I lifted it up to show him. "Let me read what it says"

'In Gorkha District, police reported that the renowned Gorkha Urn was stolen late last night. The bronze urn, which was said to belong to Mitra Lama, a well-known follower of Lord Buddha himself, was taken from a small underground vault in Gorkha Village Development Committee, Ward Number 6. Throughout most of the year, the 500 year old urn was kept in this secure place. Once a year, pilgrims from as far away as Burma come to drink out of the urn as part of a special three day religious ceremony. It is said that the urn has powers to heal and restore youth. At present, there are no leads in the case. Religious leaders from the area report that the urn was priceless. Every effort is being made by police and local authorities to recover the stolen object.'

"So what does that have to do with anything?" asked Mark. "And where the hell is Nepal, anyway? Isn't it somewhere in Italy?"

"Didn't you ever take a geography class stupid?" Thad remarked. "You're thinking of Naples. Nepal is just north of India. Mount Everest is located there—you know, the highest mountain in the world."

"Wait, he circled another article from the same paper four days later," I explained.

'Police are still looking for the Gorkha urn stolen last Tuesday from the Gorkha Village Development Committee, Ward Number 6. Two suspects have been taken into custody following an extensive nationwide manhunt. According to police, two Indian Nationals from Delhi have been charged with stealing the sacred religious artifact. Their names are Rajendra Singh and Ram Prasad Krishna. After three days of extended questioning, both confessed to authorities that they were paid 10,000 rupees each to steal the religious object. After removing the urn from the vault, they traveled south to Butwal where they handed it over to a foreign woman who paid them the money and disappeared with the object over the border into India. Her name and country of origin was not known by the men. They received their instructions by phone. An extensive search is now presently underway to recover the urn in India.'

"When was the paper dated?" asked Thad curiously. He was beginning to show an interest in the content of the articles.

"Two weeks ago," I responded. "There are two or three more articles about the urn here. It looks like they never did find it. But they did say that the woman they were looking for was probably American."

"So what's the big deal?" asked Mark in an attempt to downplay the importance of this find. "Those papers don't tell us anything about Carter or the men who killed him."

"Actually, maybe they do," said Thad. "Just think about it. This guy is a collector of antiques from Asia. He has a store in New York which specializes in that stuff. What if Carter was involved in stealing the urn? The newspaper says it was priceless. He could probably get a fortune for it here in the States. And look at the file name. It says "Nepal Project—Confidential." The word "project" implies that he had some planned activity in mind. The word confidential implies that he didn't want anyone to know about it."

"Come on, Thad, do you really think people would kill for some stupid urn?" asked Mark. He obviously had his doubts.

"Are you kidding me. In Washington D.C. teenagers kill each other for a pair of Nike running shoes," declared Thad. "The paper says that this thing heals and makes you young again. Don't you think a thing like that would be worth something to someone?"

Thad picked up the address book again and began to study it carefully. He would have made an excellent detective. He had this way of piecing together bits of information into a hypothesis. As he flipped through the pages, his left brow danced up and down. This involuntary twitch always occurred when Thad found something that intrigued him.

"What is it?" I asked, knowing that he was onto something.

"Look at this," he said full of enthusiasm. "There are about a dozen phone numbers here for people in Delhi. And check this out, this book also has a schedule in it. The day that Carter died, he was supposed to meet a guy named Mr. Keller in Front

Royal, Virginia at 2:00 pm."

"That's over three hours away from here," I said. "How did he end up in West Virginia?"

"Hell if I know," Thad admitted. "Maybe he never made the meeting."

"So what do you think the meeting was about?" I wondered out loud.

"Maybe it had something to do with that stolen urn from Nepal," said Thad as he continued to examine the address book.

"Come on, Thad," said Mark. "I don't believe any of this shit. Everything you've said so far could just be a mere coincidence."

"Well, what about this then," said Thad with a smug smile on his face. "According to his schedule, Carter was in Delhi two weeks before the urn was taken. He also was in Kathmandu, Nepal one month before that. See." He shoved the book in Mark's face.

"So what," said Mark as he pushed it away. "The guy deals in junk from all of those countries. He was probably just there on business."

"Well do you have a better explanation?" asked Thad in an irritated voice. He was obviously frustrated that Mark didn't accept his logic. "There is nothing else in this briefcase that provides a more compelling motive."

The more I listened to Thad, the more believable this theory began to sound. Maybe he was in the area trying to sell the urn. But if that was the case, why was he in Elkins, West Virginia? Why not sell it in New York or some other more accessible place? What was he doing in the forest without his car? Would someone really kill him over an old piece of junk?

"So what do we do now?" I asked feeling as if we were going nowhere.

"Wait a minute, wait a minute," said Thad as he turned to the address section again.

"What are you looking for?" asked Mark in a sarcastic tone. "Another one of your hair-brain clues?"

"I want to see if this Mr. Keller's name is in the address book," he said as he turned to the K section. There was no Mr. Keller listed in the book.

"What about his wallet?" I asked. "Maybe one of those cards belongs to Mr. Keller." After searching through the cards again, we came up short.

Thad then started looking at all the addresses starting from A. When he got to the H's, his left eyebrow once again began to dance up and down. He then looked through the rest of the pages before describing what he found.

"Well, I think I found something," said Thad as he flipped back to a page on which he had folded the corner. "There's a number and an address for a Ms. Shelly Harper. She lives at 345 Spring Street—in Elkins—Elkins, West Virginia."

"That might explain why he was in town," I remarked to myself. "Well, guys, I think we finally found our first solid lead."

*   *   *

As we slowly drove past Shelly Harper's house on Spring Street, the first thought that came to mind was that she must be one of those crazy old cat-lady types. Her lawn was two or three weeks overgrown and it looked as if the hedges hadn't been clipped for several years. All the plants in the yard were completely wild—the place was a veritable jungle. Everything about the outside of the house looked tattered, run down and out of control. I could only imagine what the inside of the house was like.

"Okay, so we found the place," declared Mark with a less than enthusiastic demeanor. "What the hell are we supposed to do now?"

"Isn't it kind of obvious?" I asked, wondering why I had to always spell everything out to the two of them. "One of us has to go up there and talk to the lady. Right?"

"It's your turn Thad," declared Mark before anyone else had a chance to speak. "Both Matt and I have already done stuff. It's time for you to join in on the fun."

"No way, not me," Thad replied as he shook his head back and forth frantically. "I drove us here. That's enough. This is Matt's crazy plan not mine. I've wanted to go the police from the beginning. I'm not getting in any more trouble, so you can count me out."

"What trouble?" I asked, not quite understanding what Thad thought we were asking him to do. "All you have to do is just go up and talk to the woman. You know, simple conversation. There is nothing criminal about doing that. Is there?"

"And so what am I supposed to say to her?" asked Thad obnoxiously. "Hey, lady, do you know this dead guy we found in the forest. Sorry guys, I can't do it." He put his arms tightly across his chest to further reinforce that there was no way he was budging.

Neither Mark nor I really thought that Thad was the right person for the job, but what irritated us the most was that everything Thad did was done to protect himself. He had this selfish habit of always looking at things from the perspective of what would happen to "him," not to "us." Even if he had volunteered to meet with her, we probably would have talked him out of it. We both knew he'd find a way to screw it up. But he never made the offer. As brilliant as he was when it came to scoring high marks on exams, his insight into what a good friend should be was always seriously lacking.

"Thad, you know something, you're a real dick you know that?" said Mark, totally disgusted. "We've saved your ass several times and you don't even make an effort to work with us."

"Screw you, Mark." Thad was beginning to feel like he was being cornered by the two of us. "It was your idea to go fishing, it was you who got us lost, and it was you who picked the campsite with the dead guy. Why should I get involved? You created this entire situation not me."

Mark leaned over to Thad and put his arm around him. I could tell that Mark was convinced that he had the perfect comeback to Thad's remark.

"Thad, let me remind you of one tiny detail. I know it was a long time ago, and you may have forgotten this minor point, but wasn't it you who yelled "shit" out there in the forest. Wasn't it your little outburst which caused most of our present dilemma?" Thad pulled himself free.

"So what, I said one stupid word, big deal." There wasn't much Thad could say in his defense.

"Well, your one little word nearly got us all killed," replied Mark. "And who was there to help you out?"

"I didn't ask for your god damn help," declared Thad. "You did it on your own."

"That's right, Thad, you didn't ask for my help," Mark explained. "You see, that's the difference between you and me. When it comes to being there for my friends, I don't need to be asked."

As much as he hated to admit it, Mark was right. At some level, Thad was grateful to Mark for helping him the night before. But he couldn't help but feel that this whole mess had gotten completely out of control. He was terrified and didn't want to get himself in any more trouble. But he also realized that by not getting involved, he was betraying his friendship with Mark and me. It became clear to him that he had to make a choice between protecting his own butt and being there for us. There was no other way around it.

"Okay, I'll go talk to the woman," he reluctantly agreed. Something inside him forced the words to come out, almost involuntarily. "But I'll tell you right now, I'll probably screw it all up. I don't have the foggiest idea what to say."

Mark and I were both totally astonished. Thad was actually volunteering to get involved? It was a miracle.

"Don't worry about it, Thad," I said with a big smile. "I'll go up and do it. You don't really have to come. Wait, on second though, let's do it together."

Before Thad could get out of the car, Mark put his hand on Thad's shoulder again and said, "Hey, good luck in there." Mark was really proud of Thad. We both were. He was finally beginning to grow up.

*　　*　　*

As Thad and I slowly made our way up the weed infested walkway in the direction of the front door, I nervously whispered to him, "Let me do all of the talking, okay?"

"Fine with me," he replied back, feeling a bit relieved. "What the hell are you going to say to her anyway?"

"I've got no idea. Maybe it will just come to me."

Up close, the house was even more of a mess. Paint was peeling everywhere, there was a about a quarter inch of dust on the window sills and the porch furniture, and you could hardly see through the windows they were so filthy.

"I wonder what kind of person lives in a place like this?" asked Thad as he looked around.

"Well, we'll soon find out." I was hoping she wouldn't turn out to be too much of a monster.

We both looked at each other before I rang the doorbell. The message we communicated without saying anything was 'I hope this all works out.'

After ringing the bell three times, we could finally hear someone approaching. The anticipation steadily increased as the person inside fiddled with the locks in an attempt to open the door. It sounded like there were at least three or four of them.

As the door swung open, I was stunned at what I saw. After seeing the condition of the house, I guess I was expecting to find some kind of old bag-lady type wearing tattered clothes and a beat-up overcoat. To my surprise, the woman standing in front of us was about twenty-five years old, tall, slim and incredibly beautiful. She had long silky brown hair, vibrant blue eyes and absolutely perfect skin. She was wearing a light blue silk bathrobe which covered her legs down to her knees. Her good looks caught me by completely off guard. I was mesmerized by her beauty. As always, when faced with someone gorgeous, my capability to say anything intelligent quickly evaporated.

After what seemed like an endless pause, just as I was about to utter something, Thad spoke up first.

"Is your name Shelly Harper?" he asked cheerfully.

"Yes it is," she replied back curiously. "I'm sorry, do I know you boys?"

"No you don't, ma'am," Thad admitted. "My name is Bob and my friend's name is Jeff. It's very nice to meet you." That was the first time I ever heard Thad lie about anything like that before.

She motioned for us to come inside what appeared to be her living room. In contrast to the yard from hell, the inside of her house was immaculate. Spread all around the room was a vast assortment of beautiful belongings, including multicolored handmade carpets scattered across fine oak floors and exotic paintings hanging on many of the walls. Most depicted colorfully dressed dancing women or romantic love scenes. Above the fireplace was a large antique wooden mirror. At the far end of the room, there was a skillfully carved showcase which accommodated a collection of statues which were similar to the ones seen in Carter's photos. The center of the room contained several pieces of furniture—a couch and three antique wooden chairs.

"Well, is there something I can do for you boys?" she asked politely.

"Yes," said Thad. "Yesterday morning we were walking down Main Street and we found an address book with your name in it. We wanted to return it to the owner. We thought that you might be able to help us."

"Who does it belong to?" she asked curiously as she reached out her hand.

"His name is Robert Carter," replied Thad. We both looked closely at her reaction.

Without blinking an eye she said, "Yes, I know Mr. Carter. He was here just yesterday on business. I wonder how he lost his book. He's usually so careful about things like that. Let me see it."

Thad pulled the address book out of his back pocket and handed it over to her. While she carefully examined it, I couldn't help but notice the collection of gold rings she had on nearly all of her fingers. With a large variety of multi-colored stones, they were probably really expensive. Having looked the book over, she handed it back to Thad.

"His address is right here in front," she said pointing it out to us. "He lives and works in Manhattan—New York City."

"Actually, we also saw that," Thad admitted. "We just wondered whether you might be seeing him again soon."

"No, he only stopped by to pick something up," she remarked casually. "He had to hurry off to some meeting in the afternoon."

"Okay, well I guess we'll just write a little note to him and send it back through the mail," said Thad. "Oh, by the way, you have a lovely home. Aren't most of these things—the carpets and the wall hangings—from India?"

"Why yes, nearly everything is from India," she said with a smile, She was pleased that Thad recognized their origin. It was obvious she had a strong attachment to all of her possessions. "Have you been there before?"

"No I haven't, but we studied about it in school last term," Thad lied. "I hope to someday travel there when I get older."

"Actually, I just came back from India a week ago," she confessed. "I was there for over two months. That's why my place is such an incredible mess. I forgot to hire someone to take care of the yard during my absence. And on top of that, I also got really sick when I got back. I've been too ill to leave my house ever since I returned."

"Where in India were you staying?" asked Thad in an attempt to continue the conversation. "Bombay, Calcutta, Delhi, Madras?"

"You seem to know your city's pretty well," she replied. "Actually, I was all over. But I spent most of my time in New Delhi, and places within Bihar and Uttar Pradesh. I used to work there so I know my way around the area pretty well."

"Is that how you know Mr. Carter?" asked Thad casually. "I noticed from his schedule that he was in India not too long ago."

For a moment, Shelly stopped and took a good look at Thad before answering. It was obvious that she was beginning to wonder why Thad was asking so many personal questions. I just stood there not knowing where to put my hands. I was so uncomfortable and couldn't wait for the conversation to end. I was usually much more relaxed when I did the talking.

"Yes, that's where I know Mr. Carter from," she replied. "He deals with art pieces from that part of the world. I sometimes help him out with his business."

"Well, I'll have to try to go there someday," said Thad as he put his hand out to shake hers. I followed his lead and did the same.

"I'm afraid I'd better not get too close to you," she said as she pulled back. "I'm still pretty sick. Actually, if you want, I'd be happy to send the address book to Robert myself."

"No, that's okay," said Thad as we made our way to the front porch. "We're both boy scouts and we are taught to try to do good things whenever we can. I'd like to send it to him myself if you don't mind. Sorry to bother you. I hope you start feeling better soon."

"No problem. Thank you for stopping by," said Shelly as she watched us leave and make our way towards the car.

*   *   *

"What the hell happened in there?" asked Mark as we both climbed back into Thad's car. "You two were in there an awful long time?"

"Hold on a minute," said Thad after starting up the engine and driving up the road to the end of Spring Street where he parked out of sight of Shelly's house.

"Okay, so what happened?" Mark repeated the question full of anticipation as he turned to look at me.

67

"Don't ask me," I laughed out loud. "Thad was the one who did all the talking."

"Thad did what?" asked Mark, not really knowing whether or not to believe me.

"I was about to say something after this woman opened the door but before I knew it, Thad was talking up a storm with the most beautiful babe I've ever seen," I explained. "I swear, you should have seen her. She was a goddess."

"Are you bull-shitting me?" asked Mark. "That place is a dump."

"I swear to God Mark, this lady was something special," I admitted. "Right, Thad?"

"She was pretty nice," he confessed.

"Shoot," said Mark disappointed. "And I missed her. Well, maybe next time. So did you find anything out from her?"

Before I could say a resounding "No," Thad once again beat me to the punch.

"Yes," he replied. "I told you guys I was right about all that urn stuff. Now maybe you guys will listen to me for a change."

"What the hell are you talking about?" I asked, not quite understanding what Thad was saying. "What does the urn have to do with anything? She didn't mention it."

"Don't you see? She's the one," Thad declared.

"She's the one what?" I asked again. "Am I missing something here?"

"She's the one who brought back the urn from Nepal," he went on to explain. "Remember what the paper said about an American woman who paid those two Indians for the stolen urn. I'm sure she's that person."

"What?" Mark and I asked in unison.

"I swear, it's got to be her. First of all, she said she was just in India. And the two places she mentioned, Bihar and Uttar Pradesh, are States in India that border Nepal. Remember she said that she was staying in those places. Second, she said that Mr. Carter was here to pick something up. I bet it was the urn. Maybe she was supposed to meet Carter in Front Royal, but because she was so sick he came to Elkins instead. And did you happen to notice her nose?"

"What about it?" I inquired.

"Didn't you see that little mark on her nose?" Thad pointed to the lower left corner of his nose near the nostril.

"Yeah, so what? She had a small zit there."

"That was no zit stupid. She had her nose pierced there. In one of those articles in that Nepali paper, it said that the foreign woman who stole the urn had a small diamond stud in her nose. Don't you see, she's the one."

It took me a while to grasp what Thad was saying, but when it finally sank in, it did seem to make sense in some ways but not in others. But after seeing her, I didn't want it to be so.

"What the hell are you guys talking about?" asked Mark who was feeling left out. "Come on, tell me, what went on in there?"

"She couldn't be involved in something like that," I said in her defense with a certain hesitancy. I totally ignored Mark's question. "She seemed to be too nice to go around stealing priceless things. And besides, she wouldn't have talked so freely with us if she had done something wrong there."

"Maybe she didn't know it was stolen," Thad explained. "Maybe she was just told to meet those two men and bring it back to the States."

"What the hell is going on here?" Mark finally demanded. By this time, he was close to losing his temper. "What are you guys talking about?"

We finally explained to Mark what we saw and heard. After hearing the whole story, Mark had a hard time believing that Thad did all of the talking.

"What got into you Thad?" asked Mark in a teasing voice. "A half hour ago you were saying you'd mess this thing up."

"I don't know. When she opened the front door and I saw all of that Indian stuff in her house, I got the idea about her going to India. Before I knew it, I just started talking to her. It was really weird. I didn't even feel nervous at all."

"How did you know that stuff was from India anyway?" I inquired. "I mean, it could have all been from China for all I knew."

"It just looked Indian to me for some reason. And it was the only explanation for how she knew Carter."

"And listen to this, Thad even lied about our names," I revealed to Mark. "You do realize that you're probably going straight to hell for that one."

"Thad lied?" asked Mark in disbelief. "Holy shit."

"It just came out," Thad said defensively. "I didn't want her to know who we were. And besides, my middle name is Robert."

"But my middle name isn't Jeff," I said as I laughed out loud again. "That constitutes a full fledged lie in my book."

"I don't know, Thad," said Mark playfully. "It starts with one tiny little lie and before you know it you will be cheating, stealing, and maybe even murdering. I'm going to have to keep a close eye on you. You're on your way down boy. The criminal gene inside of you has just been activated. It's all over now."

*   *   *

Since it was already late afternoon and we were all kind of bushed from our little adventure, Thad and I agreed we should call it a day. Finals were coming up in two weeks so we felt the best thing to do was to just stay home and try to get some

69

studying done. Neither one of us was in the mood to go out anyway. Mark, on the other hand, had his own ideas.

"I can't concentrate on school," Mark complained repeatedly. He obviously didn't agree with our proposed strategy. "I'm not going to be able to get anything done. We've been through too much so far this weekend. Shit, it's a Saturday. Let's go out and have a few beers or something to unwind. We can study tomorrow."

"You say that every weekend, Butthead," Thad reminded him. "It amazes me that you are always able to find an excuse not to complete your assignments. Actually, this is probably the first time I can remember you ever really having a truly genuine one."

"Fuck you, Thad."

"You know what?" I asked in an attempt to change the subject before it got ugly. "Doesn't all of this seem like some kind of a crazy nightmare? I mean just think about it. Two days ago, we were going to class and then in the course of a 24 hour period, we found a dead guy, almost got ourselves killed in the woods by some crazy ass gunmen, some poor guy from Bantum gets himself murdered, I broke into a motel room and stole a briefcase, and we lied to some strange beautiful lady. How can we ever top this weekend?"

"I'll be content with just staying home from now on," Thad admitted. "I've had enough excitement for a lifetime."

"You know, we're still in deep shit," I declared reluctantly. "I mean, what if those thugs are still around town. They could try to come after us. And we still don't know if that motel man called the cops on me. I say we stay out of sight for a couple of days until we figure out what to do next. What do you guys think?"

"Sounds good to me," said Thad in full agreement. "You know, with everything that happened today, I keep forgetting about last night. For some reason, I am not as scared as I was this morning."

I knew that Thad's fearlessness wouldn't stand the test of time. He had this unfortunate habit of feeling good about something bad until he had a chance to just sit around and think about it for some time. Then the thought would begin to fester inside until it nearly consumed him. I figured he was just in some kind of remission for a few hours. By tomorrow he'd be a basket case once again.

"I say we meet tomorrow morning to figure out what to do next," I suggested. "Why don't you guys come over to my house. I'll ask my mom to cook up one of her famous breakfasts and then we'll come up with a plan."

"Plan for what?" asked Mark.

"Plan for figuring out what kind of plan we need," I

explained. "How the hell do I know."

At this point, Thad dropped us both off and we called it a day.

*   *   *

For as long as I could remember, my father spent nearly every waking moment complaining about something. There was never a man who walked this earth who was more capable of finding fault in society and his fellow man than my dear old dad. If there was ever a contest, he would be voted, hands down, Elkins number one gloom-sayer. That night at dinner was no exception as the topic of conversation centered around the murdered Bantum man.

"See, I told you so," said my father feeling smug. "It was just a matter of time before those cults started coming down south. Those northern devils have been sacrificing strangers for years. I tell you, it's all that M-TV, rock music that's ruining our young folk. I told you this was going to happen. Didn't I tell you? Well, didn't I? When I was a kid we didn't have any TVs. We listened to the radio or read books, right honey? Now-a-days the world is going mad . . ."

My mother, in contrast to my father, was always as quiet as a church mouse. I used to always kid my older sister, Crisy, about how mom hasn't heard a word that father has said for the last twenty years. She just tuned him out. Every once in a while, she'd give my dad a 'yes dear' and just go on with what she was doing. If she ever really stopped and listened to the garbage that came out of his mouth, I'm sure she'd go totally berserk.

"I don't want you or your sister to watch that crap any more," my dad insisted as he pointed his finger right at us. "You hear me? And no violent, sex-filled movies either. The world is falling apart all around us. I won't have it happen in my own house. You know . . ."

At that point, I knew I had to excuse myself to avoid allowing him to start one of his famous lectures on the downfall of the American family. I had heard it all a thousand times before and just couldn't stomach the same old thing one more time, especially after what I had been through since yesterday.

"Sorry, Dad," I pleaded. "I really have to go and study now. Finals are coming up in a few weeks and I have a whole lot of work to do. I really should get started."

"Okay, go on, get upstairs and do your work," he said as he turned to my sister who as still eating her supper. She gave me a dirty look as I walked out of the room. She was hoping I'd distract him long enough for her to make her own escape.

For nearly an hour, I tried to study my geometry, but just couldn't force myself to concentrate. After all that had happened,

71

square and triangle formulas just seemed so trivial. All I could think about was Mr. Carter lying there dead on the ground. Two days ago he was alive and then boom, it was all over.

In my entire sixteen years of life, I had never seen a dead person before—at least not in real life. Sure I heard all about this business of people dying and at some abstract level knew that everyone eventually 'passed on.' But it wasn't until that moment that I verified that death was real. I guess, I didn't really believe it could possibly happen to someone—to me. I was wrong.

4

The following morning turned out to be one of those beautiful spring days you only dream about during the mid-winter months when it seems like the world will never warm up again. There wasn't a cloud in the sky as the sun emerged over the hills that surrounded our little town.

Thad and I were sitting on my front porch when Mark came running up to us that morning. Thad had this habit of always arriving early, while Mark was always around a half hour late. In fact, Mark was so consistent when it came to showing up late that I often told him to show up a half hour before I wanted him to come, to ensure he'd be there right on time.

"You guys are not going to believe what happened to me last night," said Mark completely out of breath. Whatever it was, it was obvious that Mark was real excited about it.

"So what happened, Butthead?" asked Thad. From his expression, it looked as if he wasn't sure he wanted to hear the answer.

"I'm telling you, you're just not going to believe it," Mark repeated himself. "Not in a million years."

"Well, we don't have a million years. Just tell us what happened," I urged in an attempt to get him to say what he had to say.

"Well, after Thad dropped me off yesterday, I went straight to my room. A few minutes later, my dad came storming in and began hollering and carrying on about the truck window being smashed. He was like really pissed. It took me forever to calm him down. He was in some kind of nasty mood. So I told him that someone broke into the truck and stole the radio when we were fishing. He then started yelling at me for not telling him. What the hell could I say? Anyway, about an hour later, you're not going to believe this, I looked out my window and this cop cruiser pulls right up in front of the house." Mark was getting more and more high-strung as he told the story—as if by recalling the details, what he experienced was coming back to him.

"Are you kidding me?" asked Thad as he suddenly began to feel nervous himself. "Shit, what the hell did he want?"

"I'll tell you in a minute," said Mark not wanting to get ahead of himself. "I was caught completely off guard and thought that I was nailed for sure. I even thought about climbing out my bedroom window and making a run for it. But I didn't. A few moments later, I hear this knock on the door and both the cop and my dad walked inside my room. It was that fat cop that thinks he's such a tough guy. I think his name is Officer Beller. You know the one, they call him Officer Belly. Well, anyway, they both looked so damn serious—like someone had died or something. I tell you, I've never been so spooked in my life."

"So what happened?" I insisted. "We don't need any editorials. Just tell us."

"Well, actually not much. As it turned out, my dad called the cops about the truck being robbed. He said I needed a police report for the insurance company. God, I was so relieved."

"Holy shit, man," I said feeling a bit relieved myself that it hadn't been me the cops visited. "I would have shit right there in my pants. Can you imagine if my father ever heard I was involved in any of this. He would just keel over and have a heart attack right there on the spot."

"Wait, that's not the best part," Mark went on to describe. "When I told the cop that we were all fishing on the Cheat River, he began to ask me all kinds of questions about whether I saw anything unusual going on in that area. He said they were investigating the murder of that Bantum man and said they were looking for whatever leads they could come up with."

"Shit, what did you tell him?" I asked anxiously. Mark had this habit of sometimes saying too much.

"Nothing, I told him we didn't see a damn thing," he replied back defensively. I think he sensed I didn't trust him to get it right. "I told him that we were fishing over by the bridge, miles away from where they found the dead guy."

There was a short pause as Thad and I pondered what we just heard. For a moment, the reality that the police might someday come for me entered my mind once again. I imagined them taking me away in handcuffs to cruisers with flashing blue and red lights. A crowd of whispering neighbors would be standing with their arms crossed, saying things like "I never would have believed it. I thought he was such a nice boy." My mom would be pleading with the officers to let me go. Telling them it was all some kind of horrible mistake. And then there'd be my dad—the depth of his disappointment would be engraved across his face. The vision was so terrifying and humiliating, I immediately forced it out of my mind.

"Oh, and there's more," Mark went on to say. "As the cop was leaving, my father started to ask him all kinds of questions about the investigation. As it turns out, they found the brandy bottle that I threw into the woods—or at least pieces of it. They also took a sample of the blood stains at the scene and determined that there were two different blood types—one from the victim and another one which they think belonged to the murderer. That poor fisherman must have gotten a few good punches in before they finally put him down."

"That probably wasn't the killer's blood they found there stupid, that was the blood left from Mr. Carter," Thad explained. "Remember, it was all over the ground."

"Oh yeah, maybe you're right," Mark agreed after thinking it over. "Anyway, the cop said that they brought in Jake Newman's bird hound to see if they could track the blood down. You know the dog, that small, scrawny Golden Retriever he has chained up in his back yard. Well, the dog followed the scent to a parking lot near the Park entrance. He said it was the one right near Hedgewood Road—you know, where the cops always have that speed trap on holidays."

"Did they find anything?" Thad asked out of curiosity.

"Well, they don't really know. I guess there was some drizzle late Friday night so the scent wasn't all that good. But the cop did say something about there being a bunch of tire tracks there. You know, they still think that some kind of religious cult was involved. They couldn't think of any other way to explain the 666 being spelled out with rocks and the fish being shoved down the guy's throat."

"I know that parking lot," I confessed without thinking about what I was saying. "I took Beth there a couple of times to park."

"You never told me you parked with her," said Mark as he leaned forward to hear all the juicy details. "Did she finally put out?"

"Why don't you ask her yourself." I made it a point never to discuss what happened on dates with Mark because he had this way of making even the most innocent events seem like some kind of a drunken orgy.

"So that's where Carter got out," I replied in an effort to change the subject. "Maybe those men took him there to assassinate him and he somehow got away after they shot him in the back."

"Or maybe it's the other way around. Maybe that's where they dragged his body after finding him in the woods," Thad remarked. "Let's face it, we are never going to find him. I'm sure they put him in their car trunk and took him off somewhere." There was a short pause before Thad started talking again. "You know something? What Mark just told us might actually be good news now that they found the second blood sample. If we went and told our story to the police, they'd probably believe us."

"Would you just forget about saying anything about that to anyone," Mark snapped back angrily. "We all agreed to keep quiet about this thing. So just shut up. I'm tired of hearing you talk about going to the god damn police."

"Screw you, Mark," said Thad. "Who died and made you

king turd. Besides, WE didn't all agree, YOU agreed."

It looked as if the ingredients for another one of their childish arguments was there. Thad's eyes were squinted as his face turned red. Mark's body was propped up ready for an immediate response.

"Would you two girls just clam up," I said as I fulfilled my usual referee role. "I'm really tired of listening to you fight all the time. Now we've got to figure out what to do next. We can't go to the cops without a whole lot more information than what we have. They'll never believe us. We either come up with something more substantial or I have to agree with Mark we don't tell anyone anything."

"Well, if that's the way you feel about it, I think I know what to do next," said Thad under his breath. I could tell that he wasn't sure that he should be saying anything more. He probably thought it'd get him deeper into trouble. "Last night I found out a few interesting things myself which we could use if we decided to tell someone about this." While he didn't mention who he meant by this, we both knew he was talking about the police. "First of all, our friend Mr. Carter has met with Keller three times since January. Each time was right before a trip to India or Nepal. Second, all of the meetings have been in Front Royal, Virginia. I think we need to somehow find out who this Mr. Keller person is. He might be able to shed some light on this whole mess."

"How do you know all of this?" I inquired.

"I spent a few hours last night studying Carter's address book," Thad explained. "I couldn't sleep."

"You couldn't sleep either?" I asked surprised. "Man, I tossed and turned all night. Finally after three or four hours I drifted off. And you know what, I had this nasty nightmare—a real bad one. I remember seeing those three men coming after me. I remember being trapped in Mark's truck. As they stood there staring at me, with their guns pointed right between my eyes, I knew I was about to be killed. I must have been screaming because my mom came in and woke me up. My sister and dad were standing in the doorway looking at me as if I had three heads or something. The whole thing was really embarrassing."

"Well, I slept like a baby," Mark admitted, not really understanding what the problem was.

"That's because all cavemen can sleep after carrying out some dastardly deed," said Thad obnoxiously. "It's because you lack the intelligence to know when you're supposed to feel bad about something—you must not have a conscience."

Every once in a while Thad went a little too far and Mark whacked him good. This was one of those times. Mark laid a good, solid punch on Thad's arm and sent him flying off the porch steps.

"You're wrong about that," declared Mark. "I feel really bad about having just punched you. I doubt now if I'll be able to sleep tonight myself."

"Up yours, Mark," said Thad as he got up and wiped his pants off. "One of these days I'm going to hit you back and you'll be really sorry."

"You're right about that," said Mark with a big ole smile. "I'll feel sorry for you. You'll probably end up busting your hand."

"Shut up, both of you," I scolded them. "Let's just have a truce for now. How about some food?"

"Not me," said Mark. "I've already eaten."

"Me neither," said Thad as he rubbed his arm. "I think we should go over to my father's office. He has some phone books there for Virginia which might help us locate the whereabouts of our mysterious Mr. Keller. If you guys are so intent on playing detective, then we might as well do it right."

*   *   *

After arriving at his father's office, Thad unlocked the door and Mark and I make ourselves comfortable in the waiting area. The office was situated downtown, above a small shopping complex known as Sunshine Place. Mark laid down on the couch and tossed a small pillow in the air, while I sat in the corner and flipped through a ten month old Newsweek magazine. As I checked out the dead bodies and war scenes depicted in the various photos, it appeared to me that the outside world was still in a state of utter chaos. It was sure glad to be living in West Virginia.

As usual, the place smelled like an ashtray. Thad's dad was seldom seen without a smoke in his hand. He probably went through about ten packs a day. If he could have easily handled two or three cigarettes in his mouth at a time, he probably would have even smoked more. He was a real nicotine junkie.

Thad's father worked as an "Investment Advisor." Or at least that's what he called himself. Others referred to him with much less flattering names—opportunist, trickster or even a cheat. He dabbled in insurance, the stock market or whatever else he thought would bring him a quick buck. His most enduring quality was that he was a master at spotting a financial opportunity and somehow finding an angle for himself. Whenever there was money to be made, he could almost surely be found on the sidelines. The way he was able to play on people's emotions, he would have made a terrific "used car" salesman or perhaps a TV evangelist.

While Thad worshiped his father as if he were some kind of

a god, I never thought all that much of him myself. He had taken advantage of too many people I knew over the years. It was always kind of strange to me that Thad was related to this man. Unlike his father, Thad was always such a straight arrow about everything. He never got into any trouble, studied like mad all the time, and was probably going to end up attending an Ivy-League college on a full scholarship. His father, on the other hand, never finished high school, but somehow managed to create an impression that he was educated. Maybe because Thad was an only child, his father wanted him to be everything that he was not.

"So, what are we doing here anyway?" asked Mark after picking up the pillow, he was tossing, off the floor. "This is real boring. Let's go do something."

"Shut up, Butthead," said Thad as he attempted to open the door to his father's private office. "I thought you wanted to track down Carter's killer."

Thad entered the room and grabbed a few Virginia phone books off one of the shelves. We were never allowed to go into this "special" office. Thad always said this was because his father had a top secret clearance with the CIA and often did work for the government's other intelligence agencies. I always thought the real reason was that Thad thought we'd somehow mess things up in there and get him in trouble. His father had a real nasty temper sometimes—especially if someone went through his stuff. As far as I was concerned, the closest his father ever got the CIA or any intelligence service was maybe a drive by their offices in Washington. I took everything I heard about Thad's dad with a grain of salt.

After lugging the phone books into the waiting area, we all began fingering through them. It only took Thad a few seconds to locate the K-section for the town of Front Royal.

"Shit, there are no Kellers here," said Thad in a disappointed voice. "Oh well, so much for that idea."

"Well, what about some other town?" I asked as I pointed to the different sections in the directory. I couldn't believe that Thad was giving up so easily. "Maybe he works in Front Royal, but lives someplace else. Look in Brownsville."

Thad searched there also, but again found no Kellers. It was only after looking through the directories of four other towns before he finally located a Burton Keller living in Stanford, Virginia.

"Where the hell is Stanford in relation to Front Royal?" I asked as I tried to find it on the map at the front of the phone book.

"It's about a half hour drive," said Thad, pointing it out to me. "It is also one of those really wealthy towns. You know the place, Matt. That's the area that has all of those horse stables and really expensive do-dad shops."

"So what does this tell us?" asked Mark. "Nothing!! This might not even be the right Keller. In fact, maybe this Keller guy has nothing to do with anything. You guys are barking up the wrong tree."

"Maybe so," Thad remarked. "But it's the only lead we have, isn't it? So just shut up." Thad threw a small pillow at Mark and hit him in the chest.

Mark had that bored look on his face as he went back to tossing pillows into the air. It was Thad and I who seemed interested in finding out more about Carter's death, not Mark. He would have been perfectly content to just walk away from it and get on with his life."

"Did you find anything else in that address book of his?" I asked Thad hoping for something more.

"Well, there was one other thing," said Thad as he turned to the schedule section. "Carter went to India four times since November. Before two of the trips, his schedule book shows that he had meetings with someone by the name of "BEEM." The other two times he met with Keller. It doesn't say anything else. There's no address or nothing. Kind of a strange name if you ask me. All of the letters were capitals."

"Wait a minute, wait a minute," Mark shouted as if he had some kind of a revelation. He immediately sat up on the couch. "Did you say BEEM?"

"Yes, BEEM," repeated Thad, taken by surprise. "B E E M."

"Oh, man, you remember when I said that the guy I threw down on Friday night had on a tie," Mark described. "Well, the only reason I remembered was that I saw the reflection of the fire on his tie clip when I was dragging him further into the woods. And it had the word BEEM across it. I'm sure of that."

Both Thad and I couldn't believe it. For the first time, it looked as if we were on to something tangible.

"Are you kidding?" I asked. "Butthead, why didn't you tell us this before?"

"I swear, I forgot all about it," Mark confessed. "It didn't seem all that important at the time."

"Do you know what it stands for?" I inquired. "It can't be someone's name, could it? Who puts their name on a tie clip? It's probably the name of something else, maybe a place or a business or something like that."

Both Mark and I watched Thad as he frantically flipped through the pages of one of the phone books. After only two or three minutes he lifted his head. I knew he had landed something important because his left eyebrow was at full attention and he had a great big grin across his face.

"Well, boys, it's not someone's name," Thad exclaimed. "It's the name of a company located in Front Royal." He pointed to the company's name in the phone book. "That's our link. I bet that Mr. Keller works for this company. Now we're really getting someplace."

"So what do you think it means?" asked Mark curiously. He was finally beginning to take an interest in our little quest for information which might unravel the mystery of Carter's murder.

"I'm not really sure yet, but I think it could be that Keller and others from this BEEM company were working with Carter," Thad explained. "Maybe they were involved in this urn thing. That might explain why he kept going back there before each of his trips overseas to India. Those thugs must also work for the company since that man had on a BEEM tie clip."

"So how do we find out if Keller works there or not?" I asked. "I guess we could call the place on Monday."

"Hey, wait a minute," said Thad as he stood up. "There may be one other source we can look at." Thad returned to his father's office again and this time came out carrying a huge blue book. "This might tell us what we need to know."

"What's that thing?" I asked. "It's huge."

"It's a book put out by the Chamber of Commerce for that county in Virginia," said Thad. "My father uses these reference books as part of his business. It gives you all kinds of useful information about the size of companies, what type of work they do, contact names and so on."

"How the hell do you know so much about these things?" asked Mark. "I never heard of books like that before."

"Well, when I was a kid, my dad used to take me here during the weekends when he had lots of work to do," Thad explained. "When I got bored, I always pulled books off the shelves and flipped through them. I used to look at this book a lot because I was always interested in seeing how many people worked for the big companies."

Again we watched as Thad thumbed through the pages of this massive reference volume. He was really beginning to get excited. It was almost like a school research assignment for him.

"Here it is," said Thad as he studied a page in the directory. "We are really on a roll. Mr. Burton Keller is the CEO for BEEM Inc., an export company which employs sixty-two people. And look at this, the place specializes in spare parts for defense contractors."

"CEO?" asked Mark. "What's a CEO?"

"Chief Executive Officer," I exclaimed. "In other words, he runs the place—he's like the big boss."

"It also says that they do a lot of work in the Middle East and Southeast Asia," Thad went on to describe. "There's another link."

"Did you say they were defense contractors?" I inquired.

"You mean rockets, planes and that sort of stuff?"

"No, it says that they deal mostly with spare parts for infantry equipment," said Thad. "I think like parts for trucks and tanks."

"Well, then this changes everything," said Mark as he stood up to get a look at the book. "That stupid theory about the urn doesn't make any sense anymore. Carter probably found out something bad about one of their defense deals so they iced him. Some spy probably did it. You know how screwed up those defense dealers are. You hear about things like this in the news all the time."

"I don't think so," I remarked. "Just look at the facts again. Carter travels to Virginia before each of his four trips to India and Nepal. He must have had some kind of business dealings with Keller and BEEM in these two countries. On his last scheduled trip to Front Royal, he comes all the way to Elkins to pick something up from someone who had just returned from India. As it turns out, he has a collection of newspaper articles in which he circles a description of a crime that took place in that part of the world. The name of the file is "Nepal Project" and he also writes confidential all over it. That means he was up to something there. The newspaper describes that a foreign woman gave a large some of money to some Indian men for the stolen urn. It just so happens that the person we met in Elkins is a woman who just returned from India with something for Carter. After picking up that something from this woman he is found dead in the woods. It's beginning to all fit together. Don't you see?"

"Huh, I see what you mean," said Mark as if he was finally coming around. "So Carter gave the urn over and then they killed him afterwards."

"Well, I don't know about that yet," I confessed. "Remember when we were in the woods and those three guys came out looking for us after Thad yelled out? Do you remember what the short dude said to the others?"

Both Mark and Thad shook their heads to indicate that they didn't.

"He said, 'We have to get that thing from him.' To tell you the truth, I don't think that Carter ever gave them the urn."

"Then why the hell would they shoot him?" asked Thad. "If he's dead then they might never get a hold of it."

"I don't know," I admitted. "But I still think they don't have it. If they did, they wouldn't have been looking for him in the woods. They would have just left him there to die. I'm sure he had something they wanted. Right?"

"So now what?" asked Mark. "Now that we know all this stuff, what are we supposed to do about it?"

"I think it's time to go to the cops," Thad remarked softly. I could tell he was waiting for Mark's reaction to this familiar suggestion. "I say we go to the police with the information we already have and let them sort it out. Let's face it, the cops will come looking for us at some point. There are too many things that link us to that spot that night. They may be stupid, but they're not that stupid. And remember the FBI is also helping. We will be in a lot less trouble if we make the first move."

Both Mark and I knew Thad was probably right. Thad's unusual glasses alone were a pretty compelling piece of evidence. It wouldn't take a rocket scientist to trace them to him. And then there was that bottle with Mark's and my fingerprints all over it.

"I say we keep digging deeper before we tell anyone," I urged, hoping they'd agree. "Maybe if we keep turning up clues like this, we might eventually figure out where they stashed the body. Then we can go to the authorities."

"You don't really think we're ever going to find that body do you?" asked Mark. "If they went to all that trouble to replace Carter with some other guy, I'm sure they got rid of it real good."

"It's our only hope," I explained. "We'll never be able to go to the cops until we clear up that part of the puzzle. They'll never believe us. We don't have enough evidence to support any of this."

"All this talk about bodies is making me sick," said Thad with a disgusted look on his face.

"So what next?" asked Mark as he turned and looked at both Thad and I for an answer.

"Well, I think it's time for a road trip," I said.

"A road trip to where?" asked Thad. I could already tell that he didn't like the sound of this.

"Don't be stupid, Thad," I remarked, "Where else would we go—we have to visit this BEEM place. You know, the place where our good friend Mr. Keller works."

"Are you out of your mind?" Thad nearly shouted. "Those guys are killers. Not me. I'm not going anywhere near that place. It's one thing to look through a few phone books for some information, but I'm not going after these guys."

"We don't have to go and talk to them or anything," I explained. "We'll just snoop around a little bit. You know, see if we can collect a little more information." I could tell that Mark was interested. He had that look in his eyes. He could always smell an adventure.

"So how are we supposed to get there?" asked Thad confidently, as if he knew this question would crush the idea. "My mom told me I couldn't use her car today because she needed to take my grandmother to my aunt's house. And you don't have any wheels. Besides, that place is hours and hours away from here."

"Then we'll take my truck," Mark offered. "It still runs okay."

"Yeah right, Mark," said Thad with a sarcastic tone to his voice. "Like we're really going to go and drive around that place with a truck that someone might recognize as being the one that they shot at. Real good plan. And besides, today is Sunday and the place is closed anyway."

"Oh, yeah," Mark replied as his brain tried to come up with an alternative plan.

"Then we'll have to go tomorrow," I suggested. "Thad, you always get your mother's car on Mondays don't you? We'll just leave early in the morning."

"But tomorrow's a school day," said Thad, surprised that I'd possibly suggest such a ridiculous thing. "I can't miss school. I have a math quiz during fifth period. Besides, I've never skipped before and I'm not about to start now."

"I don't think we have much of a choice," I said. "Time is running out. I think finding a way to keep our asses out of jail is a bit more important than missing a few hours of school. We'll have to leave real early in the morning so we can get there before 7:30 am—before they get to work. If we only stay for a short while, we'll be back here by around noon. You won't even miss your quiz. I'll tell my parents that I'm going fishing before school. They'll believe that."

"You can't go to school after fishing without first washing up," said Thad in an attempt to further sabotage my plan. "My mom will know something's up if I don't first come home before school."

"Then we'll all tell our parents that we'll get cleaned up at someone else's house," I explained. "I'll say I'm going to Mark's house to shower and Mark can say he's going to my house. It's the only way. We really need to take care of this mess. We can't wait any longer. You're the one who keeps saying that eventually the cops will figure it out. Well, I'm beginning to agree with you."

"So what are we going to do when we get there?" Thad asked. "All we're going to see is the outside of some stupid building. So what? There is no reason to do this thing. I say we forget the whole idea."

"Listen, Thad," said Mark. "Up till this point I didn't believe all this stuff about some urn being taken from Nepal. But now I'm nearly convinced. Everything seems to center around Mr. Keller and this BEEM Company. We have to go there and see the place for ourselves. If nothing turns up, then nothing turns up. We can't lose by just checking it out."

"You still haven't told me what we're going to do when we get there," said Thad. Thad was beginning to get that nervous look. His eyebrow was twitching as he paced back and forth.

"We'll just sit in the car in front and look around," I said. "Maybe we will recognize the guys who we saw in the woods."

"Bull shit, we didn't even get a good look at them," said Thad. "We saw them in the dark. And even if we did see them, what would we do next. I don't mind playing detective here in Elkins, but I think we're crazy to go after these guys. They're killers remember? Killers!"

"Listen, Thad," I said as I tried to change his mind. "At least if we see guys who look like them, if the cops come for us, we will be able to give them some information. Maybe they will believe us. As it stands now, our story sounds pretty unbelievable. Wouldn't you say? Go ahead and tell me what you'd tell the cops. I want to hear how it sounds."

"I don't know. We'd tell them about finding Carter's body and then seeing those men in the woods. We could then talk about the car being shot and all the stuff about the urn. There are lots of things we could say to them."

"Listen to yourself," I said. "Would you believe any of that? What will you say when they start asking where Carter's body is? And what about the fisherman? Why kill him? And what's to prevent them from charging us? They can easily find fingerprints on your glasses and the bottle which link us to the crime scene. For Christ sake, it was my red shirt which we tied to that fishing line. We'd be the only suspects. Do you want to take that risk? Go ahead, be my guest."

As much as he didn't want to accept it, Thad clearly understood my point. We were trapped. We'd be witches at a witch hunt for sure and he knew it.

"I still think it's a reckless plan that is only going to waste our time," he confessed. "I'm not going. If you guys feel you have to do this thing then go ahead, but count me out."

At this point Mark was getting irritated with Thad.

"Okay, Thad," Mark barked. "Now that we know about Mr. Keller and BEEM, what do you think we should do? What's your big plan?"

"I don't have one," he admitted. "I'll have to think about it. There has to be another way."

"Well, until you come up with one, then the road trip stands," Mark said as he got up and left the office. I also stood up and followed.

*   *   *

The rest of that afternoon was relatively uneventful. Mark and I played some hoop over at the high school, the three of us had a few burgers at Scotty's and we all went home early in the day. None of us said more than about five words throughout the entire afternoon. We were all caught up in our own individual thoughts.

While Thad was still strongly against the idea of going to Front Royal, after a couple hours of the old silent treatment, he finally caved in and agreed to take us in his mom's car. We briefly discussed a pick-up time for the following morning and left it at that. The details could be worked out as we went along.

Once at home, I buried myself in my room and again tried to make sense of my geometry homework which was due on Tuesday. After a half hour of mindlessly staring at my notebook, it dawned on me that the wheels were not turning in my brain. There was no potential for any learning that day. I was too distracted. So instead I listened to some music and then watched a few hours of late-afternoon sports on the tube. But even this couldn't seem to hold my attention.

As much as I tried, I couldn't stop myself from thinking about what had happened to us Friday night. The entire episode kept repeating itself over and over again. As much as I wanted to forget the whole thing, I realized that at some deeper level the events of the other day thoroughly aroused me. I had an incredible desire to drive to Front Royal that very moment to continue our hunt for more clues. For the first time in my life, I knew how it felt to experience real danger. I was intrigued with the thought that I might actually find myself face to face with that feeling again. I wanted to embrace it and follow a course which would take me even further into its clutches. In some ways, Thad was right. Once you've had a taste for something like this, it is easy to get lost in it.

I also came to realize that I had gotten my first good dose of the dark side of life—a world that seemed to be out there all along, but which my parents managed to shelter from me up until that point. I felt like I wanted to know more about this strange new world. I wanted to uncover its secrets. The thought of crossing over the line excited me—it was almost intoxicating.

As these feelings and emotions tumbled around in my head, it became perfectly clear to me how incredibly ordinary and boring my life really was. Everything about it was according to some kind of predetermined plan. I was like every other sixteen year old growing up in West Virginia.

But finding Carter's dead body and having someone actually try to kill me seemed to change some of that. It made me feel different inside. All of those stupid things that seemed so important to me only a few days before, now seemed so trivial. I remembered all last week I spent hours worrying whether Cindy Day was still mad at me for calling her older sister a bitch. I got a "C" on one of my math quizzes and couldn't sleep worrying that it would significantly affect my grade-point average. Next to two people being murdered and having bullets nearly graze my ass, these things seemed incredibly inconsequential.

The only thing that really scared me was the thought of being picked up by the cops. I could just see my mother's face as they took me away in handcuffs. She'd be totally devastated. My father would probably disown me. And then there'd be a few other inevitable outcomes. I'd probably never get into a decent college and I'd never be allowed to date a girl from West Virginia again, even if my name was cleared. People around here are not all that forgiving.

With all of these thoughts and feelings circulating around, I somehow managed to pass the time. By 9:00 o'clock I fell asleep from sheer exhaustion. My mind wasn't used to so much continuous activity in one day.

5

It was nearly 4:30 am when my alarm clock shattered the silence of the early morning hour. Believe me, at this time in the morning it was a rude awakening. Any other day I would have probably shut it off and rolled over for another half hour of slumber. But I was too wired to think about any more sleep. All I wanted to do was get this show on the road.

Without even bothering to brush my teeth, I threw on a pair of blue jeans and a sweat shirt, grabbed my books and headed for the front door. As much as I tried to keep the noise level to a minimum, it was virtually impossible for me to do anything in the morning without creating a small racket.

"Is that you Matt?" asked my mom as she walked by me in the direction of the bathroom. She was still half asleep—in that dreamlike state somewhere between being awake and not.

"Yes, mother," I whispered. "It's me."

"What are you doing up at this god-awful hour?" she asked with a yawn.

"Remember, I told you last night that we were going fishing this morning before school."

"Oh, yeah," she said as she rubbed her eyes. "Don't you have school today?"

"Yes," I muttered quietly to avoid stirring my father. "We're just going out for a short while. I'll shower over at Mark's house and then head off to school."

I walked over and gave her a kiss on the forehead. She wasn't awake enough to even notice this gesture.

"Well, good luck—and be careful," she said as she headed back to her room, forgetting that she hadn't made a stop to the bathroom. "Oh, does your father know you're going?"

"Yes, Mother," I admitted. "He knows. Now good night."

"Umm," she moaned as she walked back into her bedroom.

I waited for nearly fifteen minutes outside on the front porch before Thad finally arrived. For the last ten minutes I cursed under my breath as I nearly froze to death. At precisely 5:00 am, Thad drove up in his mother's 1981 light-green Chevy Impala right on time. Thad was dressed up in a full fishing outfit, complete with his high-water boots. In the back seat was a large gym bag which contained his school clothes and his usual stack of books.

"Why the hell are you wearing all of that crap?" I asked as I jumped into the front seat. "You planning on dropping your line somewhere along the way?"

"We're supposed to be going fishing," said Thad defensively. I could tell he was already in a bad mood. "If I didn't look the part, my mom would have never let me out of the house. You know she almost said no to this stupid trip. I wish she had. She kept saying that it's not safe to be going out in the woods anymore since the murder."

"Shit," I replied. "How did you get out of that one?"

"I lied," he reluctantly confessed. "I told her that I read somewhere that cults never do their ritual sacrifices early in the morning. I said it had something to do with the wrong kind of light. For some reason, she seemed to think there was some logic to this and she let me go. That was my second lie this week. I'm going straight to hell . . . I know I'm going to get caught. Actually, we're all going to get caught. You just watch."

"Shut up and drive," I said playfully. "We'll be fine. By the way, where's your dad these days? I haven't seen him for weeks."

"He's off on some big business trip to New York or some such place," said Thad. "He'll be gone for another few days. If he was home, I can tell you right now, we wouldn't be going anywhere this morning. My mom's a pushover."

Thad was right about that. A perfect stranger could walk right up to his mom and get her to agree to just about anything. She was truly the epitome of naivete.

"Do you think Mark's up yet?" I asked as we turned down his street.

"Are you kidding?" asked Thad sarcastically. "He's never been on time for anything in his entire miserable life. Oh, by the way? Who is going to pay for gas. My mom has a full tank in the car. She'll know we went somewhere if I bring it home empty. And I'm completely broke."

"Don't worry about it," I said.

"I do worry about it," he insisted. "It's my ass on the line if she finds out about this little escapade."

"I said don't worry about it," I repeated. I hesitated before explaining. "I brought the money along."

"THE money?" he asked. "What money?"

"Carter's money," I said under my breath. "Since he's the reason why we have to take this trip in the first place, it's only fair that he pay for it. Besides, after seeing the prices on those objects he sells in New York, I'm sure he can afford it."

"I can't believe this shit," said Thad as he shook his head in disgust. "You're beginning to sound like Mark. You know that Mark's going to have a complete fit if he finds out your spending it on gas and not his stupid broken window."

"I know, I know," I replied. "I'll try not to let him find out. I wouldn't have even thought to use it, but I'm also tapped out."

As we pulled up, to our surprise, Mark was actually standing in front of his house ready to go. He had his fishing pole and gear in one hand and the same backpack he took with him on Friday night in the other.

Mark had to stuff his equipment and bag in the back seat because Thad didn't have the key to the trunk. It was a bit cramped, but Mark managed to squeeze in somehow. No matter what the circumstances, Mark could always find a way to make himself comfortable.

"It took you guys long enough," said Mark as he rubbed his hands together and blew on them to warm them up. "I was freezing my nuts off here waiting for you. Hey, Thad, why don't you let me drive. If you drive, it'll take us ten hours. I can do it in three, maybe two and a half."

"No way," said Thad. "I value my life. Either I drive or we're not going anywhere."

"Okay, okay," said Mark as he tried to lay across the back seat to take an early morning nap. "Suit yourself. Wake me up when we're there."

I also found myself nodding off after only a few miles down the road. There was something about Thad's driving that always made me want to sleep—it had that warm milk before bedtime effect.

*   *   *

Thad had to shake my arm several times hard before I finally woke up. After opening my eyes, it didn't take long to realize that my back was incredibly sore from the pretzel position I had fallen asleep in.

"Matt, we've got a little problem," said Thad with a flustered voice. "We're kind of stranded here in the middle of nowhere."

Not quite understanding the gist of Thad's statement, I peered outside and noticed that we were parked along the side of the road. There was nothing but endless rows of trees all around us.

"Shit, where the hell are we?" I asked as I sat up in my seat. "And why did you stop?"

"We've got a flat tire," Thad confessed.

"A what?" I stretched my arms up in the air in an attempt to further wake myself.

"We've got a flat tire."

"Oh, shit. What time is it now?"

"It's nearly six-thirty. We are more than half way there."

"So what's the problem, let's change the tire and get going. It's getting late."

"The problem is we can't do that."

"Can't do what?" I asked not understanding what Thad was trying to convey.

"Change the tire." I could tell that Thad was bracing for my response. This was always a bad sign.

"Thad, why can't we change the tire?" I asked as if talking to a young child—slow and well annunciated.

"Don't be stupid, Matt, you know I don't have the key to the trunk. I lost it over a year ago. How are we supposed to change the tire?"

"Damn!" I shouted at the top of my lungs.

At the sound of my little outburst, Mark jumped up out of the back seat and hit his head on the ceiling of the car. He also got completely tangled up in all of the fishing equipment.

"Shit, what's the matter?" he asked as he felt for a bump. "Are we there yet? Or are you just trying to scare me half to death?"

"No, we're not there. Einstein here has a flat tire and he can't get into the trunk to get the spare out," I replied.

At that point, we all climbed out of the car to examine the situation. Thad had somehow managed to run over an enormous nail. The tire was in pretty bad shape. Once again, Thad and his usual bad luck had demonstrated his ability to locate the only sharp object for miles which could possibly interfere with our journey.

"Did you see a service station anywhere?" asked Mark while he looked around to get his bearings.

"Yeah, about three or four miles down the road there was a Shell station," Thad admitted, pointing off in that direction. "I told you we'd get caught. I have to pee."

"Shut up and pee," said Mark as he took off his jean jacket and flannel shirt. He was wearing a white T-shirt underneath. "No one's going to get caught. Now if a car drives by, I'll try to flag it down. Otherwise, I'll have to run to the service station for some help. Do we have any money with us? This is probably going to cost us a few bucks."

"I've got a little," I said as I tried to hide the fact that I was taking out two fifty dollar bills from Carter's wallet. I was never very good at keeping a secret from Mark. He always knew when something was up.

"So, I thought you two boy scouts said that we couldn't spend that dead guy's money," said Mark sarcastically. "What about his poor wife and ten starving kids? So it's okay to use it for Thad's car, but not for my truck. What about my damn window?"

"Don't worry about that now," said Thad. "This is an emergency. Without this money we're not going anywhere."

Mark nearly ripped the two bills as he grabbed them out of my hand. He didn't say anything else as he began jogging down the road in the direction of the station. I could tell he was really pissed. Mark was always sensitive to situations where he felt an injustice was committed. This was one of those times.

*   *   *

It took Mark nearly an hour and a half before he finally came driving up in a tow truck with the name Mike's Garage painted on the side. Instead of repairing the old tire, which would have taken hours, Mark bought a used one from the station for only forty-five bucks—rim and all. By the time he and the mechanic changed the tire, it was already 8:30 am.

"I don't know if I'm going to be able to turn around here," said Thad as he started up the car. I'll have to go up a ways to find a place."

"Wait a minute, what do you mean turn around?" asked Mark. "Let's get going. We're not going back anywhere. I didn't run all that way to just turn around and go back."

"We can't keep going," Thad explained. "It's already late. I'll miss my math quiz. We'll barely make it as it is."

"Screw your damn math quiz," Mark barked back angrily. "We made it this far. We're not turning back now. This is the only chance we have to do this thing."

"Well, it's my car and I'm going to call the shots here," said Thad defiantly. "I'm not going to miss any more school. We're going back."

"You want to make a bet about that," said Mark as he tried to reach for the keys from the back seat. Thad tried to stop Mark by slapping his arm. Thad's valiant display of force didn't win him any masculinity points.

"Would you girls stop that shit," I yelled. I tried to separate the two of them. "Thad, shut up and listen to me. Okay? I understand they have a fairly good high school program at that reform school in Charletsville. If we don't figure this thing out before the police do, I'm sure you'll have plenty of time to take quizzes at that maximum security facility. Okay?"

Thad paused for a moment before he drove off in the direction of Front Royal. I guess my point made a compelling argument.

*   *   *

After what seemed like an eternity, we finally arrived in Front Royal a little before 10:30 am. Our first stop was to the local McDonalds restaurant. Thad had to pee once again and Mark was convinced he'd die of starvation if he didn't eat a cheeseburger and some fries to hold him over. From there, we drove over to the town hall where I picked up a pocket-size map

91

of the area to help us find our way around.

It didn't take long to locate the BEEM Company complex. It was a short distance from the center of town, situated within the one and only industrial park. All of our eyes were fixated on the compound as we slowly drove past.

"Thad, stop the car," Mark insisted as he pointed to a place along the side of the road. "Park there. Over there." Thad hit the brakes and stopped abruptly. This sudden action nearly introduced my face to the windshield.

"Thad, you asshole, where the hell did you get your driver's license—K-Mart?" I asked. "Shit, watch what you're doing next time."

"We can't park right in front of this place," Thad exclaimed, ignoring my comment.

"And why the hell not?" asked Mark. "Look around. There are cars parked all around here."

"What if someone thinks it looks suspicious, us sitting here watching their building and all?" asked Thad, feeling a bit paranoid.

"Thad, do you really think anyone is going to notice us sitting here?" Mark asked as he looked around. "Don't worry about it. Just back up and pull into that spot there. It'll be alright."

Thad was never really much of a driver. It took him nearly ten tries before he finally managed to parallel park the car within a reasonable distance from the curb. If anything was going to draw attention to us, it was his repeated unsuccessful parking attempts. At one point, Mark was getting so frustrated, he nearly jumped over the seat to help him finish the job himself.

The BEEM complex included two concrete buildings—what appeared to be an office section and a much larger warehouse. The office building was relatively small in size with the main parking lot directly in front. There was a ten foot wire-mesh fence surrounding the entire facility. Small loops of barbed wire also were used to line the top of the fence. The place reminded me of a maximum security prison.

"So what do we do now?" asked Thad with his usual whiny voice. "We've seen the building. I say it's time to turn back."

"We're not going anywhere until we find out as much about BEEM as we can," I remarked. From the beginning, I lied when I said we were just going to park out in front. I knew we had to find a way inside the building. The night before, as I laid there waiting to fall asleep, I came up with a plan that I thought might do the job.

"And how the hell are we going to do that?" Thad inquired with a great deal of sarcasm. "Do you expect us to just waltz right in there through the front door?"

"As a matter of fact, that's exactly what I think we should do," I replied back. "Do you remember that introduction to business class we took last year? You know, with that fat teacher Mr. Shafley, the one who always had that piece of spit between his lips. Well, he told us that most companies have some kind of brochure or annual report that they give out to potential clients. We'll just go in there and ask them for a copy. It might give us some more clues about what they do in there. It will also get us through the door."

"Why would they give something like that to us?" asked Mark. "We don't exactly look like potential clients. Or are you planning on buying a few tank parts today?" Mark must have felt his comment was pretty funny because he couldn't stop himself from laughing after saying it.

"Why wouldn't they give us one," I responded seriously. "We'll just tell them that we are doing some kind of school project. I'm sure they'll hand one over. Believe me. Everyone always helps students doing school projects. It's just the way it is."

Following an argument with Thad which lasted for nearly ten minutes, it was decided. Mark and I would go inside together to get a copy of the report, if available.

As the two of us passed through the main gate and up a small walkway toward the office complex, an old security guard seemed to come out of nowhere. Both Mark and I were startled when we noticed him approaching us from behind at a rather fast pace. It was obvious, from the pissed-off expression on his face, that the guard was not very trusting by nature.

After asking us why we were there, he kept telling us we weren't allowed on the grounds. He insisted that we "exit the premises immediately" as he kept putting it. He was truly a first rate dickhead. Fortunately, as he was escorting us out, some guy in a blue three-piece suit came to our rescue.

"What's going on?" asked the suited man with a friendly smile. "You catch a few Russian spies trying to steal some military secrets again, Hal?"

"Good afternoon, sir," said the guard as he stood at attention and saluted the man. "These boys were just leaving, sir." I saw my opportunity.

"Actually, sir," I said respectfully, following the guard's lead. "Maybe you can assist us. You see, well, we are doing this school project and need a few samples of company brochures. We thought we'd come here because we heard that the man who runs this place, a Mr. Keller, was a very good businessman." I could sense that the guard was furious that we dared to talk to someone he obviously held in such high regard.

"Hey, no sweat," said the man as he reached around and patted my shoulder. I could tell he was one of those friendly exfraternity types. "Let's go see what we can come up with inside, shall we?" He then led us into a reception area near the front of the office building, leaving the guard behind.

Inside, there were pictures of all kinds of military planes, trucks and missiles. There was also a wall which contained pictures of Presidents Nixon, Ford, Reagan and Bush. The Reagan and Bush photos were both signed and personally addressed to Mr. Keller. There was no sign of any democrats on any of the walls.

"Hey, Molly," said our friend as we walked up to the reception area. Sitting behind a large mahogany desk was a middle-aged woman who wore a ratty old blonde wig. Her make-up was packed like frosting on a cake and she chewed gum like her life depended on it. It was clear that she had long since stopped caring about how she looked. "These two boys are looking for some kind of report which describes what we do here at BEEM. Listen, I'm running late again. Could you figure out what they need and take care of them for me? I'd really appreciate it. Thanks hon."

He then rushed over to a large stainless steel security door. After inserting some kind of identification card into this slot, the door opened and he disappeared inside.

"So, what do you boys want?" asked the woman in a raspy voice.

"Well, we're looking for a copy of your annual report or something which describes what you do here," I replied.

"And what do you want with something like that?" she asked as she filed one of her fingernails.

"We need it for a school project," I said. "We're doing a report on the different formats used for presenting the capability of smaller companies." The bull shit out of my mouth that day was really beginning to flow. I guess I had learned something in Mr. Shafley's business class after all.

"What school do you boys go to anyway?" she asked as she inspected her nail more closely. "And shouldn't you be there now?"

"The high school, ma'am," I responded politely. "It's a free period for us so we came out to complete our assignment. We need to collect at least ten different samples. Please lady, this project is due in two days and we are just starting. Could you give us anything that would help? We'd be much obliged."

She stopped what she was doing for a moment and looked into my pleading eyes.

"Okay, okay, here take one of these," she said as she reached into her desk and pulled out a glossy covered document which included a collection of different military equipment on the front cover. "I can only give you one, so you're going to have to share. It's last year's report, but there isn't much difference between this one and the new one which just came out."

Seconds after handing over the document, she was once again preoccupied with shaping her nails.

As I started to thumb through the brochure, I felt Mark grab my arm firmly and slowly twirl me around. When I looked up, there were three men walking in our direction. They had just come out of the security door that led into the building. It was clear from the way Mark's head was lowered that he didn't want them to see his face. Then it occurred to me that they must have been the same three men we came upon in the forest. None of us really got a good look at them that night, but when the short one spoke, I knew I was right.

"Hey, Molly," said the short guy. "Bubha, Charlie and me are heading off to the diner for some grub. I reckon we'll be back in an hour or so. If you see Marty, tell him to wait in my office. And tell him not to leave until I get back. It's real important that I meet with him today."

"Sure thing, Mr. Bradey," Molly replied. "Oh, listen, would you be a dear and bring me back some of that diner coffee? If I have one more cup of that mud they serve here, I'm going to scream bloody murder."

"No problem," said Mr. Bradey cheerfully. "I know what you mean about that stuff. It makes toxic waste seem appetizing."

Both Mark and I tried to lower our faces as they walked past. We pretended to be reading the report. For a fraction of a second Mr. Bradey paused and looked at Mark, but nothing registered. He then kept on going without looking back again.

After they left, Mark and I thanked Molly for the report and quickly walked back to Thad's car. As we strolled past the guard, Mark gave him a big wide smile. The poor guy looked like a pit bull who wanted desperately to take a huge bite out of our back sides. Thad was sleeping behind the wheel when we arrived.

"Wake up, you jerk," yelled Mark as he knocked on the window. "And unlock the god damn door. Hurry up."

"What's the matter?" asked Thad, nearly jumping out of his skin. "What happened?" He reached over and frantically unlocked the two doors.

"We were nearly recognized in there, that's what happened," said Mark full of exhilaration. Mark jumped into the back seat while I took my usual place in the front. "We saw those three goons from the woods just now. They walked right past us. Their names were Charlie, Bubha and the short one, the one I threw down, is called Mr. Bradel. Shit, I thought for sure he'd recognize me. I knew it was him the moment I saw . . ."

"Bradey," I corrected Mark. I could tell I short changed his train of thought.

"What are you talking about?" he asked.

"His name was Bradey not Bradel," I replied.

"Who gives a flying shit—Bradey, Bradel, whatever," he said. Mark was never one for details and he hated it when anyone corrected him.

"Where did they go?" asked Thad as he looked around to catch a glimpse of them.

"I saw them driving away in a big, blue Ford LTD," I remarked. "They said something about going to some diner for lunch."

I could feel my entire body quivering inside. It just dawned on me that those guys tried to kill us the other day—and they'd probably try again if they knew who we were. Seeing them brought back the fear I felt that Friday night.

"Did you talk to them?" asked Thad. He was hanging on to our every word.

"Don't be stupid," said Mark. "They talked to their secretary and we happened to be standing right there. Like Matt said, they were heading out for some food."

"Shit," said Thad. "I can't believe you saw them!"

"The guy even looked right at me," Mark explained. "I thought for sure he'd recognize me. Shit, you know, I felt like decking him again right there in the middle of the office. That sure would have been something, wouldn't it?"

Mark had that look on his face he always got right before a wrestling match. Like he couldn't wait to kick someone's ass.

"Did they give you anything in there?" asked Thad. "I saw that guy come up to you and walk you up to the building."

"They sure did," I said. I pulled out the report which I had rolled up and shoved in my back pocket. It took me a few seconds to straighten it out again. "And look at this, there's a picture of our good friend Mr. Keller here on the second page—under the CEO's address." I handed it over to Thad who began to read it out loud.

"Screw that thing," said Mark after knocking it out of Thad's hands. "Let's go find these guys. They're the ones we want."

"Are you crazy?" asked Thad, not believing that Mark was really serious. But as he took a good look at his friend's face, it was clear that he wasn't fooling.

"I'm totally serious, let's go track them down," said Mark impatiently. "They're getting away."

"Wait a minute," Thad said. I could tell that he was thoroughly amazed that Mark would say such a thing. "Three nights ago, those men tried to shoot us and you want to go after them? You want to be a hero? Well, you can count me out. We're in way over our heads now. If they find out it was us in those woods, they'll murder us for sure—right here and now. It's one thing to sit and watch a building, but I'm not looking for any more trouble. That's where I draw the line."

"Don't worry about it," Mark urged Thad in a soft voice. "They'll never find out. They have no idea we're looking for them."

That was Mark's way of trying to sweet talk Thad into changing his mind. Sometimes he even managed to succeed.

"Don't tell me not to worry," Thad yelled back. By this time, Thad was in his 'I'm not going to listen to anything you say' stance, with his arms crossed tightly over his chest as if glued in position. "You just don't get it, do you? This is not some two-bit detective movie on TV. These guys are for real. They've already killed two people that we know of and I'm sure they wouldn't hesitate to kill again. We've taken this thing as far as we can. Now let's go home and tell the cops. I don't care what they do to us anymore. I can't take this stress. I'm going back. If you want to chase those guys go right ahead—be my guest. But I'm driving home right this second. You can come with me or you can just get out of the damn car."

"Screw you, Thad," said Mark as he climbed out of the car. "Go home if you want. Be a big pussy. I'm not leaving here until we figure out a way to nail these guys." He slammed the door to the car and then started walking in the direction of the town center.

"What about you, Matt?" asked Thad. "Are you coming with me or staying here with Rambo?" I could tell that he was really upset.

"Sorry, Thad," I said while I watched Mark walk away. "I don't like it any more than you do, but I can't leave Mark here all alone. Somebody's got to watch out for him. Besides, we have to get to the bottom of this. If we go to the police now they'll fry us for sure."

"But what else can be done?" asked Thad with tears in his eyes. "You guys think this is some kind of game. I'm really scared, Matt. This is for real."

"I know, Thad. I'm scared too," I confessed. "We'll just have to see what comes up." I reached over and patted Thad's shoulder before leaving. I could tell that he wanted to grab my hand, but something stopped him. He just kept staring out the windshield.

After getting out of the car, I ran to catch up with Mark who had already walked quite a ways. Thad waited for a few minutes before starting the car. To show his anger and frustration, he tried to screech the tires as he drove off, but the car just stalled instead. As we walked away, we could hear him in the distance trying to get it started again. I never thought he'd actually do it, but he did. He drove off and left us there in Front Royal.

*   *   *

Mark and I walked along without saying a word to each other for the longest time. I wondered how we were going to get back home to Elkins and then the thought seemed to fade away. We'd get back somehow. We could always hitch a ride. The one thing I learned from the past three days was that small things like that really didn't matter much. We'd work it out.

I could tell that Mark was furious with Thad. He had this way of walking when something really upset him. He'd clinch his fists real tight, lean forward a bit and stare ahead at nothing, with this cold stone face. That warrior side, which was so a part of his personality, was clearly visible. The few times I witnessed this stance prior to one of his wrestling matches, he's usually kick his opponent's ass in a matter of seconds.

As for me, I couldn't be angry with Thad. It was in his nature to be a coward when faced with even the most mild peril. I was really surprised that he made it this far. I only hoped he'd have the common sense not to go to the police.

It didn't take us long to locate the diner. We asked a few people along the way and they all said the only diner in town was Bob's Grill. It was a few blocks from BEEM, near the center of town. Bob's was one of those of 50's diners, complete with wall-to-wall stainless steel, fire-engine red vinyl booths and table-top jukeboxes with a good collection of oldies. From the parking lot, we could see the three of them sitting in a booth right adjacent to the front door. Their blue Ford LTD also was parked off to the side.

"Great, they're here," said Mark anxiously. "Now go inside and sit nearby and try to listen to what they have to say. They'll recognize me if I go in there—it's too risky."

"Inside? Me?" I asked surprised. "Are you nuts? Let's just wait out here until they come out again."

"No way, Matt," said Mark as he pushed me in the direction of the door. "This is our big opportunity, man. Maybe we can find out something about them firsthand. All you have to do is walk in there, casually sit at one of the tables nearby, order some food and just listen to what they have to say. They'll never recognize you. They never saw you up close before."

"What are you talking about, they saw me five minutes ago over at their office," I explained. "They'll remember me from there for sure."

"Come on, Matt, be real. They didn't get a good look at you." Mark paused for a moment. "Okay then, if you feel that way, give me your coat."

"Why do you want my coat?" I asked.

"So that they won't recognize you."

"A moment ago you said that they didn't get a good look at me," I responded back. "Well, which is it?"

"Listen, Matt," said Mark as he put his hand on my shoulder. "Trust me. Go in there and everything will be fine. Now don't be such a wimp."

"Okay, okay, you win," I said reluctantly. "What are you going to do while I'm in there risking my life."

"I'll be right out here. Just don't worry. If anything happens, run like the wind. They'll never catch you. I'll see to that."

Mark's last statement didn't make me feel any better about what I was about to do.

*　　*　　*

I was terrified as I stood there trying to get up the courage to open the door and enter the restaurant. My palms were all sweaty and I was feeling so self conscious that I was sure I'd fall flat on my face. It also seemed like my heart was beating loud enough to be heard as I walked through the entrance. These guys were killers. I kept thinking that if they recognized me, I could be their next victim. But at the same time, somehow the whole idea of tracking them also excited me. All of the nervousness and exhilaration I was experiencing made me feel more alive than I ever had before.

While the place was full to the brim, I noticed an empty stool at the counter which was not far from their booth. I walked over and casually sat down. None of them seemed to notice me. I ordered a cup of coffee and a tuna fish sandwich and began thumbing through a day-old newspaper I found in front of me. With all of my concentration focused on them, I tried my best to capture their every word. Fortunately, the folks sitting on either side of me were all quietly eating their food, which made it easier for me to hear.

As it turned out, Charlie was the real tall one among the three. He was built like a World Wrestling Federation contender, complete with massive arms, a huge V-shaped chest and no neck. He appeared somewhat out of place wearing a suit and tie—a pair of shorts, a T- shirt and some running shoes would have looked more natural. Bubha, who was kind of regular size, had one very distinctive feature—he was an incredibly ugly son-of-a-bitch. His hair was haphazard and thinning on top of his head, his teeth were half rotten, and his face appeared to be a bit crooked. As for his clothes, it looks as if he's slept in his suit more than a few nights. Bradey, the smallest of the three, seemed more like a typical business person. He was well groomed and wore a tailored suit which fit him like a glove. His most distinctive trait was that he always seemed to be anxious—his leg would shake back and forth or his hand would be tapping the table. It looked as if he was an overly nervous person by nature.

At first, the topic of conversation at their table focused on the Bulls game the night before. It was obvious that both Charlie and Bubha lacked opinions while in the presence of Mr. Bradey. Whatever he said, they took as gospel without question. Once Charlie said that he felt that a particular player was really going places. Mr. Bradey, who obviously disagreed, shot him down with a mere reproaching glance.

Then, all of a sudden, they seemed to get real serious. Mr. Bradey leaned forward and quietly whispered something to his two "toadies" as they huddled around to capture his every word. I could see all of this in the mirror behind the counter. Every now and then I'd catch a word or two but nothing seemed to make sense to me.

All three of them ordered Bob's Special Burger platter. After getting a good look at it, I wished I had ordered it myself. It was a meal straight from sandwich heaven. The platter included an enormous burger with globs of cheese dripping off the side. There were so many french fries that they kept falling off the plate. While I ate my lifeless tuna fish sandwich, the talking stopped at their table as they devoured their meals. I wouldn't have wanted any of my fingers anywhere near their mouths as they sucked their food down like a pack of hungry wolves.

After the coffee came, they started talking again, this time about some meeting that was supposed to take place the following Monday. Mr. Bradey kept saying that they needed "it" before the meeting or Mr. Keller's deal would fall apart. At one point, he asked whether the newspapers were still talking about "that Elkins thing." Bubha told him that they still thought it was some kind of cult that did "the dirty deed" and they all broke out laughing.

Although I knew they killed that poor fisherman long before, hearing them laugh about it made me angry as hell. At that moment, my fear of them melted away and was quickly replaced by sheer contempt. How dare they laugh about such a thing, I thought to myself. I had this incredible urge to walk over and throw my scalding coffee in all of their faces.

Exactly an hour after they arrived, they got up and left. Mr. Bradey remembered to get Molly a coffee as promised. I waited until they were out of sight before quickly paying my check and leaving. I found Mark waiting at the side of the building with a handful of documents and a brown paper bag.

"So what happened in there?" asked Mark, barely able to hold back his curiosity. "It seemed like you were in there for hours and hours."

"Those turkeys are complete assholes," I said, full of rage. "They were actually laughing about that Bantum man's murder."

"No shit, you're kidding!" replied Mark, surprised. "Did

they say anything that would help us out."

"Not really," I admitted. "Let's find a place to sit and I'll tell you what I heard." For some reason, Mark seemed really excited about something else. It showed all over his face. "What's up with you? You look like you just won the lottery or something. And what's with the bag and the papers?"

"You'll never in a trillion years guess what I have in this bag," said Mark, hardly able to control his exhilaration.

"A donut?"

"No, stupid, come on. You can do better than that. Guess again."

"Listen, Mark, I don't know what the hell you have," I exclaimed, not wanting to play his little game. "Just tell me and put me out of my misery. I don't have a trillion years today."

He reached into the bag and pulled out a small black pistol, the kind you see in those old World War II movies.

"Wow! Where the hell did you find that?" I whispered as I forced it back into the bag. Fortunately, no one was around to see it.

"I found it in their car," Mark explained. "The stupid fools didn't lock their car so I decided to take a look around inside. And this is what I found in their glove compartment. We also now know where our good friend Mr. Bradey lives. It was his car. I got his address from his registration. See!" Mark showed me a copy of the registration.

"I don't know about you, but I think we'd better get the hell out of here," I said as I started to walk toward the main road. "If they find out that you stole their gun and papers, they might come back here looking for them."

"Oh, yeah, I never thought of that," Mark admitted.

Mark tossed the bag into my backpack and we both started running along the street that lead out of town. After about twenty minutes, we came upon a billboard along the side of the road that had a place where we could rest and talk in private without being seen. We were both panting hard after our little run.

"I can't believe you took that thing," I said as I tried to catch my breath. "Thad is right, you are crazy. What if someone saw you or they came out. These guys kill—remember?"

"Thanks for your concern, mom," Mark replied back sarcastically. "The car was parked away from everything and there was no one else around. I was in and out in about two seconds flat. Don't worry about me, I can handle myself."

"Do you think that's the gun they used to kill Carter?" I asked as I took it out again to get a better look at it.

"I don't know. It has all eight bullets in it. After finding it, I also grabbed as much stuff out of the glove compartment as I could carry. Most of it is junk—his registration and insurance information. You should see the inside of his car. It's a complete mess. The guy's a real pig."

"You and him would get along fine," I laughed.

"Compared to him, I'm a neat freak," Mark explained. "So tell me what happened in there."

I described everything I heard in the restaurant to Mark. We both wondered whether the meeting Bradey mentioned had anything to do with the murders. Mark also couldn't believe that they laughed about killing that guy. As mad as I was, it was nothing compared to Mark's fury.

"Those assholes," he said full of rage. "If I ever get my hands on them I'll rip their heads off. Did you know that the man they killed had a wife and four kids. His youngest is only two months old. I think they should all be strung up by their balls and then shot."

"I know the feeling. I felt the same way when I heard them talking. We have to make sure that these guys pay for what they did."

When we first started chasing down leads, it was to save our own butts. But now I felt we had an obligation to put these guys behind bars for justice sake.

"So what do we do next?" asked Mark.

"I don't know," I confessed. "Listen Mark, do you think we ought to keep that gun? If that was used to kill Carter and we get caught with it, they'll think we did it."

"Relax, Matt. No one even knows that Carter is dead, remember? Actually, I wanted to check out the trunk to see if our good friend Carter was there, but I was afraid they'd come out and catch me."

"Are you kidding?" I asked surprised. "They'd never put a dead body in the trunk for this long, it would stink up the entire city."

"Didn't you ever see that movie about the jewelry robbers who killed the guard and wrapped him up in plastic bags and duct tape to prevent him from smelling," Mark described. "There was also a Colombo episode where this guy murders this lady and puts her in one of those fur bags and hides her in a wall. They could have done something like that."

"Sounds pretty far fetched to me," I admitted. "You know, we better get going. It's already past 2:00 and we still got to get home. It's probably going to take hours to get there."

"I can't believe that Thad, that prick, really left us here. He's such a god damn shit. As far as I'm concerned, he is ex-communicated as my friend. He's probably at the police station blabbing about all of this right now. I swear if he tells them, I'll rip him into little pieces."

"Come on, Mark. Don't be so rough on him. That's just the way Thad is. He's scared shitless and doesn't know what to do.

The only way he knows how to deal with this kind of thing is to run from it. He wouldn't go to the police. He doesn't want anyone to find out about this whole mess."

"He's still a first class prick. He could have waited for us."

At that point, Mark and I started walking in the direction of the main road to Elkins. We decided not to start hitching until we got on Route 25. If we were real lucky, we'd get a ride right away and maybe get back before dark.

I kept wondering whether my parents found out I cut school. Over the years, I'd skipped many times, but only got caught once. But during those other times, I always covered all my bases. This time I wasn't able to work out a proper plan.

Before walking our first mile, without warning, a car coming from behind, slammed on its brakes and stopped right behind us. There was dust everywhere. Mark and I both jumped nearly three feet off the ground. We thought it was those thugs coming after us. But to our surprise, it turned out to be Thad instead.

"Thad, you shit," said Mark with a big grin. "You didn't abandon us after all. What, you couldn't find your way out of town?"

"Thad, you scared the living shit out of me, you asshole," I yelled, as I tried to stop trembling from fear. "God, I thought we were about to be executed."

"Shut up and get in," Thad demanded. After climbing inside, he sped off in the direction of home. He was obviously very annoyed with both of us. "Where the hell were you guys? I've been driving around for hours looking for you. I even went back to that BEEM place and waited there thinking you'd eventually return."

"We told you we were going to follow them to the diner," I said while I tried to brush the dust off my clothes.

"I couldn't find any diners," Thad snarled.

"It was right there in the center of town," Mark explained. "How could you possible miss it?"

"Well, I didn't see it," Thad responded back defensively.

"Did you ask anyone?" asked Mark. "I bet . . ."

"Mark, just drop it," I said in an attempt to ward off trouble. "It doesn't matter." I could sense they were about to get into one of their stupid arguments over it.

"So it looks like you guys wasted an entire day for nothing," Thad remarked.

"Well, not exactly," said Mark as he pulled the gun out of the bag and placed it next to Thad's shoulder. When Thad saw it, he nearly drove off the road.

"What the hell is that thing?" he screamed. "Get it away from me."

"Jesus, Thad, haven't you ever seen a gun before?" I asked. "It's not a snake or anything. Calm down before you get us all killed."

"Where the hell did you find that horrible thing?" Thad inquired.

"I found it in Bradey's car," said Mark in a matter of fact manner.

"Who the hell is Bradey?" asked Thad.

"He's the guy who I threw down that night," Mark explained. "Remember? We told you we learned their names when we were in that BEEM place. Well anyway, we followed them over to the diner in town. Matt went inside and listened to them, while I went through their glove compartment and found this gun."

"Are you completely insane?" asked Thad. "Get that thing out of my car. If we get caught with it, we'll all be thrown in jail. Don't you know that in Virginia, if they find an unregistered hand gun in your car that it's a mandatory one year sentence—no exceptions. And now you have your finger prints all over it. I told you we'd all be hardened criminals in a week. Look at you guys. You're now walking around with stolen guns. What's next?"

"I don't know Matt, what's next?" asked Mark playfully. He turned to me and winked. That was his way of saying let's tease Thad.

"Well, Mark, we haven't killed anyone yet," I said. "Now that we have this gun, I think we'll have to use it. Let's do a drive-by shooting or something. That would help us to expand our list of crimes."

"Sounds good to me," said Mark. "Who should we shoot first?"

"Hey, there are a few old people in that park up ahead. Should I take a few of them out?" Mark laughed.

"Shut up, shut up, shut up," shouted Thad. "You guys are really sick, you know that? How can you even joke about such a thing? You both should be committed to a reform school."

"Okay, Thad," I said. "We're sorry. We'll be good."

"Hey, why don't we add car stealing to our list," Mark whispered loud enough to be heard by Thad. "We'll just shoot Thad and take his car. That will add at least another two crimes to our list."

"That's enough, Mark," I said in a scolding tone. Mark didn't always know when to stop.

It was clear that Thad was very stressed out and wasn't in the mood for any jokes. For the remainder of the trip home we all kept quiet. Around half-way there, I took over some of the driving while Thad slept. He needed the rest to clear up all of the chaos which had taken over his mind.

We arrived home in Elkins a little after five-thirty. As it turned out, none of us got caught. I walked into my house as if nothing had happened and no one seemed to even notice me. I drove over two hundred miles, came face to face with three murderers, eavesdropped on their conversation and drove back to Elkins with one of their guns in our car and after all of that, upon arriving home, everything was the same. Somehow it didn't figure.

6

The following morning, I decided to walk to school instead of having my dad drop me off. I cut through the forest behind my house because this path seemed to always help me clear my mind. There was something about the towering trees and the natural sounds which tended to free my head from excess mental baggage.

Once again, our little adventure managed to interfere with my sleep the night before and add to my present confusion. In a dream that felt as real as life itself, I was dressed in a very ornate outfit that looked like some kind of ceremonial robe straight out of Africa. The robe I wore, with its multi-colored beads and animal skins which hung from my shoulders, went well with the large headpiece full of an assortment of colorful bird feathers. Mark and Thad were standing by my side in similar costumes. We stood before a large stone altar surrounded by massive white pillars which seemed to be reaching for the sky above. The only light came from a small fire which burned without any form of fuel and from the moon which was situated directly above us. It was a werewolve's moon—full and round in all its glory.

I remember performing a series of complicated rituals which ended by me passing my hand through the burning flame, cutting my palm, and then letting the blood drip into the fire. With every drop, the flames seemed to dance with delight. Knowing exactly what was expected of me, I walked around the blazing altar three times, counterclockwise, before saying some phrase in a language that was unknown to me. The sights, the sounds and smells made the experience appear to be incredibly true to life.

When all the various stages were completed, I closed my eyes, raised my hands to the heavens and when I opened them, there before me was the Bantum fisherman lying naked beside the altar. With a large brown trout protruding from his mouth and his eyes fixed in a perpetual lifeless stare, I knew that I was the one responsible for his death through some unknown actions I had just performed.

Upon awaking from this nightmare, my body was drowning in sweat and completely tangled in the sheets, which I had somehow managed to enshroud around me. Disoriented and confused, it took me several seconds to realize that it was only a dream and that I hadn't actually killed anyone. But for the remainder of the night, in that realm somewhere between sleep and not, I could feel that same guilt that a killer must encounter after performing a murder. The whole thing had a lasting impression on me that would be forever etched in my memories.

*　　*　　*

To get away with cutting school the day before, we all forged notes from our parents explaining why we weren't able to attend. I always had good luck with the old sore throat excuse, so I went with that one. Thad's note reminded me of a school report—it was typed and went on for several paragraphs. He was truly a newcomer to this whole process. Mark's note was straight to the point and written on a small scrap of paper. It simply stated "Mark couldn't come yesterday." What it lacked in content, it made up in simplicity. Luckily, we all managed to fool our individual homeroom teachers without getting caught. I couldn't believe how easy it was.

It was third period before the three of us were able to meet. Mr. Potter, our history teacher, was less than two months away from retirement and had long since stopped caring whether or not his students learned anything in class. Since he was late arriving once again, we had a few minutes to chat.

It was then that I discovered how much of a sacrifice Thad had made by skipping school. Up until that point, he hadn't missed a single day since entering high school. He would have received some kind of special wall plaque at the end of the year if he was able to maintain a perfect record. I couldn't help but wonder how many other students Thad must have infected over the years because he came to school sick as a dog, just so he could get some stupid award. Mark, on the other hand, probably held the school record for days missed in a single year.

"So, Mark, what did you do with that gun you stole?" Thad whispered with a worried expression on his face. "I couldn't stop thinking that someone's going to find it."

"Well, actually, I gave it to my younger brother to play with," he responded sarcastically. "He's probably got it in his mouth right now."

"God, you're really a sick person, you know that?" said Thad in disgust. "How can you even joke about such a horrible thing. Now really, come on, tell me the truth. What did you do with it?"

"Don't worry about it," said Mark in an effort to dispel any concerns. "I hid it in a place that no one will ever dare to look."

"What, in your underwear drawer?" I asked with a smile.

"Real funny, Matt, you're a real comedian today," said Mark. "At least I change my underwear once a day—which is more than I can say for you.

"And how would you know? Are you watching me undress

107

through my window again?" I replied back.

Both Mark and I got a good laugh out of our little exchange, while Thad continued to look distracted and worried about something.

"You know, with all of this detective stuff we have been doing, we still haven't really made much progress," said Thad defiantly. "I was thinking about this last night. So what if we know who those guys are and where they live. So what if we know that they might have stolen some stupid piece of junk from some two-bit country. So what if we know that there is some link between them and this BEEM company. Unless we know where Carter's body is hidden, none of it means shit. And you know as well as I do that there is no way in hell we are ever going to find that corpse."

"I'm not so sure about that," I said, realizing that Thad had just given me the perfect opportunity to present an idea I had come up with the night before. "I have this little plan I worked out last evening. You guys have to listen to the whole thing before you say anything. And try to have an open mind. Okay? So just listen."

"I already don't like the sound of this," said Thad with his arms crossed tightly across his chest in that all so familiar defiant stance of his.

"Just shut up, Thad, and hear him out," said Mark in my defense as he leaned forward in his chair to catch my every word.

"Why don't we let them lead us to the body," I suggested.

"Sure, Matt, like we are going to pick up the phone and just ask them where it is," Thad replied. I could tell he was expecting something a little more profound from me.

"Not exactly that, but close," I explained. "Listen, I saw this movie a couple of months ago where this guy killed his wife and some other dude saw him do it. After he buried the body, the guy who saw all of this tried to blackmail the killer. To avoid getting caught the killer went back and moved the body. Do you see what I mean?"

"So what happened next?" asked Mark.

"It doesn't matter what happened next," I replied. "That's not the point."

"Sure it matters," said Mark. "What happened next?"

"Okay, the guy trying to blackmail the killer didn't get paid so he went to the cops. They went to the site and didn't find the body. The blackmailer was so angry that he went over to confront the killer. After a heated argument, they got into this wicked fight and they both got shot. I think they both died."

"Sounds like a pretty stupid movie to me," said Thad.

"What can I say," I said. "It was late night TV. Forget about how stupid it was for a moment and think about it. Try to open that empty mind of yours for just a few minutes."

"So what are you saying, Matt?" asked Thad. "You think we should call these guys up, tell them we saw them burying Carter, and then follow them to see if they move the body?"

"Something like that," I said. "We have enough information pieced together to really sound like we know what they're up to. We can mention that we have the gun, describe all that we know to them, and tell them if they don't pay us that we'll turn them in to the cops."

"You know, I think the plan could work," said Mark.

Mark was the easy one. He'd go along with anything. It was Thad that would take some serious convincing.

"You are kidding, right, Matt?" asked Thad. "You really can't be serious about this."

"I'm dead serious," I responded.

"Okay then, so what happens if they don't go after the body?" asked Thad. "What then?"

"Nothing," I said. "That's the beauty of it. If they go for the body, great. If not, then we haven't lost anything, have we?"

"Sure we have," said Thad. "They don't seem to be looking for us now. If we stir this thing up, they'll start looking for us for sure."

"Looking for who?" I asked. "What makes you think they'd believe it was us who saw them do it. We were driving away at the speed of light. As far as they know, it could be anyone. And besides, they walked right by me and Mark yesterday and didn't notice us. I even sat in a restaurant three feet away from these guys and they couldn't have cared less."

"And how are we supposed to follow them?" asked Thad. "They could go looking for the body anytime. We'll be in school. We can't keep driving out there everyday."

"We don't have to do it during the week," I explained. "We'll call them up on Saturday morning and tell them that if they don't give us the money by Sunday that we'll go to the police the next day."

"I think it might work," said Mark eagerly. "We could call and follow them for those two days. If nothing turns up, then we'll just come home."

"Why are we doing this anyway?" asked Thad. "Maybe Mark's right, maybe the police will never be able to piece this thing together."

"Or maybe you're right, Thad," I said. "And maybe they will. Let's just try this thing. If nothing comes from it then we'll just give it up and take our chances. We've got nothing to lose."

"Except maybe our lives," Thad whispered under his breath. "I guess I'll have to add blackmailing to my new criminal resume."

7

The next few days seemed to just drag on. Every morning, the newspapers presented new developments in what was now being called the "Cheat River Sacrifice." A special anti-cult task force within the FBI was brought in to investigate the killing. They arrived in their fancy dark blue vans with tinted glass, loaded with all of the latest high-tech forensic gadgets available. Because of their very specific orientation, they tended to focus on the "cult" aspect of the crime instead of simply putting the obvious pieces together.

Mark's dad had an old drinking buddy named Fred who worked over at the Elkins police station, who'd regularly drop by after his shift. While he kept saying over and over again that he couldn't talk about the case, after his fourth beer, he couldn't stop himself from spilling all the details about how the "Feds" were collecting and interpreting the evidence. Mark did his best to eavesdrop on these conversations from the next room.

According to Fred, based on footprints found near the campfire, which was adjacent to the murder scene, the Feds estimated that there were at least five or six members of the cult. After measuring the size of the shoes and the depths of the impressions, it was felt that at least two of the participants were teenagers—the rest were probably full grown male adults.

They also felt that the group was not from the area. They had seen similar cases where fish were used in ritualistic killings in New Mexico and Oregon, but never in the South. One of the investigators had explained to Fred that the custom originated during prohibition when gangsters used to kill their competitors and then shove a fish down their throat. The type and size of the fish represented their calling card, which was used as a warning to others. The ritual was later adopted by a few cult groups who also used it as a kind of signature.

Around town, all anyone talked about was the murder. Children were not allowed to walk home from school or play outside in their own yards, the number of handguns purchased in the area nearly doubled, and a multitude of rumors hovered over Elkins like a black thunder cloud which at any moment would break loose.

The newspapers also seemed to have their own unique way of reporting the case. With every front-page article I read, the more crazy it all began to sound. The Wednesday morning edition of the Gazette described how Miss Lance, an old spinster who lived over on Cranberry Road, reported to the police that she thought she saw some cult members in the woods behind her house the night before. Even though she had a long history of getting "plastered" and calling the cops about UFOs and little green men who lived in her basement, this time people believed her story. I guess folks tend to believe what they want to believe.

The Elkins Weekly, which came out on Thursdays, described how Jeffrey Grover swore he heard a chanting sound coming from his barn. When he went out to investigate who was causing it, he found a dead pigeon near the door. It's neck seemed to be broken. Instead of accepting the fact that the bird probably flew into the side of the building, he told the reporter that he was sure there was foul play involved in the bird's death. Most people tended to agree.

Bart, the librarian over at the primary school, told the local papers that he had a dream the night of the murder in which he saw the whole thing happen. He was convinced that he could identify the killers if he saw them again. It was funny to me how Bart's recollection of the events became clearer with every new bit of information printed in the newspapers.

As much as the town grieved over the death of that poor Bantum man who was killed, at some level I couldn't help but feel that many people in town were somehow subconsciously excited by the whole affair. Having something bizarre like this happen in a small town tends to stir up the old daily grind a bit. The idea that evil might be lurking nearby added a little suspense to what was often an ordinary, mundane daily existence. It gave folks something new and different to talk about for a few weeks.

As for Mark, Thad and I, we gradually began to fall back into our old routines. Somehow, the reality of what had happened the week before began to diminish. It was too stressful to continue thinking about it, so our minds began to shut it out. While the three of us got together regularly, we stopped talking about the murders. Likewise, with every passing day, the events related to the killing seemed less relevant to us—as if our minds began to believe all of the stories written in the papers. With the local police and the FBI off on their wild goose chase looking for who knows what, we seemed to be in the clear. Whatever they were doing kept taking them down a trail which led further and further away from us. At that point, I was starting to feel that we didn't need to do anything more to find Carter's body after all. Mark was right, it was time to move on with our lives. Even without ever saying anything, I could sense that Mark and Thad had come to the same conclusion. There was nothing we could do for that dead fisherman—he was already gone. It was time to save ourselves.

While at some level, my conscience kept telling me that it was wrong to let those who committed the crime get away with it, these thoughts were gradually wrestled into submission by that side of myself which did its best to look after my well being.

*   *   *

It wasn't until Friday morning that something devastating happened to our false sense of security, which caused it to come crashing down. The three of us were all sitting in our second period study hall when I looked out the window and saw at least three police cruisers and one of the FBI vans pull up in front of the school. Out of the cars emerged at least ten uniformed cops and a few men dressed in plain clothes carrying walkie-talkies. I had imagined this moment a thousand times over the last week—the police coming up and handcuffing me, the trip to the station, the press—and now it looked like it was actually happening.

"Thad," I whispered, as I pulled on the back of his shirt to get his attention. When he turned around, I pointed outside. A look of sheer horror consumed his face. His expression clearly indicated his need to know what to do next. I didn't have a clue. Mark, who was sitting near the front of the class, away from the two of us, also noticed them entering the building. Without hesitating, he got up from his chair and casually walked over to where I was sitting.

"I think we've got some real trouble here, Matt," he whispered into my ear. He was cool as ever about the whole thing. "We might want to get the hell out of here. Like right now."

"Mark, you get back to your seat this very minute," said Mrs. Ryan, the study hall teacher. "You know that this is a quiet study. There are many people in here trying to prepare for their finals." She was an old bag who followed the "old school" way of teaching—discipline and order above all else.

"I'm sorry, Mrs. Ryan," said Mark with a submissive tone. "It's just that I'm not feeling very well and I was asking Matt if he had some aspirin."

"You look perfectly fine to me," she insisted. "Now go back and take your seat immediately."

As Mark made his way back to his seat, he pretended to trip, as if nearly fainting. I ran up to him and grabbed his arm to prevent him from falling. Thad, taking my lead, came up and took his other arm. Mrs. Ryan saw the whole thing, but wasn't sure what to make of it. Mark had pulled a number of practical jokes over the years and she knew he was capable of playing games with her.

"Mrs. Ryan," I said, in a concerned voice. "I think we should take Mark to the nurse right away. He doesn't look very well. This morning he was complaining that he was feeling dizzy.

It must be all of the working out he is doing for the wrestling team." As I talked, we both walked Mark over in the direction of the door.

"Very well, Matt," she said in a flustered voice. "Why don't you take him to the nurse. Thad, go back to your seat. Matt can take care of Mark by himself." At that point, Mark once again pretended to nearly fall.

"I think I should also go," said Thad sincerely. "If he falls, Matt can't handle him alone."

"Well, alright," she said angrily. "I want you both back here immediately after you take him downstairs. You hear me?"

"Yes, ma'am," we both replied as we walked into the hallway. Once out of the room, we all started running in the direction of the staircase. But instead of going down, Mark pulled us into the second floor bathroom.

"What are we doing in here?" I asked.

"Let's let them walk by first," Mark replied. "They're probably walking up the stairs right now."

"Shit," whispered Thad. "They're coming after us. Did you see all of them. They're coming after us. We'll all be dragged off to jail. What are we going to do?" Thad started rocking back and forth like a psychopath in a mental ward.

"We've got to get the hell out of here, that's what we got to do," said Mark as he looked out the bathroom windows for a way to escape. It was clear the only way out was down the stairs and past the main office.

"And where are we supposed to go?" I asked on the verge of losing it myself.

"Anywhere," said Mark. "Let's just get out of here."

"Let's face it," I confessed. "We're caught. We'll just have to tell them the truth and maybe they'll believe us."

"Yeah, right," said Mark sarcastically. "And when they search my truck and find that gun I stole from those guys under the seat, what do you think they'll say about that? And what about Carter's briefcase. You know it's still in my garage behind the tool bench. If they find that, we're all totally screwed."

"Are you crazy?" yelled Thad. "You put that gun in your truck? I thought you said you put that thing in a place where no one would find it. That's the first place anyone would look."

"I lied, okay?" Mark admitted. "So sue me."

Thad was so excited about the whole thing that he began to shake from head to toe. His breathing also increased to a point where it looked like he was on the verge of hyperventilating.

"Thad, are you alright?" I asked as I listened to his gasp for air. "Mark, I think Thad's having some kind of an asthma attack or something."

"Thad, are you okay?" asked Mark equally concerned. "Listen, Thad. It's all going to be fine. We're going to leave

113

school, go over to my house and pick up my truck and then we'll head out of town until we can figure out what to do next. We can take the gun and the suitcase and chuck them into the river some place far away from here where no one will ever find them."

By that point, Thad looked like he was ready to pass out onto the floor. Without really thinking about it, Mark and I just grabbed him and led him out the bathroom in the direction of the stairs. I guess we figured if we could get him out of the school, he'd be okay. As we were walking around the corner, all at once we were face-to-face with "them"—there in front of us was Mr. Ballick, the principal, and a small army of police officers. There was a long pause as we all stared at each other. Mark looked like he was ready to make a run for it. Thad nearly dropped to the floor.

"What are you boys doing out of your class?" asked Mr. Ballick in his usual gruff tone. "And what's wrong with Thad? He looks awful."

"We were . . ." stammered Mark. "We were . . ."

"We were just taking Thad down to the nurse," I said. "He hasn't been feeling well today so Mrs. Ryan asked us to escort him down to the medical unit. Probably just some twenty-four hour bug. Nothing to worry about, I'm sure."

"Well, make it quick," said Mr. Ballick. "There will be a special presentation in the auditorium in about a half hour." Mr. Ballick looked at his watch as he spoke. "All students must attend. Seniors and juniors will participate in the first session."

"May I ask what's going on?" I inquired, as my eyes scanned the large group of cops.

"The police and FBI just wanted to provide a little information on what people should look out for these days," he said. "There is nothing to be concerned about. It's just a routine precaution."

"I understand," I remarked, full of relief. "We'll go back to class right away. I'm glad the police are taking such an interest in our well-being. It makes me feel much safer."

Mr. Ballick nodded before continuing with his entourage toward the auditorium, while we made our way down the stairwell. Thad's recovery was immediate. When he realized that they hadn't come for us after all, he was so relieved that he started laughing. He had this tendency to laugh when he got real nervous about something.

"What the hell is so funny?" asked Mark.

"I don't know," said Thad. "I guess I can't believe they weren't coming for us. God damn, I was ready to pee in my pants I was so scared."

"At least not today," I said reluctantly. "But next time it just might happen."

114

"Well, that does it for me," said Mark. "I think it's time to finish this thing off. I don't want to go through something like that again. We really should go ahead with Matt's plan."

"I think you're right about that," I agreed, knowing exactly what he was referring to. "I can't think of any other way around it."

"Wait a minute, what plan? What are you talking about?" asked Thad, totally bewildered.

"The plan to try to get those guys to go after Carter's body," Mark explained. "It's our only hope. We'll call them tomorrow morning and then spend the weekend following them around. We can tell our parents that we're going on an overnight fishing trip again."

"And how are we going to get around?" asked Thad. "My mom never gives me the car on the weekends and Mark's truck isn't an option."

"Actually, we might be able to use my sister's car," I said. "She's flying to North Carolina this weekend to look at a college. I might be able to talk her into using her car for a few days."

"She has never let you use it before," Mark reminded me. "What makes you think she'll let you use it now?"

"Because I've got something on her, that's why," I confessed. "I found a few condoms in her purse last week. If she says no, I'll threaten to tell my dad about it. Believe me, she'll come around."

"God, that's terrible, Matt," said Thad. I could tell that he was disappointed that I'd even think of such a thing. "Blackmailing your own sister? And what were you doing in her purse anyway?"

"I was looking for a pen," I replied defensively. I didn't like Thad's tone. "Listen, I wouldn't have even thought about saying anything, but if that's the only way to get her car, then we don't have a choice."

"Shit, Matt, so who is she bopping?" asked Mark.

"Shut up, Mark," I scolded him. "She's still my sister."

"I still don't think this idea of yours is going to work," Thad confessed. "It's too much like a B-grade detective movie."

"Like I said before, if it works, it works," I replied. "If it doesn't, then we haven't lost anything. Right?"

"So when do we do this thing?" asked Mark full of enthusiasm.

"The earlier the better," I said. "We'll have to get a lot of change together and call from a pay phone. We should also write something out that we can read over the phone."

"Wait, where do we call from?" asked Mark.

"It doesn't matter, we can use the phone near the shopping center here in Elkins," I responded.

"We can't do that," said Mark. "We need to call from

Virginia so that if they do something right away, we'll be able to pick up their trail immediately. And who are we calling anyway, Mr. Keller? Mr. Bradey?"

"I think we ought to call Bradey," I insisted. "At least we know he and his goons were the ones who killed Carter. What if Keller isn't really all that involved? Didn't you say you have Bradey's address?"

"Yeah, I do. I took his car registration, remember?" Mark reminded me. "We know where he lives and I even have a phone number for him. You know, maybe we should hit them both."

"Okay, so lets call both Bradey and Keller," I agreed. "Why not make it interesting."

"So how are we going to follow these guys?" asked Thad in a very pessimistic tone. "Just explain that to me. Do you expect us to just park in front of their house and casually follow them as they drive away. It ain't going to work."

"Good point," I said. "Why don't you guys come over to my house this afternoon after school and we'll sort out all of the details. There has got to be a way."

Thad stood there looking for the words to say in order to talk us out of this scheme. But the arguments just weren't there. At some level, he too realized that there was little choice—we had to go ahead with the plan.

*   *   *

That afternoon before dinner, the three of us met at my house to sort out the details of our proposed scheme. After having some time to consider what happened that morning, Thad completely changed his attitude about things. He seemed to be willing to do anything to avoid getting caught by the cops, even if it meant tracking down Carter's corpse. Mark and I were both relieved because it was much easier dealing with Thad when he was on our side.

We decided to drive to Front Royal at the crack of dawn the following morning—before 5:00 am. Once there, Mark and I would head over to some payphones near the center of town and call Bradey and Mr. Keller at exactly the same time. This was to prevent them from calling each other and tying up the lines after the first call was made.

The statement Thad composed for us to read to them was brilliant. It went as follows:

"Dear Mr. Keller,
You don't know me, but I know you very, very well. As it turns out, I happened to see your friends Mr. Bradey, Charlie and Bubha bury a man last Friday night. I think he was the man who visits you before all of his trips to India and Nepal. I also suspect

116

your men were involved in the murder of a fisherman as well. Unfortunately, I missed seeing that one so I'll leave it alone.

The reason why I'm telling you all of this is because I am a bit short on cash and could use a few bucks. If you give me $2,000 by this Sunday night, I'll forget I saw anything. If not, I'm afraid I'll have to let someone know what I witnessed—perhaps the local authorities.

If you have any questions about whether I know what I'm talking about, just ask Mr. Bradey about his missing gun. Oh, and by the way, I understand that Nepal is very nice this time of year. I was planning to go there this summer to Gorkha District to see a famous urn, but I understand that it's missing. Any ideas?

I'll give you a call late Sunday afternoon after 3:00 pm. I'm also planning on mentioning this matter to Mr. Bradey. So long for now."

The message to Mr. Bradey was almost identical. We agreed to allow them only two days time before we called them back to ensure that they'd made their move during the weekend.

After the phone calls were made, Mark and I would then find a place to park along the main road that led toward Elkins so we could watch for Bradey's car. We decided it would be too dangerous if we tried to follow them from their own homes. Besides, there was no way of knowing which house to stake out—Keller's or Bradey's. Since we assumed the body was buried somewhere near our home town, if they passed through Front Royal in that direction, we were hoping we'd be able to spot their car and then follow them to where the body was hidden. Another part of the plan called for Thad to "stake out" the BEEM complex to wait and see if either Bradey or Keller showed up there after the calls. We figured if the two of them were going to meet, they'd probably pick their office. We knew it was a long shot, but it was the only strategy we could manage.

Since watching BEEM from a distance required the least amount of risk, Thad volunteered for the job. According to the plan, Thad would set up what Mark kept calling a "command post" across the street from the building. The day we visited there, I noticed that there was a small open field next to where we parked our car. Thad would ride his bike to the site, pick a secluded spot somewhere within the thick grass, and just watch the building and let us know whether there was anything going on. We would use a pair of walkie-talkies to communicate back and forth. If everything went according to plan, and Mark and I were able to follow Bradey out of town, Thad would stay at a local motel and we'd pick him up the following day.

To organize ourselves, we made a list of items we needed as part of our "espionage" efforts. This included a pair of walkie-talkies, a telescope to observe the BEEM building, a pair of bird-watching binoculars to watch for Bradey's car, a bike, and enough food to keep us going throughout the day. Fortunately my mother had just gone shopping—the three of us were able to raid the cabinets.

As for the wheels to get us there, I was forced to blackmail my sister into lending me her car after all. I hated to do it, but there was no other way. I could tell from her expression that she was deeply hurt that I'd stoop to such a level to get my hands on her beloved machine. As much as I wanted to explain my reasons, I knew she couldn't be trusted. I vowed to apologize to her at some later point.

Lastly, to avoid the whole pick-up hassle, Mark and Thad both decided to sleep at my house. Before hitting the sack, we watched a few T&A videos I had rented to help us relax. I even managed to get my hands on a pint of brandy from a neighbor who ran a small bootlegging operation for some of the local high school kids. As we watched our movies, we all took hits off the bottle. Even Thad managed to gulp down a few swigs.

"Do you think they'll really lead us to the body?" asked Thad after starting our second movie.

"I don't know," I responded back. "I hope so." I was caught up in the opening and was only half listening to what Thad had asked.

"Do you really?" Thad asked reluctantly.

"Do I really what?" I responded, not understanding his question.

"Do you really want to find that body," he said with a disgusted expression. "I mean, could you imagine what it's going to be like after a week. His body probably smells and has all kinds of worms coming out of it. It's probably a real nasty sight."

"You know, I never stopped to think about it," I admitted.

"Oh, by the way, do you think we should bring that pistol along with us tomorrow?" asked Mark. "I mean what if we follow them and they somehow figure out our plan. Shouldn't we have some kind of protection along with us?"

"Are you out of your gourd, Butthead?" asked Thad, once again surprised that Mark would suggest such a stupid thing. "How many times do we have to repeat ourselves—stay away from that thing. It's bad news. It will only get us in more trouble."

"I agree with Thad," I remarked. "You should leave that gun hidden away somewhere. You did hide that thing someplace better this afternoon, didn't you?"

"I took care of it," said Mark.

"That's what you said the last time," I reminded him. "Besides, we're not going to do anything that will put us in any danger. We'll play it safe on everything. If something doesn't look right, we'll just abort the mission."

"Listen to yourself, Matt," said Thad, with a laugh. "You're sounding like a Russian commando on a KGB assignment. Mission—give me a break."

8

We all woke up a little after 4:30 am the next morning and managed to somehow get ourselves ready and on the road to Front Royal for the second time in as many weeks. Even after only a few hours of sleep, I was feeling wide awake. The anticipation of what we were attempting to do had that effect on me.

We made the drive in a little less than three hours this time around. With me behind the wheel and only a handful of cars venturing out so early on a Saturday morning, it was easy to cruise at a decent speed along the country roads that led to Virginia.

"Looks like we're here," I said as I drove past the sign welcoming visitors to Front Royal. I had to shake Mark's arm roughly to snap him out of his semi-coma state. "Wake the hell up you bum—it's show time."

His head was leaning against the window with his mouth wide open and his face all crunched up. Seeing him sleep was truly a frightening experience—death's ugly face couldn't have looked any worse.

"Ohhhh shit," said Mark as he tried to stretch. "Looks like the fun is just about to begin." Mark was really looking forward to our upcoming adventure, while Thad and I were both less than enthusiastic.

"You still alive back there?" asked Mark as he tried to get some kind of response from Thad. He hadn't said a single word or uttered so much as a peep since we left Elkins. He just sat there mindlessly staring out the window. "Come on Thad, you still breathing back there or what?"

"I'm fine," he mumbled without registering any emotion.

Before allowing Mark to say anything else, I gave him a look which communicated to him to leave Thad alone. He got my message and complied this time.

Before putting our plan into action, we slowly drove past the BEEM complex to "scope out" the situation. We weren't sure what we were looking for, but it seemed like everything was pretty quiet there. I then ventured down the road half a mile or so and pulled onto a small grass covered parking area. We walked around a bit to get the old blood flowing after climbing out of the car. None of us had anything to say to each other—lately this was becoming a common scenario with the three of us.

"I guess it's that time," said Mark after a long pause. "Might

120

as well get Thad off and running. No sense waiting any longer."

Mark opened the trunk of the car and wrestled the bike out, while Thad tried to cram my telescope and the rest of his gear into his knapsack. I couldn't believe all of the junk food he was bringing along with him—Twinkies, Devil-dogs, potato chips, sodas and the like. You'd have thought he was going out for several weeks the way he crammed it all in.

While I stood there watching, Thad carried out this task with the seriousness of a seasoned soldier preparing for his next dangerous assignment in the bush. I had to laugh to myself as I watched him. He was taking this soldiering business pretty seriously. I was about to ask him if he wanted camouflage paint for his face, but decided to just let it drop. He was nervous enough without me making wise-ass remarks.

"Hey, Butthead," Thad shouted, as he went over to see what Mark was doing. "Be careful with my bike. Look, you're scratching it all up, you asshole."

"Shut up, Thad," said Mark as he handed the bike over. "I didn't scratch nothing. You're such a little baby sometimes."

"Well, if I'm such a god damn baby, then why the hell am I risking my life out there in that field today?" asked Thad with a defiant tone. "Answer me that! Why don't you go out there and I'll stay with the car where it's safe?"

"Because!" replied Mark with a big smile. He always got a kick out of Thad's little tantrums.

"Why because?" asked Thad, still expecting a reasonable answer.

"Well, because neither Matt or I are brave enough to take on such a dangerous task," he said with a serious expression which was almost believable. "You're the only one that is man enough to do it." Thad looked at him not knowing what to say. He wasn't expecting that kind of answer from Mark. It almost sounded sincere.

I had to walk to the side of the car before bursting out laughing. I couldn't believe that Thad was actually taking him seriously. Once that was out of my system, I came over and put my arm around Thad's shoulders and gave him one of those manly bear hugs.

"Good luck, Thad," I replied. "Now remember, if you see those boys from BEEM, don't you go running over there like Rambo to kick their asses. I know you want to rip them from limb to limb, but try to restrain yourself."

"Yeah, very funny, Matt," said Thad as he pulled away. "You're a regular comedian these days—about as funny as dog shit on a fork."

Before heading off, Thad shook both of our hands. You'd have thought he was going off to battle. He had on his bike helmet, a pair of dark sun glasses and his fully loaded pack. It was obvious that he was a bit traumatized by what he was about to do. While none of us really thought anything would come of it, we still sensed that the potential for danger was still there.

After struggling to balance his bike with a full pack, Thad somehow managed to ride off down the road to set up his "stakeout." Mark and I waited nearly twenty minutes before Thad contacted us by walkie-talkie to let us know that he was in "position."

"This is fox calling base, over," he said seriously. "Do you read me? Over."

"What's up, Thad," I responded back casually. "You're there already? Wow, that was pretty damn fast."

"I thought we agreed we weren't going to use names on the walkie-talkies, over," he scolded me. "What if someone is monitoring frequencies from out of you-know-where? They're in the defense business, remember? Over."

"I'm sorry, Thad," I apologized. "I completely forgot. Base over and out."

Minutes later, Mark and I slowly cruised by to see if Thad was visible from the main road. There was no sign of him anywhere. He later told us that he found a spot near a patch of tall grass where he set up the telescope. He was able to reach this place without being seen by anyone because the building across the street from BEEM had a large parking lot adjacent to the field. He hid his bike in a shallow ditch and just crawled to the site. As we drove past, we let him know we were on our way by honking the horn with a few short bursts.

Mark and I drove over to Bob's Grill before making our phone calls. The parking lot was nearly completely filled. Like most greasy spoon joints in the area, people from miles around came to enjoy a home cooked breakfast and a good coffee on their day off. You could almost smell the food cooking from several blocks away. Before getting started, I needed a strong cup of coffee so I talked Mark into going inside with me. All of that driving really wore me down. Actually, I was looking for any excuse to delay putting our little plan into action. I was beginning to have second thoughts about the whole thing.

As I sat there at the counter sipping my coffee, I looked around at all of the people wolfing down their greasy eggs, sausage and hash browns. I was truly amazed at the size of some of those people—they must have weighed in at over 300 pounds. They could live off their own body fat for months without eating and still have a good reserve for the winter. I couldn't help but wonder what a cannibal in one of those tropical islands down in the South Pacific would have said if they were to get a hold of one of those big boys.

"Come on, Matt," said Mark as he tugged on my shirt. "Let's put this play into action. It's getting really late, man."

"Hey, chill out, Butthead," I snapped back. "All in good time. It's still early. Look what time it is, it's only a little after nine."

"So what?" he added. "You know these guys might play golf or maybe they fish. We should really call before it gets any later. Besides, who gives a shit if we wake them up. Serves them right."

"Alright, alright, let's go. We'll use those two phones over there," I said as I pointed across the street to the Mini-Mart. There were two pay phones situated right next to each other directly in front of the store.

"Fine with me." Mark came up from behind and gently pushed me in the direction of the phones. "If I have to wait one more minute, I'm going to have to kick your sorry ass. Now move it."

As we crossed the street, I handed Mr. Bradey's number to Mark and then took out Mr. Keller's number for myself. We both had copies of the scripts Thad prepared for us to read.

"You know, I've been thinking, Matt," said Mark sheepishly. "Why don't you call both these guys?" He tried to hand me the paper with the number on it, but I refused to accept it back.

"No way, man," I complained. "We agreed that we'd both do it at the same time. Remember?" I was beginning to get pissed that Mark was trying to wimp out on me at the very last moment.

"I know we did, but I don't understand why it has to be that way," he exclaimed. He again tried to hand me the paper, once again without any success.

"Because Bradey might call Keller right away and then we won't be able to get through to him," I replied back angrily.

"So what?" asked Mark. "Whether he breaks the bad news to him or we do it doesn't make a difference. Come on, you do it, go ahead. You know how I am with phone calls. I'll only end up saying something which will screw it all up."

As much as I hated to admit it, I couldn't argue with Mark on this one. At some level, I wasn't sure I wanted Butthead to talk to either of them on the phone. If they said anything to piss him off, he might say something incredibly stupid which could give us away.

"Okay, okay," I said as I grabbed the number out of his hand. "I'll make the damn calls. But you owe me big time."

"No sweat, man," he remarked back cheerfully. After agreeing, he looked incredibly relieved.

With the receiver in my hand, it took me a while before I could bring myself to dial the number. I decided to call Bradey first. While I was terrified that I'd screw it up somehow, I kept telling myself that all I had to do was read the letter—just read the damn letter. There was nothing to it.

"Hello," answered a young girl. She couldn't have been more than five or six years old judging from her squeaky, high-pitched voice.

"Um, um," I mumbled. "Is Mr. Bradey there?"

"Daddy," she yelled as she dropped the receiver down. "It's for you." Hearing a child on the other end of the phone caught me off guard. I just couldn't imagine that a cold blooded killer could have kids. I was just about to hang up when someone answered.

"Yeah, who is it?" asked Mr. Bradey gruffly. I recognized his voice right off. I immediately began reading the letter, trying my best to lower my voice to sound older than I was.

"Mr. Bradey,
You don't know me, but I know you very, very well. As it turns out, I happened to see you and your friends Charlie and Bubha bury a man last weekend. I think he was the man who visits Mr. Keller before all of his trips to India and Nepal. I also suspect you and your men were involved in the murder of a fisherman as well. Unfortunately, I missed seeing that one so I'll leave it alone.

The reason why I'm telling you all of this is because I am a bit short on cash and could use a few dollars. If you give me $2,000 by this Sunday, I'll forget I saw anything. If not, I'm afraid I'll have to tell someone what I saw—perhaps the local authorities.

If you have any questions about whether I know what I'm talking about, just tell your friend Mr. Keller about your missing gun. Oh, and by the way, I understand that Nepal is very nice this time of the year. I was planning to go there this summer to "Gorkha" District to see a famous urn, but I understand that it's missing. Any ideas?

I'll give you a call late Sunday afternoon after 3:00 pm. I'm also planning on mentioning this matter to Mr. Keller. So long for now."

I waited for some kind of response after reading the statement. We didn't talk about what I was supposed to do after I passed the message so I just lingered on the line.

"I don't know who the fuck you are, but when I do find out, and I will, I'm not only going to "do" you, but your entire family," said Mr. Bradey in a cold, calculating voice which sent a ballistic chill up and down my spine. After hearing his threat, I quickly hung up the phone. It was one thing for him to threaten me, but to involve my family?

"What did he say?" asked Mark anxiously. He could tell that something had just happened. "Come on tell me, did he say anything to you?"

"He told me that he was going to find me and my family and 'do' us all," I said in a shaky voice. "God, he really scared the shit out of me." My heart was pounding, my body was shaking from head to toe and I just couldn't calm myself down.

"Holy shit," said Mark. "That guy is bad news."

"I think you should call Keller," I said as I handed him the receiver. "I don't feel up to it."

"No way," said Mark. "You did a great job. I'd just screw it up. You know how shitty my reading is. Go ahead. Don't worry about what that guy said. He'll never in a million years be able to find out who we are."

Mark was right. He just said those things to scare me. There was no way he'd be able to track us down—there was nothing to be frightened of. After getting a grip on things, I once again dialed the phone. Following about four rings, some guy picked up. After stating that he was in fact Mr. Keller, I began reading the statement, but was interrupted continuously by him asking who I was. When I got nearly two thirds the way through the script, he finally hung up on me.

As I stood there, I realized that I was once again shaking all over. As much as I tried to put it out of my mind, I still couldn't believe what Bradey had said to me. Would he actually do something to my family? That possibility never crossed my mind when we thought up this hair-brain scheme. Mark picked up on my mood and came over and took the receiver out of my hand.

"Hey, man," he said. "Don't sweat it." He then took the papers with the numbers on them and began dialing the phone again.

"Who are you calling now?" I asked surprised.

"I'm calling Bradey to see if he took the bait," said Mark. "Busy." He then called Keller and also found out that the line was engaged.

"Bingo. It looks like phase one is now officially underway," said Mark with a great big smile. He was obviously excited about the prospect of continuing our escapade. My perspective on the whole thing was much less enthusiastic. In fact, I was ready to throw the towel in the ring right then and there.

*　　　*　　　*

With our two phone calls out of the way, Mark and I drove through town and then out to the main road leading to Elkins. We parked in a secluded location which gave us a good view of all of the cars coming and going, without being overly conspicuous. It took us nearly twenty minutes before we finally

125

got in touch with Thad over the walkie-talkie to let him know we were settled.

"Thad, you jerk," I nearly shouted. "What's going on out there? Are you okay? Why aren't you answering?"

I was really beginning to get worried when he didn't respond to our repeated attempts to contact him. All kinds of horrible scenarios kept going through my mind. I imagined that Bradey drove up to the BEEM complex, somehow noticed Thad hiding out in the field and came to the conclusion that he was the one who made the calls. My mind managed to come up with a thousand and one different horrible outcomes following that.

"What?" Thad finally responded. "Who is it?"

"What the hell is the matter with you?" I screamed at him. "We've been trying to reach you forever?"

"Oh, I guess I must have fallen asleep," he said with a groggy voice. "Sorry!"

"Well, wake your ass up and keep an eye out for them," I ordered. "Bradey and Keller could arrive at BEEM any time now."

"So what happened?" asked Thad. "Did you get through to both of them?"

"Yeah, we did," I responded. "We think they took the bait. Oh, listen to this. Bradey said to me that . . ."

Before I could finish my sentence, Mark gently pushed the walkie-talkie away from my face and put his finger to his mouth. It was his way of stopping me from telling Thad something that would only end up upsetting him.

"What did he say to you?" asked Thad anxiously. "Come on Matt, just tell me."

"Well, um, nothing really," I replied back with a little hesitation. "He just wanted to know who I was. That's all."

"Oh, you know, I bet they don't even show up," Thad replied with that I-told-you-so tone in his voice. "Shit, you know I'm getting eaten up by all kinds of bugs out here. They're crawling up my legs and everything. I should have brought a blanket or something. There might not be anything left of me in another hour, over."

"Hang in there, Thad," said Mark as he grabbed the walkie talkie out of my hand. "Just hang in there, champ."

"Oh, by the way, stop using my name," Thad insisted. "Over and out."

"I'm sorry about that, Thad," I replied back, intentionally using his name just for fun. "We won't do it again. Over and out."

It turned out to be one of those long, drawn-out dog-days which seem to drag on in slow motion. There was no sign of Bradey or Keller in any of the cars passing by. After nearly five hours of nothingness, Mark tried to talk me into going back to town to call them once again to determine whether they were still at home. I thought it was a bad idea so I convinced him to give it up. The one thing we didn't count on when we dreamed up this plan was the sheer boredom that went along with just waiting for something to happen.

The lingering was especially hard on Mark who was the type of guy who just couldn't sit still for more than ten minutes at a stretch. Every now and then, he'd get out of the car and begin tossing stones into the woods or just walk around looking for something to relieve the dullness. Whenever a car passed by, we'd do our best to get a good look at who was inside. We were hoping they'd use Bradey's car so we'd recognize it easily. We knew his license plate number from the registration papers Mark had stolen.

At one point, I saw a car drive past which looked as if it could have been them, but Mark was sure the car had Maryland plates and was driven by an old man so we just went on waiting. That moment turned out to be the highlight of the afternoon.

In an effort to cope with the situation, we both managed to devour three huge bags of potato chips, two family size boxes of Twinkies, five candy bars, a six-pack of coke and a half dozen apples. It's funny how the prospect of danger mixed with nothing to do, makes a guy hungry as a bear. No wonder the cops in town were all so damn fat.

Every now and then Thad would call up and complain about something—the bugs, the hot sun beating down on him, the fear that someone might have seen him when he arrived. Mark and I tried not to laugh, but it wasn't easy. Thad was in classic form—he was truly a world class wimp. We made it a point to use his name at least twice every time he called just to irritate him. This seemed to really drive him crazy.

At around seven o'clock that evening, after nearly ten hours of hanging around, we finally gave up hope and called Thad and told him to ride his bike to where our car was parked. With no sign of Bradey or Keller anywhere, we'd had about as much as we could take. Besides, with only a few street lights along the road, it was virtually impossible to tell what kind of car was passing by, let alone getting a look at who was driving. It looked as if our plan had failed, so we decided to head on home.

Poor Thad was covered with bites from every conceivable insect known to nature. He even claimed that insects that never bit humans before began biting him for the sake of making his life miserable. Thad also ended up eating massive quantities of food to pass the time. He complained that his stomach was really hurting. I warned him several times that if he barfed in my sister's car, he'd have to walk back home.

The road to Elkins was difficult to drive at night with all of its winding curves and steep inclines as one passes through the

West Virginia hills. Since it didn't matter when we arrived, I decided to drive back slowly. I was feeling tired and a little depressed after our long ordeal.

At some level, I was glad our plan didn't materialize. What Bradey said over the phone earlier had a profound effect on me—I was really spooked. I didn't want to take the risk of getting any more involved with someone who'd threaten my mom, dad and sister.

"Shit," said Thad as he scratched the bites on his leg. "I can't wait to get home and out of these clothes. God, I feel so grungy. Remind me never to sign up for the Army."

"Don't worry, Thad," said Mark playfully. "The Army will never get that desperate. Besides, they don't accept homos."

"Is that why they turned you down?" asked Thad casually. He didn't realize it, but that was probably one of his first successful spontaneous come-backs.

"Well, we gave it our best shot," I said to keep the conversation going. "I guess we're just going to have to ride this thing out. If the police end up tracking us down, then so be it. There is nothing we can do."

"Hey, are we really going home tonight?" asked Mark. I could tell he was about to offer an alternative plan. "I told my parents that we were camping out again. They aren't expecting any of us, are they? I say we check into a motel. We have that money from Carter. Let's see if we can buy a few six packs of beer and just watch some cable TV. I've got my fake ID with me. I don't feel like dealing with my parents tonight. Come on, it's a Saturday night for Christ sake."

"Sounds good to me," I responded in support of Mark's proposal. I was also dreading the thought of walking through the front door. My mother was beginning to drive me crazy these days. She kept asking me whether I was alright. She was convinced that there was something strange about me for the last week or so. If she only knew!!

"Well, I say we go straight home," Thad insisted. "We all have a ton of homework and I hate staying in those dank motel rooms. You always find people's hair between the sheets and all kinds of nasty stains. Most motel rooms also smell like puke. They're totally disgusting."

"Come on, Thad," urged Mark. "A little pubic hair between the sheets isn't going to kill you. Besides, if we did end up following those guys, you'd have had to stay in a motel anyway."

"You know, I just thought of something," I said changing the subject. "They're probably really going to start looking for us now. After those phone calls, those guys are not going to just forget about it. Even if no one calls back to ask for the money, they now know that we know all about what they're up to."

"I'm glad," Mark replied. "It serves them right. Let them

sweat it out for a while."

"So what happens if they find out about us?" I inquired.

"Forget about it, Matt," Mark insisted. "How the hell are they ever going to track us down? Anyone could have made those calls."

"I don't know about that," I said. "Actually, all they have to do is start asking around about your red truck and they'd find out right away. Everyone in town knows that bomb you drive."

"They wouldn't think we were the ones that called," Mark insisted. "Anyone could have been out there in those woods that night and seen them bury the body. Believe me, they're not thinking it's us."

I kept quiet after that. I could tell that Thad was growing nervous again about the whole thing so I decided to just drop the subject.

"Thad, hand me one of those Hostess chocolate cupcakes," Mark demanded.

Thad handed a couple up to us and we all pigged out once again. There was nothing like a little junk food to take a person's mind off of things. As always, Mark nearly shoved the whole thing in his mouth. Before finishing it, he'd start talking and the crumbs would fall everywhere. In the "pig" hall of fame, I'm sure Butthead's picture would be hung proudly over the mantle piece.

* * *

While driving up one of the many steep hills which led back to Elkins, out of nowhere, this jet-black, four-wheel drive truck came barreling up on my tail. Whoever was driving was obviously in a real big hurry to pass. He repeatedly honked his horn and flicked his high beams. I never could stand it when people acted so damn obnoxious.

"Hey, check this out. This asshole is trying to pass me on this hill," I said as I watched the vehicle out of my rear view mirror. "This guy's a nutcase if he thinks he can pass on a blind curve like this. Look, there are on-coming cars all over the place."

Both Mark and Thad turned around to see what I was talking about. The truck continuously flicked its high beams as if ordering me to let it by.

"Pull over and let him pass," Thad suggested. "He's probably drunk or something. We shouldn't mess with someone like that."

"No way," I said angrily. "Let him wait. I hate it when people act like they own the god damn road."

For a while I managed to prevent him from going around me, but then he started coming even closer and honking his horn almost continuously. He even put on his flood lights. It got to a point where I couldn't see anything out of my rear view mirror.

"Go ahead and let this jerk pass," said Mark impatiently. "It's not worth screwing around. This guy looks like he's on some kind of drug."

"Okay, okay," I replied reluctantly. I put on my blinker and slowed down. As the truck flew by, none of us could believe our eyes. There sitting in the front passenger seat was Bradey. Charlie was driving, while Bubha sat in the back. Bradey even gave us the finger as the truck flew past.

"Did you see who that was?" yelled Mark, barely able to contain his enthusiasm. "It's them, it's them! That was Bradey and the others."

"Holy shit," I shouted as I floored the gas pedal in an attempt to keep up with them. Unfortunately, my sister's car has about as much pickup as an eighty year old man running a hundred yard dash—it just wasn't there.

"So they fell for our little plan after all," said Mark, nearly bursting at the seams. "I can't believe it. Why didn't we think of that before? Of course, they're not going to do anything during the day when there are so many people around. They decided to wait until it got dark. Haw-hoo. Shit this is great."

"You know, maybe this isn't such a good idea," said Thad with great reluctance. "I mean, what if they notice that we're following them?"

"Shut up, Thad," Mark insisted. "No one's going to find out anything. Those guys are driving too damn fast. We'll never get close enough for them to suspect a thing."

While it was clear that they were heading in the direction of Elkins, it was virtually impossible to keep up with them as they flew up and down the winding roads at such high speeds. At one point, I almost lost control of the car as I rounded a curve at nearly 60 miles an hour down a steep incline. At another spot, I almost ran over this huge woodchuck that was scurrying across the highway. I slammed on the brakes as the car screeched to an abrupt stop. The car missed plowing into the guardrail by only a couple of inches.

"Shit, shit, shit," I yelled. "That was too damn close. Man, I've got to slow down. If I trash this car, I'll be as good as dead. My sister will skin me alive."

"Come on, Matt," Mark insisted. "They're getting away. Let's move it."

"Are you kidding?" I replied. "We nearly got killed just now. I'm driving the best I can. Get off my back."

"Well, next time just run over the hairy rat," Mark insisted. "Why should three of us die to save one flea bitten rodent?"

Mark was so excited by this point, he was almost bobbing in his seat. Thad, on the other hand, seemed to be comatose in the back seat. For some reason he was unusually quiet.

130

After taking up the chase again, for the longest time there was no sign of their truck. In fact, we went for miles along the road without seeing a single vehicle anywhere.

"God damn it, we lost them," Mark complained as he pounded on the dashboard. "How could you have lost them?"

"They were only driving about a hundred fifty miles an hour, for Christ sake," I snapped back. "Nearly all of their turns have been on two wheels. If you ask me, those guys are dangerous."

"Well, I for one am glad that they got away," Thad admitted as he came out of his little trance. He was visibly relieved that our pursuit had fallen apart. "Don't you think they'd eventually figure out we were following them?"

"Shut up, Thad, and get a life," said Mark sarcastically. Mark was in no mood to give up anything just yet. He had that look in his eye that he got right before a wrestling match—he was ready to take on the entire world and more.

"By the way, where are we now?" I asked as I looked around for some kind of landmark. We seemed to be passing through a small town.

"We're pulling into Brookville," said Mark. "We're about three quarters of the way to Elkins."

"I'm really thirsty. Let's stop and get something to drink," Thad suggested. "Let's face it, those boys are miles away by now."

"Hey, look at that," I shouted as I pointed out the window. "Sorry, Thad, look over to your right. There they are. They must have stopped for some gas. Looks like we're back in action again boys."

There, parked in a small mini-mart service station, was their black truck. As we watched from the road, we could see Bubha coming out of the station's convenience store with a bag of State Line potato chips and a case of Rolling Rock beer.

"Now stay on their tail this time," Mark insisted. "If you can't drive like a man, then let me take over the wheel."

"Are you crazy? I'd rather drive like a girl than die like a man because of your crazy driving."

*   *   *

As our pursuit continued, they never knew we were following them because we always lagged so far behind. Once in awhile, we'd get to a point where we were sure we lost them again, but then there would be a long straight stretch of road where we'd see them burning up the highway. I was never as scared behind the wheel of a car as I was that night.

We made it to Elkins in a little over two hours, which was an all time record for me. If my sister ever found out how I treated her "baby" with such abuse, she'd have my head on a platter.

"Hey, why the hell are they going through the center of town?" asked Mark as we drove down Main Street. "That's not anywhere near the place where we found Carter's body."

"Maybe they hid the body someplace down along Route 4," I suggested. "There's a lot of forest along that stretch."

We followed them through town, past the main shopping complex, after which they turned down a small side street. At first, none of us had a clue what they were doing.

"Oh, shit, I can't believe it," yelled Thad. "They turned down Spring Street. They must know about Shelly!"

Thad was nearly hysterical in the back seat. The meaning of what he was trying to say didn't register at first, but then it hit me. Shelly was the woman we visited whose name was in Carter's address book—the young, pretty one.

"Who?" asked Mark. "What the hell are you babbling about? Who's Shelly?"

"Don't you remember, the woman who worked with Carter in India," Thad explained. Mark still had this blank stare on his face. "How can you not remember? Matt and I went up to her house and talked with the lady. Right?"

"Oh, yeah," said Mark, feeling a bit stupid. "The one you said was a knockout. I completely forgot about her."

Both Thad and I looked at each other with utter amazement. It had only been a week ago and Mark had already forgotten.

"They must have found out that Carter was working with her," said Thad. "Maybe they think she was the one that ratted on them. I think we really messed up this time. I told you we shouldn't be doing this thing. I told you so."

"Oh, shit, you're probably right," I admitted. "We may have put her in some deep trouble."

They drove up in front of her house and stopped. Bubha got out of the back seat and slowly walked up to her front door. As we passed by, we noticed that he seemed to be looking around as if to check to see if anyone was watching. I parked the car in the driveway of a house that had a for sale sign out in front. It looked abandoned. From there, we had a good vantage point to see what they were up to.

"Damn, damn, damn," I said under my breath. "What if they beat her up or try to kill her. We have to do something. We just can't sit here and let something happen to her."

"Let's face it, there's nothing we can do," Mark confessed. "Let's just wait and see what happens."

"I can't do that," I insisted. "I've got to do something!"

Just as I was about to get out of the car, Bubha walked back to the truck. The three of them sat there in front of the house for a long time before finally turning around and heading in the direction of the main road. I must admit, I was incredibly relieved. What could I have possibly done anyway?"

"She isn't home I bet," said Thad as I slowly drove by the house as we continued following them. "That guy was only there for a few minutes and no lights came on."

"That was a real close one," I said. I tried my best to relax. "Shit, I can't believe we brought her into this mess. Why didn't we think of that? You know, we should really warn her about all of this somehow. What if they come back again later?"

"How did they find out about her in the first place?" asked Mark.

"Well, Carter and Keller were meeting regularly before all of his trips," said Thad. "Maybe they knew that she was part of the plan."

"Or maybe they're working with her," Mark suggested. "Maybe she knows all about the murders. Did you ever think of that?"

The thought that she might be involved took both Thad and me by surprise. It wasn't often that Mark actually made us stop and think about anything. This was one of those rare times when he was able to pull off such a feat.

Could she really be involved, I asked myself. I tried to remember our visit with her. Was there anything about her that I missed—some dark sinister side that didn't come through during our meeting? She looked so innocent to me—like the girl next door. How could someone like that possibly be involved with killers? No, I couldn't bring myself to believe such a thing. Before saying anything, I looked over at Thad who was deep in thought. I read in his expression that he agreed with me. Before I could say anything, Thad broke the silence.

"No way, Mark," Thad insisted. "There is no way she is involved in any of this. When we talked to her it was obvious she didn't know anything about Carter being dead. She thought he was in New York. And besides, she seemed like a really nice person."

"He's right," I said in support of Thad's statement. "She didn't know anything. I'm sure of that."

Mark just kind of grunted. He was used to trusting our judgment, but since he didn't see her himself, he still had his doubts.

*   *   *

Our little cat and mouse game resumed as we once again passed through the center of Elkins. At the main traffic light directly in front of the town's McDonald's restaurant, their truck made a left turn up the hill which led out of town, and then another left onto Route 33 in the direction of Monongahela

National Forest. It looked as if we were finally on our way.

Fortunately, there were still a few stray cars cruising the roads. I did my best to let at least one of them go in front of me to be sure that Bradey and his crew didn't recognize us. We had already tailed them for several hours without being noticed—I wanted to keep it that way.

Every now and then one of the truck windows would open and they'd toss a beer can or an empty bag of chips outside. It looked as if they were having a good-ole time inside that truck of theirs.

"I bet those assholes are already bombed by now," I said as I watched their truck weaving ever so slightly. "They must have gone through nearly half a case of that beer they bought before."

"Shit, and they haven't even stopped to take a piss yet," said Mark anxiously. "They must have like 50 gallon bladders or something. If we don't stop pretty soon, I'm going to have a small problem myself—you know with all those sodas I drank."

"Just don't think about it," I urged. "I'm sure we're getting close to the spot."

"You know something, Matt, you're pretty damn good at all this detective stuff," Mark admitted, as he tried to change the subject. "Maybe that's your calling in life. You can be some kind of a modern day 007 spy after all of this is over. What do you think?"

"Screw that. Once in a lifetime is enough for me," I confessed.

The last automobile between their truck and our car turned off. Since we were once again directly behind them, I backed off a bit. By this time we had already entered the park area. All around us for miles was dense forest on either side of the road.

Not far from the point at which the Cheat River turned eastward, their truck roared into a small parking area along the shoulder of the road without any warning. Their sudden stop sent dust clouds in every direction. The location was several miles from where the police dogs tracked the scent a week earlier. I drove past without slowing down and managed to find a relatively secluded spot to pull over about a half mile further down.

For a long time after stopping, none of us said or did anything. We just sat there waiting for someone to make the first move. It was Mark who finally broke the silence as he opened the door and climbed out of the car.

"Okay, this is it boys," he said nervously as he took a long awaited pee along the edge of the forest. I wasn't used to seeing him so uneasy. "Let's go see what they're up to. Matt, why don't you come with me. Thad can stay here with the car. They're probably going after Carter's body right this second so we should really get a move on."

"No way, man. I don't want to see no half decomposed body being pulled out of the ground," I complained. "Why don't you take Thad with you this time? Besides this is my sister's car. She'd have a complete fit if she knew someone else was driving it."

"Who said anything about Thad driving the car?" asked Mark while tugging on my arm. "Thad will stay here with the car and he won't have to drive it anywhere. Come on, Matt, I need you. If I take Thad along with me, he'll probably yell something stupid again and we'll all be dead-meat." Thad gave Mark a dirty look.

"I don't like this," Thad blurted out with a shaky voice. "I don't like this one bit. I think this thing has gone way too far. I don't want you guys to leave me here alone. Let's just forget all of this foolishness and go call the cops. You've got to admit it, we're in way, way over our heads."

"Just stay with the damn car, Thad, and you'll be fine," Mark insisted. "If you see anything that looks out of the ordinary, just fire up the engine and hightail it to the trailer park down the road near the old granite quarry. That's only a couple of miles from here. There are lots of people living there. These guys won't do anything to you in front of all those people. Trust me."

"I still don't like this," Thad repeated. "We're too close to them. We should have driven further down the road. It's way too dangerous."

"Here, Thad, take this if you're that damn scared," said Mark as he reached behind his back and pulled out Bradey's gun.

"You asshole, you had that thing in my car all this time?" I shouted. I was really pissed that Mark didn't listen to us the night before. We told him not to bring it.

"Of course," he admitted freely. "I couldn't come up with a good hiding place at my house so I decided just to take it along with me. At least no one will be able to find it in my garage, right? Besides, what if those guys come after us. We have to protect ourselves. Shit, Matt, what's that sour look on your face supposed to mean? Just chill out, okay? It's not hurting anyone."

I stood there staring at him in total disbelief. I guess I was a little shocked to hear that Mark had been walking around with a gun all this time. All of those stories I kept reading in the papers about junior high and high school students carrying guns were probably all true.

"So, Mark, do you think you'd actually use that thing if you had to?" I asked testing to see how much of a tough guy he really was. "I mean, would you actually shoot someone with it?"

"Um, well, I don't know," he admitted reluctantly. "I guess if I had to I would." It was obvious he hadn't given the question all that much thought.

"Just get that thing out of my face and away from me," said Thad as he pushed the gun back in Mark's direction. Thad was so upset at this point he could hardly talk.

"Suit yourself," said Mark. He tucked the pistol back into his pants again. "Actually, we might need it more than you. Come on, Matt. Let's get going before they take off again."

Mark and I proceeded along the edge of the road like a pair of commandos on a top secret military mission. I kept wondering if we'd run right into them with every step I took.

As we got closer to where they were parked, I couldn't help but feel that all of this must be some kind of a bad dream. Who in their right mind would consciously track a bunch of known killers down a deserted road at night? I couldn't possibly be doing something like this. Only a crazy person would do such an incredibly stupid thing.

But as unreal as it all seemed, at another level, I knew exactly what I was doing. The excitement that it created, the sense of facing the unknown, the feeling that I was testing the limits of all I feared was somehow totally captivating to me. I was being lured by desire to come face to face with the dark side of these men, the unthinkable side of nature that had always been hidden from me along the sidelines of my sheltered life.

Finally we came to a place where we could see the truck off in the distance. Mr. Bradey was leaning against the hood as he casually smoked a huge southern cigar. While puffing away, the smoke seemed to hover above him, creating his own personal cloud which floated ever so gracefully up to the street light hanging above. Every now and then he'd reach into his coat pocket and pull out a pint of Jack Daniels whiskey which he'd swig down like grape juice. The rear hatch of the truck was open and it looked as if the vehicle was jacked up to change a flat tire. There was no sign of his two companions anywhere.

Realizing that Charlie and Bubha could be anywhere, Mark signaled to me to follow him over to a small patch of blueberry bushes. From there we had a pretty good view of what was happening in every direction.

"Where the hell did the other two go?" I whispered. "All I see is Bradey."

"They must be in the woods," Mark remarked. I could see him carefully surveying the forest for any signs of them. "Someone's got to dig up the body, right?"

"You don't think they really got a flat, do you?" I asked. Even as the words were coming out of my mouth, I realized it was kind of a stupid question.

"Naw," said Mark after studying the situation thoroughly. "They're just making it look that way in case someone comes driving past. Let's see if we can get any closer."

"No way, Mark," I said grabbing his arm.

He stared at me for a moment before pulling back. He knew from my grip that I was really serious.

We waited for nearly twenty-five minutes before we finally heard the sound of someone scurrying through the forest in the direction of the truck. It wasn't until they were almost on the road that we could clearly see that it was Bubha and Charlie. But to our surprise, they weren't carrying anything—not even a shovel.

"Shit," Mark whispered, obviously disappointed. "They don't have the god damn body. They must have buried it in the woods someplace else. I told you we should have gotten a closer look. Damn!"

"So now what?" I asked. "Do you think when they leave, we should wander around and see if we can find out where they moved it to?"

"No way in hell we'd find his body in these woods," he conceded. "It could be anywhere. Let's just get back to the car before they take off again."

Mark turned around and began to quietly make his way back. For some reason I didn't follow right away. I watched as the three of them just stood there, as if waiting for something to happen.

After a car passed by, all at once, Bubha and Charlie ran quickly back into the forest. Seconds later, they came stumbling out, struggling to carry a large, person-size black plastic bag wrapped with grey duct tape. There were a couple of shovels placed on top. They literally threw the bag into the back of the truck with a large thud, covered it with a small blanket and quickly went through the effort of taking the vehicle off the jack.

"Mark, Mark," I had whispered. "Look!" He turned around just as they were emerging from the forest with their important package.

"Holy shit," said Mark in total disbelief. "They actually did it. They dug up Carter. I can't believe it."

"So now what?" I asked, nearly exploding with nervous energy. I realized that they'd be driving off soon.

"We'd better hightail it back to the car," Mark ordered. "If they find Thad parked up ahead, they're liable to become real suspicious."

Mark and I bolted back in the direction of the car at full throttle. Because it was hazardous running through the forest in the dark, after rounding a bend out of their sight, we took to the road.

Before reaching the car, we could see a pair of headlights traveling in our direction from behind us. Mark grabbed my shoulder and literally threw me into the forest. I nearly smashed my head on a tree as I collided with the ground. We both held our breath as the vehicle came into view and then drove past. Fortunately, it wasn't their truck.

"Come on, Matt, hurry up," Mark shouted, getting up to his feet again. "The next one is bound to be them."

We both got back up on our feet again and ran towards my sister's car as if our lives depended on it. Upon arriving, we found Thad crouched on the front seat—he looked like he had crossed over that line which falls on the other side of being completely paralyzed with fear. The average ghost couldn't have displayed a whiter face. I'd never seen a person so freaked out before. I guess being left alone with killers so close by was more than he could handle.

Without hesitating, I jumped into the driver's seat, fired up the car and drove up the highway to a place where we could conceal the car down a small gravel road. I had parked there dozens of times while on fishing excursions since there was a good path that led straight down to the river. Without saying a word, we all sat there waiting for their truck to come by.

"What the hell happened out there?" asked Thad. "You guys took forever."

"They picked up the body, that's what happened," I said, not really wanting to talk about it.

"Are you sure it was a body?" asked Thad.

"Don't be stupid," Mark snapped back. "If we said they picked up a body, then they picked up a god damn body."

"So where are they now?" he asked.

"They haven't come yet," Mark replied. "They'll be here any minute. Just shut up and wait."

"And what makes you think they are going to come this way?" asked Thad. "What if they turned around and went in the other direction?"

"Shut up, Thad," Mark snapped back.

Thad was right. What if they turned around? All of our efforts would be in vain. Once again, we waited to see if fate would intervene in our favor.

"It's been nearly ten minutes," I said after looking at my watch for the twelfth time. "Shit, they probably did turn around and go the other way."

"Shit, shit, shit, shit!" exclaimed Mark, pounding on the back of my seat. "After all of this work, we lost them? God damn it."

"Come on you guys, what happened out there?" Thad insisted. "You said you saw Carter's body? What did they do with it?"

"We'll tell you about it later," I replied. I was too distracted to talk about anything. "Listen, let's drive down and see if we can catch up with them." I started the car, but Mark stopped me from turning on the lights.

"Look," he pointed in the direction of the road. "Here comes another car. If it's not them, we'll head back."

Once again sheer luck turned out to be in our favor. It was their truck alright which flew past. I pulled out without turning on my headlights after they were far enough ahead. There was nearly a full moon that night so it was pretty easy to see without them.

We only had to follow them for another ten minutes before they once again pulled over. I gradually came to a stop on a small hill which overlooked the scene. We were far enough away that they couldn't see us watching them. From where we were parked, we observed two persons from the truck jump out, open the back hatch and toss a plastic bundle into the bushes. A cloud of dust filled the air as the truck sped off leaving the two men and the corpse behind.

"What the hell are they doing now?" asked Thad. "Did you see the way they just tossed his body like that? How rude!"

"The guy's dead for Christ sake," Mark replied. "Like it really matters?"

"Maybe they're going to leave the body there," I wondered out loud. I tried my best to follow the outline of their bodies in the darkness.

"Hey, wait a second," said Mark with a burst of excitement. "Look at where they are!"

"What do you mean?" I asked. "Where the hell are they?"

"They're right in front of Bowden's Cave," Mark explained. "Don't you see? They're probably going to dump the body inside the cave."

From where we were parked, it looked as if Mark was right. I had been to the cave a few times before, but it had been years since my last trip. When their flashlights disappeared into nowhere, Mark's assumption was validated for sure.

"Why would they do that?" asked Thad. "I'm sure lots of people go in that cave all the time. Someone is bound to find his body inside there."

"No way," Mark explained. "That cave goes on forever. If they drag him into one of those little alcoves and bury him good, no one would ever find him. Besides, if they tried to bury him in the woods, some animal might come by and dig him up. There aren't any animals in that cave. And I bet within a few weeks, the cave bugs will pick his bones clean. It's a perfect hiding place."

"So at least we know where they put him," I remarked. "So now what do we do?"

"I say it's time to go to the police," said Thad in a matter of fact tone. "Now that we know where his body is hid, we can tell them everything. In fact, if we go there right now, the cops might be able to catch them in the act of burying him."

Thad's mood completely changed. He seemed relieved now that our little adventure was finally coming to an end.

"There's no time to run back and get the police," said Mark. "They might head out before we got back. If we can't find the body right away, the police are going to become real suspicious. I think we should just stay here and wait until they leave. Then we have to go inside and find the body ourselves. Only after we know for sure who they dragged in there can we go to the cops."

"What are you talking about?" asked Thad, totally surprised by Mark's insane comment. "I hope you're not really serious?"

"Hell, yes," Mark snapped back. "Of course, I'm serious."

"We know the body's there," Thad insisted. "Let the police go and find it. I'm not adding grave digging to my resume."

"For someone who's supposed to be so damn smart, Thad, sometimes you act pretty stupid," said Mark in a mocking tone. "What if that's not even Carter? What if it's some other dumb jerk that they killed the other day? Imagine if we brought the police here and they found someone else. It wouldn't be the first time. Remember the dead fisherman at our campsite?"

"I don't care what you say, I'm not looking for no dead body," Thad exclaimed with his arms clamped tightly across his chest. "If you want to find it, you go looking for it yourself. That's where I draw the line."

For a long time no one said anything. It was up to me to finally break the silence.

"Actually, I agree with Mark. I don't think we should leave here until we know for sure that they left the body in the cave. I mean, what if they change their minds or something. And besides, we need to know how long they stayed in there. If they are there for a long time, then we know that they probably went pretty far into the cave."

"So what about Shelly?" asked Thad in an effort to keep the pressure on. "Shouldn't we go now and warn her about these guys before they return there?"

"And what are we going to say to her?" asked Mark sarcastically. "Oh, by the way, some murderers are on their way over to your house, sorry to wake you up."

"I don't know what to say," Thad replied. "All I know is that we need to warn her about these men. I say we head over there right now before they beat us to it."

"Don't worry about that," I said. "Check this out. That truck of theirs just pulled up in front of the cave again."

We listened as the truck honked several times. Moments later two figures came running out of the darkness and jumped inside. Before we knew it, they were speeding up the hill in our direction.

"Holy shit!" yelled Mark. "Look, they're driving this way. Get down, get down!"

There was no time to even think about driving off—they'd be on top of us in no time. The three of us dropped to the floor of the car and made every attempt to become invisible. I somehow found myself upside down looking up at the steering wheel from below. Because the seats in my sister's car were so torn up, she placed small sheets over them to cover up the many holes. I yanked the sheet off and tried to use it to cover as much of my body as I could. Almost instinctively my hand reached up and locked the door.

It only took a few seconds before we could hear the sound of their truck approaching. At first it sounded as if they just drove past. But then the truck screeched to a stop and that distinct sound of a vehicle being shifted into reverse could be heard. Seconds later, there was a humming noise which sounded like an electric window being opened, followed by a flashlight beam being shone through our car windows.

"See anything?" asked a voice which sounded like Bradey's. "I'm not taking any more god damn chances."

"Looks pretty empty to me, boss," said one of the other men. "It probably belongs to some fisherman. Let's just get the hell out of here. I'm tired."

"Go out there and check it out," Bradey ordered. "I don't remember seeing anyone parked here when we drove by. Go on . . ."

At that point, Thad grabbed my leg to get my attention. He pointed toward the car keys in the ignition as if to signal that we should try to make a run for it. I could sense the terror he must have been experiencing by his grip which was cutting off the blood to my foot. As much as I wanted to do the right thing, I was too petrified to make a move. If this guy had his gun out and saw me try to drive off, there was plenty of time for him to blow my head off. All it took was one small mistake on my part and my life could be over. I felt it was better to do nothing and take my chances than to do something which would definitely provoke some kind of immediate response. Instead, I used my foot to slowly pull the sheet on Thad's seat over him. When he figured out what I was doing, he quickly finished the job himself. Neither one of us wanted to see what was about to happen.

The truck door finally opened and I could hear one of the men stumble out. He walked over to the side of our car and took a piss on the front tire. From the truck someone's light beam was still dancing through the windows above. I was wondering what Mark would do if they discovered us hiding there.

"Hurry up, you asshole, and check it out," Bradey demanded. "There are a couple of cars coming up the road. Come on, let's blow."

Whoever got out of the truck quickly shined the light around the inside of the car. The way Thad was lying, it looked as if he was a pile of old cloths placed on the floor of the front seat. The guy must have had one too many beers because he didn't notice anything unusual.

"I don't see shit here," yelled the man. "Just a bunch of old cloths and stuff. I think someone junked this piece of shit."

"Okay, then get back in here, let's get rolling," shouted Bradey.

Before returning to the truck, the man kicked the front door of our car with his foot for no reason. As scared as I was at that moment, I couldn't help wondering what my sister would do to me if there was a big dent in her car door. She could be equally as frightening, especially when it came to her car.

The man climbed back into the truck, which quickly pulled away. We all maintained our positions for nearly five minutes after they left. Mark was the first one to stir.

"Man that was too close," he exclaimed. "I thought for sure we'd have to take those guys on."

"How do you know they've gone?" I whispered quietly. "They could still be sitting out there watching us."

"Don't worry, I checked," said Mark. "They're miles away by now."

"Shit," I remarked. "That was the worst of the worst. I nearly pissed in my pants."

"I did," said Thad. "I want to go home. Now . . ."

"This is the second time in the last ten days that my life flashed before me," I admitted out loud. "I hate reruns."

"God, I'm still shaking," Mark confessed.

"So, Butthead, you were actually scared?" I asked, somewhat surprised. "Another first. I thought nothing phased you."

Before starting the car, I got out to look at the damage. There was a small dent in the car door. Although few people would ever even notice it, I knew my sister would. She'd think her car was completely totaled. When she finds out, I couldn't help but wonder whether I would have been better off being caught by those good ole boys.

"I'm dead meat," I admitted. "My sister is going to have my head on a stick."

"Forget about that," said Mark. "When you eventually explain what happened she'll forgive you."

I got back behind the wheel, started up the car and drove off. Thad wasn't kidding, he had wet his pants. He was too shell shocked at the moment to be embarrassed by it.

"Go straight instead of turning around," Mark instructed. "They may have pulled over up the road. If they see this car again, they might try to go after us. There's nothing along that road for miles. We'd be sitting ducks."

"But if we go straight, it'll take us twice as long to get

back," I complained.

"Listen," said Mark sternly. "We just nearly got caught because we were careless. I don't think we should take any more chances at this point. Do you? We're too close to finishing this thing off. Up ahead there are a number of places we can pull into if there's a problem."

Thad was still too traumatized to agree or disagree. I drove straight.

"So what would you have done?" I asked Mark.

"Done about what?" he responded back.

"What would you have done if they found us there?" I repeated the question.

"I would have shot him right in the head," he admitted.

"Sure you would have."

"I guess we'll never know, will we," he said before the conversation withered away into silence.

It took me nearly forty minutes to reach Elkins. The entire way home I couldn't believe what had just happened. We solved the case. I began to imagine how proud everyone would be of us. We'd be town heros. Maybe they'd give us some kind of presidential medal or something for all of our good work.

Several times I looked over at Thad. He had fallen asleep. The pressure of staking out BEEM all day, chasing down criminals and then nearly coming face to face with death drained his little grey cells. I had exactly the opposite reaction. I was so wound up, I probably wouldn't sleep for a month.

Mark stared out the window and every now and then made a comment about something as if nothing out of the ordinary had just happened.

"You know, I could really go for a slice of pizza, Matt," he remarked casually. "I wonder if the Pizza Hut is still open. Don't they stay open late on Saturday nights. Let's go get something to eat. And then . . ."

Instead of answering him I just kept on driving. As always, Mark was in rare form.

*　　*　　*

I was truly relieved that this day would soon be coming to an end as we pulled back into Elkins for the second time that evening. It was already well past eleven o'clock and I was both physically and mentally depleted—my batteries were low and in need of a serious recharge. I could hardly wait to climb into my bed for a good night's sleep. Fortunately, all of the late-night food-joints along the strip which led into town had already locked their doors so I didn't have to yield to Mark's insatiable appetite for more junk food.

Looking back on the events of the day, there was something

almost unreal about the whole episode—I had to repeatedly remind myself that it actually happened.

"Matt, Matt, slow down," Thad shouted as he pointed toward Spring Street. "Turn down there."

I was startled to hear Thad speak. I hadn't seen him awaken from his comatose sleep. As I pulled over to the side of the road, I knew exactly what he wanted us to do.

"Come on, Thad, it's really late, let's just go home," I urged, hoping to change his mind. "You're not really thinking we should go and talk to Shelly at this late hour, are you? Look at the time."

"We can't go home until we warn her about those killers," he insisted. "They could still be around here somewhere. In fact, they might be over at her house this very second. Who knows what they might do to her."

"I thought you said you wanted to go home, Thad?" Mark asked in a mocking manner.

"I do," he admitted. "But there is no way in hell I'm going to get a wink of sleep thinking about whether she's going to get murdered because of those stupid phone calls we made this morning."

"Those stupid phone calls got our asses out of a whole lot of trouble," Mark reminded Thad. "And besides, I didn't see you having any trouble sleeping just a few minutes ago."

"Those calls also nearly got us killed at least twice tonight," Thad defended his statement, ignoring Mark's second comment. "And it could get someone else killed too. We have a responsibility to warn her."

"I don't know, Matt," said Mark with a big sarcastic grin. "Actually, I think Thad has the hots for this babe. After you save her life, Thad, maybe she'll want to marry you and have your babies. You big hero, you."

Before Mark could reach over the seat and do something stupid like rubbing Thad's head or pinching his cheek, Thad leaned forward out of his reach. Mark was incredibly predictable after making such statements.

"Actually, Thad may just be right about this one," I finally chimed in, once my conscience had a chance to review the possibilities. "Maybe we should try to warn her somehow."

"Or how about this for a plan?" asked Thad, sensing an opportunity to go even further. "Now that we know where Carter's body is buried, let's just go over to the police station and tell them everything we know right now. That way we can get this whole mess all over with and the police can worry about saving Shelly. That will solve all of our problems in one swoop."

"Shit, Thad, are you deaf or just down right stupid?" asked Mark, clearly annoyed at Thad's persistence. "I told you before and I'll say it again, we can't go to the police until we see for

144

ourselves that it's Carter's body. What if that wasn't his body they dumped in the cave? Maybe they killed someone else we don't know about. Imagine if we brought the police there and it was some other poor fool. For all we know, those guys could be driving around right now, as we speak, picking up dead bodies all over the god damn county. Who the hell knows how many people they've wasted."

"You're really serious about us digging up that body?" asked Thad, still unable to believe it. "I thought you were joking before. You mean to tell me you expect us to crawl into that cave and dig up a body that has been dead for over a week? You're real funny, Butthead, real funny. I'm not going into no cave. I'll suffocate in there."

I remembered Thad's fear of confined places. Once when he was a kid, his cousin locked him in a closet for nearly twenty minutes. When he finally let him out, Thad couldn't stop hyperventilating. I could still recall the color of his face—it was a light blue shade. He looked like death itself.

"You chicken shit," Mark replied "You're such a wimp."

"Screw you, Butthead," said Thad. "You . . ."

"Shut up, both of you, just shut up," I shouted.

I was in no mood to listen to their childish cackling. I must have caught them off guard because they both had a startled expression across their faces.

"First off, we are not going to the cops tonight," I continued. "So just get that idea out of your mind, Thad. There is no way we are going to say anything to them or anyone else until we've had a chance to get all of our facts in order and we all know what we're going to say. Don't expect our visit to the police to be an easy one. Believe me, they are going to question the hell out of us. As for going into the cave, as much as I hate the idea, we've got to get a look at that corpse. If you don't want to go inside, then you can wait in the car and act as our lookout for all I care. So just forget about that for now—we'll worry about it in the morning. Now that those things are settled, what are we going to do now? Are we going to make a visit to Shelly or not? Let's just decide that or I'm going straight home right this very second."

"I vote that we go home," said Mark as he raised his hand.

"What about you, Thad?" I asked. I could tell from his eyes that he was hoping I'd support him on this one.

"So someone's actually seeking my opinion?" he asked sarcastically. "I already told you what I want. Going to see her is the right thing to do."

"So what about that little accident you had back there," Mark reminded him. "How is your little girlfriend going to react when she sees that little wet spot in your crotch."

"Screw you, Butthead," he responded back. "I'll pull my T-shirt out. She won't see anything. You know something, you are really a first rate asshole. You know that?"

"Oh, such big words," Mark replied. "Uh, you really hurt my feelings."

"Okay, just shut up," I intervened once again. "This is what we'll do. We'll drive by the house to see if there is any sign of those men. If we don't see them and her lights are on, we'll go up to the door and talk to her. But I don't think we should tell her very much. Just enough for her to realize that she might be in some kind of danger."

"Sounds like a plan to me," Thad agreed. Mark just mumbled something and kept quiet after that.

I started up the car and slowly drove down Spring Street toward her house. I decided that if I saw their truck, I'd drive straight to the police station despite what I had just said. There was nothing else we could do to protect her.

Fortunately, there was no sign of their vehicle anywhere near Shelly's home. But there were a few lights shining brightly on the front porch and in her living room. It looked as if she might still be up.

"Look, her lights are on," said Thad, full of excitement. "Great, let's go!"

I couldn't believe how anxious Thad was. I had never seen him so gung-ho to do something like this before. I think Mark was right, Thad must have had some kind of a crush on this woman. After having seen her, I couldn't blame him. I, too, could fall in love with a woman like that.

"Mark, you stay here," I insisted as I climbed out of the car. "She already knows me and Thad. One look at that ugly face of yours and she'd really become scared."

"Hey, wait a minute," Mark protested. "I want to see what this babe looks like."

"You'll see her next time," I replied. "Now drive the car up the road and wait for us. If their truck pulls up, you're going to have to let us know somehow."

"How the hell am I going to do that?" he asked.

"You've got a brain, right?" I asked. "Figure something out."

I could see that Thad was about to make an obnoxious comment about Mark's brain or lack of it, but for some reason he kept it to himself.

"Listen, you guys," said Mark in a serious voice. "Whatever you do, don't tell her that much. I'm really serious. We probably shouldn't be saying anything to her about the murders. We don't know how involved she is. Just warn her about those men and get out of there. Don't tell her the whole story. I still don't like this one bit. It might get us in more trouble somehow."

Thad and I looked at each other and smiled. It was clear to

both of us that Mark just didn't understand. If he had seen her, he'd know that she couldn't be involved. If she did take those things in Nepal, I couldn't believe she knew they were stolen. She seemed like such a sweet girl—a real angel.

* * *

"Thad, are you going to do all the talking?" I asked, hoping he'd take on this responsibility. "You did a really great job last time around. Why don't you do it again?"

"Don't worry, I'll do it," he responded back nervously. "Just wish me luck."

"Good luck, Thad! By the way, do you have any idea what you're going to say to her?"

"Haven't a clue," he admitted as his hand reached out to ring the doorbell. I noticed that it was shaking something fierce. He also kept looking down to see if his T-shirt fully covered all of his front side.

Standing on Shelly's front porch, I still couldn't believe that the outside of this nasty house could possibly look so incredibly elegant inside. It was like there were two worlds separated by the house's thin wooden wall—the ugliness of the outside world with its pealing paint and caked on grime, and the beauty of her own little fantasy world which she had created from the treasures she had brought back from India over the years.

Thad rang the bell several times before someone finally approached the front room. Before making her presence known to us, I noticed her peering out of a small window, in the living room.

"What do you want?" asked Shelly through the front door a few moments later.

"Ms. Harper," Thad said very politely. "It's us, we're the ones who found Mr. Carter's wallet last week. Remember? Could we talk to you for just a moment. It's very important."

"It's late," she complained. "Can't it wait until tomorrow sometime?"

"Like I said, it's really, really important," Thad persisted.

For a moment we didn't hear anything, as if she was trying to decide whether or not to open the door. Finally, she gave in to our request and began undoing at least half a dozen locks before swinging the door open. She was obviously not thrilled to have visitors like us disturbing her at such a late hour.

Seeing her standing there, only a few feet in front of me, sent a wave of desire throughout my entire body. Barefoot and dressed in a loose T-shirt that barely covered her torso, she looked like a goddess who had come alive straight from one of my most erotic fantasies.

"I hate to break it to you boys, but it's a bit on the late

147

side," she grumbled. "What's so important that we couldn't talk about it in the morning?"

"Um, um," muttered Thad in an attempt to find the right words. "We think, um, we think that you might be in some kind of danger."

"Danger?" she asked surprised. "What are you talking about? What kind of danger?"

She motioned for the two of us to come inside, before closing the door.

"Well, there are some men who came by your house tonight," Thad replied. "We know that they've done some really bad things and we think they might be coming after you."

"What men?" she insisted. "What are you talking about?"

"Well, there are these three men from Virginia," Thad explained, feeling pressured to say more than he wanted. "They work for a company called BEEM. Mr. Carter used to . . . I mean Mr. Carter has done some work for them in the past. Have you ever heard of this place before?"

"No, never," she replied back anxiously. "What are the names of these men?"

"Mr. Bradey, Bubha and Charlie—we don't know all of their last names," Thad admitted. "Do you know any of them?"

"No, I've never heard of them before," she conceded. "How do you know all of this? And how do you know they came over to my house tonight?"

"Well, it's really kind of hard to explain." Thad was beginning to have trouble finding the right words to say. "We think they know you have been working with Mr. Carter and we think they are coming to see you about . . ."

Thad stopped in mid-sentence. He didn't want to give that much information to her, but somehow it just came out. His statement must have hit a raw nerve with her because all at once she became very agitated and began demanding an immediate explanation of what was happening.

"Who told you all of this," she demanded. "Tell me! How do you know these things? I want some answers, right now!"

"It doesn't matter how we know," Thad replied back, surprised by her sudden outburst. "We . . ."

"Yes it does matter, yes it does matter!" she shouted. "You come into my house at nearly midnight, you tell me that I'm in danger and then you don't tell me how you know all of these things. Have you been following me around?"

"Listen, Ms. Harper, we don't want to cause you any trouble," I finally jumped in to help Thad out. "We can't talk about the details now. All we know is that these three men who came to your door have done some very bad things. We just wanted to warn you to be careful. They have hurt some people and we think they might try to hurt you too. Now that's all we can say. We're really sorry we bothered you."

Shelly walked over and sat down on a massive, hand carved wooden chair with inlaid camel bone. I grabbed Thad's shirt and tried to pull him toward the door. He resisted. We both realized that we should have discussed what we were going to say before talking to her. It was apparent that our approach, or lack of it, was all wrong.

"Okay, we'll be going now," said Thad reluctantly. "We're sorry we bothered you."

"No, wait," she shouted as she jumped up out of her seat. "Please stay. Just for a moment."

Thad looked at me before saying yes. I was feeling really uncomfortable about the whole thing, but I also hated that we were about to leave under such strained circumstances. We were both feeling that the whole idea of talking with her was a complete disaster. But it was already too late—there was no turning back.

"Please, tell me whatever you know," she requested in a soft voice, completely changing her tone. "I need to know the details. It's only fair, okay?"

"We really can't," I admitted. "It's really late and we're very tired. Maybe tomorrow. We need to first talk to the police about some things and then maybe after we'll be able to explain everything to you in detail."

"The police?" she asked. "Why are you going to talk to them? What do the police have to do with all of this?"

Thad looked at me before answering. He was seeking guidance on what to say. The blank stare imprinted on my face provided little help.

"Like he said, we really can't talk about it now," said Thad. "But it has nothing to do with you."

"Why can't you talk about it?" she persisted. "I promise I won't say anything to anyone. Please, it's very important that I hear what you know. How can you help me if I don't know who it is that I'm supposed to be hiding from and why?"

"We really don't know that much," I said in an attempt to change the subject so that we could get the hell out of there. "Listen, we'll come back another time. Just watch yourself."

I grabbed Thad's shoulder and gently pushed him toward the door.

"Okay, okay—one minute," she said. "Just . . . please, before you go to the police tomorrow, come and see me first. Okay? You said that you came here to help me. If so, then help me. It is very important that I know more about what you're talking about before you tell your story to anyone. Please, I don't want to get all caught up in anything, especially if it has to do with the police. I know it's late and I know you don't want to talk to me now. But you've got to promise me that you'll come by tomorrow morning for coffee. I won't discuss this with anyone and I'll be real careful until then. And you don't have to tell me anything you don't want to, or can't. I just need to know what is happening—especially if it has something to do with me. Please?"

Thad and I looked at each other once again. What could we say? She was pleading with us. This was the first time in my life that a beautiful woman pleaded with me. If she was ugly it would have been easier. But she was gorgeous. It couldn't hurt if we told her some of what we knew, I rationalized in my mind. Besides, we'd be telling the police right afterward anyway. What harm could there be? I was convinced that she was somehow a victim in all of this.

"Okay, we'll come by tomorrow morning," I said. "But we can only stay for a few minutes. What time should we be here?"

"Come anytime. It doesn't matter. Just as long as you show up."

"Okay then. We'll come over some time after eight."

"Thank you so much," she said looking very relieved. "I really appreciate it. Thanks again. Oh, you are going to come to me before you talk to anyone, aren't you?"

"Yes," Thad agreed. "We'll talk to you first. See you tomorrow, good bye."

"Bye," she said. "Oh, by the way, do you boys live here in town."

"Yes, ma'am," I responded.

"Close by?"

"Over near . . ." Thad started to say before I pinched his arm.

"We live way over on the other side of town," I said, not wanting her to know anything else about us just yet.

"Well, we'll see you again tomorrow," she said before closing the door behind her.

*   *   *

"So what happened in there?" asked Mark eagerly through the car window, before we even had a chance to climb inside. He was ready to bubble over with anticipation.

"Go ahead, Thad, you tell him," I said, not wanting to be the one to break the news. I knew Mark was going to have an absolute fit when he found out we agreed to meet with Shelly the following morning.

"Well, um . . . we just told her that some guys might be coming after her and that she might be in some danger," Thad explained after a long pause. "And, well, she wants to know more about what we know."

"What do you mean?" asked Mark, clearly confused by Thad's lack of clarity. His eyes kept jumping back and forth in an attempt to get a better reading from either one of us. "Come on, what is that supposed to mean? What the hell did you guys say to her?"

"Nothing . . . really," Thad mumbled under his breath.

At that point, it was all over. Painted across Thad's face was this expression which revealed he was trying to avoid saying something. Even in the dark, Mark picked right up on it—it was as if he could somehow smell what Thad was thinking.

"You didn't tell her anything . . . did you?" Mark asked, hoping that the answer to his question would be a definitive no.

"We haven't yet, but she wants us to come back here tomorrow morning so we can explain what we know to her before we go and tell the police," Thad admitted. "Okay? I said it. Now you know."

"Yeah, real funny, Thad," said Mark half joking. "Like we're really stupid enough to tell some strange bimbo about those murders."

"That's exactly what I mean," said Thad seriously.

Mark began to laugh again, but when he saw that Thad and I both had straight faces, he stopped abruptly. "You can't be serious about this. We just can't go and blab everything to this lady. You don't know anything about her. Besides, we've already found out that she might be a thief. Who knows what other crimes she might have committed."

"Well, it's too late now," Thad confessed. "We told her we'd stop by tomorrow before visiting the cops. And we also said we'd tell her more about what happened."

"Are you guys for real?" asked Mark. He just couldn't believe we'd do such a dumb thing. "We're not telling anyone anything until after we talk to the god damn police. Just get that through your fat head. And I can't believe you mentioned anything about going to the police to her. Shit, what else did you say to her anyway?"

"Nothing, Mark," I said in Thad's defense. "We told her we'd come by tomorrow and talk to her. That's all. We didn't make any promises to her about anything. She was really scared about what we told her. She just wants a better handle on what's going on. Let's just drop it for now and get out of here."

"What makes you think we can trust this bitch?" asked Mark as he turned on the car. "We don't know anything about her. Let the police go and see her in the morning. Shit, I told you we never should have come here. It was a real mistake."

By the way he "screeched" the tires as he sped away driving my sister's car, I could tell he was well beyond being merely pissed off.

"Cut it out, Mark," I said with conviction. "And just slow down. This isn't your god damn truck. Now listen, both Thad and I trust this woman. And believe me, she's no bitch. She's actually a nice person. I'm serious, I think . . . I mean I know we can trust her."

"I'll tell you what I think," Mark finally burst out. "I think we should get up early in the morning, head over to the cave, dig up Carter's maggot filled body and then hightail it right over to the cops. You can just forget about going to see her or anyone else. Just think about it. She could be one of them for all we know. She could even be on the phone to them right this minute telling them everything."

"But we promised her," Thad said quietly.

"What?" Mark snapped back.

"We promised we'd come back," Thad admitted. His head was looking down as he made this statement. He was bracing for Mark's imminent response.

"I thought Matt just told me that you didn't make her any promises," he replied back sarcastically. "What other promises did you make to her? Did you promise to go to jail for her too? And you guys think I'm a dumb jock. What the hell were you thinking about in there? I told you not to do this thing. I told you so."

"Let's just forget about it for now and worry about it tomorrow," I suggested, hoping to drop the subject. "I'm dead tired. It's been a long day for all of us."

Mark clearly didn't want to end the conversation. But for some reason he just sat there driving. Thad and I exchanged glances, but it was hard for me to give him a supportive look. As much as I wanted to be angry at Mark for being so unreasonable, I knew that what he was saying was true. Going and visiting Shelly only made things more complicated than they had to be.

By this point my brain had converted over to being about as useful as a plate of mashed potatoes. I was tired of obsessing about all of this. All I wanted was for it all to come to an end, and soon.

After dropping Thad off, Mark and I headed over to his place for the night. It was much easier to explain to his parents why we didn't end up camping than it was to describe it to my folks. My parents would have been overly suspicious. Ever since the night we found Carter, my mom has been forever asking what's wrong with me. She was constantly coming over and feeling my forehead to see if I had a fever or something and would say things like "What's the matter, Matt, you just don't seem right to me these days." The fact that I started having nightmares for the first time in my life also made her wonder what was going on. There was no explanation for my bizarre behavior.

In response to my mom's concern for my well-being, my father even came into my room one night to have a little father-son talk with me. Before getting right to the point, I had to listen to an hour of idle chit-chat—kind of like verbal foreplay for him. After what felt like an eternity, he finally got around to asking me if I ever used drugs before. Even after saying no outright, he went on to lecture me for another hour on the evils of using intoxicating substances. As always, the conversation eventually deteriorated into a description of the downfall of the American family. Actually, it was talks like this which could easily drive a person to taking drugs.

As usual, Mark's mom and dad were already in bed. Mark's father always called Saturdays his "date" night. Whenever he made this comment, he'd make a big smile and wink once or twice. It didn't take a rocket scientist to figure out what he meant by that.

We both collapsed into our beds without even bothering to change or brush our teeth. It took nearly all of the energy left in me to remove my shoes. Mark didn't even bother to make the effort.

"Matt, you know something, this has got to be one of the strangest days in my life," said Mark as I laid there waiting to doze off.

"No shit," I responded back. "What would you have done if that guy came up to the car and found us inside? I mean they could have just taken out a gun and shot us all dead."

"I don't know. I usually don't know what I'm going to do until it happens. I don't think about it, it just comes to me. I probably would have had to shoot the guy."

"Shit, I forgot all about that gun of yours. Did you have it out when that guy came up to the car?"

"Hell, yes. I had it pointing right at him," he said as he lifted his arms to show how he held it. "I would have shot him right between the eyes."

"That's the second time they nearly caught us." A shiver went down my spine as I recalled the two events. "Either we're pretty good at hiding or they're just down right blind."

"I think they're blind," said Mark. "You know I never thought Thad would hang in there this long."

"I know what you mean. Listen, about this Shelly lady. I think we should try to see her tomorrow morning. I think she might be able to help us."

"Yeah, how?"

"I don't know. Although she said she doesn't know anything, she might be able to fill in a few of the missing pieces."

"Like what?"

"Like, maybe she can tell us something about the urn. I still think she was probably the one that took it from Nepal to here. Maybe she knows what Carter wanted to do with it."

"Shit, Matt, who cares?"

"Aren't you curious? Maybe she can give us some answers."

"And maybe she can't. Listen, up until now we've managed to keep this thing our own little secret. I don't like the idea of bringing anyone else into this mess. She just probably wants to save her own ass from getting in trouble. She'll just try to talk us out of going to the police."

"She'll never be able to do that. We've got the upper hand here. Come on, Mark, what's the big deal?"

"There is no big deal. I just think we ought to leave her out of it. Like I said, let the police handle it."

"I thought you said before that the police were all a bunch of incompetent fools," I replied back sarcastically. "And here you are talking about them as if you're good buddies with them."

"Screw you, Matt," he responded back. "Shut up and go to sleep."

At that point, the conversation came to an end. I could hardly keep my eyes open and I didn't have the strength to argue with Mark.

9

The following day started out cold, wet, and dank, which I felt was somehow appropriate for the gruesome task which lay before us. The thought of going after a corpse, that had been dead for over a week, was not high on my list of things to do on a Sunday morning. I felt like a grave digger going off to do his dastardly deed.

At half past six, we swung by Thad's house to pick him up. We found him pacing nervously in front of his house with the same high-strung puss on his face he always got right before a major exam—he looked as if he was about to throw up any second.

As for me, I hardly slept a wink—a terrible nightmare once again interrupted my sleep. In this dream, Mark and I were digging in some obscure corner of a cave where we had located a large brown tombstone. It was the kind of gravestone found in the old section of the town cemetery. The ones used to mark the plots where the men killed in the Civil War were laid to rest. There were no words across the front to identify who was buried beneath.

After clearing the dirt away from a large cement vault located several feet below the surface, Mark and I slowly lifted this giant lid off the top. All of the weight lifting I had done over the years finally paid off since it didn't take much effort to accomplish this task. When I finally brought the lantern over, I fell backward in horror after beholding the contents of the tomb. It was me lying dead inside with my arms crossed over my chest as if in some kind of vampire position.

I woke up from the dream and was unable to doze off for the rest of the night. For some reason, I felt that if I fell asleep again, I might never wake up. I was also convinced that this vision, which came to me in my sleep, was probably some kind of a bad omen.

"So, Matt, did you bring a flashlight?" asked Mark as I drove in the direction of our destination—Bowden's Cave. "If you didn't, I've got an extra one here in my pack. It's one of those real big mothers."

Mark didn't bother asking Thad because he knew there was no way in hell he'd be joining us inside the cave.

"Yeah, I got one," I replied back. "So, Butthead, what about this Shelly thing? Did you give it any more thought last night?"

"What about it?" he replied back, as he continued checking

his gear to see that he had everything he needed. I sensed that he was really getting tired of this topic. "We'll find the dead guy, see the police and then go talk to her. Okay? What is there to think about?"

"How about this for a plan? We find the dead guy, talk to her and then go to the police," I said expecting a major argument. Thad was listening closely to see what Butthead's response would be.

"Whatever!" he replied back in a matter of fact tone. I think he just wanted the whole thing to go away.

I took this as a compromise on his side and decided not to push my luck—the subject was immediately dropped.

As I made my way down those familiar roads which lead out of town, Thad stared blankly out the backseat window. He seemed to be off again in his own little dream world. While I felt like something was really bothering him, I knew enough to just leave him alone when he was in one of his moods.

We drove down Route 33 for several miles and then turned down Cheat River Road, which ran parallel to the river. The fog that morning was unbelievably thick. Several times I was forced to slow down almost to a stop as we rounded a sharp corner. At one point, out of nowhere, an enormous cement truck came barreling down from behind and nearly forced me off the road. Mark took the whole thing in stride, while Thad didn't even seem to notice that anything out of the ordinary had just happened.

"Shit," I said. "I hate those trucks. It's a wonder more people don't get killed by those assholes."

"Just chill out, Matt," Mark replied.

"You try driving in this fog. I can't see a damn thing two feet in front of my face."

"Then just slow down for Christ sake. What's the big deal?"

I didn't bother saying anything back for a while. It would have been pointless to get into an argument with Butthead over something so stupid. Besides, as we got closer to the cave, I found myself becoming more and more anxious.

"So, do you really think we'll find him in there?" I asked Mark reluctantly.

"We'll find him in there alright," said Mark, beaming with confidence.

"Maybe we should go somewhere and get some breakfast first," I said hoping to further postpone the inevitable. "I'm really starving."

"We'll have breakfast after it's over," he insisted. "If you eat something now, you might barf it all up in the cave if the guy really stinks."

Nothing was going to prevent Mark from immediately completing this task. He was funny that way. Once he got something into that little mind of his, that was it—there was no turning back.

As we pulled up in front of the cave, I turned and looked at Thad. He was terrified. I could read in his expression that he was feeling the same way I was—the dead should be left to rest in peace.

"Thad!" said Mark sternly. "Now you stay with the car. You should probably cruise up the road a ways and find a place to park. If anyone comes and asks you what you're doing, just tell them that you couldn't see in the fog so you pulled over. Pretty simple, huh?"

"Well, what if a cop stops and asks me for my registration and finds out that the car doesn't even belong to me?" he inquired. Thad could always be counted on to come up with some tough questions.

"Then sit in the passenger seat and tell them that you are waiting for Matt," said Mark after a long pause. "Tell them that he is fishing or something."

"Sounds real believable," said Thad sarcastically. "Why would anyone just sit in the car while their friend went off to go fishing."

"Okay, Thad, if that's how you feel about it, I've got a better idea," Mark responded angrily. "Here, take this light and you can go into the cave and dig up that maggot filled corpse and I'll stay here with the car. That way you won't have to worry about anyone asking you anything, okay?"

"Never mind," he said, sliding over into the driver's seat. "I'll think of something."

Before Mark and I could reach the mouth of the cave, Thad had already driven off.

*   *   *

The entrance to the cave was very narrow. Mark and I both had to get on our hands and knees and crawl for nearly fifty feet before we finally reached a large chamber which had a ceiling high enough for us to stand up. It was cool and damp inside. All around, we could hear the rhythmic sound of water dripping down to the soft, slippery earth below. The darkness was blinding.

Along the far side of the chamber was a small stream which transversed the cave. Upstream was a footpath that led deeper into the belly of the mountain which towered over the site.

While there was a part of me which didn't want to have anything to do with our dead friend, at some deeper level I was beginning to feel very excited about the whole thing. That thrill of once again facing the unknown was kind of exhilarating. These two feelings were both so strong and so completely contradictory, I didn't have a clue what was going on in my brain.

"This is the only trail," said Mark as he pointed his flashlight upstream. "They must have dragged him off in that direction."

"How do you know that's the only way?" I asked, while my flashlight danced around the chamber, looking for other passages.

"Haven't you ever been in here before?" asked Mark.

"Yeah," I replied back. "But I never went further than this spot here. And I was usually pretty drunk."

"You wimp," said Mark, passing his light in every direction looking for any sign of the body. "I've been in here a million times—maybe more. There is really only one way to go—up that path. Along the way, there are a few small diversions, but none of them amount to anything. Down stream the path only goes about ten or twelve yards before it gets so narrow you can hardly move. You know something, I almost got stuck down there once."

"Oh, yeah, how?" I asked, not really caring.

"I tried to see where it went and I just got stuck. I was with Jack and a few of his friends from Bantum. We brought a half keg of beer in here one night after a ball game and all got really plastered. We decided to use this place because we thought the coach would hear about it if we partied out in the woods somewhere. He always seemed to find out when we broke training."

"So how did you get yourself unstuck?"

"I don't know. I just did. For a while I was scared shitless. But I was with a bunch of football players. They managed to yank me out of there somehow. I got all bruised up in the process. Oh, and listen to this. There was this other time when I tried to climb up this hole and my leg got all twisted up. That was ten times scarier. I tried forever to free myself with no success. I was sure I'd never get out of there alive. I would have starved to death in here."

"What are you talking about? You came in here by yourself and climbed up some stupid hole?"

"Sure, all the time," said Mark. He looked at me as if he couldn't understand why I'd ask such a ridiculous question.

"You know, Butthead, there is something about this whole cave thing I still don't understand. Why not just dig another hole somewhere in the forest and bury him there? They must know that crazy people like you wander around this place, climbing in holes and what-not."

"Like I said yesterday, this is a perfect place," said Mark as we began walking in the direction of the path. "Not too many people really come in here and if they found kind of an isolated place, no one would ever find the body. Believe me!"

"Maybe you're right. By the way, weren't you scared walking around here all by yourself?"

"Naw, not at all," Mark admitted. "There's a lot to see in here if you take the time to really look around."

"Butthead, the scientist. Who'd ever believe it?"

Mark and I made our way up the narrow path that followed along the stream. The ground was moist and slippery beneath our feet from water seeping along the walls. Several times I nearly fell on my ass. At one point, we had to jump over the stream in order to continue to follow the trail. Mark made the jump with ease, but it took me a few minutes to get up the courage to follow. We were at least ten feet above the water and the ledge was very meager.

"Come on, you pussy," Mark laughed, as he reached his hand out to help me across. "If you fall, you'll probably only break a leg—maybe an arm. I'm sure you'll survive. Course you might limp for the rest of your life, but . . ."

"Shut up, Mark. I'm not a cave dweller like you. This is the first time I've ever done this before. You have Neanderthal blood in you. I don't." I finally made the jump and survived.

Whenever we found a small alcove along the way, we stopped to see if it looked as if the ground had been disturbed. I made sure that Mark was always in front of me so that he could take the lead. I had no interest in being the one to locate the body.

"Anything?" I asked as Mark came out of a small crevice in the wall.

"Nothing," he said, feeling disappointed. "It has to be up further, I guess."

"You know something, I don't think they brought the body this far. We've been walking for nearly thirty minutes now. They weren't in the cave all that long. Remember?"

"It's got to up this way," he exclaimed. "Where else could it be?"

"Hey, wait a second. They couldn't have gone this far with Carter. How could they have gotten the body across that stream back there? There is no way they could have passed it over. The ledge was way too small. And it would have been impossible to throw the body that distance."

"So where the hell is it then? I looked in every crack and hole along the way. And they couldn't have put him in the stream. We would have seen it in there. It's only a few feet deep and I've been checking the whole time."

As I thought about what it must have been like to drag a full-grown man's body into a cave, it suddenly dawned on me. I pointed a flashlight to the ground and noticed that there was something missing that should have been there.

"Mark," I said full of excitement. "If you were going to take a body into a cave, how would you do it?"

"What are you talking about?" he asked, not fully understanding the jist of my question.

"How would you bring it inside?" I repeated. "Think about it. You need at least one hand to carry the light, right? And it's too difficult to lift and hold a body with one hand, especially if you're walking on a slippery surface."

"So?" asked Mark, still confused by my train of thought. Mark was never one for serious problem solving.

"Don't you see? They must have dragged the body. Right? And if they did, then where's the trail? It's not here. If we can go back and find it, it should lead us right to where the body is buried. God, I can't believe we didn't think of that before."

"Maybe whatever kind of bag they used was too thin," Mark suggested. "Maybe if they dragged it, it would tear and the guy would just ooze out all over the place."

"Huh, it could be," I said as I thought it over.

Mark was a master at finding the potential horror in all situations. For a split second, I visualized Carter's body trickling out and nearly gagged at the thought.

"But I'll bet I'm right," I continued, after focusing again on our situation. "I'll bet they had to drag it at least some of the way. They weren't in this cave all that long. They couldn't have gotten up this far, buried the body and then got out so fast. It has to be closer to that big chamber."

After mulling it over, Mark finally turned around and started walking back toward the entrance.

When we arrived back in the large chamber area, I walked over to where we crawled in and immediately noticed a thick trail about two feet wide with foot prints on either side.

"Shit," I said. "Look at this. I was right. Why didn't we think of this when we first got here?"

A chill ran through my body as I realized that we were nearing our goal.

Mark came rushing over and carefully inspected the scrape mark which created a small path in the dirt. We both followed the trail with our flashlights. We had gone the wrong direction before—the trail led downstream to the place where Mark had once gotten stuck. As we followed along, it all seemed to make perfect sense. It was much better to put the body in a place where most people wouldn't go.

*   *   *

Within a matter of minutes, Mark managed to locate a small mound within the narrow tunnel that lead downstream, which had obviously, only recently, been covered with dirt and rocks. While they did their best to make the spot look natural, the surrounding area had clearly been disturbed.

"That's got to be him, you know," I said as I turned away. "Oh, shit, I really don't want to see this."

"I know what you mean," Mark confessed, as he crawled over to inspect the pile of dirt and rocks more closely. "So now what?"

"I say we go and get some breakfast and call it a day," I replied back half joking—half serious.

"Let's just do this thing and get the hell out of here," said Mark with a determined tone in his voice. "We're on the home stretch, Matt. Soon this mess will be over with and we'll be laughing about it. So do you want me to do this thing or what?"

"Hey, go ahead, be my guest," I said, feeling very relieved that he was the one who volunteered. "I'll hold the light while you dig."

"Oh, shit! You know something, I forgot to bring the damn shovel along with me. What the hell am I supposed to dig with?"

"You can clean your fingernails when you get home."

After a long pause, Mark began pulling rocks and dirt away from the small mound which was only a few feet from the stream. It didn't take long to feel something wrapped up in plastic beneath the surface.

"Well, Matt. I think I found him. I can feel something plastic down here. Yep, it's a body alright."

"Hurry up, Mark." I found myself becoming more and more antsy. "Find his face, make sure it's him and let's get out of here."

"Well, then keep the flashlight straight man," he complained as I tried to steady my arm. By this point, I was really feeling freaked out.

It took him a while to move enough earth away before he could pull the body out from under the mound. When he finally accomplished this task, he realized that they had buried Carter feet first—Mark had pulled the corpse out of the hole by his head. While I tried to repress the thought, for a fleeting moment, I visualized his head coming off. Gross!! Once again, I nearly gagged.

The body was wrapped up in layer after layer of Hefty garbage bags and grey duct tape. The way the tape conformed to his remains, the package almost looked like some kind of Egyptian mummy.

"How am I supposed to see his face?" asked Mark. I could tell he was beginning to have second thoughts. "There's like about ten inches of tape and plastic wrapped around his head."

"I don't know. Can you peel it off?" I asked impatiently. "Come on, just hurry up and do whatever you're going to do."

Mark reached into his pocket and took out a small, imitation Swiss Army knife he often carried around with him. He slowly began to cut the tape and the plastic with the care of an experienced surgeon. I tried to keep the flashlight steady as he went through this process, but my hands were shaking so much I couldn't hold it still. I was absolutely terrified. This would be the second time in less than eight days that I found myself face to face with a dead person—the same dead person.

After cutting through the last bag, the smell of decaying flesh finally seeped out. Mark got the first whiff of it and nearly threw up. I wasn't so lucky. I vomited about ten times—or at least went through the act of vomiting. Having not eaten anything, there was nothing in my stomach to bring up.

"Come on, you asshole, get over here," Mark shouted. "I can't see anything. Flash that light on his face."

Mark had placed his flashlight down to free up both of his hands and couldn't seem to find it.

I walked over and pointed the light in the direction of the corpse's face. As much as I didn't want to look, I knew that my curiosity would eventually get the best of me. So I did. As anticipated, it was Carter alright. His face looked much different than before. It was completely white and drained of any color. His eyes and mouth were both wide open, as if he wanted to say something to us.

Having confirmed his identity, Mark tried to put the plastic over Carter's face again and push the body back where he found it. But before he could finish, he got so grossed out that he began crawling out of the space he was in.

"Screw this," he said, disgusted by the whole thing. "I've got to get the hell out of here now!"

Before we knew it, we were both racing in the direction of the cave opening. We fell to the ground and crawled out of the cave as if we were being chased by someone. Once outside, it took us a while to adjust to the bright light. The early morning fog had completely lifted and it looked like an absolute perfect day—at least weather-wise.

Mark immediately ran over to a small pool of water near the cave's entrance, dropped to his knees and began washing his hands frantically. I couldn't blame him. If I had touched that bag, I would have done exactly the same thing.

"Holy shit," said Mark. "That was, by far, the nastiest thing I've ever done in my life. I actually touched that thing. Shit!"

*   *   *

Mark and I headed up the road and located my sister's car parked about a quarter of a mile away. Thad was sitting on a large rock which provided an excellent view of the river down below. His back was to us when we came upon him.

"I trust you found what you were looking for?" Thad asked

without turning around.

"Yeah," I responded back. "He was there alright."

"How bad was it?" he asked as he tossed stones into the forest. I could tell that he was feeling guilty that he didn't go into the cave with us.

"Pretty bad," I admitted.

"Looks like it's all over," said Thad. He stood up and brushed the dust off his pants.

Mark walked over to the car and just leaned against the side and stared out into the woods. He seemed completely dazed. I had never seen him so withdrawn. It was a bit disconcerting seeing him like this.

"Does anyone have a cigarette?" asked Mark.

Thad and I just looked at each other in total amazement. Mark didn't smoke. He never had and always talked about how it was such a gross habit—sticking that miniature smoke stack in your mouth. Neither one of us could figure out what got into him.

"Hey, Butthead," I said as I came over and put my hand around his shoulder. "You okay, man?"

It took him a moment before he finally answered.

"Yeah," he mumbled. "I'm peachy." He tried to force a smile, but it looked contrived.

"Hey, it's all over man," I said patting his back. "We did it. We solved the mystery. I guess that makes us pretty good detectives. You think they'll make a mini-series about this someday?"

"Sure thing," he responded back.

*   *   *

During the ride back to town, none of us wanted to talk about Carter or anything else for that matter. We all got caught up in our own individual thoughts.

As I negotiated the winding road which seemed to hug the river's indecisive turns, I began to wonder about Carter. Who was he? What was he like when he was still alive? Did he have a family, friends, pets? Did anyone miss him? Was he a good person or a fiend like those BEEM boys? Was the world any different now that he was dead? Would the world be any different when I eventually died?

It's funny how insignificant life seems when you come face to face with death. Carter died and the world still rolled on. In some ways, I kind of always felt that when I died, everything would come to a screeching halt. As if my life was so incredibly important that if I were to kick the bucket, it would be a big deal in some way. But seeing Carter's lifeless body lying there on the cave floor, it occurred to me that maybe my life was nothing special to anyone, but myself. The fact that I was like everyone else around me, with nothing special to distinguish me from the rest of the cattle, came shining home. For some reason, being so incredibly ordinary somehow frightened the hell out of me.

It took us only a short time to make it back to Elkins. My sister's car was nearly out of gas so I pulled into one of those mini-mart gas pump places to fill it up and to grab something to drink. I guess digging up dead guys makes a person thirsty.

While filling up the tank, I inspected the dent on my sister's car door. I couldn't help but cringe. As much as I tried to convince myself that it wasn't all that noticeable, it would always seem to come back into focus. I feared her wrath nearly as much as I feared those good ole boys from Virginia. She'd hold this one against me for the rest of my life.

"Okay, where to next?" I asked as I handed Mark and Thad a cup of coffee I had bought in the station's grocery section. They were those jumbo sized ones which would provide enough caffeine for an entire regiment and more. Since Carter's money was paying for it, I didn't think he'd mind if I splurged a bit.

"Okay, now, let's go visit Shelly," said Thad. He looked at Mark to see what his reaction would be.

"Are you still thinking about seeing that stupid woman?" asked Mark. "Come on now. Let's just forget about her and go to the police." For a moment, Thad just stared at him with a look I had never seen on his face before.

"No way!" he finally said with a determined voice. "I'm tired of letting you have your way all the time. It's always Mark's way or nothing. Well, I'm really sick of it. This is a democratic country we live in, with democratic ways. Up until now you've forced your god damn plans on us. I'm tired of being pushed around by you."

I couldn't remember ever seeing Thad take on Mark like this. With his clinched fists and his unyielding stare, I felt like he was about to pounce on Mark.

"What the hell brought all this on?" asked Mark surprised. He, too, was caught off guard by Thad's uncharacteristic frontal assault. "What's your problem anyway?"

"You're my god damn problem," he snapped back with his mouth twitching with sheer determination. "I think we should go to see Shelly. We told her we were going to come by and that's exactly what I'm going to do. If you have a problem with that, then just drop me off and I'll go see her by myself."

Both Mark and I looked at Thad in utter amazement. His eyes were on fire and his nostrils were close to flaring. It almost looked like in another second he was going to just explode. He stood his ground and didn't look as if he was going to back down. I guess deep down inside, there is a wild man in all of us—even Thad.

"Okay, okay, just relax, Thad, don't have a fit on me now," said Mark when he realized that there was no sense in arguing anymore. "We'll go see your girlfriend if that's what you want. Shit, Thad, what's gotten into you? Matt take that coffee away from him or give him decaf next time. He's about to blow about a dozen fuses any second."

"Okay, then, let's go do it," I said, satisfied with the outcome. I fired up the engine and started driving in the direction of Spring Street.

As we got closer to her house, I began to really think about Shelly. The more I thought about it, the more I was really glad we were going to see her before visiting the cops. There were still so many holes in our story which lacked an explanation. For example, why did they kill Carter? Who had the urn and what did it have to do with Carter's death, if anything? What would a defense company want with a stolen antique? The list of other unknowns seemed to just go on and on. I wanted to understand everything. While I wasn't sure what the outcome might be, there was no one else we knew of who could even begin to answer these questions.

"Oh, shit," yelled Mark. "Shit, shit, shit."

"What is it, what is it?" I asked. For a moment I thought something horrible had happened. I immediately looked in my rear view mirror to see if I'd find Bradey's truck following behind us.

"I left my god damn flashlight in the cave," Mark confessed. "Remember how we ran out of there after we wrapped his body back up. I must have left it on the ground. We're going to have to go back and get it."

"I'm not driving all the way back there and going in that cave again," I said emphatically. "You couldn't pay me enough money to turn this car around. Just forget about it, the police will find it. If you want to go back and get it, be my guest. But you're not doing it in this car."

"But, that's my dad's flashlight," said Mark in a panic. "He'll have a fit if I lose it. He's had that thing for years."

"Then I'll just have to buy him another one," I said. "Just forget about it. There's no way in hell we're going near that cave again."

Mark didn't say anything as I drove off through town towards Spring Street. I could tell that he was going to obsess about it until he got it back. But I was in no mood to go all the way to the cave for a worthless five dollar piece of hardware. Once in a lifetime was enough.

10

We arrived at Shelly's place a little past 9:00 am—only an hour later than what we promised. I parked the car up the road a ways just in case those BEEM boys came back while we were still inside. Although I was pretty sure they wouldn't recognize the car, being so close to the end of this thing, I wasn't about to take any more chances.

All three of us made our way toward the house this time around. Mark insisted on getting a good look at this "so-called" beauty he had heard so much about. Despite all of the many positive things we had said about her, he still had his doubts. He told us it was time to size up the situation for himself—first hand.

While making our way up the brick pathway to the front porch, I caught a quick glimpse of Shelly peering out the front window. She had obviously been waiting for us.

"How the hell could anyone so beautiful live in a dump like this?" asked Mark, as he stood on the porch and looked around at some old wooden furniture scattered about. He rubbed his fingers across a battered chair and was surprised at how much dust it collected. "Are you sure she's not some kind of dog. I mean really. If Thad thinks she's nice looking I'll bet she's probably . . ."

Shelly opened the door at precisely that moment and stood there in front of us, in all of her glory. She was wearing a pair of faded, tight-fitting blue jeans which clearly accentuated her thin waist and well-rounded curves, and a bright pink T-shirt which left little to the imagination. The fact that she wasn't wearing a bra did not go unnoticed by any of us. Her hair was tied up in a pony tail with a large blue ribbon which flopped from side to side as she spoke. She looked absolutely stunning—even more so than on any of our other visits.

"Thanks so much for coming over," she said, extending her hand out to Thad. After shaking mine, she turned to Mark.

"I don't believe we've met before. My name is Shelly. Please, won't you all come inside."

Mark didn't say a word. He just stood there with his eyes practically popping out of his head. He was completely awe struck. It was a clear case of "lust" at first sight.

"Please come over here and sit down," she said, motioning us in the direction of her living room. "Before getting started, can I get you all something to drink? Some coffee, tea or perhaps a soft drink?"

"I'll have some coffee," Mark replied. Thad and I both declined. We had just finished drinking those mega cups of coffee and I already had to pee. I was feeling anxious enough as it was without another dose of caffeine.

"How do you take your coffee?" she asked Mark.

"Black please . . . with milk and sugar," he said confidently. Thad and I both got a kick out of Mark's lame attempt to sound grown-up.

"Please make yourself at home," said Shelly, before heading off toward the kitchen. "I'll be back in just a few minutes. And feel free to look around if you'd like."

"So, what did I tell you, Butthead," I said, grabbing his arm and shaking it. "Is she fine or what?"

"Holy shit, man, she's a real babe alright," Mark confessed, biting one of his knuckles. "She can't be from around here. She doesn't have a mustache. And besides, she's way too classy for these parts. And shit, did you see that bod of hers? She's a goddess."

Mark was always complaining how ugly the girls were in Elkins. He'd often compare them to those from other high schools he'd seen during his out of town wrestling matches. It was always funny to me how the girls from other schools were seen as being so much better looking than our own—the old greener-pastures- elsewhere syndrome, I guess.

"Man, this is a really cool place," I whispered, while wandering around the room from one object to another. "Look at all of this weird stuff everywhere."

We all aimlessly strolled about, looking at the paintings on the walls and the wide range of interesting nick-knacks scattered throughout.

"This place is like a god damn museum," said Mark, picking up a small statue of Lord Ganesh which he found on one of the many wooden end-tables scattered about the room. He then hurried over to something on one of the walls which immediately caught his eye. "Hey, check this out. She's got a bunch of tiny porno paintings all over this wall. Holy shit, look at these things."

Thad and I both rushed over to where Mark was standing. At that age, whenever the word porno was mentioned, We'd all come running. On the wall was a small collection of very detailed paintings on what appeared to be some kind of white material which resembled bone. Each of the paintings depicted a man making love to at least three women in some pretty bizarre positions. A Chinese acrobat would have had trouble achieving most of the poses. It was all very graphic. None of the dirty magazines hidden under my bed came close to displaying anything so erotic.

"I wonder what my mom would say if I put one of these paintings in our living room over the fireplace," I said with a laugh.

"If I put one up, my dad would place his chair right in front of it and never watch the TV again," Mark responded.

"Don't you know what these are?" asked Thad in a matter of fact manner. "They are miniature paintings depicting scenes from the Karma Sutra."

"Karma what?" asked Mark, with his head cocked sideways, the way a dog does when he hears a high-pitched sound.

"Karma Sutra, dummy," Thad repeated. "It's this really famous book written in India many centuries ago about the art of 'doing it.' These paintings are very popular in India. They are considered an art form."

"Well, I don't care what you say, they look pretty pornographic to me," Mark admitted while inspecting them closer—for their artistic value, of course. "So, how the hell do you know about this book anyhow? Do you have one stashed in your closet? Have you been holding out on us, Thad?"

"Haven't you ever seen those 'Kama Dupa' pictures Thad's mom keeps over the mantel," I said as I elbowed him. "Oh, I'm sorry, those were photographs of his parents 'doing it.' It's art you know." Thad just turned to me and gave me one of his glaring "that's disgusting" expressions.

"Actually, I saw these paintings in a book in Washington D.C. last summer," Thad went on to explain. "I think it was at the Natural History Museum bookshop. This massive volume had about a thousand pictures of these kings screwing in all different positions. Back then, these guys had hundreds and hundreds of concubines so they had lots of practice."

"What's that, some kind of disease or something?" I asked half serious. "Sounds like those big warts old fat ladies get between their toes."

"Concubine means prostitute, you moron," Thad described in a condescending tone. "God, what planet are you guys from?"

"You know something, maybe this lady is really into sex," said Mark optimistically. "What kind of person puts this stuff on her wall? Who knows, maybe she'll go out with me and I'll get lucky? Man, I'd love to be one of those guys in those paintings with her. Could you imagine doing it with . . ."

When we heard her returning from the kitchen, Thad and I scurried to find a place to sit. Mark was right behind us, but all of a sudden just stopped in his path. For some reason, he kept staring at something on one of the walls. It looked like he was in some kind of a weird trance. Neither Thad nor I could figure out what he found so intriguing. I wondered whether he saw an even more revealing painting. But all at once, his expression became incredibly serious before he finally took a seat against the far wall.

"Here you go, black coffee with milk and sugar," she said as she flashed Mark a great big smile. Mark didn't say anything back, not even "thank you." I couldn't understand what had gotten into him. Only seconds before, he seemed to be in a good mood and then all at once he got real somber.

Our host didn't initially notice his abrupt change. She walked over to one of the chairs and sat down. I could tell she wasn't feeling very relaxed by the way she sat on the edge of her seat and kept playing with a small ring she had on one of her fingers. She'd repeatedly take it off and then put it in between her two pinkies, twirling it around nervously.

"Well, I'm not sure where to begin," she said timidly. "This is all a little awkward for me. You boys didn't . . . didn't mention what we talked about to anyone yet, did you? I mean, you . . ."

"No, ma'am," said Thad in a reassuring tone, before she could finish her statement. "We promised we'd talk to you first, remember?"

"Yes, I remember," she admitted. "But, what about other people? Did you tell anyone . . . uh, do others know anything about what you know—your friends, family members, anyone? Maybe you mentioned it to them before yesterday?"

"No, ma'am," I replied this time around. "We haven't told a living soul anything. Swear to god."

After hearing this, she smiled again and settled back in her chair. There was something about her facial expression that struck me as being a little unusual. It almost looked as if she wanted to laugh out loud about something. Not knowing what it's like to be around an attractive woman, I just thought that's the way they acted.

"Well, then," she said, leaning forward again, clasping her hands together. "Let's talk. Maybe you should start by telling me more about those strange men you said might be coming after me. What do you know about them?"

Instinctively, Thad and I looked at each other in an attempt to clarify what to reveal. Once again, we had completely forgotten to discuss how much to confide in her. As for Mark, it didn't look like we were going to get any guidance from him. He was still off somewhere in his own little world. His uncharacteristic behavior was really becoming kind of bizarre—it almost looked like he was possessed by some kind of demon.

"Before we talk about that, I was just curious, did anyone come to see you since yesterday after we left?" asked Thad, breaking the silence. "I mean those men we told you about."

"No, no one came by," she admitted in a very animated manner, with her hands moving about as she talked. "You boys really scared me with that story of yours. I tell you, I double bolted all my doors and windows and hid under the covers the whole night. I was so frightened, I hardly slept a wink."

"Sorry about that," said Thad sympathetically. "We just didn't want anything to happen to you."

"That's real sweet," she replied back.

She reached over and patted Thad's arm several times. You'd have thought from the expression on his face that he just had his first kiss. Of course, that was probably Thad's most physical moment with a member of the opposite sex to date.

"Oh, and we forgot to ask you something yesterday," I added. "Um, I take it you never met those men before? You know, the ones we described." I felt compelled to ask once again, just to make sure she was being straight with us.

"Actually, you did ask me that last night. Remember? I told you already, I don't know anything about them." She seemed a bit annoyed that I'd repeat that particular question.

"Oh, yeah," I said, feeling embarrassed. "I must have forgotten. Sorry!"

"Now, please, enough of this chit-chat," she said seriously. "Tell me all about these men and what you know about me. And please start from the beginning."

"Well," Thad started. "Well, um, you see we were in the woods last Friday night on a fishing trip. Actually, not the Friday that just happened, the one before that. And, well, we were going to Mark's uncle's cabin when . . ." Before Thad could finish his sentence, Mark abruptly cut him off.

"Actually, Miss Harper, there isn't much to tell you." His voice had a very aggressive edge to it. "We were out in the forest and we noticed these three men near the location of where someone was murdered last week—someone from Bantum, a fisherman. Maybe you read about it in the newspaper. Anyway, we thought the men who came to your door might have had something to do with it. That's about it. There is really nothing else to tell."

It was strange to see Mark acting more cautious than Thad. He was usually the first one to blab out every detail, but something seemed to really be holding him back. I still couldn't figure out what he was so interested in. He kept staring across the room. I tried to follow his gaze, but there didn't appear to be anything out of the ordinary there—a few wall hangings, a couple of paintings and a large, antique mirror. Whatever it was, he was really captivated by it. Even Shelly began to look behind to see what had caught his attention.

"Last night you said that those men came to my house," she continued, directing her statement at Thad and me as she ignored Mark's comment. "How could you possibly know that?"

The conversation seemed to be jumping all over the place. One minute she'd focus on a given topic, the next she'd be on to

170

something else.

"We were . . . we were following them," I said with a bit of hesitation, not knowing how Mark might react. "We were trying to . . ." I didn't finish my statement immediately. I needed time to decide how to better phrase it.

"You were trying to do what?" she asked impatiently. The conversation was quickly beginning to deteriorate.

"It's not important!" Mark insisted before I had a chance to respond. She was again taken aback by his intrusive style. Actually, we were all kind of surprised by it.

"Please tell me, what were you trying to do?" she asked, focusing on me again. She was clearly annoyed by Mark's constant interruptions.

"Nothing, that's it, there is nothing else left to say," said Mark, before I could respond.

"Would you just shut up and let him speak," she shouted in a scolding voice, turning toward Mark. "I'm not talking to you. I'm talking to him. Okay?"

Thad and I were both a bit shocked by this unexpected outburst. It seemed so out of character for her.

"Well, excuse me," Mark replied back sarcastically.

It was really unlike Mark to be so incredibly rude. Neither Thad nor I understood what was going on between him and Shelly. But the tension was mounting by the second. The room had an explosive feel about it.

"Yesterday you said something about Mr. Carter working for someone, and because I'm doing work for him, they'd be coming after me," she continued as she looked back and forth between Thad and I. "What was that all about? And why are you following these men? I thought we agreed we'd talk about this. That's why you came over here this morning. Wasn't it? Please, it's important to me. Won't you tell me what's happening so I can better understand?"

"We just knew they were up to no good," said Thad, struggling to find the right words to avoid upsetting Mark again. "That's all. We think they may be bad men who were involved in . . ." Mark cut Thad off for the third and final time.

"Who else is in this house with you now?" asked Mark suddenly, as he jumped out of his seat. "Who's in that room back there?" He was looking toward the kitchen door.

"There's no one here but us," she acted surprised. "I live alone and . . ."

"You're a god damn liar," Mark shouted, looking toward the mirror on the wall. His hand was shaking as he pointed to the mirror and then to the kitchen door. "I thought I saw you whispering to someone before you came back in here with my coffee. I wasn't sure about it until I just saw that person's reflection again—just now. Someone's standing by that door. Let's get the hell out of here, something's not right." From where Mark was sitting, he could clearly see the reflection into the next room.

Thad and I jumped up immediately. Instinctively, we all turned toward the front door. But before we could make our escape, two men came running out from a small side room which led to the dining area. It was Bubha and Charlie. They stood in front of the door with a smug, self-satisfied look imprinted across their faces. Bubha had a small pistol in his hand which was pointed right at us. Charlie just stood there with his arms crossed in front of him, like a bouncer at a night club.

When we turned to look for another way out, someone else entered from the door that led to the kitchen. He was wearing a pair of bright green golf pants, a white polo shirt and a small checkered cap. I always hated people who wore that kind of outfit. They were usually such snobs.

At first I couldn't make out who this person was, but then it struck me—it was Mr. Keller, the president of BEEM. I remembered his picture from the company brochure. He had put on a few pounds and his hair was a lot grayer, but it was him alright. He was also carrying a small pistol in his hand.

"Shit," yelled Mark as he frantically looked around the room for a way to escape. There appeared to be no way out. We were completely trapped. If he had been alone, Mark probably would have made a run for it somehow. But he was not one to leave his friends behind. Before long we all found ourselves huddled together in the center of the room like a bunch of cornered animals.

"What do we do now? What do we do now?" Thad whispered as he cowered behind me. The sheer terror he was feeling raised the tone of his voice by several decibels.

Before we could answer Thad's question, there was one more little surprise—the infamous Mr. Bradey casually strolled into the room and stood beside Mr. Keller. He had a half eaten donut in his hand which he polished off in a single bite. Upon seeing him, I nearly bit my tongue. All at once, the memory of what he said to me on the phone the day before came flooding back—he said he was going to get me "and" my family. All I could hope for was that he'd forgotten that whole episode.

"I wouldn't try anything stupid," Bradey suggested, with a crooked smile on his face which clearly displayed his sheer satisfaction at our present situation. "You are liable to get yourselves hurt. Now sit down there and just shut the hell up."

Despite his command, none of us were able to move. We were all still huddled together. Mark stood in front, as if to shield us from whatever danger might come our way. He was always kind of protective that way. I could see his eyes still darting in every direction. It looked like he was trying to find

172

that magic tunnel which would allow us to flee to safety. Every possible scenario was being calculated, but no such escape route materialized.

There was nothing we could say or do—they had us good. We were setup by that bitch. I couldn't believe how stupid we were to trust her. Butthead was right all along. We should have listened to him and just gone straight to the cops. When I looked around to see where she was, I couldn't find her anywhere in the room. It looked as if she slipped out to another part of the house during all of the commotion.

"Well, well, well," said Bradey sarcastically, as he casually strolled right up to us. "What do we have here? A couple of real smart guys. Thought you were the Hardy Boys for a while, didn't you?"

He stood directly in front of Mark and looked right up at his face for a long while. It was like he was studying him. He then looked at Thad and me for a moment, but immediately turned back toward Mark again. I knew Mark wanted to deck this guy right there on the spot. I prayed over and over that he wouldn't do anything foolish.

"I thought I told you boys to sit," Bradey commanded, pointing to a small couch in the center of the room. In unison, we slowly edged our way over to the sofa, but continued to stand. "I said sit down, now!"

The sheer force of his voice was enough to compel us to finally comply. Both Bubha and Charlie came over and stood behind us.

"So you boys seem to think that I'm some kind of bad guy," he said playfully, while pacing back and forth. Mr. Keller took a seat on the other side of the room. "You know, that really, really hurts my feelings. Am I really a bad person?" He directed the question to all of us. As expected, none of us ventured an answer.

"Bubha, you know me pretty well," he continued, with poignant sarcasm. "Am I really a bad person?"

As he asked the question, he leaned over and put his face inches from Thad's. Up close, his eyes looked crazed. He really seemed to be enjoying this little taunting game of his.

"No, boss," Bubha replied back. "You're a regular angel."

"You hear that boys?" he asked. "I'm a regular angel. And you know something, I think that Bubha and Charlie over there are also angels. Well, then, so why do you suppose these boys think we're such bad people then? Oh looky here, this one's crying. Look at the little cry baby. Isn't she cute."

Thad's body shook from top to bottom with each successive wave of tears. Bradey used one of his fingers to lift Thad's face so that he could see it. Thad tried to turn away, but Bradey grabbed his chin hard in an effort to hold it in place.

"You leave him alone, you bastard," yelled Mark as he lunged at Bradey with his fist raised high. His motherly instincts seemed to have kicked in—he was on fire with rage. I had seen that look on Mark's face a thousand times before. It usually resulted in someone getting their ass severely kicked. But before he could make any headway, Bradey's goons grabbed him from behind. He only backed off after Bubha placed his pistol to Mark's temple and cocked the trigger.

Bradey walked over to Mark, who was now on his feet, pushing aside a small coffee table so that he could stand face to face with him. He stared into Mark's eyes for a long time before suddenly pounding Mark with some kind of Karate kick to the face. Mark fell right to the floor, as a steady stream of blood trickled out of his nose. If I had blinked that very moment, I would have missed the whole thing. It happened so fast—none of us saw it coming.

"That's for last Friday night you piece of dog shit," said Bradey, showing his sheer pleasure at settling the score. "You know you ruined one of my best shirts. That wasn't very nice, was it?" He then proceeded to kick Mark in the ribs several more times for good measure.

Mark lay on the floor, doubled over in pain. It almost looked like he was unconscious. While I desperately wanted to do something to help, I was paralyzed with fear. And besides, what could I have done anyway?

"So, Mr. Cry Baby," said Bradey, turning back toward Thad. "Why don't you describe to me what you were about to tell our good friend Shelly. It sounded like you had all kinds of interesting things to say about us."

Even if he had wanted to, there was little chance Thad was going to speak. He was so traumatized, he was on the verge of having an asthma attack—he could hardly breathe, let alone talk.

"Hey, I'm talking to you, boy," Bradey shouted, grabbing Thad's chin again. With Thad grasping for air, it was pretty evident he wasn't going to be of any use for quite some time.

"Looks like our little cry baby friend can't talk just now," he declared, turning toward me as an alternative. "So what the hell's your name?" When I didn't answer, he persisted. "I'm sorry, I couldn't hear you."

"My name is Matt," I whispered.

"Oh, yes . . . that voice, that voice," he replied. "Let me see, where have I heard that voice before? Could it have been on the phone? Maybe, like yesterday morning? Please refresh my memory, Matt. Did you call me yesterday? Say around seven or seven thirty in the morning?"

"No, sir," I replied. My lip quivered as I spoke.

"Sir?" he asked sarcastically. "He thinks I'm this horrible person, but yet he still calls me sir? How very strange. These boys must be confused."

He stopped talking for a moment as if to size me up before starting again.

"You know something, I think you're a god damn lying bastard," he continued, putting his face real close to my ear so he could whisper to me. "I think you remember our little talk, don't you? Didn't I say I'd find you? And do you remember what else I said? You know, the part about your family. Well, you know something, I really meant it, you piece of shit. Oh, and I hope you have a sister. I can't wait to tell you the nice things I plan on doing to her."

Him talking that way about my sister and family, completely changed my whole attitude. I couldn't stop myself from exploding in anger.

"If you touch anyone in my family, I swear I'll rip you apart," I shouted, as I tried to throw a punch at him.

Someone grabbed me from behind and threw me back down on the couch. Before I knew it, one of his goons had me in a head lock. All three of our captors started laughing at my momentary display of valor. They were like a bunch of cats entertaining themselves with a cornered mouse, just before the kill.

"Those are pretty strong words there, Mr. Matt," Bradey remarked in that obnoxious tone of his. "Oooooh, I'm trembling with fear. Very, very strong words. But I'm afraid you're a bit out numbered. Between your little cry baby friend who isn't going to do anything, and that big one on the floor next to your feet, it looks as if you're aaallll alone. So go ahead then, try and take a piece of me. Give it your best shot. You saw what I can do with my feet. I welcome the opportunity to give you another little demonstration."

As I watched Mr. Bradey in action, it occurred to me that there was something "not right" about him. While he had that good-ole boy accent, he just didn't talk or act like someone from the South. With his expensive clothes, big words, and his arrogant way of expressing himself, it was almost like he was trying to change his roots and be like some kind of big shot city person from up North. That made me hate him all the more.

"You know, you can't get away with this," I shouted, as someone held my arms from behind. "We lied to Shelly about not talking to the police. They know all about you. We told them everything before coming over here. I'm sure they'll be driving up any minute now. You just wait and see."

Once again, all three of them laughed out loud. Mr. Bradey reached down, took my chin in his hand and just stared at me. Without seeing it coming, he slapped the top of my head real hard. Whatever he did, hurt something awful.

"Sorry to disappoint you, Matt, but Charlie over there was

parked out in front of the police station since late last night when we heard you guys stopped over here," Bradey described. "He was just waiting to see if you boys would show up. As it turned out, he just got back from there only a few minutes ago. According to him, since last night, no one except a bunch of cops have gone in or come out of that station. There was no sign of you boys, that's for sure. You know, it was real nice of you three to follow through with your promise to Shelly. For the life of us, we wouldn't have known where the hell to look for you. That would have made things so much more complicated."

"We didn't visit the police in person," I continued my lie, in a desperate attempt to convince them. "We called them on the phone and told them everything. They know all about you and the people you murdered."

"Well, there you go again," said Bradey, shaking his head as if disappointed. "I just don't think so! You see, a while back I used to live near this town. I know those boys at the station real, real good. Used to hunt with some of them—still do sometimes. One of my buddies there, who works the grave-yard shift, told me this morning there were no calls last night. He was sitting there by the phone all evening so he'd be the one to take it. So once again, I caught you lying to me. You know I really don't like it when you do that."

He grabbed my chin again, this time squeezing it so hard I thought my jaw was going to crumble. I tried to pull away, but his grip was too tight.

"Oh, and by the way, I have another little question for you," he continued. "When Charlie drove up a few minutes ago from the station, he said he recognized a car up the road that looked very familiar. He parked right behind it actually. Swore to me he'd seen that piss green, poor excuse for a car somewhere before. Charlie, didn't you say you saw that car somewhere?"

"Yes, boss," he replied back with a smile. "I reckon I have."

"So where was it that you saw that piece of shit?" Bradey asked as he continued taunting me. His obnoxious way of asking questions that he already knew the answers to, was really irritating.

"Um, didn't we see it parked along the side of the road, kinda near that cave we visited last night," Charlie replied. He obviously liked it when Bradey included him in these little mind games.

"Now, isn't that very, very interesting," replied Bradey sarcastically. "A few moments ago, I heard you tell Shelly you followed us here. And now we know you were also near Bowden's Cave. Now, that's really a very big coincidence. Unless, of course, maybe you boys have been following us all along. Yes, I think you must have been following us for a long while, which means that you know so much more about us than we know about you. Am I right about that, Mr. Matt? How about telling me what you really know about us. I think we'd all be very interested in what you had to say. Wouldn't we boys?"

Mr. Bradey had this nasty habit of spitting whenever he talked. Every three or four sentences, he'd splatter my face with a small glob of white goo. As much as I wanted to wipe it off, I couldn't seem to induce my hand to move up in that direction. It was frozen by my side.

"Well, boy?" he asked, leaning toward me. "What do you have to say?"

I didn't answer. My brain couldn't focus on anything. These guys had already slaughtered two people that I knew of, they had threatened to kill me and my family, and they had beaten Mark pretty bad. My mind was way beyond the point of just merely feeling overwhelmed, as the stress of our present predicament increased by the second.

"Cat got your tongue, boy?" asked Bradey, with that snide tone of his. "Well, I guess if you were out there last night, you probably know all about our little package delivery. I should have figured it out earlier. It wasn't until I heard about that junk car of yours this morning that it finally came together." He paced back and forth like a seasoned interrogator, while he thought about what to say next. "You know something, you boys got a lot of balls. I respect that. Over the years, a whole lot of people have tried to catch me doing all kinds of things, but I don't think anyone has gotten as close as you have. I must say, I'm pretty damn impressed. I mean, you know about the fisherman, you know about that low-life Carter, you even mentioned on the phone something about Nepal. If you hadn't come here, I'd probably be on my way to prison right this very minute. Isn't it funny how beautiful woman always get in the way of our plans."

Mr. Bradey's little speech about how much he admired us reminded me of those corny old World War II movies. The triumphant general raves about how much he respected his captured counterpart for putting up such a commendable fight, right before taking him out in the back to deliver a bullet to the head.

Just then, something compelled Mr. Keller to get up from his seat and stroll over to where Bradey was standing.

"Okay, Bradey," Keller declared impatiently. "Enough is enough. Pick that one up off the floor and put him back on the couch and let's get on with this thing."

Charlie and Bubha came around, picked Mark off the floor and tossed him next to me on the couch. I noticed there was still some blood trickling from his nose. I had never seen his body so placid before—he looked half dead. I watched closely to see if I could determine some sign of his condition. His head tilted in my

177

direction for a second and I saw something that totally amazed me—he winked several times. It was obvious that Mark was pretending to be hurt worse than he was, maybe to throw them off guard. He must have had some kind of plan, I thought to myself. I wondered if he still had that gun with him.

"Well, then," Keller started with a heavy southern accent. He cleared his throat several times before going on—as if he were about to begin a long speech. "I'm afraid you boys have created a little trouble for me. You see, I'm what you might call a powerful man in these here parts. I run my own business, have good relations with a whole lot of important people, and I can't have anyone going around saying harmful things about me or my friends. Your phone call yesterday really had me bothered, if you know what I mean. If any of this ever got out, it would be very embarrassing for me, my family and my business associates. That's why it's a good thing that we found out about you boys before it got out of hand. You should have just left this thing alone—just dropped it from the beginning. You really don't know what you've gotten yourselves into here." He paused for a moment before continuing. "Well, then, now that I've said this, I don't want to play any more games with you three. I want to hear what you know and I want to hear it right this second. So let's stop with all of this funny business and just get down to it. Okay?"

"If I tell you what you want to know, will you let us go?" I asked, knowing I'd never get an honest answer to this question.

"Well, let me put it this way," Keller explained, after thinking it over. "If you don't start talking pretty soon, you're not going anywhere—maybe ever again. Do you understand what I'm saying, boy? Now, let's just get down to business here."

"That's not good enough," I replied back defiantly. "I want you to tell me what you plan on doing with us or I ain't saying nothin."

"I don't think you're in a position to demand anything, you little shit," said Keller, trying hard to hold back his anger. "I'm telling you, you're in a heap of trouble here. You'd better just do what I tell you and watch that mouth of yours. You hear? Or I'm really going to get fired up. And trust me on this one boy, you don't want that to happen."

Keller nodded to Charlie who took his gun and pointed it to the side of Thad's head. Thad was in no condition to say anything. In fact, through his swollen eyes, I'm not even sure he knew the gun was there. As for Mark, he was still doubled over on the couch. It looked as if it were all up to me.

Before saying anything, I tried to work out in my mind how much information to reveal. I had to tell them enough to satisfy their curiosity, without making it look as if we knew more than we did. It was only after Charlie cocked the trigger on the pistol, that the words began pouring out of my mouth, almost involuntarily.

"Okay, okay I get the message," I said frantically. "Well, you see, it all started last week. Last Friday, um, we set out to go to Mark's uncle's cabin inside the park. When we got into the woods, we somehow got lost and weren't able to find the place, so we decided to head home. As we were walking through the woods, we spotted these guys by the campfire." I pointed toward Bubha, Charlie and Mr. Bradey. "When we saw that they had guns and stuff, we tried to circle around, but they heard us. Mark had to jump Mr. Bradey because he was coming right toward us. Me and Thad ran off and we all met at Mark's truck. Two of them, I don't know which ones, must have followed Mark. They shot at us as we were driving away."

Mr. Keller looked at Bradey, smiled and then came over to me and slapped my face. He hit me so hard that I fell to the floor. I could taste a small drop of blood forming on my lip. For some reason, instead of frightening me, it made me real pissed off. Something deep inside was beginning to bubble with rage. I really wanted to hurt that fucker. This guy was playing with my life. He was threatening to snatch something away that wasn't his to take.

"I'm afraid you didn't start from the very beginning," said Keller without any real emotion. "You failed to mention how you knew about Carter. In that phone call of yours, you mentioned something about seeing him get killed. And what about the fishing line and that torn T-shirt you put around his dead body. Now, I'd like you to please start from the beginning and stop screwing around with me or I'll be forced to do something ugly. Do you understand me, boy?"

"Okay, okay, actually, we didn't see Mr. Carter get killed," I said softly. Keller lifted his hand to strike my face again. "Wait, wait, wait! We didn't see him get killed. We found his body in the woods. We had settled in for the night at this camp site after we got lost. When Mark went to take a piss, he found Carter sprawled out dead. We got real scared so we decided to head on home. We put that fishing line up to mark the spot for the police. I swear, that's what happened."

"I don't think I believe you, boy," said Keller with a disappointed expression across his face. He shook his head several times as if to indicate that what I was saying didn't quite add up. "I think you're lying to me again. If you didn't see him killed, why were you trying to blackmail us?"

I had to think for a moment. They already knew my sister's car was near the cave site. I had to tell them the truth. What else could I do? They had me cornered.

"Um, actually, we made up that blackmailing story to get your guys to go after Carter's body," I said reluctantly. "I once saw someone do this on a TV show—you know, that show Columbo? We weren't after any money. Honest!! That Friday night we found Carter, we called the cops and told them about his body in the woods. We didn't leave our names because we didn't want to get all wrapped up in this thing. The next day we read the papers and realized that someone had changed bodies on us. Since we thought the cops might eventually figure out that we were there, we wanted to find a way to clear our names. If we went to the police and told them about finding Carter in the woods, and we couldn't locate him, they'd think we were making it all up. We thought they'd think we killed that guy from Bantum—that fisherman. We needed to find Carter's body first. So after making those phone calls yesterday morning, we waited in Front Royal for Bradey and the others to drive to Elkins and we just followed them there."

"So you called us up and these three led you straight to the body?" he asked, somewhat surprised. "So that's why you boys were parked near the cave. You must have seen everything then?"

Keller said nothing for a long time before turning toward Bradey and this time slapping his face. This unexpected turn of events really took me by surprise. Why would he hit one of his own, I wondered.

"You moron," he shouted, waving his hands in all directions as he spoke. "You call yourself a god damn soldier and you let a couple of zit-faced kids fool you into leading them straight to that body and you didn't even know they were there? I ought to kick your sorry ass right back to Virginia. God damn it. This really burns me up. Shit, what the hell am I paying you for?"

It was obvious that Bradey was furious by this direct assault on his character. He was not accustomed to having his competence questioned, certainly not so publicly. He glared at me with such hatred, it sent a shiver up and down my spine. His eyes were calling out to me, letting me know that at some point, not right away, but later, he'd seek his revenge. I knew he wanted to have a piece of me right then and there.

"Well, that explains a few things," said Keller, shaking his head in amazement. "So tell me, how did you find out about me then?"

"We have Carter's schedule book," I confessed. "We went through it and found out that he was supposed to meet with you the day he died."

"What? Where did you get his schedule book from?" he asked with his eyes clearly expressing disbelief. "He didn't have it with him that day. Are you lying to me again?"

I hesitated for an instant before answering. I was surprised that Shelly hadn't mentioned to Keller our first meeting with her. She knew we had that book with us. Maybe she forgot.

"I said, where the hell did you get that god damn schedule book from?" he continued, wanting an answer immediately. "Okay, go ahead and plug his friend then if he doesn't want to talk."

Thad gasped after hearing this directive. It sounded like he stopped breathing. I was afraid he'd die from sheer terror. Once again, the words just started spilling out.

"Wait, wait, wait," I shouted. "I got it from his briefcase."

"His briefcase? He didn't have a briefcase with him either."

"We didn't find it with him. We found it later in his motel room." I knew what he was about to ask me, so I answered before he had a chance to say it. "Let me explain. After finding Carter in the woods, we took his wallet to give to the police. When we read in the newspaper that they didn't find his body, we went through the wallet and found a credit card slip which had the name of the motel he was staying at. He was paid up for three or four days. It was the Gateway over on Main Street. Anyway, I went over to the motel and managed to talk myself inside his room. That's where we got the schedule book, from his briefcase."

"Of course, his briefcase," said Keller, full of optimism. "So what else was in the case?"

"A bunch of papers and some other stuff."

"What kinds of papers and other stuff?" he insisted, as his anticipation began to rise.

"Nothing really, just papers."

"There you go again," Keller replied, irritated by my vagueness. "You seem to have forgotten about that little phone call you made to me yesterday morning. You said you knew about Nepal and specifically mentioned Gorkha District. Well then, how did you know about that? Did those papers have that information in them? Huh?"

"Well, actually, there were a few newspaper articles about something stolen from Nepal—some old thing. We guessed it had something to do with Carter going back and forth to India and Nepal all the time."

"And how did you know he went back and forth to India and Nepal?" Keller seemed to be very intrigued by the many pieces we were able to fit together.

"His schedule book had all of that stuff in it," I replied. "You know, dates when trips were taken."

"Okay now, once again, I want you to stop for a moment and tell me everything you found in that case of his. And I mean everything."

"Um, well, like I said, there were those newspaper articles. Oh, and there were also a handful of photographs of old stuff from India and other places—all kinds of bowls, cups and statues. Some of them had the name of the object, where it was bought, and how much it cost written across the back."

"Photographs?" asked Keller, clearly interested. "That's it! He always photographed everything for his records. Where are these photos now?" The way he reacted, I could tell that these pictures were somehow very important to him.

"We hid them away with the other stuff from the briefcase," I said, as I reexamined our situation. "We put them in a place where someone would look, if something were to ever happen to us."

"Where?" he demanded, grabbing me by the collar and shaking me hard. "You better tell me now or I'll have to take care of your friends. You hear me? Now where are those god damn photos?"

"Fuck you!" I replied back defiantly. "If you touch any of us again, I swear to god, you'll never see them. You got that?"

It occurred to me from his passionate reaction, that Keller might want those photos bad enough to bargain with us. He let go of my collar and just stared at me before turning around and walking back to his chair. I tried to remember what the photos looked like. There were about fifteen or twenty of them in the pile. Then, all at once it hit me.

"So, you want the picture of the stolen urn from Nepal, don't you?" I asked, hoping that my guess was on the mark. The expression on his face confirmed my hunch.

"Yes, I want that picture," Keller admitted angrily. "So, I imagine you also know about the three urns and the little game that Mr. Carter tried to play on us to acquire more money. That greedy bastard. You seem to know every other detail."

My blank expression betrayed my lack of knowledge on this particular subject. He once again stood up and walked over to where I was sitting.

"So, you don't know about that, do you?" he asked, studying my face. "Well, then I'll tell you anyway. I paid Carter a large sum of money to acquire a special object from Nepal for one of my business associates overseas. This particular object, which is known as the "Gorkha Urn," was just wasting away in a tiny, insignificant village in the middle of nowhere. After arranging to bring it to the States, Mr. Carter decided that our agreement wasn't good enough for him. So instead of giving me just one urn, he gave me three of them which looked nearly identical. Although one of them was quite precious—the other two were ordinary and had no value to anyone. To squeeze more money out of me, Carter decided that he should be paid an outrageous fee for identifying which one was the original. Well, somehow things got out of hand and after a heated argument, Carter got hurt—badly hurt. I assure you it was an unfortunate accident that was not meant to happen. So now you can see why I would be very interested in seeing those photos. They may help me to identify the original piece from the rest."

For the life of me, I couldn't understand why Mr. Keller would confess all of this. He could have said that he wanted the photographs without mentioning any of the details. As far as I was concerned, he made a grave error in doing so. I now knew I was in a position to work out some kind of horsetrade.

"So then, maybe we can make a deal with you. You let the three of us go and we'll give you your precious photos and the briefcase. It's the only way you'll ever get what you want from us. Take it or leave it!"

I sensed Bradey took offense that I would make such an audacious statement. It was clear that he still hadn't gotten over my embarrassing him.

"You're not going to let this punk talk to you like that, are you?" asked Bradey, lifting his hand to strike me again. Keller reached up and gently lowered it down.

"Let's hear what the boy has to say," he announced. Before continuing, he sat down in one of the chairs across from us. "I'm a reasonable man. So what do you propose?"

"I know you want us all out of the way. I don't want to die so I'll promise that we'll give you the pictures and anything else that belongs to Carter. In return, you'll have to let us go. All three of us will swear to never say anything to anyone ever. Honest!"

All of the men except Keller laughed out loud at my suggestion. Keller just sat back and stared into my eyes.

"What makes you think we want you 'out of the way'?" he asked gently. "You're just boys. We don't want to bring any harm to you three. Like I said, Carter's unfortunate death was an accident. That's all. We never meant to bring him any harm."

"Yeah, bull shit," I hollered, pointing to Mark. "Just like your goon friend accidentally beat the shit out of him. And explain this to me, how do you accidentally shot someone in the god damn back? If you didn't think we had anything, you'd have killed us long ago. We may be young, but we're not totally stupid. Besides, two minutes ago you threatened to shoot Thad in the head. So don't give me any of that crap."

Keller quickly switched subjects. His credibility on this score was not very convincing.

"So according to your little plan, if we let you go, what's going to prevent you from telling the police everything you know?" asked Keller. "You can just head over there any time and tell them about Carter and Nepal, and what could we possibly do about it? How could we trust you three to keep up your end of the deal?"

"If we tell them anything, then you can come after us, right? Like I told you before, we don't want to be dead. We've got our whole lives ahead of us."

"But if you tell them, we'll be the ones in jail, won't we? How are we supposed to come after you if we're all behind bars?"

"You said before that you had lots of friends everywhere," I reminded him. "I'm sure you'd find a way to get back at us. Wouldn't you? So we just wouldn't ever say anything, that's all.'"

Bradey came up and whispered something into Keller's ear. Those evil eyes of his just glared at me as he spoke. I was sure I didn't want to go along with whatever plan he'd come up with. He was the type of person who wanted to finish things off once and for all—no loose ends. His way would have been to shoot one of us in an attempt to get the rest to tell him what he needed to know.

"Okay," said Keller reluctantly. "We'll make a deal with you. You give us the briefcase and anything else you have related to Carter and we'll let you go unharmed."

Bradey's mood seemed to have transformed into something different—he was more relaxed than before. This made me feel even more uneasy.

"That's it?" I asked surprised. "You're going to let us go just like that?"

"That's all there is to it," said Keller, opening his arms. "All we want is the briefcase and those photos. Course, you'll have to stick to your end of the bargain."

"And what's going to prevent you from going back on your word?" I finally asked. "I mean you can come after us just as easy as we can go and tell the police."

"You're just going to have to trust us," he said with a forced smile. "I'm an honorable man. And besides, you really don't have much of a choice, do you? We're going to just have to trust each other on this one."

"So, what now?"

"It's pretty easy," said Keller, pointing toward the door. "You go and get the stuff and after giving them to us we'll let you all go."

"You mean we can all just walk out that door right now?" I asked, hoping to further clarify our position.

"Don't be ridiculous," Keller answered. "You go and get it and then we'll let your friends leave only after you hand it over to Mr. Bradey."

"I can't do this alone," I insisted. "I need Thad to come with me. He knows where everything is hidden."

I thought it was best to get Thad out of there as soon as possible. With him out of the way, I was sure Mark could escape on his own. Thad looked like he was on the verge of some kind of nervous breakdown. His entire body was quivering as if he were naked in a winter storm. I had never seen anyone look so terrified. His skin was the color of white milk.

"No, I'm sorry I can't let you do that," said Keller. "He stays here. You go alone. I'm sure you'll manage to locate what you're looking for."

"But why not?" I persisted. "You'll still have Mark."

"Because I said so, that's why," he replied in a stern, uncompromising voice.

"Then let Thad go alone. I'll stay here."

I could sense that Thad was grateful that I was trying to get him out of there. For a moment, his body stopped quivering as he waited for Keller's response. I couldn't believe how noble I was being.

"Sorry," said Keller. "I don't trust him. He's more concerned about himself than you two. He stays. And by the way, you have exactly one hour to collect everything. That includes the address book and anything else you may have taken from Carter. After you've found them, I want you to call here and we'll tell you where the exchange will take place." Keller turned around and motioned with his hand that he wanted Bradey to give him a pen. He then wrote out a number and handed it to me.

"Why don't I just come back here?" I asked.

"Because we won't be here, that's why. This is to prevent you from making a run for it and going to the police and bringing them back."

"So where should I meet you then? I need to know."

"We'll let you know later. Now get going. Your one hour begins starting now."

"I need more time," I pleaded. "One hour just isn't enough time."

"That's all the time you have," said Keller. "If you don't call us in one hour I'm afraid your friends . . . and one more thing. Mr. Bradey is going to follow along. If you try anything foolish he'll radio back and your friends will be finished. You understand me?"

"No way, no way in hell," I blurted out. "If he comes along with me I have nothing to bargain with. What's to stop him from taking it right away and . . . no way. If I so much as see any of your men when I'm out there, the deal is off. Either I do this completely on my own or I'm not doing it at all." They must have really thought I was a complete idiot to suggest such a ridiculous thing.

Mr. Keller walked over to Bradey, led him to the other side of the room and began talking with him. They both turned their backs on us. At the same time, Bubha and Charlie didn't seem to be paying any attention to anything. Seeing an opportunity, I slowly leaned over to see if I could get away with talking to Mark. To my surprise, no one stopped me.

"Are you okay?" I whispered.

"I'll live . . . I hope," he whispered back. "What are you

going to do?"

"I haven't a clue," I admitted. "If we bring them Carter's stuff, they're going to do us all." All at once a possible solution to all of our problems flashed through my mind. "Do you have that gun with you now?"

"No, it's in the car." I could tell that Mark would have killed to have had that gun with him at that moment—literally.

"Shit," I replied. "That could have offered some hope."

"Forget about that," Mark insisted. "I don't care what he said about letting us go. It's never going to happen. Find those things and go straight to the police. They might be able to work with you to track us down. I'll do my best to see if I can manage to escape with Thad."

"It's too risky," I replied. "There has to be another way."

"That's the only way," he insisted. "They're never going to let us walk. You said so yourself."

"I know," I said reluctantly as I checked to see if Keller and Bradey were still talking. They were. "I may have another plan. When I get into your garage, I'm going to write up everything we know about these guys and put it on top of your father's tool box. If something happens to us, at least someone will know who to look for. That could also be our little insurance policy. If they don't let us go after we give them what they want, I'll tell them about the note and maybe that will convince them. Is there any paper around in your garage?"

"Look in the top drawer of the tool bench," he suggested. "There's always paper in there. Listen, as part of the exchange, don't give them everything. Hide the address book somewhere. Put it with the letter. You can use both things to bargain with later. I know they're going to double-cross you. And watch out for Bradey. I'm sure he's going to try and follow you. Don't let him or we're all dead."

"Oh, I almost forgot. Where's all of Carter's shit hidden?"

"It's behind the tool bench, covered with an old blanket," Mark explained. "Wherever you go, take the gun along. Use it if you have to."

"Is anyone home now?" I asked.

"No, everyone's at the flea market. They . . ."

"Hey, cut that out," yelled Bradey as he turned and noticed us talking together. "What the hell's wrong with you guys? Are you crazy letting them talk like that? Now shut them up."

Charlie and Bubha came over and separated us.

As I left the house a few minutes later, I wondered if that was the last time I'd ever see my two best friends again.

11

I slowly opened the door and climbed into my sister's car. With trembling hands, it took me several attempts to insert the key into the ignition. Much of the mental energy I had used to maintain some semblance of control inside the house suddenly evaporated, and for the first time in many years, I broke down and sobbed like a small child who had lost something precious. I not only cried because my friends were still in danger—I also cried because my world felt like it was crumbling around me on all sides. My reality was no longer a playground for all of the wonderful things that were going to happen to me. All of a sudden everything took on a new face—it was now rough and coarse with jagged edges to be feared. Reality's ugliness, which had always been lurking around every corner, finally revealed itself to me. I felt compelled to look over my shoulder for the first time in my life.

I managed to somehow pull myself together when I realized that time was wasting. I still couldn't believe they actually allowed me to walk out of there alive. I was free! At some level, my most basic instincts kept telling me to just run away. To head off in any direction and drive to some place safe. I wanted to forget about briefcases, photographs, and urns from far away lands and the danger which hovered over such things, and just get on with my life as a teenager living in a small town in West Virginia. But it was too late for all of that. The sinister cloud which surrounded such things had already penetrated that little bubble which used to shelter a person like me. There was no escaping it.

I forced myself to start the car and drive off. Fearing that Bradey might try to follow me, I had one eye glued to the rear-view mirror the whole time. I pulled down a few small side streets just to make sure I didn't miss him. By this point, my fear had transformed itself into acute paranoia. As far as I was concerned, every car was suspect. I saw Bradey's face in every person behind a steering wheel who passed by. After reaching Cross Street, I doubled back down the alley behind the Agway Farm Supply depot and then stopped in front of Ben's liquor store. There was no sign of him anywhere.

I was surprised at the number of people out and about that morning. Some were coming from church, while others seemed to be doing a bit of shopping at the convenience stores scattered around town. More than a few I knew waved at me as I drove past. For some reason, I couldn't bring myself to wave back.

As much as I wanted to do the right thing, it took all the courage I could muster to drive in the direction of Mark's house. Throughout my entire life, whenever I had a major problem, I'd go running to my parents. There was a certain security in knowing that they'd always be there for me. But this time they couldn't help. It was up to me to decide how to proceed. I really felt like I was on my own for the first time in my life and I didn't trust myself to make the right decision. I wanted someone there to verify that going to Mark's garage instead of the police station was the right thing to do, but there was no one I could turn to.

Another five minutes passed before arriving at Mark's place. His family lived in a relatively remote area—their nearest neighbors were separated by a stretch of forest on either side. Both his parents relished their privacy. His dad's truck was gone, but his mom's station wagon was parked in its usual place. I could tell from the way the curtains were drawn that no one was home. I had seen his mother go through her "departure" ritual enough times to spot the tell-tale signs.

Instead of parking directly in front of the house, I drove past and turned down an old gravel logging road which provided a bit of cover. I took one more look around before leaving the safety of the car. The gun Mark stole was stuffed down my front pocket. I wondered whether I'd be forced to use it.

I started walking along the side of the road towards Mark's house, but then decided it would be much safer if I cut through the woods. Luckily Mark's garage was located near the back of the yard, far from the house and the main road. Actually, the structure was more like a storage shed than a garage. Mark's dad built it years ago to house all of the accumulating junk the family no longer needed, but was unable to bring themselves to throw away. Mark only took it over after buying that dilapidated truck of his. Since the thing broke down nearly every other week, he needed a place to repair it which would protect him from the elements.

For as long as anyone could remember, Mark's mom always complained about how ugly the shed looked. To hide it from the rest of the world, his dad finally broke down and planted a bunch of hemlock trees all around it. Years later, these trees had nearly engulfed the entire structure.

As I stood outside the shed, I took one final look around to see if anyone was stalking me—there was no sign of life anywhere. I used the side door to enter because it was more secluded from the road. I reached up, snatched the key from above the door frame, and undid the lock. Nearly everyone in town knew about that key. There was not much need for security in Elkins. no one ever stole anything in this neighborhood.

I pushed open the door and desperately searched for the light switch. It took me more than a few tries to finally locate the lever. Even after visiting the garage nearly a million times, I still had trouble finding the god damn thing. For some reason, it always seemed to be in a different place. I locked the door behind me.

There were piles of junk everywhere—bicycles, lawn mowers, patio furniture, truck parts—to name a few. Mark, much like his father, was incapable of throwing anything away. He could always come up with a hundred reasons why something might be needed someday in the future. After negotiating my way around a maze of debris scattered all over the floor, I finally arrived safely at my destination, his tool bench.

The briefcase, which Mark had stashed behind the bench, was relatively easy to locate. After removing this horrible, smelly blanket which was draped over the back of the bench, I stuck my hand down behind there and blindly felt around for it. I cringed at the thought of all the years of crud I must have touched as my fingers fumbled around aimlessly. At last, I managed to find the handle and bring up the case from behind.

With Carter's things now in my possession, it was time to move on to Plan B. As it turned out, it took me forever to get my hands on a few sheets of paper to write down our story. Mark had told me to look in the top drawer of his tool bench, but all I found was a collection of oil stained newspapers, a half pint of blackberry brandy and a few vintage Playboys he had stashed there to hide from his mom. After nearly giving up hope, I searched in Mark's truck and discovered his math notebook stuffed under the front seat. Not surprising, there was nothing written in it so I decided to use it to document our little adventure.

Like many students in town, I was never all that good at whipping up an essay. I'd always freeze when put under pressure and this time was no exception. Nothing at all was coming. I knew how important it was to write everything, but I just couldn't manage to get a single word down on paper. As the minutes continued to soar by, I became more and more panicky. What the hell was I supposed to do? They only gave me an hour and I had already used up more than half of that time.

Then, as if my worst nightmare had come to life, something totally unexpected happened—I heard the sound of people walking along the gravel driveway in the direction of the shed. Who could that be, I wondered. Mark's family never returned from the flea market until after five. Could it be them—Bradey or one of his goons? Could they have followed me here somehow? I knew if they caught me with Carter's briefcase, I'd be as good as dead.

I frantically looked around, realizing there were only three ways out of the garage—through the side door which I came in, the front door which would have taken too much time to unbolt, or out a window. As I tried desperately to decide what to do next, I could hear whoever it was approaching the side door. It was lucky for me that I remembered to lock it earlier.

Without a moment to spare, I decided my only chance was the window. But after pulling it open, I came to realize the bushes surrounding the shed had grown so close, it would have been nearly impossible to escape without getting caught. Instead, as if a guiding angel had come along and offered me a way out, I found myself dropping to the floor with Carter's briefcase in hand. I then quietly crawled under Mark's truck. I had seen this move used in the movies a dozen times. It was the only thing that came to mind at such short notice.

Someone gently jiggled the handle a few times before finally kicking the door open. From where I was lying, I could see two pairs of shoes just standing there by the entrance. There seemed to be an endless pause before anything happened. I couldn't help but wonder if they heard me scurrying around inside.

"Shit, where the hell is he?" shouted Bradey, totally surprised at not finding me. "Look over there. He couldn't have gotten out of here without us seeing him. We've been outside since he arrived."

One of them made his way around Mark's truck in the direction of the open window. His shoes made a squeaky sound every time he took a step. He nearly tripped several times as he tried to avoid all the piles of junk scattered across the floor. At one point, he was literally standing less than a yard away from me. The dust stirred up as he walked nearly caused me to sneeze. My heart raced out of control as I tried desperately to hold it back.

Realizing how desperate my situation had become, I pointed the pistol right at his foot. I figured if I had to, I'd shoot him there first and then after he fell, I'd pop him again in the chest. I'd shot guns many times before, but the thought of shooting another human being had me totally freaked out.

"He must have climbed out over here, boss," said Charlie. He stuck his head out the window to see if there was any sign of me. "This window is wide open. Maybe he heard us coming. I'll bet he's on his way to that car of his. It's a good thing you took his keys."

I reached down and felt my front pocket. I completely forgot I left the keys in the ignition in case I had to get out of there in a hurry. Obviously, they discovered my sister's car parked down that road.

"God damn shit," said Bradey, grinding his teeth with rage. "I swear, I'm going to kill that kid with my bare hands when I catch him." I could hear him kicking things all around as I struggled desperately to maintain my sanity.

"So what do you want to do now?" asked Charlie. "Do you think he's going to that other guy's house? Does his wallet have the address in it?"

It was obvious they had used Mark's license to track down his house. That possibility never occurred to me.

"I don't know," Bradey snapped back, throwing Mark's wallet against the wall. He didn't say anything for a while as he contemplated his next move. "Okay now, this is what I want you to do. Take that piece of shit car of his and drive it over to the cave with the others. And for god sake find a way to hide it in the woods someplace. We'll get rid of it later. I'm going to park in front of the police station to see if he shows up there. Oh, and I want you to stop somewhere and call Shelly. Find out if he's contacted her yet. If he hasn't, tell her to give him my cellular phone number. I'll swing by the motel and pick up the phone on my way to the station."

"What's the number?" asked Charlie.

"You stupid fool. How can you not know that number? Idiot. It's 245-9945. Now write it down."

"Um, I don't have a pen."

"God damn it," said Bradey, throwing his pen at Charlie, who used it to write the number on his hand.

"Boss, why don't you call Shelly," Charlie suggested. "You know what to say better than I do."

"Because I don't have my phone with me now and I asked you to do it. Okay?"

Charlie didn't say anything for a while. Bradey was extremely pissed off. He knew enough not to push, especially when his boss was teetering on the edge of completely going ballistic on him.

"What do you think that kid's going to do now?" Charlie finally asked, in an attempt to change the subject. "Do you really think he'll go to the cops?"

"Hell if I know," Bradey exclaimed, a bit calmer. "But I don't think he'll go to them. This one's not stupid. He knows we're serious about hurting his friends. I'm sure he'll probably try to make some kind of deal with us. Now get going before it gets too late. And make that call immediately."

"What about his buddies?" asked Charlie. "What do we do with them?"

"Don't do anything until I tell you. We still need them for now. Just hole up in the cave. I'll figure something out later."

"You know, there's one other thing. Keller's going to be really furious that this kid got away from us."

"Screw Keller," said Bradey. "Him and his god damn old junk. We're in the defense business. He never should have made a deal to steal that thing in the first place. If he had just paid

Carter that extra money, none of this would have happened. Cheap bastard. Now, let's just get the hell out of here."

I waited for a long time before I could muster up the nerve to climb out from under Mark's truck. It felt safe under there. After finally doing so, I realized my shirt was completely drenched with a combination of motor oil and transmission fluid from the truck's multiple leaks. Unfortunately, that was the least of my troubles.

So they had no intention of keeping their side of the bargain, I thought to myself. They were coming to finish me off for sure. Now that I knew what to expect, I felt I needed to re-think my next move. I immediately made my way over to the tool bench and opened the briefcase to see what was inside once again. I flipped through the pictures and located what Keller was so excited about—photos depicting three different urns. It was easy to see his dilemma. They were all nearly identical in size, shape, texture and color. On the backside of each photo was written the location where it came from. Two were from Lalitpur District, Nepal, while the third one came from Gorkha District. That was the stolen one. I inspected the photos more carefully, noticing that the Gorkha urn had a tiny arrow pointing to a V-shaped crack along the rim. There were no other obvious differences which could have distinguished them apart.

I looked at my watch and noticed it had already been nearly an hour since I left Shelly's house. Realizing that I needed to do something fast, I collected all of the photos, stuffed them back into the case, grabbed one of Mark's work shirts to cover my oil stained clothes and headed off in the direction of my sister's car, just to make sure. As expected, Charlie had driven off with it. It looked like I was on foot for the time being.

It occurred to me that if I walked around town with a briefcase in my hand, it might look a bit odd to people I knew. So I decided to find a suitable hiding place for Carter's stuff other than the garage. It didn't take me long to come up with the perfect location—an old tree fort in the woods behind Mark's house. When we were kids, we used to spend much of our time playing inside there.

It had been nearly five years since I last climbed up those rickety wooden steps to the platform up above. With every step, the recollection of the many hours spent there seemed to come flooding back. I remembered the day we decided to build the structure. How we wandered around scouring the neighborhood for old scraps of wood. How Thad's mother found out and forbid him from ever going up there because she felt it was unsafe. And then there was the time we all had our first cigarette together. Thad got sick as a dog and nearly fell off the edge. As all these old memories drifted in and out of my mind, the need to rescue my friends became even more compelling. It was all up to me—I couldn't let them down.

I climbed inside our little sanctuary from the outside world. To my surprise, it seemed incredibly small. I always remembered it to be so spacious. Before hiding the briefcase in one of the corners, I retrieved one of the imitation urn photos and Carter's address book. The rest I stashed there to bargain with at a later time, if necessary. I figured if they knew I had at least one of the photos, they'd believe I could also produce the other two.

Since I couldn't trust Bradey to honor his part of any agreement, I decided to see if I could rescue Mark and Thad from the cave by myself. I had two things in my favor—a loaded gun and the element of surprise. They didn't know I overheard their conversation in the garage. If worse came to worse and I got caught, I figured I could always whip out the photo and hope for the best. No matter what I did, they were going to try to double-cross me anyway, so I had to be prepared.

To pull off my plan, I first needed to get Bradey out of the picture. He was too crafty and unpredictable. I decided to call him and set up a bogus appointment to meet someplace in town. While he waited, I'd head over to the cave. Once Mark and Thad were freed, we'd all drive off to Bantum or some other town, and report what was going on to the police. There was no other option. After working out the details in my mind, I ran back to Mark's house to use the phone. Although I knew where the key to the house was hidden, I used a small rock to break one of the back door windows to make it look like a robbery. I also decided to take his mother's car. There was no other way to get my hands on a set of wheels in such a short time. This would also indirectly get the police involved as they searched for the stolen vehicle.

Per Bradey's instructions, I called Shelly's house first. I was afraid if I didn't make the call straightaway, they might do something to my friends. I tried to hold back the rage I felt for that bitch as I dialed the number.

"Hello, hello?" asked Shelly, after picking up the receiver. "Who is this?"

"It's Matt," I responded back coldly. There was a long pause before she finally said anything. I could tell she felt more than a little awkward talking to me after all that happened.

"Where are you?" she asked nervously. "You know you didn't follow through with your part of the deal. You were supposed to call back within an hour."

"Screw you, lady," I remarked, full of hatred. "Look who's talking about fulfilling deals. I suppose you heard that your two pals, Mr. Bradey and Charlie, from Keller's little goon squad came looking for me. Let's just say that held me up a bit."

"I was told to give you a number to call," she said, ignoring my comment. "It's 245-99 . . ."

"I want my friends to be let go," I demanded, before she could finish. "And if anything happens to them, I swear on my grandmother's grave you'll all rot in jail for the rest of your lives, if I don't kill you first."

"Mr. Keller gave his word to you. If you give us those photos they can go. If you hadn't run off like you did, they'd be free by now. Mr. Bradey was only trying to save time by . . ."

"Are you for real?" I yelled over the receiver. "You really believe they're going to let us go, just like that?"

"Why not?" she asked naively.

"Because they're all killers, that's why," I replied angrily. "They've already killed two people that we know about and they also want us dead."

"I don't believe you," she said with a certain degree of hesitation in her voice. "Who did they kill?"

"They killed your good friend Carter and they also killed that fisherman who happened to be in the wrong place at the wrong time. Don't tell me you don't know anything about that."

There was another prolonged lull. I sensed from the way she was breathing that what I said upset her.

"I don't believe a word you're saying," she admitted. It sounded like she was confused. She had that shaking sound to her voice. "Carter's not dead. He left a message for me on my answering machine, just yesterday. He's in India. And I know you and your sick friends killed that other man. I saw the proof."

"They told you that?" I asked surprised. "They're lying to you. They want you to believe that we are some kind of sadistic monsters, but we didn't do anything. They killed that poor guy and they're trying to frame us for his death."

"I said I saw the proof," she repeated herself.

"What proof?" I demanded. "What the hell did you see?"

"They found your friend's glasses at the scene of the crime—the one with the thick lenses. I saw them myself. Mr. Bradey also told me he saw you carrying out some kind of ceremony right after killing that man. That's why they chased after you that night. They were only going to catch you so they could turn you over to the police."

"Are you for real?" I vented out loud. "How stupid can you be? I don't know who the hell left a message on your machine, but it wasn't Carter. Check it out. Go ahead and contact him in India, you'll never find him cause he's dead. And as for your so called proof, sure we were there, but we found your friend Carter dead, not that other guy. That other man was killed later and then placed nearby our camp site to frame us. Carter's body was moved someplace else. That's why we followed them last night, to find out where they buried him so that we could clear our names."

"They told me you'd try to lie about it. Now I don't want to talk about this anymore, just call the number I gave you."

"If I'm lying, then why the hell would we have come over to see you?" I asked. "Why would a bunch of no good cult members risk our own necks for a total stranger if we were cold blooded killers? Explain that to me. If your pals hadn't come over, we'd be at the police station right now."

"You only came over because you wanted to find out if I was associated with Mr. Keller and his friends," she finally admitted. "Since they knew about your little murder, you were trying to find out about them through me."

I couldn't believe what I was hearing. She really seemed to buy into all this crap. It was their word against mine and she obviously believed them. It was like she was brainwashed or something. It was obvious there was nothing I could possibly say to change her views.

"Give me that number again," I insisted.

"It's 245-9945. You should phone right now. He's expecting your call."

"Just one more thing," I said defiantly. "If you read in the newspaper tomorrow that three high school kids were found dead in some alley somewhere, I want you to remember this little talk. You understand? I'd also do some serious thinking about your friendship with these guys. After they take care of us, I'll bet you're next on their list. You can count on that."

There was no response on the other end. It took her a long time before she finally put down the receiver. I sensed that what I said had some effect on her.

*　　*　　*

It took me several attempts before I was finally able to get through to Bradey on his cellular phone. I figured he was probably talking to Shelly or maybe one of his so-called buddies at the Elkins police station. There was a lot of static in the background and a persistent humming sound which made communicating a bit difficult. I practically had to shout into the receiver to be heard.

"Bradey here," he answered gruffly, obviously in a foul mood.

"It's me . . . Matt," I muttered. "I have the stuff you want."

"So where the hell are you?" he hollered. I could feel his hatred for me over the phone. His voice left little to the imagination.

"Wouldn't you like to know," I responded back defiantly. "Now listen to me. Do you know where the Elkins High School football field is?"

"Yeah. What about it?"

"I want you to pick me up there at noon. I'll be standing directly in front of the ticket box, the one near the northeast gate. You can then take me to where Mark and Thad are and we'll make the exchange."

"We told you one hour," Bradey reminded me. "No way am I waiting until noon. And I don't think you're in any god damn position to call the shots here."

"Well, if some asshole hadn't driven off with my car, maybe I'd have been there a little sooner. Any ideas who might have taken it?"

"Noon is over ninety minutes away," he replied, ignoring my comment. "I'm not waiting that long. If you know what's good for your friends, I wouldn't mess around with us like this. Now tell me where you are and I'll pick you up."

"Fat chance. If you want Carter's precious photos, you're going to to have to do it on my terms. Oh, and by the way, I want some assurances from you that when I get there, you'll follow through with your side of the bargain."

"Mr. Keller never breaks a deal."

"I'm not worried about Keller," I said under my breath.

Before he could say another word, I hung up. I was sure Bradey must have thought I was a complete idiot to agree to meet him at some location without asking that Mark or Thad be present. Any sane person would have demanded that they be waiting in the car so that a swap could take place out in the open, at some public spot. But for this to happen, he'd have had to go and get them, which would have disrupted my plans. The idea was to buy some time while I headed over to the cave. It felt like the phone call had achieved this objective.

12

It took me almost a half hour to get my hands on everything I felt I needed for my little rescue attempt. Along with Carter's photo and schedule book, I stuffed a flashlight, matches, a few candles, the pistol and some bug spray into an old knapsack I found in Mark's bedroom. I figured if I had to, I could use the spray as "mace" to blind Bubha and Charlie. I also grabbed Mark's shotgun off the living room wall. From the layer of dust along the top, it looked as if it hadn't been used for quite some time. The last item I needed, the 10-gauge shells, took me forever to find. I nearly ransacked the entire house before I found them stuffed in an old shoe box in the hall closet on the top shelf. After I had finished, the house really looked as if a prowler had been through there.

As I sped away in his mother's 1984 Chevy stationwagon, I realized that my criminal resume had grown even more impressive—I had just added breaking and entering, burglary, and grand theft auto to my inventory of crimes. I was hoping I wouldn't have to add any more items to the list—namely first degree manslaughter.

I made the drive to the cave in record time, breaking more than a few land-speed records along the way. I could hardly believe how well that old wagon handled when put to the test.

Upon arriving in front of the cave site, there didn't appear to be a single car parked anywhere. For a split second, I couldn't help but wonder whether I had somehow made a horrible mistake. Should I have gone to Shelly's house, I asked myself. Maybe I should have gone to the police. What if they decided to hide Mark and Thad someplace else. Or maybe there was another cave that I didn't know about. The multitude of possibilities began to poison my confidence in the scheme I had committed to. I became nervous as I drove up and down the road in search of some sign—any sign that they were nearby.

Finally, after making my third pass, I decided to turn down a small dirt road, not far from the cave's entrance. The road served as a kind of parking area for the local boys. While the climb down to the river was steep and a bit hazardous, the fishing was said to be first rate early in the morning and late in the day. Or at least that's what I'd always been told. Since it was late-morning, there was not a soul around. I drove to the end of the road, not far from the steep slope which led to the river, so as not to be seen from the main highway. To avoid making the same mistake again, I took the car keys with me this time around.

For a long time, I leaned against the stationwagon as I tried to sort out what to do next. As the range of possible scenarios swirled around in my head, I happened to look over in the direction of the path that led down to the river, when I noticed something lying on the ground—it looked like a set of car keys. I walked over, picked them up and realized that they were the keys to my sister's car. How did they get here, I wondered. There was no sign of her car anywhere. Without the keys, there was no way to drive it. So where could it be?

Then it struck me. I remembered Bradey telling Charlie to take care of the car—what about the river. As I walked closer to the edge, I realized that there were tire impressions in the dirt leading right to the edge of the slope. My stride grew faster with the increased pace of my heart. What I saw, upon reaching the rim, confirmed my worst nightmare. Down, far below, wedged between a couple of oak trees was my sister's car. They had actually pushed the sucker off the edge. They must have been trying to sink it in the water down below, but somehow missed their mark.

It took me no time to descend the steep sloop to where the car was positioned. It was beyond being "just totaled"—it was a complete wreck. All I could think about was Mark and Thad. What if I found them dead in the back seat? I started praying to God that they were not in the car. It took all my courage to open one of the doors—there was no sign of them. I then took the keys and made my way to the trunk. A vision of them being mutilated inside crossed my mind as I reluctantly turned the key. Once again, they were also not there. Although I realized that my sister was going to literally skin me alive for allowing her precious vehicle to be destroyed, in the context of what had happened, I couldn't imagine her not understanding.

This deliberate act of destruction further clarified what these men were capable of doing. They were evil down to the core. I was convinced they wanted us dead and they weren't going to stop at anything less than that. Up until that point, I kept feeling I could somehow reason with them. But seeing the wrecked car, it was evident that if any of us were going to survive, I'd have to be as ruthless as they were. I couldn't take any chances. If I had to, I'd shoot to kill—all of them. It was perfectly clear to me—it was either them or us.

*　　　*　　　*

Since there was no telling where Mark, Thad, or the others might be, I was extra careful as I made my way along the road toward the cave's well-exposed entrance. I must have looked like

"Rambo " with the pistol sticking out of the front of my belt and Mark's shotgun up against my shoulder. Several times, I had to dodge into the woods to avoid being seen, as a car raced past.

My mind seemed to waver back and forth somewhere between fear and utter terror. To overshadow these feelings, I had to dig deep within myself to scrounge up the half ounce of courage which kept me moving forward. But with every step closer to the cave, I found my bravery quickly fading. To keep me focused, I prayed that some good-ole-boy would find my sister's car down beside the river. That would at least result in the cops coming out to investigate. The thought of having someone backing me up provided some semblance of relief, even if the chances were highly unlikely.

The cave's opening, which was situated along the side of the road in plain view, seemed somehow different to me than it had that same morning. Peering into the darkness, it felt like I was about to enter something evil and sinister—hell maybe. I reluctantly crept inside a short ways on my hands and knees. There didn't appear to be any sign of life within.

Before I knew it, that little voice inside my head which usually kept me out of trouble, tried desperately to talk me out of what I was about to do. The longer I lingered, the louder came the call for reason. "What if this is the end of the line for you, Matt," it whispered to me, in that convincing voice which I had learned to trust throughout my life. "Could you be doing something which might result in your demise? There are probably a hundred scenarios that could result in favor of a bad outcome. It isn't too late to turn back. You can drive down the road to the Bantum police station and get help. You can even call from a local phone. Yes, that's the only logical, sensible, rational thing to do. Going inside all alone, would be reckless and irresponsible. It's suicide—pure and simple. They'll manage to kill you for sure. Run Matt! Save yourself. Turn around and sprint like hell. Run for your life!!!"

Just as I was about to throw in the towel and take the coward's way out, I heard someone laughing deep inside the cave. It was Bubha's laugh—crude and piercing like a baboon's. Mark and Thad must be in there, I thought to myself. This new sliver of hope snapped me out of the spell which had seduced me, as if someone had come along and slapped my face hard. I'm doing this thing, I decided. I'm going inside. There's no other way around it.

After a final check to make sure the pistol and rifle were loaded and in working order, I began crawling through the small passage which led to the much larger chamber further inside. I stayed as close to the cave wall as possible so that no one would notice me coming. The ground was soft and damp beneath me, making it easy to maneuver without being easily detected.

By the time I reached the first bend, I caught a glimpse of a bright light shining from the inner chamber. It had that crisp appearance, like it came from one of those propane lanterns. While I could clearly hear Bubha and Charlie laughing about something, from where I was situated, it was impossible to see them just yet. Inch by inch I made my way closer. With less than twenty-five feet left to go, I got my first look at Bubha. His back was facing me as he played a hand of cards. There was no sign of Mark or Thad anywhere. With the ten gauge directly out in front of me, my finger twitched as I repeatedly felt for the trigger.

I spent several minutes plotting my next move. I figured if I shifted over to the other wall of the passage, I could almost get right up on them before springing out. The idea was to lunge out suddenly, demand that they put their hands in the air and if they made any sudden moves, to cut them in half with the shotgun. I kept repeating to myself that I had to shoot if they tried to do anything funny. It was either them or me. Once these details were sorted out, I felt a whole lot better about my chances. It was time.

As I was moving over to the adjacent wall, something totally unexpected occurred—I heard Bradey's voice yell from the entrance of the cave. I couldn't believe it. He didn't go to the stadium as planned—he came here instead!
SHIT!

"Hey, Bubha, Charlie, are you in there?" Bradey shouted, with a cautious voice. "Bubha, you asshole, answer me!"

My entire body was totally paralyzed with fright. Before I knew what was happening, Bubha had stood up and started walking in my direction with the propane lantern in hand. I had the shotgun pointed right at him. Just as I was preparing to make my presence known, the on-coming light revealed a small crevice in the wall directly behind me, which was large enough to conceal myself. It was as if someone or something had come along and opened an invisible escape hatch. Instead of taking a stand just then, I found myself wedged in this crack for dear life.

"Mr. Bradey, is that you, boss?" asked Charlie, trying his best to shine the light down the narrow passage that led to the outside world.

"Who else would it be?" Bradey responded, making his way through the cave's narrow passage. I could hear him cursing the entire time. At the very moment when he passed by me, I realized that I could have just blown him away—but I couldn't bring myself to do it. I had to admit, the temptation was mighty strong.

"Did you see any sign of that other prick?" Bradey continued, wiping the dirt off his trousers after entering the inner chamber which was high enough for him to stand. "What's his name, I think it's Matt." As always, his voice sounded like he was well beyond the threshold of being merely a bit irritated.

"No, boss," confessed Bubha," still surprised to see his master. "I thought he was supposed to meet you somewhere. Didn't he call?"

"He called alright," Bradey explained. "That asshole is playing games with me again. He told me to meet him at the football stadium in an hour, but something didn't seem right so I decided to come here instead. And then I found this piece of shit station-wagon parked down the road. It looks like the same one we saw at that house we were just at. I'm sure that little shithead heard us talking about the cave when we were inside the garage. I know he's around here somewhere. I can feel it in my bones."

"We didn't see anything," Bubha admitted. Charlie stood there and shook his head in agreement. "What could he do by himself, anyway?"

"Hell if I know," Bradey hissed. "But I don't trust him. He's a clever little shit. Let's get the hell out of here now, before we're forced to find out. Grab those two and let's move it. I left the truck out in front. At least he hasn't gone to the police yet."

"How can you know that for sure?" asked Charlie.

"Do you see any cops walking around here, stupid?" asked Bradey in a patronizing tone. "Oh, by the way, where's that little prick's other car anyway? I didn't see it parked anywhere around here."

Bubha and Charlie looked at each other, but neither one of them ventured to respond. They wanted that particular question to just go away quietly.

"Well?" asked Bradey, sensing that there was something wrong. "Where the hell's that car?"

"It's kind of . . . in the river," Charlie admitted with his head lowered.

"Wait a minute, did you say it's in the river? What are you talking about?" Bradey couldn't believe what he was hearing.

"I pushed it into that river outside there," Charlie muttered reluctantly, under his breath.

"You did what?" asked Bradey, without making an effort to restrain his astonishment. He started pacing anxiously back and forth in front of the two of them. He looked like a time bomb seconds before it detonated. "You put his car in the Cheat River? That river isn't more than three feet deep at any given point. What the hell are you talking about?"

"Well, um, I pushed it over the edge near this parking area," said Charlie. "You told me to take care of it. There was no other place around to hide it. I thought someone might see it just sitting there, so I . . ."

"Shit!" yelled Bradey, before Charlie could finish. As

expected, the impending explosion finally occurred. "And can you see it there in the water?"

Neither Bubha nor Charlie offered an answer. They both looked as if they were preparing for the worst—as if by admitting that the car never made it to the water, the wrath of Bradey would come thundering down upon them like the hand of some angry demon.

"I said, can you see it?" Bradey repeated the question, with his two fists clinched tightly in front of him.

"Well, boss, the car somehow hit a tree and stopped," Charlie finally declared. "It never made it completely down to the river. But don't worry, you can hardly see it from up above. It's all surrounded by bushes and shrubs. I swear, it'll be okay."

"It'll be okay?" Bradey repeated to himself. "I don't have to worry, he says?"

Bradey just stood there not saying anything for a long time. Both Charlie and Bubha lowered their heads like school boys who had just been caught breaking one of the cardinal rules. Without the slightest warning, Bradey did something that totally shocked me—he threw a side kick at Charlie which sent him crashing down to the cave floor. He then proceeded to beat the living shit out of him. Charlie never once tried to get up or fight back. He took every kick and every punch. When it was all over, Charlie laid there without saying anything. He looked half dead, as a low moaning sound faintly escaped from his bleeding mouth.

"You stupid fools," Bradey howled, walking over to Bubha. "After work, there'll be dozens of fishermen walking down that hill to the river. Ten minutes after finding that car, this place will be crawling with cops. What if they find that Matt kid? You want to go to jail for the next thirty years? I can't believe how god damn stupid you two are. I just can't believe it. Now grab those two boys and let's get the hell out of here before we get ourselves caught. We're going back to Virginia, now! It's not safe here."

"What about Carter's body?" asked Bubha.

"Did those kids find it?"

"Yes, boss. Charlie and me buried it again, but it still smells in here. And if that other kid knows it's in the cave, he could find it again."

"There's nothing we can do about it now. There's no time. We'll worry about it later."

Every once in a while, you get the feeling like a given moment represents the right time to do something. At precisely that moment, I knew I had to make my move. With what light was available, I climbed out of my little hiding place and proceeded to the large chamber where they were all gathered. Charlie was still on the ground moaning in pain, while Bradey and Bubha were off doing something out of sight. I was pretty certain that Mark and Thad were there based on what Bradey had just said.

"Slop right there and put your hands where I can see them or I'll blew you away," I yelled, as they came into view. The words didn't come out exactly the way I wanted, but they got the message across. Their hands immediately flew up without hesitating. I held the shotgun hard against my shoulder, aiming it at the back of their heads. I obviously caught them completely off guard—especially Bradey. He was totally taken aback. He kept turning his head around to catch short glimpses of me.

I noticed that Mark and Thad were sitting on the ground, not far from where my two captives were standing. They were both bound and gagged, with their backs up against each other to keep them upright. Mark's face was beginning to swell from all of the blows he received at Shelly's house. He looked something awful.

"Now, I want you to turn around slowly," I instructed. "And if you so much as twitch a finger, I swear I'll blow both your heads off. You hear me?" They both reluctantly complied.

The cave had an unusual stale stench. While it wasn't foul smelling, it was very unpleasant. At first I couldn't put my finger on it. Then I remembered Carter. It must have been the smell of his body decomposing under the earth. I nearly gagged at the thought of it.

"Okay, now, I want you to move away from them!" I insisted. I could tell I was making them nervous by the way I jerked the gun around. "Over there, next to Charlie. Now move it." They slowly edged over to where Charlie was lying on the cave floor. By the way he sat himself up, it appeared he was coming back to life.

"So, I see you managed to track us down once again," said Bradey as if nothing out of the ordinary was happening. "I must say, you never cease to amaze me, Mr. Matt. Maybe you should come work for me. I could use a good boy like you. So what do you think? How'd you like to make some real money?"

"Just shut up," I demanded, while making my way over to where Mark and Thad were sitting. They were both clearly overwhelmed with relief.

As I reached down to untie them, I realized I had a small dilemma. I couldn't easily unbind them and keep the gun pointed at my three prisoners at the same time. I needed someone to help.

"You, come here," I said, pointing the gun in the direction of Bubha. "Untie these two now. And hurry up."

Bubha started to walk over, but Bradey grabbed his arm to stop him. "I'll do it," said Bradey softly. "I tied the knots so it'll be much easier for me to undo them."

"No way," I replied. I put my head up against the gun as if I were preparing to fire. "Stay where you are. I want him to do it."

I knew what Bradey's feet were capable of. I wasn't going to take any unnecessary chances. There was no way I was going to trust him to do anything.

Bubha came over and clumsily untied Mark. Once freed, Mark pushed Bubha aside as he quickly released Thad himself. Bubha stumbled back over next to Bradey, with his hands still propped high in the air.

"Take this," I said, handing Mark the pistol.

"Are you all alone?" asked Mark, full of excitement. Another one of Mark's brilliant questions. He managed to figure it out for himself. "God that took a lot of balls. Man you're a god damn hero, buddy. It looks like we're even now."

Thad stood directly behind Mark and I. He must have been crying up a storm. His eyes were watery, bloodshot and nearly swollen shut.

"Do you think they have any guns with them?" I whispered to Mark.

"I don't know," he responded back. "I'd better check it out. Cover me. And don't accidentally shoot me."

"Let's just get out of here," Thad pleaded, before Mark could make a move. "I can't stand being in this place another second. I just can't take it anymore. Please Matt, get me out of here."

"We'll be outside in a few minutes, Thad," I exclaimed. "Don't worry, everything will be fine. I promise you."

"Why don't you just shoot them all," Thad suggested. "Go ahead and shoot them in the leg or something."

I had never seen Thad act like this before. He was always "Mr. Non-Violence." I wouldn't have dared given him a gun at that moment. In the state of mind he was in, I was afraid he'd shoot them all without hesitating.

"Okay, now, this is the plan," Mark shouted, cautiously making his way toward the three of them. "I want you two to get down on the ground. And keep your hands where I can see them. Okay?"

"You don't really think you boys can get away with this, do you?" asked Bradey with a smile from cheek to cheek. Mark couldn't resist the temptation—he gave Bradey a sharp punch to the side.

"Shut up, you prick, and drop down before I shoot your head off," Mark demanded. I could tell he wanted to take Bradey on right there and then—karate, or no karate he was ready.

"Mark," I said firmly. "Leave it alone. You hear me?"

"You'd better listen to your little friend," said Bradey defiantly. "Or you're liable to get yourself hurt again."

Bradey and Bubha slowly dropped to their knees and then laid down face first. Their hands were sticking out in front of

204

them. Mark grabbed the propane light and brought it close-by so he could better check for weapons. Bradey had a gun in a holster near his chest. Bubha's was hidden in an ankle holster. Mark then walked over to Charlie who was only half aware of what was going on. He was still in a daze from Bradey's little beating. Charlie was clean—he didn't appear to have a gun or any weapon on his person.

"I think that's it," said Mark, coming back over. He was about to hand one of the pistols over to Thad, but I took it instead. "Now what do we do?"

"We've got to give them over to the police," I declared. "We can put them in the back of Mark's mom's stationwagon. I don't want to use their truck. There might be more weapons stashed inside of it."

"You've got my mom's car here?" asked Mark surprised.

"It's a long story. I'll tell you about it later," I stated, trying to think of the best way to get them outside without providing them with an opportunity to make a run for it.

"Shouldn't we tie them up?" Mark whispered. "What if that maniac tries to throw another one of his ninja kicks?"

"Then we'll shoot him dead," I said, aiming the gun towards Bradey to demonstrate I was completely serious. "If he tries anything funny, I'll just blow him away. In fact, I hope he makes a move. It'll give me an excuse to waste him." I made the statement loud enough so he'd hear me. With Mark and Thad there to back me up and a double barrel 10 gauge shotgun firmly in hand, I began to feel like I was the man—nothing could stop me now.

"I think Thad's right, we should just shoot them all in the leg and leave them here to rot," said Mark, in an attempt to further taunt our three prisoners. "Better yet, let's just finish them off. That's what they were planning on doing with us."

"That's enough," I insisted. "Let's just get this over with. Okay, now I want you three to get up slowly! You, too, Charlie." They all gradually got to their feet. "Now one of you grab that lantern. And no funny-business." While I directed this command to Bubha, Bradey leaned over and picked up the propane lamp off the ground himself.

"I'll go first so they don't try to run for it," Mark volunteered. "You two take the rear. Why don't you give Thad one of those guns."

Despite Mark's suggestion, I wasn't about to comply. I was afraid Thad might accidentally shoot me with it—or maybe himself.

As Mark began walking toward the passage leading to the outside, Bradey made his move. He hurled the propane lantern clear across the room, right into the stream. All at once, the cavern became pitch black. What happened next was a bit of a blur. I could hear them scurrying around in the darkness in front of us. They were getting away, I thought. In all of the confusion that followed, I somehow pulled the trigger causing one of the two barrels to ring out a shot. The kick from the gun nearly knocked me off my feet. Thad let out a scream that could have raised the dead.

Before I knew it, someone grabbed me into their arms and picked me right off the ground. From the feel of it, I could tell it was Mark. He had Thad in one arm and me in the other. He made off with us in the direction of the stream and then stopped abruptly just before entering the water. I could hear it trickling down below my feet. Then, as if someone had hit the mute button on the entire situation, the cave became dead silent—there wasn't a sound to be heard from anyone. I later discovered that Mark's hand was covering Thad's mouth. Thad even tried to bite him to get Mark to release his vise-like grip. He couldn't breathe.

After placing us down on the ground, Mark gently tugged the shotgun out of my hands. At first I couldn't figure out what he was up to. Why the hell were we hiding from them? We were the ones with the guns?

He then reached down, picked up a medium size stone and tossed it in the direction of the cave's entrance. The moment it hit the ground, three shots rang out from the other side of the cave, spraying the area where the rock had landed. Shit!!!! They had guns too and they were still inside the cave. How the hell did Butthead know? Mark immediately responded by firing the second barrel off in their direction.

"Shit!" someone yelled out. "I'm hit. God damn it, boss, I'm hit. My leg!" I couldn't make out which of them it was, but he seemed to be overcome with pain.

Without a moment's hesitation, using the sound of the flowing water as a guide, Mark seized both of our arms and gradually led us quietly upstream. We moved at an incredibly slow pace, so as not to create a sound. Fortunately, the ground was very soft beneath our feet, thus allowing us to move with stealth.

After having gone nearly ten feet, we heard a rock being tossed in our direction this time. It landed inches from my foot. We made no effort to respond. It was their turn to try to fish us out. I just stood there waiting for the bullets to fly. None came. My biggest fear was that Thad would lose it and do something stupid. But somehow he managed to remain completely silent.

"Boss, you've got to help me," I heard someone call out. "I'm hurt bad. Come on, boss. I can't move. If you . . ." The mysterious shot that rang out in the darkness, caused an immediate end to his pleading.

Mark had to cover Thad's mouth again to stop him from

crying out. By this point, Thad's reactions had become totally involuntary. He was beyond mere fear—he had become a complete zombie, shaking from head to toe like a naked man in a blizzard. Mark waited a few moments before moving on. He and I both had to prop Thad up as we led him in the right direction. I could feel his legs giving way with every step. He even had the smell of fear all about him.

Since it would have been impossible to follow the steep trail which ran adjacent to the stream without a light, before long, we soon found ourselves knee deep in water. We walked at a snail's pace to avoid making any noise at all as the water flowed past. My finger strattled the trigger of the pistol, ready to fire at anything that moved.

As the walls along the stream closed in at different points, Mark was forced to take charge of Thad on his own. I trailed close behind. Mark did his best to let me know when there was a low ledge or a protruding rock up ahead. He managed to locate most of these obstacles by first bumping into them himself.

We walked for a long time in the darkness before Mark finally stopped and whispered something into my ear. "Do you have a flashlight in that bag of yours?"

"Yeah, I do," I replied, struggling to pull the knapsack off my back. "And a bunch of candles and matches."

After leaning Thad against the wall, Mark opened the bag and fished out the light with little trouble. He turned it on for just a moment to see if it worked.

"This will do. What about shells? Did you bring any extras with you?"

"Yes, I brought a whole box."

Mark reached inside, snatched two 10 gauge shells and reloaded the shotgun. He then pointed the light upstream for several seconds, as he attempted to get his bearings.

"Do you think we should use that thing?" I asked, afraid we might be discovered. "What if someone spots it?"

"I don't know. We're probably far enough along now. I don't think they can see us. Besides, what else can we do. I keep bumping into things. It's not safe without it."

"How the hell is Thad doing?" I whispered, walking up to him. "Thad, are you okay man?"

There was no answer. He was still too freaked out to respond. He stared back at me with this blank, empty expression as if he were blind, deaf and dumb.

"I couldn't get him to say anything either. I've tried a few times."

"Come on, Thad, just say something, anything," I persisted, shaking his arm.

"He doesn't look very good to me," Mark admitted, as if Thad weren't even there. "I've never seen him like this before.

It's like he's in shock or something—like he's one of those walking dead zombie types you see in movies. You know how he is about confined spaces."

"Thad," I said, gently shaking both shoulders as I tried even harder to get him to answer. "Thad, are you okay?" There was no reply. At that point, I finally gave up.

"He'll probably be alright when this is all over," Mark muttered. "Listen, when this light goes on, we're all going to have to move fast. You'll have to help me move Thad along. We still need to put distance between us and them. Okay?"

"Don't you think they're long gone by now?" I asked, hoping for an optimistic response. "Why would they come after us when they could just run away?"

Mark handed me the flashlight and asked, "You want to go back there and find that out for sure? Believe me. They're coming for us. If they don't, they know we're going to send them all off to jail. That's why. If they can get us out of the way, then they'll be . . . hey wait a second! Don't move!"

"What?" I asked, nearly panicking. "What is it?"

"Shhhh, shut up and listen!" Mark scolded me. Once again, he got real serious. We both listened in the darkness.

This time, I heard it. There was a soft splashing noise off in the distance. It sounded like there was somebody trudging through the water behind us. Every once and a while a small flashlight beam would dance around, before being quickly extinguished. Someone was definitely tracking us.

Before I could react, Mark abruptly grabbed the flashlight back and then softly pushed my shoulder in the direction of a wall. Fortunately, we were at a point where the stream was wide and shallow, with plenty of head room. Without making a sound, I gently grabbed Thad's hand and guided him backwards until we were both flat against the side. He didn't seem to know what was happening.

For some reason, Mark remained in the center of the stream. I couldn't figure out why he didn't take cover with us. Why was he just standing there right out in the open? I could hear him cocking both barrels of the shotgun with the greatest of ease. I just stood there listening. The sound of someone approaching came again and again—this time even closer. And then, whoever was there, turned on his flashlight once again.

When a shot finally rang out, I couldn't tell who fired it. And then I heard a large splash, as someone fell into the water. What happened? Did someone just shoot Mark? It all happened so fast. Without a light, there was nothing I could do. I was helpless. I grabbed the pistol from my pants and held it straight out with both hands. My finger wanted desperately to pull the trigger—if only to release some of the overwhelming anxiety I was feeling.

"Mark," I whispered in desperation. "Mark are you there? Come on, answer me. Are you okay?"

"Shut up," he finally responded. "I'm fine. Whatever you do, don't turn on a light."

"I don't have the light, you've got it."

Nearly five minutes passed before Mark went off in the direction of the splash. He didn't say a word. From behind a small pillar located within the stream, he first surveyed the area downstream to check out if there was anyone else following us. There didn't appear to be any others. He then scanned the water until he found what he was looking for. After going over and inspecting the body, he returned with a somber expression across his face. While I couldn't tell for sure, it almost looked like he had tears running down his cheeks—I couldn't remember ever seeing him look so upset.

"Are you okay, Mark?" I finally asked. "Who did you hit?"

"It looks like I wasted Bubha," he muttered softly. "I blew half his face off."

"Holy shit, man," I responded in amazement. "Do you think Bradey's still out there somewhere?"

"I don't know," he admitted. "I don't know. But we'd better not take any chances."

Mark shined the light upstream as he walked ahead. Thad and I followed along a few yards behind. Every few steps he'd turn the light off and peer back to see if we were being trailed again.

As I stumbled along through the water, my mind tried to piece together what had just happened. Bubha was dead. And it sounded like we heard someone else get shot earlier. That had to have been Charlie because he kept calling out the word "boss." That meant that Bradey was probably still alive. Would he come looking for us, I wondered. Would we all get out of this thing alive?

We walked for another ten minutes or so before stopping at a point where the stream took an abrupt turn to the left.

"This is as far as we go," Mark explained. "I've never been beyond this point. It's too dangerous."

"Shit, man," I said. "What the hell are we going to do now? Just sit here and wait?"

"You got a better plan?" he snapped back. "You said you had some candles in that bag. How many do you have?"

"Ten or twelve," I responded.

"Good, give them over here." He reached out his hand.

"What are you going to do with them?" A couple fell into the water as I tried to pass them all over at once.

"You'll see."

Mark walked over to the other side of the stream and then climbed up a slight ledge until he reached what looked look a small natural platform. The spot was covered with old beer cans a few empty Nacho bags. It was obviously one of Mark's old party spots. He lit several of the candles and then quickly returned to where we were standing.

"Okay, now this is the deal," he said, pointing the light to where there was a small ledge behind us. "We're going to sit up there and just wait. If someone comes, we can see them from here, but they won't be able to see us. They'll think we're on the other side where the candles are. We shouldn't use the flashlight anymore. We're going to need the batteries to get us out of here later."

Mark and I both helped Thad up to the spot. After getting settled, the last thing I did was to look at my watch. It was already three o'clock in the afternoon. I couldn't believe how late it had become. A couple of times I started to say something to Mark, but he kept telling me to just drop it. I guess if I had just killed someone, I wouldn't be in much of a mood to talk about it either.

*　　　*　　　*

Six candles later, Thad was fast asleep and Mark was finally ready to open up.

"What time is it?" he asked quietly. His voice sounded strained and weary.

"Can I use the light to see?" I asked.

"Go ahead."

"It's almost five-thirty," I replied. "Can I ask you a question?"

"What?"

"How did you know those guys had guns back there? You know, after Bradey threw the lantern into the water. How could you possibly have known?"

"I didn't," he admitted. "I guess I figured something was up when they didn't try to leave the cave when they had the chance. If I didn't have some kind of weapon, that's what I would have done. Wouldn't you?"

"But how did you know they were still in the cave? There was so much commotion inside there going on?"

"I was standing right next to them when it happened. I heard them moving around."

"That was really good thinking," I said. "You know, you saved us once again."

"I didn't even think about it. I just did what I had to do. That's all."

"Well you still saved our lives . . . Butthead, what next? Do you think we'll get out of this in one piece?"

"I don't know." I could tell something was bothering him.

His voice sounded tense.

"Hey, Mark, are you alright?" I asked. There was a long pause before he finally answered.

"Not really," he confessed. "You know, I just can't believe I killed that guy. He had his gun pointed straight at me. What else could I do? God, I feel really bad about it." Mark paused before going on. "You know, while I was tied up back there, all I could think about was wasting them all. The thought of getting back at them was all I could think about. I imagined tearing them apart with my bare hands. But now that Bubha's dead, I feel really shitty about it. I actually took his life away. I also shot Charlie back there. That's two in one day."

"But you didn't kill him," I said. "It was Bradey who murdered that guy in cold blood—he wasted his own god damn friend. The guy's a monster."

After fighting to hold it back, Mark finally gave in to the overwhelming sense of guilt he was feeling and broke down and began to cry. I was totally unprepared for this. I didn't know what to do to help him. It felt too awkward to think about holding him in my arms, so I just let it be. Guys just don't have an outlet for showing they care for each other. Maybe if it had been Thad, it would have been different.

"Listen, Mark, it was you or him," I finally blurted out in an attempt to do something to ease his conscience. "He was coming to kill us for sure. There was nothing you could have done."

"Thad was right," Mark finally remarked. "We should have just probably shot them all in the leg and left it up to the police. At least he'd be alive now."

"There was no way of knowing Bradey was going to throw that lantern. Listen, it's over. You did what you had to do, right?"

"I guess so," he finally admitted. "But I still feel like shit."

*   *   *

Another hour dragged on before I caught a faint glimpse of a flashlight beam moving its way in our direction from downstream.

"Holy shit, Mark," I whispered, pointing to the dancing light. "Oh, God, it's Bradey. He's coming for us."

"Shit, we've got to get the hell out of here," Mark replied, as he tried waking Thad. He had to slap Thad's face several times before he finally responded. He must have been having a bad dream because when he opened his eyes, he let out another one of his hair raising screams—the kind that could easily raise the dead. Mark and I were absolutely mortified. This time it was my turn to cover Thad's mouth with my hand, as we both dragged him off the ledge into the water.

Before we knew it, the approaching light seemed to be coming at a much swifter pace. All I could think of was Bradey—the madman. He was coming to butcher us. Instead of following through with our plan to ambush him, we lost our nerve and made a run for it. Our fear exploded into an intense state of paranoia, thus transforming Bradey into something much bigger than life. I couldn't stop myself from imagining him as one of those big screen villains like the terminator, who couldn't be killed by mere conventional means. What could WE possibly do to stop someone or something like that? We were just a couple of kids.

We didn't get very far upstream before Mark finally grabbed my shoulder to stop me in my tracks. It sounded as if someone was shouting from behind.

"Whoever is in there, identify yourselves," came a voice off in the distance. "We are representatives of the Elkins Police Department." I was about to reply back, but Mark stopped me.

"How do we know you're cops?" Mark yelled back suspiciously.

"Please, identify yourselves," the voice demanded, not answering the question.

"First tell me who you are," Mark insisted.

"My name is Officer John Galliway," the policeman replied. "Now, we aren't here to hurt you. Just put down your weapons and come out with your hands raised high in the air."

"Hey, wait a minute," Mark shouted back. "We didn't do anything. We're the good guys. Those men . . ."

"Fine, whatever you say," said the cop, not allowing Mark to finish. "If you have any weapons, please just put them down and come out slowly with your hands raised in the air, and no one will get hurt."

I could tell that there were more than a few of them by the multitude of splashes they were making. I could also hear the sporadic sound of police radios firing off. Inside the cave, these radios produced little more than static. As far as I was concerned, they sounded like genuine cops to me.

"Shit," Mark whispered to me. "They think we're god damn criminals for Christ sake. Stupid cops always get everything wrong. They're such idiots. I told you they were good for nothing."

"Well, what the hell do you expect," I said sarcastically. "There are at least three dead bodies out there. Of course, they think we're god damn killers. Come on, it's all over. Let's just do what they say and go turn ourselves in. At least we'll be safe with them. The whole thing will sort itself out sooner or later. You'll see."

"But what if this is a trick or something?" asked Mark, still wanting to remain back. "I mean, how do we know they're really cops?"

"Don't be stupid, Mark," I exclaimed. "Who else would they be? There must be at least ten of them. What, do you think, Bradey went and got reinforcements? And listen, can't you hear those radios. Of course, they're real cops. Someone must have found my sister's car near the river. I'm sure as part of their search, they came in the cave and found Charlie's dead body. Now they are here. So come on, it's all over."

"I hope you're right," said Mark reluctantly.

"Trust me on this one."

Mark walked over and placed the shotgun on the ledge, along with the three pistols we had collected. To keep Thad's hand up, I took one of his wrists and Mark took the other. By this point, he could hardly walk at all, he was so traumatized.

As we rounded the bend in the stream, there were at least four or five flashlights shining directly in our eyes. We were blinded by the intense light, unable to see who was standing there in front of us. I went to shield my eyes, but one of the policemen demanded that I put my arm back up again. I sensed from his voice, that he was extremely anxious, as if we were highly dangerous convicts.

For the first time in my life, I came to know what it felt like to be treated as a criminal. While one of the older cops yelled out orders to the others, at least three of them came up to me in bullet proof vests and threw me hard up against the cave wall. Following a thorough search for weapons, all three of us were handcuffed. I tried talking a few times, to let them know that they were making an enormous mistake, but they kept telling me to shut up and save it for later. The hero's welcome I had anticipated did not come as expected.

13

Everything that happened from that point on continued to be somewhat of a blur to me for many years to come. With people splashing in the water, radio static sounding off spontaneously around us, and numerous conversations on all sides by men who were more used to handing out parking tickets than dealing with murder cases—the setting was more than a bit chaotic.

On our way out, we were forced to walk right by Bubha's lifeless body, which was still lying faceup in the water. The police weren't able to move the corpse until the coroner arrived to issue an official death certificate. I noticed a small streak of blood emanating from his mangled head, thus creating the appearance of a red ribbon gently trickling down the stream. A photographer was there taking shots from every conceivable angle. The manner in which he took the pictures, with such energy and enthusiasm, it almost looked as if he enjoyed his work. I kept seeing camera flashes going off in my head well after passing this hideous scene.

Once outside the cave, Mark, Thad and I weren't able to see or talk with each other for more than a few days. We were all taken in separate squad cars to the Elkins police station for our initial processing. That's when the real nightmare began—mug shots, fingerprinting, being placed into jail cells, cops staring at us like we were wild animals. And then there were these endless interviews with some guy who kept telling me he was my lawyer and that he was my only hope. I could tell he was convinced I was guilty of everything. All the people around me seemed to feel that way. They hated us—I could read it in their loathing stares. We were all treated like shit—pushed around, slapped, verbally abused—as if we were mass murderers or even worse.

The minutes, hours and days that followed were the most trying of my life. As the attention surrounding the case began to grow by the hour, the three of us were transferred to Charletsville. This was done, they said, for security reasons—whatever that meant.

It took nearly three full days before the police and FBI finally came to the realization that we were the victims in all of this. They interviewed us over and over again, and then some more. Each of us reacted in our own way to the questioning process. Thad could hardly make a single statement without breaking down and crying. While Mark, unable to deal with such a heavy dose of authority, wavered between being helpful to reacting defensive and abusive towards those who he felt were totally incompetent—which for him, was just about everyone. This left me to toe the line. I did my best to cooperate with the countless lawyers, district attorneys, and special investigators—thus providing a clear, concise description of every tiny detail I could remember. The investigators also did thorough checks of all of our backgrounds, including interviews with just about anyone we had ever come in contact with, going back to our primary school days. The whole process was totally humiliating and degrading from the very start.

On the second day, a "shrink" was brought in to give us a vast array of goofy psychological tests. After being shown a bunch of ridiculous ink stains and asked to tell what we saw, it occurred to me that maybe someone should be examining the brain of the guy giving the tests. Boy did he seem to have a few loose screws.

Part of the reason for the extra long delay in clearing us was because the law enforcement folks just couldn't come to accept that we weren't involved in some kind of crazy cult conspiracy resulting in the deaths of Carter, the fisherman, Bubha and Charlie. Even after explaining again and again about how we found Carter's body that first night, and how the fisherman's death was all an elaborate deception by Bradey and his men to throw the authorities off the real trail, they still refused to accept our version. It was too much of an embarrassment for them to admit how wrong they had been. Besides, according to their data, we all seemed to fit some kind of computer profile the FBI had developed for identifying suspected cult members—and, of course, computers never make mistakes. They were so convinced we were lying to save our skins, they kept drilling us in the desperate hope that we'd eventually crack and confess the real truth—allowing them to avoid being openingly criticized.

What further added to this situation was the question of why we didn't just go to the police station in the first place. Over and over again they kept asking—"If we were truly innocent, then why didn't we report what happened to them that first night? What were we hiding?" When I listened to myself trying to explain our reasons, I had to admit, my explanation sounded more than a bit lame. For some reason, the fact that we left an anonymous call that night didn't seem to win us any points.

Back in Elkins, the entire town waited anxiously for some kind of news about our guilt or innocence. They all wanted to know whether we were heroes or fiends. Our arrest and everything that followed, was surrounded by a cloud of secrecy, thus adding to the suspense. I later learned that more than a few rumors circulated around town ranging from us having sacrificed teenagers in other counties following out-of-town wrestling matches, to us being possessed by the devil and in need of an exorcism. In a short time, the news of our little ordeal was even picked up by the regional press. There were enough bizarre twists to the whole thing that made it newsworthy—the kind of stuff that good ratings were made of.

My parents and sister came to visit me in Charletsville several times while I was still in custody. While they did their best to be supportive, I sensed that my dad and sister had their doubts. I could tell from the miserable expression on my father's face that he wanted desperately to believe my side of the story. It was my mother who kept them from losing faith. She knew I was totally incapable of doing all the things we were accused of and she made these views clear to anyone who would listen. During one of her visits, my sister described how mom nearly punched out this old fat lady who made an insolent comment about me. I found it hard to imagine my mother with her fists raised high, ready to deck some old bat. I wished I could have been there to see it.

*　　　*　　　*

Over time, the many pieces of evidence which supported our version of the events began trickling in. Between the police and FBI, the twenty odd-plus investigators assigned to the case left no stone unturned, uninspected, unreviewed, or uncovered.

After confiscating Mark's truck, the forensic boys found a bullet lodged in the back tail-light. While it was too damaged to provide any useful information, it did confirm our story that someone shot at us that first Friday night. They spent a lot of time looking for the second bullet which shattered Mark's back window, but unfortunately they never did locate it. The fact that Mark's dad called the police in to report the broken glass helped support our account, especially after they found Mark's radio—the one that was supposedly stolen—stuffed behind his tool bench.

While investigating the site where the truck was allegedly pelted, they found fragments of plastic which matched the tail-light. They even discovered the two piles of rocks Thad and I stacked on the ledge, as we waited for Mark to return from the woods that fateful night.

A careful inspection in and around Mark's garage provided support for some of our statements related to Bradey, Charlie, Bubha and the BEEM organization in general. They found Bradey's insurance papers and the BEEM annual report exactly where we told them to look. Likewise, they found Bradey's and Charlie's fingerprints scattered throughout the garage. The stains on the shirt I was wearing the day I was arrested also matched the oil found under Mark's truck.

As for Carter's eelskin briefcase, which contained the photos, newspaper clippings and other information related to the stolen urn, the investigators easily located it stashed inside the old treehouse. After a great deal of persuading by the police, the Indian couple who owned and managed the Gateway Motel reluctantly admitted that I snatched the briefcase that Saturday morning. They hadn't reported the incident to the local authorities, fearing that they might be held accountable for this theft because they were the ones who had allowed me to enter the room.

To verify the events that supposedly took place in Front Royal, the Feds took a road trip out to Virginia. Their first stop was the field across from the BEEM building. According to Thad, he described that they'd find a collection of empty junk food packages to mark the spot where he set up his little stake-out. As expected, the area was littered with a vast assortment of Hostess "Twinkie" and "Devil-Dog" wrappers, and empty Coke cans. Mark's description of the BEEM tie clip was also easy to corroborate. Last Christmas all of the male employees were given one at the annual holiday party—that and a hefty bonus.

The waitress at Bob's Grill remembered me from a photo shown to her. She even managed to track down the bill for my tuna fish sandwich as well as the bill given to Bradey, Charlie and Bubha for their burger specials. She recalled the three of them because Bradey gave her a real hefty tip. During their return drive to Elkins, the FBI also verified that Mark purchased an old used tire for Thad's mom's car from a small service station along the way.

When it came to Shelly's house, the evidence was mixed. To verify that the three of us had been inside her place, we were asked to recount what we saw. Independently, we all described her living room with great accuracy. However, the cops were unable to locate a single fingerprint in that room—not even Shelly's own fingerprints could be found. Someone had obviously wiped the entire room down before the police had arrived.

Unwilling to completely disregard their cult conspiracy theory, the FBI special agents assigned to the case focused much of their investigation on the four dead bodies. As for Charlie and Bubha, they spent nearly two days investigating the evidence in Bowden's Cave for any available clues which would discredit us. They were convinced that the cave was the perfect place for clandestine rituals to take place—especially after finding three dead bodies there. But once again, our account was easily substantiated. The circumstances surrounding the death of these two men matched the information provided by us. Bullet holes were in the right place, foot prints confirmed where everyone was standing, the propane lantern was found in the stream, and the forensic information from the bullets seemed to all tally in our favor.

Likewise, it was clear that Mr. Carter was not killed in the cave. The second blood sample taken from the site where the fisherman was found dead, matched with Carter's own blood. Using information provided by Mark and I, several hound dogs were brought in to sniff out the place where Carter was initially buried in the forest. It took less than an hour to uncover the shallow hole.

It was also determined that the gun used to shoot Charlie in the cave was the same one used to kill Carter the week before. The forensic lab was able to confirm that the bullets found in both bodies came from the same weapon. Since none of the three pistols we had in our possession gave a similar match, they had to conclude that someone else blew those two away—most likely Mr. Bradey.

Upon checking police records from around the region, the Feds discovered that both Bubha and Charlie had rap sheets that went on for several pages. They had both worked for small-town mobsters in Atlanta, Georgia before hooking up with Bradey, a returning war veteran who received a dishonorable discharge for getting caught throwing Vietnamese prisoners out of helicopters in "Nam." He was one of the few who ever got charged with pulling off this little stunt. He spent several years in jail for this offense, before being released on good behavior.

As for the fisherman from Bantum, his murder remained a mystery. There was no new evidence to link his death to the three of us or to anyone else for that matter. While we tried to explain to everyone that Bradey and his boys had killed this man to frame us, this account was not taken seriously, even after we told them what I had heard them talking about at that restaurant in Front Royal.

Initially, the stolen urn theory we had come up with did not go over well with any of the investigators. For a long time, they all seemed to discount it as being totally irrelevant—a mere fantasy on our parts. All they could think of was "cult this" and "cult that." Even after describing in great detail how we concluded that Shelly and Carter worked together to steal the urn from Nepal, how Carter tried to extort more money by providing three identical urns instead of the original one, how Keller and Bradey were willing to trade Mark and Thad for the photos to determine which one was authentic so they could sell it to some wealthy arms dealer—they just couldn't seem to make the connections. I spent countless hours describing all of the tiny clues we uncovered which supported this hypothesis. It was only after their initial attempts to come up with an alternative explanation failed, that they slowly started to take us seriously.

Because our account of how we patched together all of the bits and pieces of information sounded like it came from a cheap detective movie, we were repeatedly asked to describe the many steps we followed. They even made each of us use Carter's address book, the phone books and the Chamber of Commerce publication to show them exactly how we came to know about all of the different pieces. I could tell this one asshole FBI agent named Joe was totally convinced I was lying. After about the tenth time of going through the many steps, he started pointing out measly variations in what I described, as if by doing so, I'd eventually trip up, break down and tell the truth. What a jerk he was.

As the case continued to unfold, the FBI and State Department finally contacted the US Embassy in Kathmandu, Nepal to follow up on the stolen antique theory. The Government of Nepal verified that a sacred urn had been taken from Gorkha District several weeks before. Upon hearing that the Feds were trying to locate this important religious relic, the Prime Minister himself sent a formal letter requesting that it be returned to Nepal immediately, if recovered.

When all of the evidence was compiled, analyzed, reviewed and summarized, they ultimately let us go. But to a certain extent, the damage had already been done. The people of Elkins were convinced we must have been guilty of something. Why else would it have taken so long to release us?

*   *   *

As it turned out, there was never even a trial for any of the deaths. Bradey and Shelly disappeared after the cave incident, leaving Mr. Keller as the only other living person accused of being involved in the case. According to the FBI, Shelly must have managed to get out of the country and was probably somewhere in India. With nearly 900,000,000 people living there, it wouldn't have been hard for her to merely evaporate into the vast crowds. There was also no sign of Mr. Bradey—as if he disappeared off the face of the earth. We were told later that he had spent at least two years as an intelligence agent in the war behind enemy lines. The FBI and others informed us that if he didn't want to be found, nobody was ever going to catch up with him—he was too good.

The one person who managed to completely wriggle his way out of the scandal was Keller—the big man himself. He had an alibi for everything, with plenty of witnesses to back him up. In time, he was able to present himself as a victim. No one could believe such an upstanding citizen would be caught up in such a horrible set of crimes. He, too, blamed Bradey for everything that happened. He explained that Bradey was hired to provide security for the BEEM Company. He said he had no idea that Bradey, Charlie and Bubha had police records. If he had known, he never would have hired them. When asked about our story that he was at Shelly's house, he kept saying that we probably mistook him for someone else—it was a simple case of mistaken identity.

Fortunately, he never made an attempt to discredit us. In fact, he was very supportive in his own way. He even offered to cover our legal fees out of the kindness of his heart. Once again showing what a benevolent soul he was.

When it became clear that we'd never be released until our account of the events jived with Mr. Keller's, at the urging of our lawyers, we all finally admitted that maybe he was right—maybe we had mistaken him for someone else. We all conceded that it was probably someone who looked like Keller in Shelly's house that day. With no fingerprints or witnesses to support us, it was his word against ours and our credibility was not above reproach. Despite this little alteration to reality, we all knew the truth in our heart of hearts.

As for the three urns, they were never recovered. Keller admitted that he was planning on buying an urn from Carter, but he had no idea that it had been stolen from Nepal or anywhere else for that matter. In fact, he kept saying he didn't even know where Nepal was on the map. He went on to describe that he sometimes bought antiques from Asia as an investment, but admitted that he didn't know much about them. He just liked the way they looked on his mantel over the fireplace.

As for Carter, the authorities confirmed that there was a missing person's report filed in New York City by Carter's wife and business partner. They knew he went to West Virginia to complete some deal, but they didn't know where. When he didn't return and there was no word from him, they both got worried—it wasn't like him not to call regularly.

We never did learn all that much about him. But according to the newspapers, he was considered to be a well-known scholar specializing in artifacts from South Asia. His antique store was said to represent a very prosperous business.

No one was ever able to explain why he was shot that first Friday. Since all of the witnesses were either dead or missing, all anyone could do was speculate. Maybe he got into a fight with Bradey, who shot him out of anger. Or maybe he had a gun himself and there was some kind of shoot out which resulted in him being hit. It was only after a number of years, that this mystery was finally explained to me. But let's not get ahead of ourselves just yet.

*　　*　　*

For the most part, the events that took place that spring changed us all, in one way or another. Out of the three of us, Mark seemed to adjust the best. Despite the fact that he killed someone, it didn't take him long to convince himself that there was no other choice—it was pure self defense. He quickly went back to his old ways as if nothing ever happened. His career as a wrestler, however, was never quite the same. He was no longer able to muster up that killer instinct which resulted in so many wins. At some level, his unconscious mind seemed to prevent him from totally letting loose on his opponent, probably out of fear that he might somehow hurt another human being once again.

Thad, on the other hand, never fully recovered. After being released, he spent nearly a month in what his parents kept calling a "summer retreat." We all knew what they meant by this. Not long after being discharged, his family decided to move up north. Following this, things with us were never quite the same. Now and then the three of us all got together, but the visits were strained and we could never really recapture that old rapport we once had.

As for me, I too walked away a different person. I no longer trusted those around me. I came to realize that I was just as vulnerable to the undercurrents of good and evil as anyone else. My false sense of feeling that nothing could touch me was replaced with the reality that the world was basically a dangerous and sometimes evil place. I began to take things a lot more seriously.

One of the hardest things for me to accept was that my family also changed toward me. While my sister eventually forgave me for allowing her car to be trashed, this was only after I ended up paying her back twice what it was worth. My dad also seemed to treat me differently. I think at some level, a part of him harbored the slightest bit of doubt that the things they said about me might be true. While I understood why he might feel this way, I could never forgive him for not totally believing in me.

Finally, the fact that Bradey was still lurking out there left us all feeling a bit insecure. We couldn't help but wonder whether he'd someday come back to Elkins to seek his revenge. He became the boogy man for all of us—the hidden shadow that prowls in every dark alleyway. As time went on, this feeling lessened, but not enough to prevent us from constantly looking over our shoulders to see if we were being stalked. He also came to visit the three of us in our dreams as if to constantly remind us that he was now a permanent part of our lives.

PART TWO

14

"You know, it sounds like he's in pretty terrible shape," said Mark, as we drove up Route 95 north, through New Jersey.

"I'm sure he'll pull through this thing," I replied back, trying to force some kind of encouraging response. "His mom said there is still a good chance he'll fully recover."

"You know, Matt, I still don't understand why the hell he did it," Mark confessed. "I mean, I thought he was over all of that. The last time I saw him, he was really excited about starting his junior year at Cornell. He also said he hadn't had one of those bad dreams in nearly six months. Shit, he had it all—a fully paid scholarship, he was going to one of the best schools in the country, his grades were excellent. I just can't believe with all that going for him, he'd just throw it away. It doesn't make any sense to me."

"I can't figure it out myself," I admitted. "When my mom told me about it, I was completely blown away. Well, I guess when we get to the hospital, maybe we'll learn something more. Who knows."

It was really pouring cats and dogs that night. Several times, Mark was forced to pull over to the shoulder of the road when it became nearly impossible to see anything through the windshield. For a Friday night, the traffic was remarkably light. With several places in the area already reporting low-level flooding, we were one of the few cars brave enough to venture out. Most people were sensible enough to just stay at home—where we probably should have been.

But we didn't feel we had much of a choice. Thad was in the hospital with two broken legs, a nasty head injury, and a multitude of other wounds across his mangled body. He had been in a coma for nearly 36 hours now. The doctors were still uncertain about his overall prognosis which, up until now, hadn't looked overly encouraging.

While a note was never found, the school officials suspected it was a suicide attempt. Over the years, there had been many other students who had jumped off one of the steep cliffs not far from the main campus. Having been found at the base of such a cliff—what else could they conclude? And then there was Thad's history of being depressed sometimes. In addition to seeing a shrink at least once a week, on occasion, he took some kind of medication to help him control his mood swings. When all of these facts were added together, there were few other explanations to account for what might have happened.

223

With the windshield wipers relentlessly pounding up and down like a pair of African tribal drums, I found my mind slowly drifting back to the days when Mark, Thad and I were inseparable—during the period before that terrible Friday night when we first stumbled onto Carter's dead body. Those had been some of the best times of my life. After Thad's family moved up north, things were never quite the same with the three of us. Nearly four years had passed since then, as our lives had all gone down separate paths.

As for Mark and I, we both finished school at Elkins High. After struggling through my senior year, I somehow managed to get accepted into a local college with the help of my baseball coach. Nearly two years into the program, I finally settled on psychology as a major. I found myself spending more and more time trying to understand why people behaved the way they did—to comprehend what motivated them to say and do things which seemed out of character. Psychology offered me a chance to better understand the human mind in general, as well as my own.

To earn enough money to pay off my tuition, I took on a part-time job at a local grocery store stacking milk products—nights and weekends. My parents felt that this experience would help me to "build character." Actually, I hated working as a grocery clerk. I always felt like such a "dweeb" every time I saw someone I knew. It was incredibly embarrassing walking around with one of those goofy, green aprons hanging down around my neck. But what else could I do, I needed the money and the flexible hours allowed me time to keep up with my studies.

Although Mark was offered more than a few wrestling scholarships, both in and out-of-state, he decided not to attend college after all. He had given up on anything remotely resembling an education. He decided instead to take a full-time job at a local factory which put out billions of tiny ball-bearings each year. While he constantly complained how shitty the work was, I could tell at some level, he was pretty happy with the arrangement.

Mark also fell madly in love with Tracy Nanes, this girl from Deep River—a small town west of Elkins. According to all accounts, the two of them are planning on getting married sometime in the fall. Mark met Tracy at one of his wrestling matches during his final season. After a quick "romp" in the back seat of a friend's car, it was love at first lust. She was a bit on the plump side, with long blond hair and greatly exaggerated curves—which were all prerequisites in Mark's book. With an IQ hovering in the low 90s, nearly everyone agreed that she was just right for him. The fact that she had screwed nearly every guy on the Deep River wrestling team didn't seem to phase Mark one bit. He used to say he liked a girl with experience—it saved having to break her in himself.

*　　*　　*

We managed the journey from Elkins to Ithica, New York in a little over twelve hours. By the time we arrived, a little before 8:30 pm that evening, the rain had begun to taper off. After stopping and asking for directions at a local gas station, we finally located the hospital where Thad was staying.

"How are you, Matt?" asked Thad's mom, as she came up to greet me in the hospital corridor. "Where's Mark? I thought you were both driving up together?" She looked incredibly haggard from endless hours of worrying and a general lack of sleep.

"He'll be here in a few minutes," I said. "He had to stop off at the restroom."

"How was your drive up? It was raining like mad a few hours ago."

"It was fine, Mrs. Cooper."

I was beginning to feel really uncomfortable for some reason. I didn't know what to say to her. I was hoping Mark would hurry up and arrive to bail me out.

"The doctors did a CAT scan this morning," she remarked, trying to produce a reassuring smile. "There doesn't seem to be any serious damage to his brain—just a bit of swelling."

"That's good," I replied, fidgeting as I tried to stand still. "Has he woken up yet?"

"No," she admitted.

Her head dropped slowly as the tears began to roll off her cheeks. Not knowing what else to do, I reached out and gave her a reassuring embrace. Over the years, she had given me hundreds of hugs. Whenever I skinned my knee or fell off my bike while visiting Thad, she was always there to provide me with a bandage or a kind word. It was very strange to find myself switching roles with her for the first time.

"Hello, Mrs. Cooper," said Mark, after finally arriving. I noticed he had a small piece of toilet paper stuck to the bottom of his shoe. "How is Thad doing?" It was evident that he also didn't know what to say under such trying circumstances.

She was too choked up to answer. She pulled Mark over and gave him a hug before speaking again.

"You know, I don't believe what they say," she said as she took out a handkerchief to wipe the many tears away. "Thad wouldn't have tried to take his own life. I know my own son. He'd never do such a thing. Besides, I spoke with him hours before it happened. He was really excited about some special science project he had just started."

"Did anyone see it happen?" I asked. "Could he have

225

somehow slipped and fallen?"

"That's the strange thing, he fell off a small ledge which had a large railing," she described. "He'd have to climb over the rail."

"Well, maybe he was sitting on the rail?" I asked, even though I knew Thad would never do such a thing. He was terrified of heights.

"Maybe, that's what happened," she whispered. I could see that our conversation was upsetting her even more.

"Can we see him?" I finally asked, in an attempt to change the subject.

"Yes, of course." She led us down the hall, into his room.

It was hard for me to see Thad lying there with all of those tubes and wires attached to him. His face was pale with a number of cuts and scrapes across his nose and forehead. Wrapped around his head was an enormous bandage. It looked like they cut off all of his hair. Mark and I just stood there and stared at his motionless body for a long time before finally sitting down. Neither one of us knew what to do next—so we did nothing. We stayed in his room for nearly an hour before finally heading out.

As luck would have it, we managed to locate a small bargain motel not far from the hospital. After settling in, we went out for a couple of beers—we both felt like we really needed to throw down a few.

"So what do you think?" asked Mark, following a long pause.

"About what?" Mark was a master at asking vague questions.

"What his mom said. Didn't you hear her? She told us she didn't think he jumped. Well, maybe he didn't?"

"So, what's your point?" I asked. I was exhausted and in no mood for one of Mark's guessing games.

"I don't have a god damn point," he snapped back. "I just asked what you think. Christ, do you have to analyze everything I say? Shit, you're going to make a great shrink someday."

"So you don't believe he jumped either?" I eventually asked.

"I don't know what to think. For all I know, he could have been given a helping hand over the edge? Did that possibility ever cross your mind?"

I knew exactly what Mark was implying. I didn't want to think about it—I didn't want to believe it was even remotely possible. But once said, I couldn't get it out of my mind. Could our "friend" be back to even the score? Was the boogy man lurking out there in the shadows? Were we next on his hit list?

*　　　*　　　*

The following evening, just as Mark and I were preparing to

go out for a bite to eat, the phone rang. It was Thad's mom.

"What's the matter?" I asked, full of anticipation. I couldn't help but think the worst. "Did something happen?"

"It's Thad," she said, barely able to hold back her excitement. "He woke up. We found a note in his hand beside his bed."

"Wow, that's really great news." I was incredibly relieved. "Is he awake now? Can we see him?"

"He's sleeping again, but the doctors say that this is a very encouraging sign," she explained. She sounded much more relaxed than before. "I think everything's going to be okay. Maybe having you boys stay by his side this morning helped to snap him out of it. Thank you so much for coming up. I'm so grateful that Thad has such good friends."

"Did he say anything to anyone?" I asked out of curiosity.

"Well, no," she confessed. "We just found a piece of paper in his hand, but it was surely his handwriting."

"What did the paper say?" I asked, hoping it would shed some light on the whole affair.

"Well, um, he wrote the word PUS," she said reluctantly.

"PUS?" I asked, not knowing whether I heard her right.

"That's right," she conceded. "We don't know what it means, but the doctor said that people coming out of a coma often don't make much sense."

"Well, okay, Mrs. Cooper, Mark and I are on our way." Mark was standing behind me throughout the call. He already had his coat on and was waiting by the door.

"So what's all this about PUS?" asked Mark.

"Who the hell knows," I replied, having no idea what to make of it all. "Thad woke up and wrote that word on a piece of paper. Maybe we'll find out what it means when we get there."

*   *   *

Mrs. Cooper was talking to one of the doctors when we arrived. Thad's father was even there. I hadn't seen him for many years. When he saw us approaching, he got up from his seat and headed down the hall in the opposite direction. Ever since our little West Virginia fiasco four years before, he refused to speak to us. He blamed Mark and I for getting Thad in trouble and for ruining his reputation in Elkins.

"I can't tell you how happy I am," she said, coming up and giving us both a big reassuring embrace. She noticed Mark watching her husband walk away. "Don't worry about him. He's just a big sour-puss. He's worried about Thad. Forget about it. He'll come around."

"Can we see him?" I asked. It just seemed like the appropriate question to ask at that particular moment.

"No, I'm sorry. The doctor suggested that we wait outside his room until he wakes up on his own. The nurse will let us know if there is any change in his condition." Thad's mom handed me a small pad which had a pen attached. "This is what we found in Thad's hand. Tell me what you make of it."

"Mrs. Cooper, please forgive me, could you come over here again for just one more minute?" asked the doctor who was standing outside Thad's door. "I just have a few more items to discuss with you."

As she walked away, I looked at Thad's note. Sure enough, the paper had the word PUS written across it. It was Thad's "chicken scratch" handwriting alright. Mark and I both looked at it not knowing what the hell to think.

"Maybe in his state of mind he was having a wet dream and wanted to write what he was thinking about—the word Pussy," Mark whispered into my ear.

"Shut up, you pervert," I replied back. "So, I guess we should plan to stay one more night. Can you spare a day off from work?"

"No sweat," said Mark without hesitating. "What about your classes on Monday?"

"Screw school," I responded defiantly. "I could use a short break. Besides, I wouldn't be able to concentrate much with all this stuff going on here."

Mrs. Cooper, Mark and I all sat in a small waiting room for nearly two hours. While Mark thumbed through two year old women's magazines looking for photos that showed some skin, I just sat there trying to figure out what Thad was attempting to communicate by writing down those three letters—PUS.

At a little past 9:00 pm, Thad's mom finally decided to return to her hotel, which was only minutes from the hospital. She had spent most of the night before and all that day by Thad's side. She needed a few hours sleep. The nurse promised to call if there was any change in his condition.

Mark and I decided to pop down to the hospital cafeteria for a bite to eat before heading out ourselves. While the food was nothing to write home about, it was at least cheap. As always, Mark's plate was overflowing with enough grub to feed a small army.

"Are you sure that's going to be enough nourishment for you Mark," I asked sarcastically. "I don't want you to go hungry on me now. You probably won't be eating anything for another ten hours or so."

"If it isn't, I can always go back again," he replied with a mouthful of potato chips.

"You do that, Mark. You just go and do that." His serious response to my teasing forced a smile across my face.

"So have you figured out Thad's note yet?" asked Mark,

grabbing the pad out of my hand. "You've been staring at that thing forever."

"Can't say I have," I admitted, snatching it back again. "Maybe he had PUS in his throat or something. What the hell do I know?"

"Or maybe it's some kind of code," said Mark casually. "Have you tried changing the letters around?"

"No. What do you mean, changing the letters around?"

It sounded like another one of Mark's hair-brain ideas. But at that point, I was willing to try just about anything.

"Give me that pen and a piece of paper and I'll show you."

I handed Mark Thad's pen and went through my wallet and found a business card I had picked up at the garage where my dad's car was fixed. Mark took the pen and the card and attempted to write something.

"This pen is a piece of shit," he said as he tried to get it to write. "It's out of ink. Give me something else to write with."

I took back the pen and tried myself with no success. Then it struck me—Thad's pen was out of ink!!! Before Mark could blink an eye, I was up racing over to the cashier.

"Excuse me, do you have a pencil?" I asked in desperation. The middle-aged woman behind the counter looked at me like I was a lunatic. "Please, I need a pencil. It's really important. Do you have one? It's a matter of life or death."

"I have a pen, will that do?" she asked, holding the pen out in my direction.

"No, I need a pencil," I insisted. The woman opened the cash register and frantically looked around under the tray.

"Wait, here's one," she said, pulling it out and handing it over.

I nearly grabbed it out of her hand. By that point Mark had come over to see what had gotten into me. I took the pencil and began to lightly scrape the lead across the area from where the "S" was written on Thad's paper, to the opposite side. By doing this, I was able to expose the faint impression of three additional letters "HED." When put together, the word spelled "PUSHED." None of us were able to see the entire word because Thad's pen had run out of ink as he was writing.

"Holy shit," I said, as we both stared at our little discovery. "Thad was trying to say that he was pushed. Someone tried to kill him. You don't think this person would try to go after . . ."

Before I could finish my statement, Mark was off racing for the door. I was right on his heels.

In the back of my mind, I knew who was most likely responsible. There was only one person who it could be—Bradey. For years I wondered whether he was going to exert some form of revenge on us. With an ego like his, there was no way he could just walk away and ignore what we did to him. It looked as if he had finally made his move after all these years.

Mark pounded on the elevator buttons with no success—the doors just wouldn't open. Feeling like we couldn't wait another moment, we took the stairs instead. When we arrived on the intensive care floor, we both raced in the direction of Thad's room.

"Hey wait . . . where are you two going?" yelled one of the floor nurses in a commanding voice. The woman would have made a terrific squad sergeant in the army. She was built like a two-by-four with a face to match. "Hey, you can't be up here now, stop right where you are this minute! This floor is off limits after ten." She wattled behind in an effort to catch up with us.

I had to open three or four doors before I located Thad's room. With so many rooms along the floor, I couldn't remember which one was his. When we finally found him, he was lying there with some medical person standing over him. Whoever it was had on a pair of baggy green surgical scrubs from head to toe with a mask across his face. Since he was wearing glasses and cap which completely covered his head, it was virtually impossible to make out who he was. From where I was standing, it looked like he was injecting something into Thad's IV line. He casually turned around, briefly looked at us and then proceeded to complete his task as if everything was as it should be. It was only after the nurse arrived that we realized that his presence was something out of the ordinary.

"What the hell are you boys doing up here?" yelled the old nurse as she grabbed our collars in an effort to pull us out of the room. "I told you that . . ." Before she could drag us through the door, she looked up and saw the other person standing over Thad with a syringe in his hand. "And who the hell are you? And what are you doing here on my floor? The doctor made it perfectly clear that this patient isn't going to receive any medication. Jesus, what the hell is going on here tonight?"

There was no response from him. Without showing any sense of urgency, the stranger carefully capped the syringe, casually walked into a small toilet near the back of the room and shut the door behind him.

"Wait a minute," I said, turning to the nurse. "You don't know who that person was?"

"No, but I can tell you I am surely going to get to the bottom of it right this very instant," she insisted. She was obviously flustered by all of these intruders messing around on her turf. "Now, I told you that . . ."

"Holy shit," I yelled, pulling away from her grip. "Mark, that must have been Bradey." I turned to the nurse, grabbing her by the hand to get her attention. "Now listen to me. Someone is trying to kill our friend. I don't have time to explain all of the details right now. Just get a doctor up here and find out what that man just injected into him. I think it was probably some kind of poison. And for god sake call the police. Please, I'm totally serious about this. This is an absolute emergency."

"But . . ." she started to say.

"Just do it," I demanded. "Get a doctor in here now and call the police. Or you are going to end up with a dead patient." The poor woman was totally bewildered.

By this time, Mark had already run over and kicked the door to the bathroom open. I could tell he was out for blood. As it turned out, it was a common bathroom—there were entrances from Thad's room and from an adjacent room on the other side. Whoever it was, just walked right out the other door. Mark and I ran through the bathroom, past several startled patients and into the hallway. And there, waiting patiently beside the elevator was our man. When he saw us running in his direction, he made off for the staircase instead.

The pursuit that followed resembled a scene from one of those hospital mystery movies. We chased him down four flights of stairs and ended up in the basement—a dimly lit hallway lined with innumerable pipes and wires going off in every which direction. It felt like we had just entered some kind of "Starwars" spacecraft. There weren't any other people around.

"Where the hell did he go?" I asked, looking back and forth in both directions. "You know this is stupid. We really shouldn't be going after this guy. For all we know, he probably has a gun with him."

"No way," Mark replied back. "Those doctor clothes don't have any pockets. And besides, I don't think he was expecting anyone to walk in on him like that. If we don't find him, he'll go underground again and he'll just come after us at some later point. We've got to find this jerk right now or we'll both be dead. He's not getting away this time."

"So what do we do if we catch up with him?" I asked sarcastically. "Tell him he's under arrest?"

"We kick the living shit out of him," Mark replied full of adrenalin. "That's what we do. There are two of us and only one of him."

"That's easy for you to say. You're a god damn wrestler. This guy knows Kung Fu, remember? What am I supposed to do to him?"

"Hey, looky here," said Mark as he walked over to a small janitor cart parked along the wall. "Take this. If you see this guy, just beat the shit out of him with it." Mark handed me a toilet plunger.

"Are you serious? What am I supposed to do with this, plunge him to death?"

"Okay then, if we see him, we'll just shout or something. I'm sure the cops are on their way down here right now."

"This is total bullshit," I said angrily. "I don't think . . ."

"Just shut up and stop your damn whining. Now let's split up. He could have gone either direction. You go that way and I'll go down here. If you see anything just start yelling and I'll be right with you. Like I already said, we can't let him get away this time or we're both dead meat. We've got to think about Thad, too."

"But . . ." I tried to reply back before Mark abruptly cut me off.

"Just do it, Matt," he demanded, heading off in the other direction.

As I cautiously proceeded down the abandoned corridor, I noticed that there were rooms on either side with names like "Maintenance Supervisor" or "Medical Storeroom" printed across the front. I turned the handle of each door, but found them all to be locked. My heart and soul were truly not in this.

I couldn't believe I was all alone in the basement of a hospital with no one around, trying to track down a killer who had combat experience with a plunger in my hand. The more I thought about it, the more I realized that there was something inherently wrong with this situation. I didn't care what Mark said, this was a job for the police—it was time to get the hell out of there, and fast. After finally giving in to that rational voice within my head, I found myself running back in Mark's direction.

My desperate attempt to locate him was short-lived. As I came upon the elevator area, the masked person we were searching for stepped out from behind a huge laundry cart with a gun in his hand. Without saying a word, he aimed the weapon right at my head with one hand as he pushed a wheel chair over in my direction with the other. It was obvious what he wanted me to do—I was to sit in the chair. Everything around me in the hallway went blank as my mind centered on the barrel of that gun. I was completely paralyzed with fear.

"I know who you are, Bradey," I exclaimed. There was no response. Since the lighting all around us was poor, I couldn't see well enough to catch his reaction.

After dropping the plunger to the floor, I reluctantly sat down in the wheelchair. What else could I do? If I tried to yell I was finished. I also couldn't run off without getting a bullet in my back. I remembered what happened to Carter. Once again Mark's instincts were completely off-base—our little friend here did have a gun with him after all.

The elevator door opened and he pushed me inside. I watched as he pressed the ground floor button. I could feel the barrel of the gun against the back of the chair. The manner in which he held the pistol, it was easily concealed.

For some reason, it didn't seem to phase anyone in the hospital that I was being pushed through the lobby by someone who looked like they were ready to step into surgery—complete with a surgical mask, cap, and a pair of gloves. As the wheelchair approached the security guard who was sitting behind a small desk near the automatic door, I could feel the barrel of the gun being pressed even harder against my spine. The message was clear—if I tried anything, I'd be dead. Knowing Bradey, I was convinced he'd make do on this threat. Over to the side, near the registration area, I noticed there were a couple of cops talking to the nurse we met in Thad's room, but she didn't notice me. She was too busy recounting her version of what had just happened in Thad's room. It was almost as if we were invisible to everyone around us.

Once outside the entrance area, Bradey tugged on my arm to let me know that my little chair ride was over. He then led me over to the main parking lot where I was directed toward a new Ford Escort. It was obviously a rental—it had that rental smell. Throughout this process, Bradey didn't utter a single word to me. All of his messages were communicated through simple gestures.

He handed the keys to me and motioned for me to unlock both the front and back doors of the car. After having me sit behind the wheel, he climbed into the back seat with the gun still pointing at my head. I ended up doing the driving. Whenever he wanted me to turn, he'd tap my shoulder to indicate the direction.

For some reason, up until that point, I didn't seem to feel anything. It was as if I was in a state of complete shock. Maybe it was because everything happened so incredibly fast. But after getting behind that wheel and finding myself driving away from the hospital, my emotions seemed to catch up with what was happening. All I could think about was him taking me down some dark, deserted road and putting a bullet through my forehead. Once again, all the terror I felt that day in the cave came flooding back. I kept remembering the hatred that gleamed from Bradey's eyes every time he came in contact with me back then. I knew he wanted me dead. So this was it. He had come back to even the score. I had been living on borrowed time all these years.

"Where are you taking me?" I finally asked. I really wasn't expecting an answer. "Please, don't . . ." I couldn't seem to get the words to come out. I tried again. "So what do you want? Are you going to kill me like you tried to kill Thad?" There was still no response. "Well, you might get me, but Mark knows who you are. The cops will eventually track you down. I can promise you that."

I decided that when the car eventually came to a stop, I was going to make a run for it. My palms were sweating, my heart was racing—I was trying to prepare myself for the most important moment of my life. There was no other way. I looked at the door handle and memorized how it worked. Fortunately, the door was unlocked. I figured I'd rush out, cut across to the other side and then just run like hell. As my plan was being finalized in my mind, our ride came to an abrupt end. He had me pull into the parking lot of a tiny, beat-up motel not far from the Cornell campus. I parked the car in front of room number 9 as directed. Our little journey had lasted less than ten minutes.

He must have realized that I was contemplating something because he got out first and then indicated that he wanted me to exit while he held the gun right up against my skin. There was no way for me to run without being shot.

Walking together, he slowly escorted me up to the motel room door. I was given a set of keys and expected to unlock the door. Once inside, he closed the door and locked it, and motioned for me to sit on a wooden chair next to the bed. The room was small and dingy. With the exception of a bed, a couple of chairs and a tiny black and white TV on a dresser, there was no other furniture.

By this point, I was beginning to panic—I felt like I was about to have some kind of a nervous breakdown right then and there. The anticipation of what he was going to do to me was unbearable. Was this really the end, I asked myself. I bent down and started to sob.

"Well, we finally made it," said my captor.

As I mindfully listened to his voice, there seemed to be something terribly wrong—it almost sounded like a woman's. I remembered Bradey's voice well. It was rugged and gruff—nothing like what just came out of this person's mouth. As I tried to understand what was happening, I watched as he removed his cap, mask, glasses and gloves. To my surprise, it wasn't Bradey at all—it was a woman! She had short black hair with olive facial features. I knew I had seen that face somewhere before, but I just couldn't place it. Who was this woman and why did she just abduct me?

"I can see you don't recognize who I am," said the stranger, coming closer to allow me a better look. She was smiling—almost laughing as she spoke. "Course I've made a few changes since the last time you saw me. Back then I was a blond, had much longer hair and my skin was a bit lighter. It's amazing what a little hair dye and some skin bronzer can do to bring about a brand new look. Wouldn't you say, Matt?"

"Shelly?" I asked, totally surprised. Even with her new appearance, she was still stunning as ever. Her face had that timeless beauty that couldn't be easily erased with only a few cosmetic alterations.

"You know, I really can't believe how stupid you are," she remarked, sitting down on one of the chairs directly in front of me. She toyed with the pistol as she talked. I couldn't help but notice that her finger was always on the trigger. "You actually thought I was Mr. Bradey. That's pretty funny. I guess you haven't been with too many women in your life. Huh, Matt?"

What could I say, she was absolutely right. How could I have failed to notice that she was a woman. I guess I was convinced in my heart of hearts that it was Bradey so I saw what I expected to see. Besides, I had my back to her most of the time.

"If you had said something earlier, I'm sure I would have figured it out," I said, feeling a bit defensive.

"Well, Matt. That's the beauty of it," she laughed out loud. "Since you thought I was him, you blindly followed every little thing I directed you to do. If you had thought it was just some stupid woman, I bet you would have tried to do something heroic. Right, Matt? All you boys are exactly the same!" I sensed a hint of contempt in her last statement.

"So what's with the new look?" I asked sarcastically. "I think you've been living in India too long. You're starting to look like one of the locals."

"Well, you see I really don't have much of a choice, do I?" she replied back coldly. "Ever since you boys went to the police four years ago, I've had to give up a few things—like my old life and everything I owned. I'm still a fugitive remember?" I could sense there was more than a little resentment coming from her voice.

"So what do you want with me?" I asked, not really knowing whether I wanted to hear the answer.

"It's actually quite simple," she said, walking over to a small carrying case before pulling out a large white shopping bag. "I want you to do me a favor and tell me which of these three is the original."

"Original what?" I inquired, unable to see what was in the bag. She reached inside and took out the three urns from Nepal. I immediately recognized them from the pictures I had seen years before.

"Your friend Thad told me that you were the only one who saw Carter's photos and knew how to tell them apart," she explained in a soft, gentle voice. The hostility she displayed seconds before seemed to just evaporate. It was as if she could turn on and off her emotions at will. "As I said, it's very simple. You tell me which one is real—the one from Gorkha—and I'll see that nothing happens to you."

"Yeah, right," I snarled. "You probably said the same thing to Thad and look what happened to him."

"What happened to Thad was an unfortunate accident," she admitted with an expression of remorse. "We were just having a

235

little conversation, but when I told him who I was, he just went berserk and somehow slipped. I tried to stop him from climbing over the railing, but he was like a crazy man out of control. I don't think he knew what he was doing. I swear, that's the god's honest truth. He was just terrified by me I suppose."

"That's not what Thad said. He wrote down on this piece of paper that he was pushed."

"That's impossible." She seemed surprised that I'd make such a statement. "He hasn't woken since arriving at the hospital."

"And how would you know that?"

"Because I know," she said softly.

"And what were you doing in his room tonight?" I demanded. "I bet you were trying to kill him with that injection so he couldn't tell anyone about you pushing him over that cliff."

By this point I was full of rage. I remembered how she betrayed us the last time. I wasn't going to fall into her trap again. I had to keep reminding myself that she was a complete liar—everything that came out of her mouth was sheer crap. But it seemed like the more angry I got, the more relaxed and composed she became. It was really irritating.

"You've got it all wrong," she replied as she stood up and paced back and forth in front of me. She had that "concerned parent" expression all across her face. "I was just giving him a small sedative to keep him asleep for a bit longer. I didn't want him telling you I was here just yet. I used to be a nurse in India. Your friend is perfectly fine. Believe me. I wouldn't do anything to hurt him. I'm not like Bradey. I swear. I knew you and Mark had come in town and I was trying to figure out a way of meeting with you. As it turned out, you managed to make this task a whole lot easier. I didn't want to use the gun, but I couldn't think of any other way. You do understand, don't you?"

"So who are you working for this time—Bradey, Keller?" I asked, not really expecting an answer.

"Neither," she responded back casually. "Keller doesn't want to have anything to do with the urns anymore and Bradey is dead."

"What? How do you know Bradey's dead?"

"Because I was the one who killed him," she admitted, showing no sign of regret.

Once again I was caught completely off guard. It was hard for me to accept that this woman standing in front of me could ever have done anything like that to anyone else. She just didn't look like a criminal, let alone a killer. That girl-next-door face of hers was deceptive.

"I'm sorry, I don't understand. You did what?" I asked in total disbelief.

"Just what I said. I killed him. I stabbed him to death."

I couldn't manage to get any more words to come out of my mouth. It all just seemed so incredible. My face must have betrayed my utter astonishment at the news.

"Please, let me explain," she pleaded, sitting down in the chair again. "I don't want you to get the wrong idea. It really wasn't my fault. Believe me. Bradey had the three urns and wanted to sell the one from Gorkha to one of Keller's old business associates. That's why Keller had Carter arrange for it to be stolen in the first place. Keller set up this whole deal in order to get this massive defense contract for BEEM from some rich businessman living in the Middle East. The man was some kind of Sheik or something, and had a great deal of power and influence in certain circles. He also had this passion for important religious artifacts from around the world. The arrangement was simple, if Keller delivered the Gorkha Urn by a given date, he'd receive a defense contract worth millions, which would have made him and his company wealthy for many years to come."

I watched closely as she spoke. She seemed sincere in what she was saying.

"So what happened to Bradey?" I asked, not knowing where her explanation was heading.

"You see Bradey didn't know which one was the original either. So he somehow managed to track me down in India. I was hiding out in a small village in Rajistian where I had a few friends. He knew that if he sold the wrong one, the buyer would eventually find out and he'd really be screwed. He told me he'd go halves on the money if I could pick out the correct one. Since I was the one who smuggled them across the Nepal border, he thought I could tell them apart if I really put my mind to it. Because I really needed money to bribe the local officials to extend my visa, I just picked one of them and told him it was for real. After convincing him I was telling the truth, he tried to strangle me to death to avoid paying up. Luckily, there was a pair of scissors on a table which I managed to use to stab him in the throat. I got him right in the jugular—another advantage of being a nurse. The people I was staying with helped me to get rid of the body. So now he's dead and I have all three urns. And all I want to do is sell the original and get on with my life. I found a buyer here in the States who is willing to give me a very good price. So that's my story. It was self-defense—pure and simple."

Shelly stopped talking as a tiny tear rolled down her cheek. At that very moment, it looked as if I might be able to make a run for it. She seemed distracted and a bit vulnerable. But as if she anticipated what I was thinking, she lifted the gun and pointed it right in my direction again.

"Don't even think about it."

"I'm not going anywhere," I said, raising my hands in the air.

"So now you want me to help you? Tell me, what's to prevent you from killing me if I point out which is the Gorkha Urn—assuming, of course, I could do that." I was looking for some kind of guarantee from her that I'd get out of there alive.

"Listen, all I want is the information," she said candidly. "I don't want the authorities coming after me for murder. Once I know which is the real one, I'll sell it for enough money to get out of here forever. Don't worry, I don't want to have anything to do with you or anyone else. All I want is the money."

I studied her face for a long time before answering. I was looking for some reason to believe in what she was saying. She had already betrayed me once before at her home in West Virginia. I didn't want the same thing to happen again.

"Bull shit," I finally said. I was still less than sixty percent convinced I could trust her. "If I tell you what you want to know and you let me go, what's to stop me from going right to the police and having you picked up."

"Absolutely nothing, I expect you'll do that," she said with a confident smile. "I'd do the same thing if I were in your situation. But by that time, I'll be long gone. Believe me, no one will find me once I'm out of here. I've worked it all out. So please. Let's just get this over with so we can both get on with our lives. Come on, which one is it?"

"Wait a minute, not so fast," I said, hoping to slow things down. I needed more time to think it through. "So what happens if I refuse? Or what if I do what you did to Bradey and just pick any one of them."

"Then I'll just leave for now and you'll never know when I might come back into your life again. Maybe you'll be married. Or maybe by that time you might have some kids. How would you like knowing that at any time in your life I might return to bother you about this matter? And maybe by that time I'll be so bitter and angry that I'll start getting real mean. How would you like that hanging over your head?"

"Are you threatening me?" I asked.

"Smart boy," she said with a big grin. "You figure it out for yourself. Well, what is it going to be? All you have to do is point to the right one and all of this will be over. And please, don't try to fool me. Sooner or later I'll find out that you lied to me. Remember what I said about coming back, well I mean it."

I looked at her closely as I thought it all over. She already admitted to me that she killed Bradey. She didn't have to do that. In fact, if she had done it maliciously, she never would have mentioned it. And then there was Thad. Knowing how screwed up Thad had been over the last few years, it wouldn't have surprised me that he'd totally freak out after coming in contact with Shelly. On the other hand, what if I tell her and she tries to kill me? And if I don't tell her, will she really come back someday? She already turned up after four years. Yes, she probably would. I kept asking myself, do I trust her? What she said seemed to make sense. But should I tell her what she wants to know?"

I looked at the three urns carefully. It wasn't difficult for me to determine which one came from Gorkha. The small V-shaped crack was easy to spot. It was as if I'd seen it a thousand times before.

"By the way, if you were the one who smuggled these things out of Nepal, how is it that you can't tell them apart?" I asked out of curiosity.

"Carter had the two men who stole the urn from Gorkha give me all three at once. When I picked them up, I had no idea that one of them was stolen. Actually, I thought they were a set."

"Yeah, right," I replied back sarcastically.

"I'm totally serious. Carter called me from New York right after returning from Nepal. He explained that he bought these three pieces from some dealer, but felt it would be difficult for him to get them out of the country through customs because they were very old and valuable. Nepal has these strict rules about antiques. He told me he had them stashed at a friend's place near Butwal bazaar in Southern Nepal. He asked if I'd travel from Delhi to pick them up for some money—good money. Since I was short on cash, I agreed. I crossed the border at a point where there was no checkpost, took a bus to Butwal, picked up the three urns and headed back for India the way I came. I'd done this for him a few times before. As it turned out, the day before I arrived there, the urn was taken. I was in Delhi before the story even broke in the papers. Carter then asked if I'd bring the urns to the States. Since he agreed to pay for my airfare and all other expenses, I took him up on his offer. Once home, I got real sick. Remember? That's why I was still around when you came to see me. Otherwise I should have immediately returned to Delhi."

Her explanation cleared up a few things for me. For example, it explained the reason why the outside of her house was such a mess when we visited her years ago. She wasn't regularly living there at the time and no one was taking care of the property.

"So then, how could Carter even tell them apart?"

"Like I said, he was in Nepal a few weeks before they were taken. He went to Gorkha District where he managed to bribe one of the caretakers to let him take a photo of the urn. He then went and bought two others that looked identical from a shop in a place called Patan. It's a small city adjacent to Kathmandu, the capital city of Nepal. The men who stole the original were given these two others to hand over to me. I guess he figured his little scam—you know having three instead of one—would earn him some extra money from Keller. As it turned out, it just got him killed."

"So tell me about that then."

"Tell you about what?"

"What happened to Carter? I still don't understand why he was shot in the first place."

"How would I know? I wasn't there."

"Come on, someone must have told you what went down."

"I told you, I don't know about that."

"Listen, Shelly, I might be able to remember which is the original urn if you can somehow answer that question for me. Now just think about it for a second."

"Well . . . I heard a few things about it," she said reluctantly. "But I'm not sure if it's true or not."

"So tell me what you know anyway. That's all I ask."

"Well, to begin with, Mr. Carter was trying to extort an additional $50,000 from Mr. Keller for telling him which was the original urn."

"$50,000? How much is that thing worth?"

"The Gorkha Urn is priceless to the right person."

"So, what happened next?"

"Mr. Carter phoned Keller from New York telling him that he wanted at least twice the amount agreed upon. Keller was furious about this. As far as he was concerned, a deal was a deal. When a compromise couldn't be worked out over the phone, Carter agreed to come down to Virginia to settle the problem face to face. You see Carter knew that Keller was going to probably earn millions on this deal. Keller went around bragging about this. Carter just wanted to get a better piece of this action."

"So why did he come to Elkins instead of traveling directly to Virginia?"

"Because I had the urns at my house. Since I was sick, I couldn't bring them up to New York as planned."

"So then what?"

"Well, when Carter came to pick up the urns, I tried to get him to tell me which one was the original."

"Why would you do that?"

"Because Bradey, Charlie and Bubha were all standing in my kitchen, that's why. They said if I didn't help them, they'd contact some people in India to make sure that I was denied access into the country ever again. I knew they were capable of doing this since BEEM had contacts all over the world as part of their defense work. Bradey did the same thing to me the time you boys came over to my house. I didn't want to go along with them, but what else could I do? India is my home now. Besides, back then I didn't realize how violent these men were. It never occurred to me that they'd actually hurt anyone. I swear."

"Did Carter tell you which one was real?"

"That's kind of a stupid question, isn't it? Would I be here if he had told me?"

"No, I guess not. So what did he talk about then?"

"Carter spent most of the time laughing and joking about how stupid the BEEM people were. Unfortunately, there was no way for me to warn him that Bradey and his men were standing ten feet away. Bradey heard every word of this. When he finally had enough, he came out of the kitchen, grabbed the urns and drove Carter away. That's the last time I ever saw Carter. Actually, I was convinced that he had returned to New York. Mr. Bradey called the following morning and said that the matter had been worked out. I also got this call on my answering machine from someone who said it was Carter. He briefly described that he was going away for a week or so and not to worry about things. Whoever it was, really sounded like Carter to me. When you boys came that day with Carter's wallet, I thought he had just dropped it. I had no idea he was dead. Honest!"

"How did Bradey know that Carter was going to visit you in Elkins?"

"Actually, I don't really know for sure. Maybe Carter mentioned it on the phone. All I know is that they were there a half hour before Carter arrived."

"So how did he get himself killed?"

"I don't know." There was a real reluctance in her voice.

"Just tell me what you heard," I persisted.

"Well, since it was still early in the day, I heard they took Carter to the Cheat River area which you know is pretty deserted. Only a few cars drive by there at any given time. The three of them apparently tried to threaten Carter into telling them which was the original urn. But Carter wouldn't say a word. He knew how much Keller needed the urn for his big business deal. He just sat back with that New York arrogance of his and kept insulting Bradey right to his face. At some point Carter just opened the door to the car and said that he was going to start walking back. He told them that when they were ready to pay him what he wanted, they could find him up in New York City."

"So why would they just let him go like that?"

"What else could they do? Carter really had them over a barrel. Bradey didn't make due on any of his earlier threats. A couple of times he put a gun up to Carter's head and threatened to pull the trigger, but he never did. Carter knew he was in total control of the situation."

"So how did he get shot then? If he never told, why shoot him?"

"As Carter walked away, Bradey threatened again to shoot him for real. Carter turned around, gave him the finger and just kept on walking. Bradey was so incredibly pissed off by this point, he couldn't stop himself from pulling the trigger. He had this uncontrollable temper sometimes, especially if someone compromised his ego the way Carter had. After all the insults, he just couldn't stop from taking a shot. The bullet hit Carter in the backside of his shoulder. Instead of falling down to the ground, Carter panicked and ran off into the forest. Actually, I'm told it really wasn't such a bad wound. If Carter had gone for treatment, he probably would have been okay. But after running off, he was so terrified, he eventually just died of shock and loss of blood. He was a city boy you know—not much experience in the woods."

"So why couldn't they find him out there?"

"I don't know. It's a big forest, I guess. Maybe they misjudged which direction he went."

"When did you find out all this stuff?"

"Bradey told me about it all while in India. I was curious myself. I couldn't believe how freely he confided in me. It was almost as if he was proud of what he did. The man was really sick if you ask me."

"So what about the fisherman. Did he tell you why they killed that guy?"

"Um . . . no." Once again her facial expressions reflected her hesitance.

"Bull shit, you must have heard something," I said angrily. "I'm not telling you anything about the urns until you give me the scoop on that."

There was a long pause before Shelly finally broke down and described what she knew.

"Well, I heard that after the three of you drove off in the truck, they noticed that the fisherman had witnessed everything. Seeing two men running down the street shooting pistols at a fleeing vehicle terrified the poor man. When he turned and began to run, not knowing what else to do, they caught up with him and dragged him into the woods. For some reason, Bradey beat the man so hard he died right there on the spot. Having found the trail of Nacho chips to your camp site, they switched bodies and then dragged Carter to some other place where he was buried. The rest you already know from the papers."

"Wow, that's an incredible story."

"Okay then. I told you what you wanted to know. Now it's your turn. Which is the Gorkha Urn?"

"Wait, one more thing. If you were forced into doing all of these things, why didn't you just turn yourself in? They wouldn't have had much on you. I'm sure you would have gone free."

"Bradey told me that day you boys came to my house that if

I confessed anything to the police, he'd see that I was "eliminated." You can guess what that means. If I couldn't tell my side of the story, they'd blame me for everything so I decided to just go underground. I didn't have much of a choice."

"So let me see if I've got this straight," I asked, hoping to better understand what was about to happen. "I tell you which one is the original and you then take off and leave me, Mark and Thad alone forever."

"It's as simple as that. You tell me what I want to know, I'll tie you up and then I'm out of here. You've got to trust me."

"Wait a minute," I said surprised. "You didn't mention anything about tying me up."

"Come on, be reasonable," she smiled. "I need a little time to get away. You understand, don't you?"

"Tell me something," I said. "You weren't really going to shoot me, were you?"

"If you tried to run I would have," she declared emphatically. "At least in the leg."

"I don't believe you." At that point, I made an attempt to stand up.

"Just try me," she said seriously, pointing the gun right at my chest. Her hands were shaking as she prepared herself for anything.

"Okay, okay, I get the picture." I sat down again. "I guess I'm ready to do this thing."

"Fine, but I've changed my plan. I'm going to tie you up first and then you can tell me what I want to know. Please Matt, let's not play games with each other. I don't want you to get hurt. Okay? This thing has already claimed enough victims."

She walked over to her bag and pulled out a small wad of nylon rope. She motioned for me to sit in a small wooden chair next to the window. While she held the gun in one hand, she somehow managed to tie a pretty firm knot around my hands and legs. I could hardly move.

I didn't resist as she completed this task. I was convinced that this was the only way out. I'd tell her which was the original urn and she'd stay out of our lives forever. It just wasn't worth trying to put her in jail. Why should I care if she sold some stupid piece of junk from some far off land? In some ways, based on what she said, I felt that she was a victim in all of this too.

"So what if no one finds me here?" I finally asked. "Or what if I have to take a pee or something?"

"I'm afraid that's your problem," she admitted. "The cleaning lady will be in here tomorrow morning around seven. Don't worry, you'll be fine." She patted me on the head like a little puppy. "If you have to pee, just pee. Believe me, it's not going to kill you."

"Now, which one is it," she asked, full of anticipation. "Remember, there is no advantage in lying about this. I'll only end up coming back again. And as I already said, the cops will never be able to track me down. So let's have it now. I told you everything I know. It's your turn. Which is the original?"

I took one more look at her before deciding what to do next. Her face was as beautiful as ever. There is no way she would do anything to me, I thought. How could she hurt me? At that moment I decided.

"It's the left one," I said confidently.

"Why that one?" she asked, picking it up to get a closer look.

"See the V-shaped crack on the rim. That's how you tell it from the rest. Carter's photo had an arrow pointing to that crack with the name Gorkha written on the backside. The other two photos had the name Lalitpur, or something like that, marked on them."

"Good boy," she said as she walked to her bag and pulled out a large handkerchief which she tied tightly across my mouth before I could say anything.

"Well, I guess it's time for me to run off now."

She carefully packed the urns and threw a few clothes that were scattered around the room into her bag. She then took a small handtowel and carefully wiped everything down—to remove her fingerprints, no doubt. To my surprise, she changed her scrub outfit right in front of me. She had wrapped a large ace bandage around her chest to flatten out her breasts. She looked incredible standing in front of me in nothing more than her underwear. She had an unbelievable body.

After making one last inspection of the room, she carried everything out to the car parked in front. It took her nearly ten minutes before she finally returned and just stood there staring at me with that beautiful face of hers.

"You know, you surprise me, Matt," she said, pulling out a small syringe from her pants pocket. "I thought you were going to be more of a challenge. But I guess you're as stupid as all the rest."

She reached out and squeezed my face lightly, shaking it back and forth several times before walking behind the chair I was tied to. It was clear that something had just changed. Her eyes had this crazed, almost evil appearance. All at once, I no longer felt safe. I tried desperately to release myself, but by that time she had already managed to inject something into my right arm.

"You see, Matt, I'm afraid I wasn't being totally honest with you a few minutes ago. Despite what everyone believed, I never left the States for India after all. Instead, I spent most of the last four years working as a nurse on an Indian reservation out west in Arizona. No one would ever think of looking there for a fugitive like me. As for Mr. Bradey, he didn't really come looking for me. I went looking for him. Two months ago, I tracked him down through someone from BEEM who knew where he was hiding out. I fucked the guy a few times and he agreed to contact Bradey on my behalf. It was as simple as that. When he heard I was looking for him, Bradey arranged to see me one afternoon. We agreed to meet at this old farm house in Deep River which had been abandoned for many years. I knew Bradey had the three urns, but didn't know what to do with them—he had no contacts in the antique world like I did. Well, to make a long story short, I told him I could identify the original Gorkha Urn and also help him find a buyer. When he showed up that day, I drugged his coffee, shot him in the back of the head with his own gun and managed to drop his sorry ass down an old well on the property. So why did I do it? Well, I guess you could say that Bradey was a major asshole. Besides, killing him was the only way to get my hands on the urns."

I couldn't believe what I was hearing. She seemed to be taunting me with her story. Could it be true?

"You see, Matt, you're just like all those other men," she said in disgust. "You believed every word I told you a few minutes ago. You're so stupid." She laughed out loud again. "I must be a great actress. And yes, you were right. I did push Thad off that ledge. I thought for sure he was gone. When I found out he was still alive, I had this brilliant idea. I knew you three boys were such good friends so I kept Thad sedated to see if you and Mark would come up to visit. Every five or six hours I'd manage to sneak in there somehow and give him a shot. And believe me, it wasn't easy to do this with his mother sitting there all the time. And sure enough, you two boys came as planned. Thank you so much for following through like a good little lamb."

"And then there is your situation," she continued, standing in front of me, grabbing my chin once again. "Your friend Mark thinks that Bradey was the one in Thad's room. Thus, when they find your dead body in this room, they'll think Bradey did it. A few minutes ago, I managed to change the name in the register book to Mr. James Bradey. I bet you didn't know that James was his first name. I also changed the license plate number written there to Kansas GT243. As always, the motel owner was fast asleep behind the desk. He's a mindless drunk. Since I used a pencil when I checked in, it wasn't all that difficult to change it to pen. That ought to keep the police going for a while. And when the hotel clerk describes a dark haired woman who checked in, they'll think it was Bradey's girlfriend. Or maybe they'll think it was his wife. Who cares. You see I've covered all of my bases. You've made it real easy for me, Matt. I really appreciate that.

Well, I guess it's about time for me head out of here forever."

"Oh, by the way, the sedative I gave you should be starting by now. Don't worry, you won't feel a thing. You'll fall asleep and then your heart will slow down and then just stop. It's the same amount I gave your friend Thad an hour ago. I guess you could say that this is my payoff to you two for ruining my life."

As I listened to what she was saying, I tried to free myself. But whatever she injected into my arm made it nearly impossible for me to move. My entire body felt so heavy. That was it, I was fading fast and there was nothing I could do about it. I had trusted her. I believed every word she said to me. I believed it because I wanted to believe that there was some good in her. But the more I watched her, the more it became obvious that Shelly was truly a disturbed person. How come I never saw this before? I walked right into her web and now my life was slipping away. While I could tell she was still talking to me, I could no longer concentrate. I was trying desperately to hold on—to fight for my life. But at some point . . .

15

"Hey, man," said someone standing over me. "We thought we lost you there for a while."

At first I couldn't recognize the voice. After opening my eyes, everything around me was a complete blur. My head ached so bad it felt as if it might explode into a million pieces.

"It's me, Mark. Guess what, the doctor said you're going to live after all. Too bad, Matt, I know how much you wanted to hang out with that Grim Reaper dude."

"Where the hell am I?" I asked. Nothing seemed to make sense to me. My throat was so dry, I found it nearly impossible to talk. Every word got stuck to the side of my mouth.

"You're in the hospital," Mark explained. "You've been out cold for nearly fourteen whole hours. Do you remember anything that happened yesterday?"

I was still disoriented. The last thing I remembered was driving over to the hospital to visit Thad. And then I was in the cafeteria. And then it all came back to me—Thad, Shelly, the shot . . .

"Shit, how's Thad?" I asked. "Is he okay?" I immediate sat up in a panic.

"Don't worry about him, he's fine," said Mark. Mrs. Cooper was standing next to me holding my hand. I didn't even realize it. After giving me a kiss on the forehead, she rushed out to inform the nurse that I had finally awakened.

"Did anyone catch that bitch?" I asked turning back toward Mark.

"We sure did," he replied with a big smile which completely consumed his entire face. "She's now in jail. You won't have to worry about her anymore."

"Shit, how did you ever find me there?"

"You're never going to believe this, but I swear it's all true. You know when we were down in that hospital basement. Well, I walked all the way to the end of the hallway looking for Bradey, but didn't find anything so I started back. When I got near the elevator shaft I saw Shelly standing there with that gun pointed at you. After she put you into the wheelchair, I managed to follow you both upstairs and out to the parking lot."

"Did you know it was Shelly right away?" I asked out of curiosity.

"No, but I knew it wasn't Bradey. After watching her, I could tell it was a woman."

"That's funny, I thought it was Bradey until she removed her mask and cap in the motel," I reluctantly admitted.

"You need to spend a little more time with the opposite sex, Matt," Mark laughed, slapping my shoulder. "I'm beginning to worry about you."

"So what next?"

"Well, since I thought I'd lose you if I tried to get help from the police, I just followed behind to see where she took you. You had the car keys, so I ended up driving off in an ambulance which was parked near the emergency area. I'm surprised you didn't see me following behind. When you guys pulled up into that motel, I parked across the street at this gas station and used the ambulance radio to call for help. Within about eight or ten minutes these asshole cops arrived and they tried to arrest me. It took me forever to convince them that you had been kidnapped. It was only after calling Thad's mother at the hotel, the nurse at the hospital and even the Elkins police, before they finally believed what I was saying. That's why it took so long to rescue you. I tell you, all police are the same—they're all so moronic."

"So then what?" I asked, urging him to go on. "The last thing I remember was her sticking me with that needle."

"Actually, the cops managed to get there just as she was about to drive off. You should have seen her. Man it was great. She went absolutely berserk on them. It took about five guys to hold her down. I swear she started foaming at the mouth. She was really, really pissed off. You sure know how to get a woman excited, huh, Matt?"

"But what about her gun? The one she used on me. She didn't pull it out?"

"No," Mark confessed. "She didn't seem to have it when the cops drove up. Maybe she put it in the trunk or something. Man you should have seen her. And as for you, my friend, you're lucky to be alive right now. She nearly killed you and Thad with that stuff she injected into your arm. It was really pretty scary. The ambulance I stole had to rush you off to the hospital. She injected you with enough sedative to knock out a small herd of elephants. They ended up giving you a bunch of shots to counter the effect. The doctor said it was touch and go there for a while."

"You know she told me that Bradey is dead," I said. "She actually admitted to killing him."

"Really, she's one screwed-up lady," said Mark. "Oh, by the way, your parents and sister are on their way up here. I guess the whole town heard about the story already."

"Shit, not again," I remarked under my breath. I remembered what happened the last time around. "We've got to go through all that again?"

"No, you've got it all wrong," said Mark full of excitement.

"Listen to this. You and I are being put up as heroes. After my mom got the news that you were going to be okay, she went right over to the town paper and gave them the complete story. She called and told me that we both made the front page this morning."

"Knowing your mom, I bet she had us leaping tall buildings in a single bound," I remarked.

The doctor walked in with Mrs. Cooper and the attending nurse.

"So, I see you've decided to come back to the world of the living," said the doctor. I couldn't help but feel that his comment was a bit out of the ordinary for a medical person. "We're going to keep you here at the hospital for a few days of observation. But you'll be fine." He grabbed my wrist and took my pulse—the standard doctor thing to do, I guess.

"I'm so glad to hear that," said Mrs. Cooper. "You know, Matt, we're moving you over into Thad's room later. He's also awake and talking up a storm. He's really looking forward to seeing you boys. Thank you both for all your help." As expected, this statement was followed by one of her predictable hugs.

*　　　*　　　*

Two nights had passed since Shelly's attempt to permanently sedate Thad and me. According to my doctor, everything was fine with me, and I was free to be discharged from the hospital the following morning. My parents had come up from Elkins along with a few of my friends and we were all going to drive down to West Virginia together.

While Thad was still in a lot of pain, he seemed to be in good spirits most of the time. The night before, he admitted to me that his biggest fear over the years had been that Bradey would someday come after him. He had recurrent nightmares about this happening. This anxiety had a real negative influence on his life. But now that he found out that Bradey was dead, his entire outlook on things changed—like a massive cancerous tumor had been successfully removed from his throat, thus allowing him to breathe freely again. Likewise, knowing that he had almost been killed twice, but managed to beat death both times, also gave him a new lease on life. I hadn't seen him so relaxed in years.

That night, after all of the nurses, doctors, family members and friends finally left us alone, Mark somehow managed to sneak back into our room. It was just the three of us again.

"So, you boys are going back to Elkins tomorrow?" asked Thad. "Shit, how can you live in that flea bitten, poor excuse for a town?"

"Fleas got to live off someone, I guess," I confessed.

249

"Hey, listen," said Mark. "When you two "wimps" get out of bed, why don't the three of us go up to my uncle's cabin for a weekend of fishing. We can get lost in the woods again. I'm sure there are plenty of other dead New York antique dealers out there. Wouldn't it be fun to go through all of this again?"

"Shut up, Mark," said Thad as he threw one of his pillows at him. "You're a real funny guy. You ought to be on TV or something."

"So, Butthead, what's in your pocket?" I asked. I pointed to a small brown paper bag bulging out of his jacket.

"Well, I guess since both of you were able to get yourself sedated, I thought it was only fair for me to go through the same experience," he said, pulling out a pint of Wild Turkey from his coat. It looked like he had finished nearly half of the bottle already.

"Hey, man, wait a minute," I complained. "Give me some of that shit." Mark came over and handed me the bottle and I took a big swig. "You want some, Thad?"

"You know something, you guys are really messed up down to the bone," said Thad in disgust. "I swear, neither one of you is going to amount to anything if you continue drinking that swill. And, Matt, you're probably going to end up in a coma if you mix booze with the remnants of that sedative in your body. I tell you, if I .. .."

*   *   *

And so the three of us came together once again as good friends that night. In some ways, the experience of those few days seemed to reinstate the bonds we once shared. With Bradey and Shelly no longer lurking in the shadows of our lives, there were no more ghosts in any of our closets. We were free again.

From that night on, we resumed our friendship from where it had been derailed that Friday night over four years before. While we all went our separate ways and lived our separate lives, we made a point of getting together at least once or twice a year to talk about old times and new. And as might be expected, life went on!

THE END

EPILOGUE

After the police took my statement, much of what Shelly told me was validated over time. The police were able to track down Bradey's body at an old farm located in Deep River. Just as Shelly had said, he had been shot in the head and thrown down an old well. She used his own gun to do the dirty deed.

Apparently, Shelly exhibited a long history of anti-social behavior going back over twenty years. During the trial, one of her high school teachers used the term sociopath to describe her actions. From an early age, she was said to be a compulsive liar who'd say and do anything to get what she wanted, irrespective of the consequences. All she cared about was herself. Her teacher also described her as being incredibly cruel. During her junior year in high school, Shelly was accused of dowsing her neighbor's dog with gasoline and setting it on fire because "the dog barked too much?" Shelly's family managed to get the charges dropped based on a lack of evidence. It wasn't as if she came from a bad home or was molested by someone at an early age. Nothing like that ever happened to her. She was just an evil person—a bad apple.

After graduating college, Shelly somehow managed to lie her way into a Peace Corps slot in India, but was kicked out because she was caught stealing artifacts from sacred temples. The local authorities wanted to throw her in jail, but the U.S. Embassy managed to bail her out.

Instead of returning to the States, she went underground and remained in India for a number of years. She eventually ended up marrying an Indian man, but he abandoned her after six months. That's when she started working for Carter. Since she spoke nearly perfect Hindi, he used her to go from village to village in search of old Indian antiques for his shop in New York. When she collected enough of this stuff, Carter would travel to Delhi to arrange for it to be taken back to the States.

Shelly was never a nurse after all. As part of her Peace Corps experience, she spent a lot of time working around health posts. There she learned how to give injections and treat minor illnesses. Years later, she got a volunteer job as a nurse working in a local hospital in Rajistian. While she didn't last more than a few months there, she spent years telling people she was a trained nurse. It was all part of the big lie—a lie that she came to truly believe over time.

After inheriting the house in Elkins following her aunt's

death, Shelly moved much of her stuff to West Virginia. The yard was always such a mess because she never spent more than a few weeks there in between trips back to India.

The trial lasted for over six weeks. Fortunately, I only had to spend a couple of days testifying about what I knew. Following the closing arguments it took the jury less than an hour to come back with a guilty verdict. Three weeks later, she was sentenced to life in prison, with no opportunity for parole.

As for the sacred urn, it was eventually returned to Nepal. Upon its arrival, a group of about a hundred and fifty residents from Gorkha were there at the airport to receive it. The entire crowd escorted the urn in a large bus caravan back to its original resting place, where there was a massive ceremony to celebrate its return home.

About the Author

Born and raised in Newington, Connecticut, Matthew Friedman completed his degrees at Central Connecticut State University and New York University. As a professional in the field of international health, he has worked and traveled to over thirty countries around the world. For the past six years, he has been living and working in Kathmandu, Nepal as a Health Technical Advisor for USAID. His first novel entitled *Tara* (Vikas Publishing), focused on the tragedy of child prostitution in India.